D0408384

LARGE
PRINT

*Also by Belva Plain*

After the Fire
Looking Back

# BELVA PLAIN

# HER FATHER'S HOUSE

BOOKSPAN

**LARGE PRINT**

EDITION

Copyright © 2002 by Bar-Nan Creations, Inc.

All rights reserved under International and
Pan-American Copyright Conventions.
Published in the United States of America by
Random House Large Print in association with
Delacorte Press, New York, and simultaneously
in Canada by Random House of Canada
Limited, Toronto.
Distributed by Random House, Inc.,
New York.

0-7394-2751-2

This Large Print edition published in accord
with the standards of the N.A.V.H.

# HER
# FATHER'S
# HOUSE

# Prologue

One day when I was four years old, a girl in school told me that my mother was not my real mother.

"Your real one's dead," she said.

Is it not strange that I cannot remember what explanation my father gave me when I ran home? I only remember that it was raining hard. I was all wet, and at the front door the cat was crying to be let in.

# PART
# ONE

# Chapter 1

∽◦∾

## 1968

His name was Donald Wolfe, Donald J., for James, and he was twenty-five years old when he joined the stream of eager youth that from every corner of the country, every year, pours into the churning human sea called New York. If it is ever possible, or even makes any sense to say that someone's geographic origin can be visible on his person, then it made sense to say that Donald looked like just the man to have come from healthy small-town or farming people in some cold place like North Dakota— which is exactly where he had come from.

He was tall, brown-haired, and large-boned; his brown eyes were thoughtful and calm. On the streets of New York during those first months, he walked with slow deliberation through the impatient crowd, taking his time to estimate the height of a building or pausing to wonder at the heaped-up splendors in the shop windows. Untempted, he merely wondered.

Once only was he tempted. In a bookstore's window lay the *Writings of Thomas Jefferson,* bound in dark red leather. It was expensive, yet the price did not faze him too much, for he hoped to build a library and he also felt that he owed himself one treat, so he bought it.

Never in his life had he had so much money at his command. Having graduated second in his class at law school, he had been hired as an associate in the New York office of an international law firm. Although others in the firm complained that the city, with its high rents, expensive restaurants and entertainments, left them beggared, he, because he did not go to expensive restaurants and always bought standing room or the cheapest seats at theaters, felt rich. His clean, two-room apartment on the fifth floor of a nineteenth-century walk-up building, with an interesting view of the lively street, was satisfying to him.

Sometimes in window glass he would catch a reflection of himself on his way to work, wearing his correct dark suit with his briefcase at his side.

"I can't believe what's happened to me," he

would cry out to himself, and then be amused at his own simplemindedness. Who do you think you are, anyway, Donald Wolfe? Why, there are dozens of young men just like you in any one of these towering buildings along the avenue.

Yet they were not all quite like him. Senior partners were surely known to be sparing of praise; still, before the year had passed, he had already received a good deal of it. One of the seniors, a punctilious, middle-aged man whom a few of the younger people in the office had secretly labeled "typically white shoe," took a liking to him. But even if Augustus Pratt had not taken that liking, Donald never would have scoffed at "white shoe"; to begin with, he was not exactly sure what it meant, but if it did mean what he thought—a certain old-fashioned, formal courtesy—he would have found no fault with that.

One evening at the conclusion of *Aida,* Donald came upon Mr. Pratt in the lobby of the opera house. He was accompanied by a woman, obviously his wife, with their three half-grown children.

"Why, hello, Donald. I never knew you cared about opera."

"I do, although I still don't know much about it."

"It's never too late and seldom too early to

learn. If I'd known you were here," he said as they walked out together, "we could have had some refreshments. Where were you sitting?"

"On top. As high as you can go."

"Oh. It was worth it, I'm sure, in spite of the seat."

"Yes, sir, it was."

"Well, see you in the morning. Good night, Donald."

More than once when in a later time he reflected on the chain of events that had moved him through the years, Donald wondered how differently things might have turned out if he had not met Augustus Pratt that night at the opera.

*Was it the fact that I shared his tastes that impressed him enough to present me with two good seats for the rest of the season? Had that led to those informal conversations which, in their turn, had led to more swift assignments and promotions, and that, in a roundabout way had led in the end to Lillian, to marriage, and the deadly ruin that came after it?*

Pratt had grown up in a small town in northern Maine. His father, like Donald's late mother, had been a teacher. He, too, had left for law school, borrowed and worked his way through it, and never returned to the small town. It was this fa-

miliar background that made Donald feel particularly comfortable in his presence.

"Yes," Pratt said in one of those conversations,
"Dakota sounds much like Maine. A hot July
and August, then a long winter. My brothers and
I worked all day in the potato fields. We worked
so late sometimes that our mother brought our
dinner to us in a pail. You, too, I suppose?"

"Except that I had no brothers or sisters, either. Mom had a summer job when school was
out. When I got back from the farm where I
worked, I'd make supper. If she got home first,
she'd make it."

"You don't mention your father. Or am I in-
truding with the question?"

"Not at all. He died in France in 1944. I was
a year old."

"To have a son, and never see him grow up,"
Pratt murmured, then gave Donald a penetrating
look.

"You would have pleased him, Donald. Our
profession, despite the abuses of some lawyers,
still demands the highest honor and trust. You
are going to be an honored name within it."

Donald was to remember another day, two years
later.

"How would you like to go with me to

Singapore next month? There's a bank matter there that's come to life again. We'd thought it was nicely settled, but it isn't."

"Like it, Mr. Pratt? Until I came to New York, I'd never been farther than the state capital. Oh yes, I'd like it!"

Pratt had smiled. Donald never forgot that smile, a little pleased, a little amused, and even perhaps a little bit—well, fatherly.

"You'll see a lot more than Singapore in your time, Donald."

There was so much that he needed to see, and do, and learn! The world was a thousand times larger and fuller than he could have imagined. In the courtroom as part of a team accompanying a senior partner, he saw the human tragedy and the human comedy as he had never seen them. The variety of people! The poverty and the riches! The astonishing evil and the innocence! And above it all was the majestic quest for justice.

At his desk he sat and studied the postmarks on foreign correspondence. The very names on them lured him. London and Paris evoked grand boulevards; Suriname, Bombay, or Malaysia evoked wet heat, dim rubber forests, or red-and-gold bazaars. The firm's clients had profits, losses, and myriad problems all over the world. Here were complicated puzzles with much at stake—not to mention his own job if he were to err in a report to his superiors. . . .

The bright years rolled one into the other. In the fifth year, he was approaching the time when a young lawyer either "makes partner" or knows that he never will.

"I can't talk about it yet, but I assume you have a pretty good idea," said Augustus Pratt, and changed the subject. "Do you ever think of marrying?"

Donald was startled. They were five miles above the Atlantic, flying home. And they had just been talking about the Federal Reserve. Anyway, the question was more personal than one would generally expect from Mr. Pratt.

"No," he said, stumbling over his reply. "I'm in no hurry."

"Well, you've been with us going on six years. And you haven't met anyone? I thought maybe that English girl you always see when we're in London. She seemed quite lovely that time I met her."

"You liked her," Donald said mischievously, "because she looks like Mrs. Pratt."

"Ah yes, maybe she does, a little. We'll be married twenty years next month." A soft expression crossed Pratt's face. It was remarkable to see that softness appear on features usually so firm as to have been carved. "Yes, yes, Donald, a sound, loving marriage is a man's blessing. Someplace right now there's a young woman who is going to give you great joy in life. And let me add that she will be one lucky woman."

"Well, we'll see," said Donald, wanting to end the subject. "But up till now, I haven't ever felt about anyone that I'd want to spend the rest of my life with her. Without that, I certainly wouldn't marry her."

# Chapter 2

Scattered among New York's stone towers are a number of small, green oases, with seats in the shade or in the sun, depending on one's choice. Throughout the day, people come to them to read or eat a sandwich lunch, or simply to sit.

About half-past four on a warm afternoon late in April, Donald sat down in one of these oases and opened the newspaper. He was unusually tired; he had been in the office until midnight the night before and had then spent the greater part of the day in court. Debating within himself whether he ought to go back to the office or whether, it being Friday, he could afford to go straight home, take off his shoes, and stretch out, he put the paper down and shut his eyes against the lowering sun. His mood was mingled; there was the satisfaction that came of having skillfully presented a convincing argument before the court; also there was the pity that he could not help but feel for the poor guilty devil who by now must be sitting in jail, quivering as he awaited the term of his punishment.

A bright, girlish voice woke him from his thoughts. "Your briefcase is about to fall and spill out all your papers."

So it was. He had placed it carelessly on the very edge of his knees. Now, in haste, he retrieved it and mumbled his thanks.

"Very nice of you. I should have known better."

Directly in his line of vision sat the owner of the voice, the owner also of two very large and very blue eyes. He smiled appropriately, returned to his newspaper, and read a column. When he looked up as he turned the page, there she was again, a smart young woman wearing black and white; her skin was also very white against her black, upswept hair. About twenty-five, he guessed, and went back to the newspaper.

The next time he looked, she was eating an orange. She had placed it upon a magazine, and with a tiny knife—mother-of-pearl handle, he thought—was cutting it into sections. These she ate with unusual delicacy, and with the same delicacy, having wrapped the peel in a paper napkin,

dropped it into the trash can at the rear of the little park.

*Elegance.* The word flashed into his head as he
watched her. She was small, but not undersized.
She was erect and graceful, as if she were dancing. When she sat down, her ankles were crossed
so that her pretty shoes hugged each other.

He looked away, but not before he had caught
her glance, which then made it necessary to say
something.

"I certainly appreciate your noticing my briefcase. The last thing I need is to have any of these
papers blow away."

"Legal documents, oh yes. One of the people
in my firm lost some last week in the subway,
and it was pretty awful."

"Your firm? You're a lawyer?"

"Heavens, no. Just a secretary, a legal secretary
to Mr. Buzley. Buzley of Anaheim, Roman and
Roman."

"You shouldn't say 'just' a secretary. We could
hardly work without secretaries."

"Well, true enough. By the way, I'm Lillian
Morris."

"Donald Wolfe. I'm with Orton and Pratt."

She smiled. "A far cry from Mr. Buzley. Pop
singers and movie stars versus international
strategies. But Mr. Buzley's very nice to me, and
I shouldn't say that, should I?"

"No, you shouldn't. But I won't quote you."

She laughed. Her laugh was a real one, not the affected giggle he so often heard. There was something about her that delighted him. He suddenly had the feeling that in another minute she would get up and leave. Surely there must be something he could say to detain her.

"It feels like an early spring. I mean, it will be if this keeps up," he said, and was at once ashamed of his dull remark.

"Yes, it does," she agreed.

For the life of him, he could think of nothing more to say. But then when she actually did stand up, opening her mouth perhaps to bid good-bye, he thought of something.

"I'm walking east. Is that your way, too?"

When she replied that it was, he berated himself for his stupidity. What if she had said west? How then would he have been able to accompany her?

They crossed Park Avenue. "I always wondered," said Lillian, "what those apartments are like inside. The doorways with the awnings and the doormen look so impressive. I've heard that some apartments have twelve or fifteen rooms, or even more."

Augustus Pratt's apartment had fourteen rooms. Donald could have told her about the mahogany library there, or the long dining table under the brilliant chandelier. But the subject did not seem important enough to take his mind from the thought that on Lexington Avenue, only a few steps away, there was a little place with tables on the sidewalk and wonderful pizza, or—

"Are you by any chance hungry?" he inquired.

"Yes, to tell the truth, I've only had breakfast this morning and that orange just now."

"How about keeping me company? I'm starved."

"I would love it."

Having had a large lunch with a group of lawyers between court sessions, he was hardly hungry. But at the table on the sidewalk, he managed to eat a fair-sized piece of an excellent pizza. The ordering of food, the discussion of choices, and the comparisons among various recipes and restaurants, followed by a brief selection of a sorbet, relieved him of the need to make good conversation. He did not remember ever, before now, having struggled to "make" conversation! Words had always come easily to him. Was a lawyer not, after all, a wordsmith?

Lillian was making comments on the passing scene: an unfamiliar foreign car, a woman wearing a fashionable suit, and a man leading a pair of handsome standard poodles. She spoke vivaciously, but not too much so; hearing her, he only half heard; he was observing her instead.

She made small, expressive gestures with her hands. He disliked women of whom he often thought that if their hands were ever tied, they would be unable to talk. But now he watched those hands, the long fingers and the pale, oval nails. Raising his eyes, he saw a necklace of small pearls lying between the rise of round breasts under a fine white blouse. He saw a firm chin and full lips that, for some odd reason, recalled the taste of warm raspberries. The nose was a trifle too short. The cheekbones were perhaps too high, although it was said, was it not, that high cheekbones were to be desired? So then they were not too high! And the eyes, lake blue, lake deep! And the dark, thick hair piled high, the crown on a proud, proud head.

The man with the poodles came walking back. One dog, too close to the table, brushed against Donald and sniffed his plate, for which behavior the owner apologized profusely. But Donald, filled with a sudden and curiously warm happiness, only stroked the dog's head.

"That's all right. He reminds me of the dogs I once had. Not poodles, but setters. The same size, though."

When the man smiled and went on his way,

Lillian smiled, too. "Isn't it interesting how babies and dogs break the ice?"

"Break the ice?"

"Pull people together, I mean. If I hadn't been here, that man would probably have lingered awhile with you, talking about dogs. You looked so happy all of a sudden, when you were stroking his poodle."

She's keen, he thought. She doesn't miss much. No doubt she was observing the flush on his heated cheeks. She might even know perfectly well that it was she herself and not the dog that had put it there.

But now, having at least one thread to catch on to, he used it to seize hold of the conversation. "I grew up in a country town. I had dogs and a horse. I still get sentimental about them, even about a policeman's horse, when I see one."

"Tell me about your home."

She knew instinctively, or perhaps had been taught as she grew up, that the way to please is to let people talk about themselves. It was an innocent trick, after all, and much more considerate than monopolizing the conversation with long accounts of one's own ambitions or grievances.

"It was in North Dakota. Very spare, wide, grand scenery. In many ways, I miss it. I could just as well have been a rancher or a farmer, like my father."

"So how did you end up as a lawyer in the big city?"

"I don't know. I was only ten or twelve when I made up my mind to go to law school. Maybe it was my schoolteacher mother, encouraging me. She, and all the books in the house. We didn't have any money, but somehow we bought books."

"How long have you been in New York?"

"Almost six years, all of them with Orton and Pratt."

"You'll be a partner before long."

"Who knows? But I hope so. I love the work."

"It must be wonderful to feel that way about your work. I don't hate mine, but I certainly don't love it, either."

"What would you rather be doing?"

"Painting. I've taken art lessons, and while I'm not awful, I've learned that I'm not good, either."

"Maybe you need better training," said Donald, aware that he knew nothing about the subject.

"I tried that. I even went to Italy for six months, in Florence, going to classes, soaking up the atmosphere. The best thing I got out of it beside the pleasure of being there was learning to squelch all foolish hopes. I came home almost broke. I used up almost all the insurance that came to me after my mother's death. Then I went to work for Mr. Buzley."

Thinking, but not sure, that he was seeing a glimmer of moisture under her round white eyelids, he said gently, "It isn't easy to lose your mother. I know about it."

"But you have to accept, don't you? Accept and keep moving." She looked at her watch. "Excuse me, I don't want to leave, but my housemate is going to have a major extraction at the dentist's, and I promised to go with her. Thank you so much for this treat. I've loved talking to you."

"Would you like to have dinner with me to-morrow night, Lillian? I have a feeling that we have more to say to each other."

He had a tentative appointment for the next night, but he was going to break it because he was not going to let go of this woman.

"That would be wonderful, Donald."

"Give me your address and telephone. Here's my card. It's proof of my identity, so you can check. It's for your safety," he added when she protested.

"Nonsense," she said. "Your face is proof enough of my safety. I'm a very good judge of people, Donald."

They were going in opposite directions. When at the first corner he turned to look back, he saw that she was doing the same. Then they waved to each other and walked on.

⌣

Perhaps because this was their second meeting, or because of the surroundings, quiet space, comfortable chairs, and the lighting so soft and subtly pink, there was no hesitancy between them.

"So we're both orphans," Donald said. "And both only children. I think about it sometimes, although not too often. But whenever I do, I'm aware of being alone at the end of a chain. There are some third cousins on my father's side, but they live in Wyoming, and I've only seen them once when they came by our way. But my life is full, and always has been. I had a great childhood. The only pain I have is that neither parent lived to see me graduate from law school. My mother had been talking for years about that day."

Why was he telling her all this, he a private person not given to revelations about himself? But she had seemed interested and had pressed him to talk about himself.

"Now what about you?" he asked. "You grew up on Long Island, you said. I haven't been on

Long Island more than twice, and then only for an hour each time. I've read about it, though."

"You read about the mansions, and the beaches. An awful lot of it is just rows of little houses side by side, where, they tell me, the potato fields used to be. That's where I grew up. Suburbia. You must have read about suburbia, too."

"Yes, all kinds of supposedly learned articles. They don't praise it much, and I'm generally suspicious of that nose-in-the-air attitude."

"They're not altogether wrong, believe me. Suburbia can be dull beyond belief. As soon as I could get away, I did, and went as far as I could."

Her eyes were sparkling. She had determination. Imagine a young woman, alone in the world, taking her ambition and her little money, all she had, to gamble it on her future in a country where she didn't know man or woman! There she sat, as sure of herself as any well-protected young woman living on Park Avenue. He had learned enough about New York to recognize that her clothes were fashionable. She wore a fine watch, and why not? She had nobody to care for but herself.

Nevertheless, it was a dangerous world. One accident, one illness, one misstep, and a defenseless person all alone is destroyed. Thinking so, he fell silent.

"You're a gentle soul," Lillian said suddenly.

He was touched, and he laughed. "You've never seen me in a court fight."

"I don't mean that. I mean that if your heart is touched, you can be terribly hurt, more than most people."

Yesterday, when he was fondling that dog, she had sensed his mood. "What are you doing, psychoanalyzing me?" he asked.

"No, nor flattering you, either. You're too intelligent not to see right through that. No, it's simply that I like you, and so naturally I'm interested in you."

"Are you interested enough to prolong this evening, after we've had our coffee?"

"Yes, very. Unfortunately, we can't go back to my place because tonight's Cindy's turn to have a friend."

"Then we'll go to mine—that is, if you don't mind climbing four flights of stairs."

Cindy's turn. Was it not ridiculous that having met this woman only yesterday, he should feel a pang of jealousy and wonder whom Lillian brought to those rooms when it was her turn?

They climbed the stairs, and he opened the door and switched on the light. Seldom did he have visitors here, but he was meticulous, and for his own sake, kept his home in order. So here they were, his two little rooms, filled with books and simple mementos of his journeys: a hand-woven cotton rug from Turkey, a Chinese screen to hide the closet-sized kitchen, and three engravings of eighteenth-century Paris, bought at a bookstore on the Left Bank.

Lillian exclaimed, "It's lovely! The cobalt blue paint and that grass green lamp, the chair—all just right. I'm amazed. Most men don't know about colors. Most people don't, for that matter."

"Well, I assure you that I'm one who doesn't. I merely copied the idea from a window on Madison Avenue. I thought it looked nice."

She drew back the curtains and looked out into empty darkness. "I was wondering whether you had a view, and that's why you moved so high up."

"No, if I wanted a view I'd move to the twentieth floor in one of those new buildings on the avenue."

"Why don't you?"

"Too expensive, when I started out. I had to pay off my college loans and start saving. Then by the time I was free of debt, I was used to it here. There wasn't any reason to move. I work in a fine office, I go out into the world, and when I do have an evening at home, all I need are my books and my music records. I'm satisfied. It's clear sailing for me."

Why was he telling her all this, too?

"You must have two hundred albums on those shelves. Opera—do you like opera?"

"Very much. Do you?"

"I went when I was in Italy, but never here. I suppose it's the same."

"We'll go sometime. . . . Why are you smiling?"

"Because you're taking it for granted that I'll go with you."

"That's true. I am."

"Well, you're right. I will."

"Good. Better to be honest with each other from the start instead of just guessing."

"Then give me a drink. We'll drink to that."

"Wine, or what?"

"Wine, please. Or anything. It doesn't matter."

"Be comfortable," he said, motioning toward the only upholstered chair."

"No, you take it. I like to sit on the floor. I'll lean against your knees. I'm comfortable that way. I insist. Would you like some music?"

"Not now. Just silence, and the wine. It was cold walking here."

She leaned with confidence against him. When he looked down, he saw two twinkling diamonds in her earlobes; her fragrance was faint as a whiff of summer. He had known her only a little more than twenty-four hours. A sense of unreality swept over him.

She spoke softly, hesitating. "I was thinking that thirty-one hours ago we didn't know each other, and here we sit."

"I was thinking the same."

Then silence returned. Donald's thoughts were whirling. He wasn't used to moving quite so fast, although many men—possibly most men—were. There were of course times when he had done so, but not with a woman like this one; this one was by turns outspoken and reserved, by turns reflective and vivacious; he knew only, as he had known when they met, that he did not want to lose her.

She stood abruptly. "Let's see the rest of your house."

"House? There's only one other room."

"Well, show me."

There was just the narrow bed, made up in tight army style, a dresser, and a small table with a lamp and a pile of books on it.

She looked and nodded. "Monastic. No cobalt and green. This is your other side."

Arranged on one wall was a series of historical prints: Custer's Last Stand, the Lincoln Memorial, Lee's surrender at Appomattox, and Washington taking the oath of office in New York.

After examining each one, she turned to him. "You're a very interesting person, Donald Wolfe."

"And you," he replied.

"You're not a monk, are you?"

"No, not at all."

They stared at each other. My God, he thought, this is different. I never—

"I'm twenty-six," she said. "I'm not a virgin."

"I didn't think you would be."

"It's you who've done this to me. I don't want you to think . . . I'm not really . . ."

"That's all right. That's all right. Come here."

Past midnight, he found a taxicab and took her home to a modest apartment house.

"The next time, Lillian? When shall it be?"

"Any time."

"Tomorrow, then."

"Tomorrow."

He walked home, although the cab could have taken him back. But he needed to move, to feel the night air, and to come back to reality. So he told himself.

Emotion! All the women, beginning with girls in high school up to last month's charming friend in Paris, who still, after two years, hoped for him to say something definite—all of them, and never anyone like her. So smooth, so cool, and still so fiery!

"*Lillian,*" he said aloud, and the sound of the name took visual shape as sounds sometimes did for him, so that as he walked he was able to see it before him, a presence white and silken, shimmering through the darkness: *Lillian.*

# Chapter 3

If he had ever had to fill out one of those questionnaires in which you were asked to answer such perplexing subtle questions as, "Do you consider yourself happy?" Donald would not have hesitated to write yes. He took a plain view of life. It was supposed to present problems and one was supposed to solve them if one could. For a long time now, he had had no problems. His health was excellent, his profession was in every way rewarding, he had agreeable friends, and the world was a splendid place. So yes, simply put, he was happy.

Yet never, as spring moved toward summer, had the world been so splendid. Of course he had read those old sayings about how the world seems to smile on lovers, and of course he had thought that was all sentimental nonsense, yet now he had to admit that it was quite true. Strangers whom he passed on the street all seemed to be smiling; people held doors for him and said "good morning" in such a friendly way; the weather itself was especially wonderful this year, and the city never more beautifully arrayed with tulips everywhere and a sapphire sky overhead.

A free hour away from Lillian was a wasted one. Sometimes they met for a sandwich lunch in the pocket park where it had all begun. On Saturdays when he was not catching up on work and always on Sundays, they roamed through the city. They took brisk walks around the reservoir in Central Park, they took a boat ride around Manhattan, they visited the medieval marvel of the Cloisters, where she began his education in art. At the Metropolitan Museum, she led him in big leaps through the ages, from the Egyptians through the twentieth century. She did not know that although he wanted to absorb what he was seeing, most of the time he was more aware of her than of anything else. He was charmed by her velvet voice, her earnest explanations, and the white frill around the neck of her summer dress.

"Now you see," she said one day on the one time he visited her apartment, "now you see why I shall never be an artist."

Fastened by tape to one whole wall were oils and watercolors done by Lillian. Looking them over, he was not quite sure how to be both frank and truthful.

"Well," he began, but she did not let him finish.

"Don't spare me. I know better. They look like greeting cards, don't they? Answer yes or no."

Her eyes went straight to his. There's no point fooling her, he thought. People won't ever be able to fool her.

"Yes," he said.

"Thank you for being truthful. It's easy to get along with people who tell the truth." She sighed. "I'll tell you something, though. If I'm ever rich, I'm going to buy paintings. I'm going to wake up in the morning and look at beautiful things." She motioned to the wall. "I really want to take these horrors away, but believe it or not, Cindy wants them up. When I move out of here, whenever that will be, I'll leave them for her, and good riddance."

He could have said also, but naturally did not say, "Good riddance to Cindy, too, when you move."

Beside her somewhat coarse manner, which might be forgiven because no one had ever taught her anything else, Cindy was cynical and hard. A strange companion for Lillian, he thought; and very delicately, he suggested so.

Lillian shook her head. "No, no. You don't know her. She's a very, very good person. She's had terribly hard luck. I pay three quarters of the rent here. She has nothing. And I'm used to her ways." She laughed. "When you work in Buzley's office, you meet all sorts."

It was this brief visit that gave Donald the impetus to make some changes. In a brand-new building not far from his present quarters, he found two attractive apartments typical of the ones occupied by those of his unmarried friends who did not live downtown in a loft. One, on the twenty-ninth floor just beneath the penthouse, had a grand view of Manhattan's entire width from east to west; the other, on the third floor, had a view of the traffic on the avenue. The design of each was identical, the only difference, a considerable one, being the price. Reasoning that money was better off invested than being handed out every month to the landlord in exchange for a view, he chose the lower floor and quietly went ahead with his plan.

At this point, he stopped being frugal. Don't be a miser, he said to himself. You're living in New York. Get a decorator. These rooms were

to be a fit setting for a lovely woman. The bedroom must be feminine; it must remind her of a
garden. The "extra room" must fit his needs for
big chairs, a huge desk for the work that he
brought home, and shelves for his by now considerable library.

The young decorator apparently sensed that
Donald was in a frantic hurry, and he worked
with amazing speed. Soon then came the day
when the last curtain was hung and the surprise
could be revealed.

Lillian was enchanted, as he had known she
would be. On their first evening, she arrived
with a perfectly cooked dinner and six gardenias,
which she set floating in a shallow dish at the
center of the table. She looked around the room
and sighed, "I can't believe I'm here. It's so
beautiful. Poor Cindy, I feel so guilty about leaving her alone. She'll probably be moving soon,
she says, and I do hope so. She has a new man,
but I don't know about him. Anyway, you
wouldn't like him."

"How do you know I wouldn't?"

"Oh, I know you pretty well, darling, pretty
well."

He laughed and took another helping of
dessert, and felt that he was living on top of the
world. What peace! And afterward, the soft new

bed in the cool room under the blue-and-white covers.

⁓

Donald's friends, when he began to introduce Lillian to them, were all impressed. She was charming. Many of the men were lawyers; she had the good sense not to offer opinions on the strength of what she had learned as a legal secretary. Some of them were married, and she had the patience to listen to lengthy anecdotes about babies. Above all, she was friendly and, as one of the men joked to Donald, "Best-looking girl in the room, yet none of the other girls hated her."

One day his closest friend in the office, Ed Wills, who already had two children and a third on the way, asked him frankly whether he was "serious" about Lillian. Had he, or was he planning to, ask the big question?

Yes, he had done some thinking about that. He had been playing with the idea of making an immediate proposal. Why wait? They were living together in a cozy home and were as good as married. Yet something, most likely his innate conservatism, held him back from doing anything quite so abrupt. They had met, after all, only three months ago. On the other hand, people had always made hasty marriages, and

many of them had worked out just as well as
any. Again on the other hand, most people did
take a little more time and live together for a
while before they took the step. Might it not be
irresponsible, even somewhat adolescent, to
rush into something after an acquaintance of
ninety days? Did Ed agree? Yes, Ed did agree.
Three months was a short time, and you never
knew. . . .

Ultimately, though, Donald had no doubt,
none at all. One day, testing himself, he had even
sat down and done his best to separate head from
heart. Had she any discernible faults? For every
human being on earth has faults, isn't that so?
Was she a little bit stubborn? Maybe, but only
maybe. Was she a bit fanatic about art? Well,
maybe again, but if you had to be fanatic about
anything, art was no bad choice. He gave up.
She was marvelous. She had everything: beauty,
intelligence, humor, refinement, kindness. Look
how she cared for that poor soul, Cindy! Yes,
she had everything. And chuckling, he wondered what faults she would find in him were
she to make the same kind of list.

Lillian's two-week vacation came in August.
Cindy and she were going to a spa in New
England. She teased Donald: "You'll be pleased

to know it's for ladies only. No gentlemen allowed in."

Puzzled, he asked how she could afford it. "And I suppose you're treating Cindy, too?"

"Yes, but it's not as painful as it sounds. In fact, it's not painful at all. Mr. Buzley gave me a bonus for extra work, combined with my Christmas present that I had asked him to keep until next summer so I wouldn't spend it."

"Save it. Put it away. Let me pay for the treat."

"No, no, you already do so much for me, living here where I do. But thank you, anyway."

He had not seen Cindy since the one visit she had made to the new apartment. It had bothered him to think that he was perhaps the cause of separating Lillian from her friend. What kind of a snob was he? Yet he knew very well that he was almost as far from being a snob as anyone could be. At the same time, whenever he broached the subject of inviting Cindy, Lillian made it clear that she did not want the visit.

"Listen, Donald. You two are poles apart, so why try to force you together? Forget about it."

Well, let them enjoy their two weeks of luxury, the massages and swims, the dinners and mountain hikes, the girl talk, although what those two young women had in common to talk about, he could not imagine.

August had never lasted as long. He met new

clients, went out to eat with some of the men at the office, and returned to an apartment grown deadly silent and suddenly too large. Never in his life had he felt so strong a need for another human being.

Then while she was still away, two things happened. The first was his advancement to a partnership in the firm; it meant a name at the bottom of the letterhead and a considerable increase in earnings; it meant, more than anything, enormous respect. The second thing was an unexpected conference in London—and the decision that, he realized when at later times he thought about it, was hastened because of his going to London.

Waiting for him there was the same young woman whom Augustus Pratt had once admired. Well, Donald admired her, too; he was indeed very fond of her, as he had from time to time been fond of another young woman in Paris, and also of more than one back home. But never had he misled any one of them to think in terms of marriage.

Therefore, he was unprepared for the reproof that was given to him over drinks at the end of a day in the London office.

"I am getting married next month and moving to Edinburgh," she told him, "so we are not likely ever to meet again, Donald. And since that's the case, I feel free to speak my mind. I really loved you, Donald. I would have married you if you had asked me. Each time we were together, I was hoping you would before you left again for home. When you didn't, I swore to myself that I'd ask you the next time you were here. I guess I had too much pride, false pride, to do it. After a while I got tired of waiting and found another man. We love each other, and I am very, very happy."

For a minute or two, Donald was unable to find a response. She was looking straight at him and surely was aware of the burning heat in his cheeks. She was, in her poise and dignity, quite lovely; she had always been lovely. Yet seeing her at that moment, all he could feel were a deep regret and guilt for having so clumsily hurt her.

"I'm sorry," he said. "I didn't know. I never thought. Please forgive me if you can."

Back at the hotel, he fell into a panic. Had he been taking Lillian for granted? Taking his leisurely time on the grounds of their short acquaintance? The way other men, even his own friends, glanced at her—how long would she wait for him? He looked at the clock and at the telephone. It was early afternoon at home, so she would be at the office.

"You frightened me!" she cried. "Are you all right?"

At the sound of her voice, a feeling somewhere between relief and laughter choked his
own voice. "Listen to me. It's important. You've
been away, now I'm away and it doesn't make
any sense."

"What doesn't make any sense? What are you
talking about?"

"That we aren't together, don't you see? We
need to be together, we're perfectly matched.
Dammit! I'm not coming up with the right
words. Oh, Lillian, I miss you! Make believe I'm
on my knees before you right now and I'm
handing you a box with a ring in it and I'm asking you to set the date. And make it soon. I
mean soon, thirty days and not a minute longer.
Will you?"

"Oh, darling, I'm crying. I'm sitting here in
the office crying. I can hardly talk. But I don't
need thirty days."

He flew home with a ring from one of London's best jewelers in his pocket. Every so often
when he touched the small velvet box, he felt a
surge of pride, and more than that, of gratitude,
as he saw himself again departing from his
hometown, boarding the plane to New York,
and buying the leather-bound *Jefferson* on Fifth
Avenue. Now he was climbing up in the world,
traveling all over it, and soon would be coming
back every night to the most marvelous wife in

the prettiest little home anybody could desire. And he thought humbly, I hope I deserve it all.

∽∾

Lillian's plans were short and simple. She suggested that they be married in a clergyman's study and leave at once for a honeymoon in any place that Donald should choose.

He, on the other hand, while agreeing about the ceremony, did suggest that they make more of a celebration out of their wedding day by giving a gala dinner to their friends in some gala place.

"But I don't know any of your friends except Cindy and a couple of people from your office," he added.

"That's because I don't have many friends. You know I live quietly. I'm as much of a stranger in this city as you were when you first arrived here."

"But you have relatives on Long Island. You said you had a lot of them."

"Did I? Then I was exaggerating. Anyway, I never see any of them."

He was curious. "You never said why you don't."

"They're not my kind." Lillian shrugged. "We're entirely different. We have nothing in common."

"But you do have one thing in common. You have some of the same ancestors, blood ties."

They were both reading in the room that Donald liked to call "the library." From where he sat he caught in the lamplight a small, ironical twist on Lillian's lips, and it made him feel stubborn.

"Blood's thicker than water? Cliché," she said.

"A cliché is a cliché because there's truth in it. After my mother died and I was truly, totally alone, I can't tell you how much I wished I had somebody who belonged to me. He could have been almost anyone but an ax murderer and I would have welcomed him."

"Well, you do have those third cousins out in—where is it?—Nebraska?"

"Wyoming. And I've seen them one time in my entire life. But your relatives live on Long Island and you grew up practically next door, you said."

"Nevertheless, I don't want them."

The firm tone was irritating. "Who are these people? What's this all about? Why the secrecy?"

"They're just people, for heaven's sake! What are you hinting at, that they're all convicts or something? They're just plain, ordinary people."

"Of course they are. But can't you say something about them? What do they do, for instance?"

"I don't know what they do. I'll find the address and phone, since you're so persistent, and you can find out all about them yourself. Just please stop foisting them on me."

"I'm not 'foisting' anything at all on you, Lillian. But I must say, you're a little bit touchy today."

"I'm not touchy! You're pestering me. It's not like you."

He was nonplussed. Here we are, we who love each other beyond words—yes, beyond words, he thought—and we're quarreling over nonsense like this. Perhaps after all he really was making a fuss about nothing. Don't be a pompous jackass, Donald. If for some reason she wants to be rid of these relatives, what difference need it make to you? What business is it of yours?

Yet he could not resist one more remark. "You never even talk about your parents."

"They're dead."

"Is that a reason never to talk about them?" he asked very gently.

"What is there to say? She was a housewife, he was a salesman, and they lived, just lived, the way millions of people do."

All of a sudden, he saw a flashback of himself at ten or twelve, on the day when, rummaging perhaps where he was not supposed to rummage, he came upon the telegram from the War Department: *We regret to inform you . . .* He had just stood there staring at the piece of paper in his hand with the world gone strangely still and gray around him. Of course she did not want to talk. Why open the wound to bleed again?

He went over and put his arms around her. "Forget it, darling. What a stupid quarrel! We're both nervous and overexcited, that's all it is. So let's have our little party right here. I'll have my group—they're all crazy about you. And you'll have anybody you want, or nobody."

"Just a few favorites from my office, and Cindy with her boyfriend. Unless you mind having them?"

"Of course I don't."

"Well, you're not very fond of her, so I thought—"

"No, I'm not fond of her. But I haven't a thing against her, which is altogether different. She's your friend, and that's enough. You know what? I just thought of something. I have to introduce you to Mr. Pratt. Get off from work a few minutes early one day, tomorrow if you can, and stop in for a minute. I want to show you off."

❧

"I found her," Donald announced to Mr. Pratt the next morning. "You've been urging me, and now I'm doing it. We're being married at the end of the month."

On the shelf behind the other man's smile and handshake stood the photograph of his family. Even more than his achievements in this office, the picture seemed to define the man, as if to say: *This is what it's all about. Love, loyalty, family.* And now, I, too, thought Donald. Lillian and I, a family.

"She's going to call for me here this afternoon. If it's convenient, I'd like you to meet her."

"Convenient? Donald, I'd be really hurt if you didn't introduce me."

So she came, and the introduction was made. In her plain, dark blue dress, with pearls in her ears and gloves on her hands—for as she later explained, she had assumed that so proper a man as Augustus Pratt would approve of gloves—she was perfect. Everything, from her well-modulated voice to her well-chosen words, was perfect.

It bothered Donald the next morning that Augustus Pratt, such a master of language, had so little to say.

"A beautiful young woman. How long have you known her?"

"We met in April. Sort of love at first sight."

Pratt nodded. "I wish you everything I could wish for my own son, Donald."

He could have said more, couldn't he? He could have been warmer. Donald was slightly annoyed. But then, sometimes when he was preoccupied, Pratt did have a way of turning down the thermostat.

Events moved happily along. They were married on a golden day in a mahogany-paneled study just off Fifth Avenue, each with one friend from their respective offices as witness. Then through the mild afternoon, they walked back hand in hand, up the avenue toward the park, and turning eastward, arrived at their home where a welcoming crowd was waiting.

The apartment overflowed with splendid autumn flowers. The caterers, who had been recommended by Mr. Buzley, had supplied them, along with superb food and the best champagne.

"I can't believe you didn't invite him," Donald whispered to the bride.

"He wouldn't enjoy the company. He's twice our age. Anyway, his wife is terribly sick at home."

Nevertheless, he had sent his wedding gift, a silver service for twelve that Lillian described as "Danish silver, about the best there is."

"I wouldn't know," Donald said.

"It costs a fortune, I can tell you, but he thinks nothing of it. He's always doing things like that for people. All the time."

The party was lively. First the women all wanted to look at the gifts that Lillian had tactfully stored away. Then someone found the record player and added music to the pleasant hubbub of talk, toasts, clattering china, and popping corks. People were all feeling very, very good.

Toward the end of the evening, Cindy got drunk and had to lie down in the bedroom, where she managed to smear a faceful of garish makeup on the silk pillow shams. Her current boyfriend, in T-shirt and jeans with hair rippling and beard rumpling to his shoulders, stood out among this gathering of ties and jackets. Nevertheless, everybody enjoyed him, and Donald observed that he "added an exotic note" to the scene.

"Come to think of it, he may be smarter than any two of us here put together. On the other hand, he may not be. God bless him, anyway."

So, full of champagne and good humor, he closed the door on the departing guests, set the alarm clock in time for an early departure to Vermont, and took his wife to bed.

# Chapter 4

They decided that because the semester had already begun, Lillian would wait until the following fall before starting to work on a master's degree in art.

"It's what you really want," Donald said. "So what if you can't be Mrs. Renoir or Mrs. Picasso? You'd do wonderfully in an auction gallery or a museum. With all you already know, you're halfway there. All you need is the degree. And in the meantime, I think it's fine that your boss will let you work three days a week to keep yourself busy."

"Howard Buzley is absolutely the best."

"I really should meet him sometime, don't you think?"

"You wouldn't like him."

"Why do you always say that?"

"I don't always say it."

"Well, you sometimes do. Anyway, why wouldn't I like Buzley when he's been so good to my girl?"

"He's just not your type."

"What on earth do you think my life is like, that I just go around selecting clients who are 'my type,' whatever that is?"

Lillian laughed. "All right, I'll arrange it sometime. But seriously, what am I going to do with the days I don't work? I'm already starting to feel pampered and lazy."

"It won't hurt you to take it easy for a change. Do some reading and get a head start on your course. Go out with some women, have lunch, make friends."

"You know what, Donald? You're a darling. You're too good to me."

Good to her? How else could he be but good to her?

Every evening when he opened the door and stepped into the hall, he caught sight of the table. Always it was a picture for a luxurious magazine, set with a little pot of flowers, proper china, and Howard Buzley's Danish silver. Often the food was something unusual, culled from the shelf of cookbooks that she had begun to collect.

"I've never done any serious cooking," she

told him, "but now that I've begun, I want to do it perfectly."

"You do everything perfectly."

One day when he came home, she was all excited. "You can't imagine where I was today. In the penthouse! Oh, you should see it, Donald! I had no idea. It's a regular ranch house, a spacious one with a garden so big that you'd think you were out in the suburbs. Oh, I knew what a penthouse was, of course, but actually seeing one is something else."

Definitely not interested in penthouses, he was interested in her enthusiasm, which was always delightful.

"I'm all ears," he said.

"You know that tiny dog, the Yorkshire terrier we sometimes see in the lobby? Well, he belongs to the people in the penthouse. Sanders, their name is, and this morning, the boy who takes the dog for a walk lost him. I can't imagine how, oh yes, the hook that fastens the leash to the collar wasn't on right and the dog ran away. Well, I happened to be in the lobby just going out, when the boy came back practically out of his mind. Stupid! Instead of going after Spike— isn't that a name for a big, tough, six-pound dog?—he came running home. So I went out and raced down the street, turned the corner, and there were some fellows walking away with

Spike. Now *they* really were big and tough. I gave a shriek, 'That's my dog!' which attracted a lot of attention, so they dropped Spike, I grabbed him, and ran home.

"Well, Mrs. Sanders, Chloe, wouldn't let me go. I had to go upstairs with her, have a second breakfast, take a tour of the house which is incredibly beautiful, including Spike's nook, where his basket is upholstered to match the room."

Donald smiled. She was so charming, rosy, out of breath, and full of her story.

"Remember that day when I said dogs and babies break the ice? If it hadn't been for Spike, we'd never have done more than nod to each other in the elevator, if that. She wants us to come up one evening soon. He's on Wall Street. Frank Sanders."

"Yes, one of the biggest new names in the city. Made a few hundred million before he was thirty. Too rich for us, Lil."

"Oh, do you think so? I hope not. Of course, when we have to invite them back—oh, I don't know—I did say that we're just married and will soon be looking for something larger."

"Not soon. It'll be a while before we do anything like that. You shouldn't have said it."

She answered quickly, "I didn't mean that I don't appreciate this apartment, because you know I do. You aren't annoyed, are you?"

No, he was not annoyed, and he said so. Rather, he was surprised by this evidence of insecurity coming from so sophisticated a woman. And then he thought, there are bound to be many surprises, aren't there? Consider that starting a marriage must be something like opening a new book; as you turn the pages, unexpected scenes and situations will be revealed.

"So you'll accept if they invite us?"

"Of course I will."

The Sanders were leaders among the young group who, like themselves, had made enormous quick fortunes. They were friendly and never could thank Lillian enough for her rescue of Spike. Clearly, they were taken with her, Donald saw. But then, most people were. For how often did one meet a human being so filled with alert and joyous energy as Lillian was?

So, on rare evenings when they were home, the Sanders—soon to be simply Chloe and Frank—invited Lillian and Donald to have some after-dinner coffee and dessert on their marble coffee table in their forty-foot-long living room. Once in a while they came downstairs to the Wolfes'. Therefore, it was not as astonishing as it might have been when invitations to gallery openings, teas, benefits, and gala charity dinners began to arrive in the mail. Chloe Sanders apparently had decided to sponsor the interesting newcomers.

Most of these events turned out to be for Lillian in the daytime, since Donald, unlike many of the men in circles like these, was a worker with long hours, into which great balls and banquets seldom fit. But she, an unknown from the city's outer rim, was gradually being drawn toward its center. And Donald, seeing her pleasure, was glad.

⁓◦⌇

Often, much later, whenever he tried to find a pattern behind events and a reason for the pattern, he would wonder whether this friendship—or was it just acquaintance?—with these people could have been the moving cause. But no, he would usually argue, an event is simply the result of a situation's meeting up with a particular character or temperament. In short, it would all have happened, anyway.

⁓◦⌇

Perhaps it had been negligent of Donald not to have discussed with his wife in greater detail the ever-present subject of money. But because he felt himself to be prosperous it hadn't seemed important.

One day he came home to find a painting on prominent display between the windows.

"What's this?"

Lillian wore the proud look of a mother with a new baby. "I bought it this afternoon. Do you like it?"

"Yes, oh yes I do."

It was a small-sized oil, suitably framed in what looked like old wood, of a winter scene with angular, dark branches and slender, short new growth half buried in blue-white snow, all these wrapped in a stillness of silvery gray air.

"Waiting for spring," he said, stepping back for a better view. "I have a sense of late winter, of thaw. Maybe it's February. Where did you find it?"

"At that showing this afternoon. I couldn't take my eyes away. And it was a very good buy."

"Really? How much?"

"Seventy-five hundred. It's worth much more. It's old. Nineteen-ten."

"Seven thousand, five hundred— Lillian!"

"For goodness sake, you know what prices art commands these days. You've been around enough with me to recognize a bargain."

"That depends on the point of view, the ability to pay."

"I don't understand. I've not been extravagant, have I?"

She was staring at him as if she could scarcely believe him.

"No, but—come on in here to my desk. I need to show you some figures that I guess I should have shown you before this. Look here."

Drawing on a pad, he made a simple chart: so much for income, so much for taxes, the remainder subdivided for rent, insurance, daily living, and savings.

"We have to start some real saving. Oh, we can live well, we do live well, but we have to be prudent. There will be children who will need money for their education. So we need to discuss all our big purchases, like this painting, for instance, before we go ahead."

She did not answer at once. Frowning a little, she stood at the desk, caressing her smooth hands while she appeared to be studying her rings. It was a habit she had very lately developed, and it bothered him.

"I thought you made much more than this," she said.

"I don't know what made you think so. It's a very handsome income."

"I didn't mean that it wasn't a great deal of money, of course I didn't. I meant that if I had known this, I wouldn't have been in such a hurry to take the painting. But Chloe kept saying, 'For heaven's sake, treat yourself. You're dying to have it,' and I was embarrassed to walk away without it."

"But how did you pay?"

"Chloe did. She gave them a check, so now we owe her."

Feeling a strong rise of anger, he waited to let it subside before he should say something that he might later regret.

"I can pay part, Donald. It won't be much, but I still get salary every week from Buzley, don't I? So I can help."

Making amends, she stumbled over her words. And when he saw her condition, his anger actually did subside.

"No," he said, "I'll take care of it. Only next time, let's talk it over first. Agreed?"

"You can call it a birthday present and a Christmas present combined for the next few years, Donald," she said, now almost in tears.

She was so contrite that he even began to feel sorry for her.

"Leave that to me. In the meantime, we'll enjoy the painting together. It'll be our treasure," he added, and actually began to feel good about the whole matter.

Then suddenly later in the evening, she told him something else. "Do you remember the opera gala, Donald? The Sanders and their group have taken boxes as usual, and Chloe can get us two seats in her aunt's box. Actually, she's Frank's aunt, Gloria Sanders. You've read about her."

"I haven't. What's she done?"

"Not done, exactly. But she goes everywhere, to all the openings. She's always in the newspaper. She's ages old, but she doesn't look it."

"What opera are they having that night?"

"I don't know, I didn't ask."

"Well, I'd like to know what I'm going to hear before I buy tickets."

"I'm sure it will be wonderful, whatever it is. The important thing is to be there. It's the occasion that counts."

"Not to me. How much are these seats?"

"They're expensive, but nowhere near what the whole box would cost."

"I should hope not. How much?"

"You see, I didn't know anything until tonight about what to spend." She looked at him doubtfully. "And so I said yes. They're a thousand dollars each."

Objects, the lamp, the new painting, and on his lap the typewritten document over which he had been laboring, all spun slightly before Donald's eyes.

"I'm sorry, but you'll have to change your mind about accepting," he said. "We'll go if you want to, but we'll sit in our usual seats. As seats go, they're B-plus. We don't have to have A seats in the boxes, plus a donation."

"You're angry, Donald, and I'm sorry."

"I'm trying not to be angry. You didn't know. But now you do know, and it won't happen again."

"No harm done?"

"There's never any harm done between you and me."

                          ∽◦◡◦∽

The opera was *Tosca*. It had become one of Donald's favorites, not only through these past few years of operagoing, but also because of a childhood memory, when his mother had used to turn on the radio for the Saturday afternoon broadcast. The house had been very small, and from his room he had been able to hear what was to him merely a jumble of voices, violins, and drums. Now and then, though, he had been summoned to listen to something that, his mother said, must not be missed. Most of the time, he would have preferred to miss it, but occasionally, something did catch his ear, a stirring march, or a woman's voice as pure as a flute. So when the first time he heard "Vissi d'arte," he knew he had heard it before.

Now on this festive evening, he was to hear it

again. Here in this splendid hall he sat with his lovely wife glowing in crimson silk, while on the other side of the orchestra pit, a musical drama of incredible tragic beauty was being played. A thrill quivered through his nerves. He felt as if he was being given all the best that life has to give.

In this exultant mood, he stood among the crowd in the lobby between the acts. "She's the best Tosca I've ever heard. Of course, I've only heard one other," he said, laughing at himself. "What are you looking at?"

Lillian had turned to peer at a group standing near the bar.

"Over there," she whispered. "Quick! There's the Sanders' aunt I was telling you about. That emerald pendant—can you believe it? Eight carats at least, maybe ten. Have you any idea what it's worth?"

"None at all," he said.

Whether or not his tone had revealed his abrupt change of mood, he could not tell because she continued her train of thought.

"It must be great to sit like royalty in a box and let your jewels glitter. When you come down to it, there's nothing like opera for dignity. It has a kind of stateliness, don't you think?"

"I guess so," he said.

The next morning was Sunday, so there was

time enough to lie in bed and think while Lillian slept. He knew her face in every detail and yet, what did he really know of *her*? Or anybody? *A secret inside a riddle inside an enigma.* He had been stupid to let himself be hurt by something as trivial as her relative indifference to *Tosca*. What, Donald, is she supposed to be? A carbon copy of you? Who do you think you are, anyway?

Still, it was something that bothered him. By the time she woke up, he had decided to tell her.

"I had a bad dream. I felt that you were drifting away from me."

"That's crazy," she said with her head on his shoulder. "Absolutely crazy."

"I guess it is. But I do wish you'd make some other friends beside people you've met through Chloe. I don't mean that you should give them up, only that it would be nice if you went out in the afternoons with some different people. A little variety . . . you know what I mean?"

"It's hard to make friends in this city. Everybody's too busy with their own affairs. I'm lucky that Chloe's done so much for me."

"What about my little group? Ed's wife. Or Susan. Or Polly. You especially liked Polly, you told me."

"I do see them now and then. But they all

have a kid or two, or else they're pregnant and can't talk about anything else."

He felt himself smiling up at the ceiling. "Maybe that tells you something. Or is it too soon?"

"Donald! We were married last September. What's the rush? Anyway, I'll be starting work on my degree. One thing at a time."

Something compelled him to keep holding on to the subject. With his next remark, he surprised himself, for he had not planned to make it.

"You see quite a good deal of Cindy, don't you?"

"A good deal? No. But I do keep in touch with her. Why? Do you mind?"

"I would have no right to mind whom you see. But as it happens, I don't mind. I think it's interesting that you can feel comfortable with two such extremes, Chloe Sanders and Cindy. By the way, how is she?"

"The same. She finds a lousy job, she keeps it for a week or two, and loses it. If she could stop drinking—but she can't."

"And you keep helping her."

"She's a good soul. I can't stand by and let her drown."

Kindness like this could not help but touch one's heart. "You wonder," he said, "if Cindy had come out of Chloe Sanders's home, would she have been different? A question that everybody asks, and it has no answer. But if there's any way I can help your friend, I will. Just tell me."

"You're a good man, Donald. So good that you're making me sad."

"Sad? Good Lord, I want you to be happy. I want you to be the happiest woman in New York."

Spring was late that year. Cold rain, driven by powerful winds, sped through the gray streets.

"Everything gray," sighed Lillian, standing at the window. "It's depressing."

She had been making these remarks all week, and he was tired of hearing them. "No, it's just winter," he said firmly. "And there's nothing we can do about it."

"Easy for you to talk. You'll get on a plane and fly away, come home, and fly out again."

"I don't always enjoy it. Not always," Donald said. "But I have no choice."

"It seems to me that once in a while you could say no."

"That's too ridiculous to deserve an answer. You know better."

"All right, I do know better. But you can't

imagine what it's like being alone here. It's horrible. You look out of the window and all you see are walls. If we were higher up, at least, you'd have—"

His thoughts interrupted her. *She never liked the apartment. She only pretended that she did.*

"We miss so many things. I do, at least. Nobody asks a woman alone to go out for the evening. Those tickets for the Plaza dinner went to waste because they only gave you two days' notice to fly to Geneva."

It was true that he had been away unusually often during this, the first winter of their marriage. Orton and Pratt had among its clients a company that had been defrauded of hundreds of millions by a man who was still at large. He had been seen, or reports had come in from people who claimed to have seen him, in places as various and scattered as Brazil, Switzerland, and Beluchistan. The company's subsidiaries had interests forming a complicated web that kept a dozen lawyers like Donald busy all over the globe.

"I work for an international law firm, remember? There's nothing I can do about it, Lillian. Or that I want to do, either," he added.

He had not meant to be curt. He wanted peace and contentment, and since he worked for it, it seemed to him that he deserved to have it.

And wanting just to shut everything out, he closed his eyes and laid his head on the chair's pillowed back while a heavy silence like a fog crept through the room.

When he woke up again, there she was, willowy in her slender skirt while one graceful hand toyed with her long necklace, reminding him somehow of one of her favorite paintings; as usual, he failed to remember the artist, some Frenchman, he was very famous. . . .

This has got to stop. I am too touchy, he thought, and surely not for the first time. Why do I let every little tiff trouble me so? Lighten up! What did I expect? A snug little love nest with never a cross word? People aren't like that. I'm not like that. She's not like that. This is marriage. This is life.

"I'll do what I can," he said. "Don't you think I'd rather be here with you than anywhere else in the world? Don't you know that?"

With outstretched arms, she came to him. "When you talk like this, I feel so sorry, Donald, so ashamed of myself. You're too good to me."

He did do what he could. In June, somebody who owned what was said to be a fabulous estate in Westchester was giving a party to which Donald and Lillian, no doubt by way of the Sanders connection, were invited.

Early in the month, he gave Mr. Pratt the date. "I was wondering whether, since we're probably going to have a meeting soon again in Geneva, whether it would be possible to work around that date a bit? My wife—well, you know how it is, she has her heart set on going to this party. I don't even know the people or anything about them."

"You haven't heard about Tommy Fox? About the few billions he made in Mexico? No? Well, it's a couple of years back, and I guess you forgot." Pratt twinkled. "Or you don't keep up with the social news. Well, tell your wife not to worry."

So it was that on a fine, cool evening long before sunset, Donald and Lillian drove out of the city in a sumptuous, attention-getting, imported sports car. He had asked her to rent a car for the occasion, and this was her choice. It suited the occasion, she said. It was worth a hundred and seventy-five thousand dollars.

"A hundred and seventy-five? It's not much larger than two trash cans tied together, in my opinion."

"Well, it's a two-seater, what do you expect?" She laughed. "And it can go over one hundred twenty miles an hour, I'm sure you'll be glad to know."

"Great! I'll try it as soon as we're off Riverside Drive."

She was full of excitement. Her dress matched her eyes, he remarked. Not exactly, she said. The dress had violet mixed with the blue, and the color was called "periwinkle." Around her throat lay a narrow diamond necklace about which there could have been some fairly heated discussion if he had not made up his mind that nothing would mar this event, or any event in the future.

"Chloe insisted on lending it to me," she had explained. "You see, what happened is that Frank just gave her another one for her birthday. Of course it's very different from this one, but still she really didn't need it. So now she has two, and she said there's no reason why this one should go to waste when she wants to lend it to me for tonight."

Donald's mother would have said that borrowed jewelry was tacky. It was funny how a man who seldom gave thought to his old life anymore could suddenly find a quirky memory like that one popping into his head.

Nevertheless, the necklace was an enhancement, drawing the eye to the pure curve of Lillian's chin, to the red of her plump lips and the blue of her eyes. Men would look at her this evening; they always did. Well, let them look. He reached over and for a moment or two held her hand.

The house that they reached was enormous and obviously quite new. White Corinthian columns gave it the look of a Southern plantation; the huge, double front doors, heavy and dark brown, were definitely Victorian, while from each side of the main building there jutted a flat-roofed wing that could easily be mistaken for a storage warehouse, he thought, except for its vast plate-glass windows.

Pretty awful, he thought. His work had taken him to some great mansions here and abroad, and none of them had ever looked like this.

At the rear of the house on a wide open space that apparently had been cleared out of the surrounding woodlands, a colorful crowd moved about, while waiters in contrasting white moved among them carrying trays.

"What a picture!" Lillian cried. "They've invited two hundred fifty people, I heard. Oh, Donald, look at that—"

*That,* to their right down a gentle slope, was a sizable pond near the edge of the woodland. At its center rose a quaint gazebo of wooden filigree such as one may see in an old-fashioned garden.

"Do you swim out to it?" she wondered.

A man, passing and overhearing, replied, "No, it's just for water lilies and for beauty." Laughing, he added, "For algae, too. But everybody wants a pond these days. They've already had their pools forever. By the way, am I supposed to know you? I'm Roy Fox, Tommy's brother."

Introductions were made, hands were shaken, and the three walked on toward the enormous tent in the distance.

"We're very close old friends of Chloe and Frank," Lillian said.

"Are you? Then we must have met before. I'm a people person, and yet I've got a bad memory."

"Oh, there you are," Chloe Sanders called out. "I said to Frank, those are the Wolfes in that stunning little Italian number. When did you get it?"

"We didn't. We rented it," Donald said.

"To try it out," Lillian explained. "To see whether we like it enough to buy it."

Something trickled down Donald's neck. It was so warm that it could well have been a few drops of water, but it was not; it was shame. Why did she say things like this as if people couldn't see right through her remark? On the other hand and for all he knew, perhaps they didn't see.

Frank Sanders now came up. "Place is jump-ing. I never knew I knew so many people. Take two steps and there's old Ray, or Charlie, or somebody. It's a great crowd. They've got two top bands—I forget the names—but later on there's going to be entertainment by the Dig Down Wheezers. They cost a dime or two!"

"I'm starved," said Chloe.

The crowd was drifting toward the tent. It was a huge construction whose walls were of sheer white silk. Losing touch with the only couple they knew, as the Sanders were immediately sur-rounded by friends, Donald and Lillian found themselves at a table with strangers. They were all strangers to one another.

Not the top echelon, he thought with some amusement. They're on the fringe, like us. They're the leftovers.

Lillian was perplexed that they were not sit-ting with any of the women with whom she had become acquainted at the charity luncheons, and he saw that she was hurt. She did not understand that status here was assigned according to net worth, but since this was neither the time nor the place to explain that, he merely said that it was nice to be meeting new people. A pretty young woman across from them was telling everyone that they had never before been at a party like this.

"It's so lovely of them to invite Rick and me. Our children go to the same day camp with theirs, that's how we know each other. Of course, we're neighbors, too, or sort of neighbors. Our house used to be the gardener's cottage on that big place across from here."

Donald liked her honesty, and her husband Rick's simplicity. He was a lawyer, a sole practitioner here in town.

"Oh, Orton and Pratt," he said when Donald, in answer to his question, had to give the name of his firm. "A lot of pressure must go with a job in a place like that, I imagine."

"Donald is one of the partners," Lillian said unnecessarily.

Why did she have to talk like that? She used to be so tactful. It was on his lips to tell her privately just how unnecessary and even boastful her remark had sounded, but thinking better of it, he drew her instead onto the dance floor and into the flow of the music.

"It's very smart of them to have two bands," she said. "The rock band will alternate with this one every half hour or so. In that way everybody will be happy."

Her face, turned up toward his, was like some gleaming tropical flower that he knew he had seen somewhere, perhaps in a botanical garden. The music lilted; he was swept into a sense of total harmony. How then was it that in a matter of seconds, this harmony could be broken by a trivial remark?

Lillian spoke softly. "We go well together, don't we?"

"We do," he said.

"You're happy. You didn't think you would like it here this much."

He smiled. "You read my mind, don't you?"

"I do. You mustn't take everything so seriously, Donald. That's your trouble."

"No," he said, "that isn't my trouble."

Just then someone tapped him on the shoulder. "I'm cutting in. It's allowed, didn't you hear?" The man was slightly drunk, or not so much drunk as just "feeling good." "Why should you monopolize the best-looking woman in the room?"

Because she consented to the man, Donald let her go. Back at the table he watched, and seeing that she was quite safe, rejoined the conversation.

At the far end of the table, a stout man who was probably younger than he looked was holding forth. "Have you any idea what an affair like this costs? First they get party planners to put all of it together. Twenty thousand for starters for the planners. Then after that, the sky's the limit. Take a look at the flowers on this table. Just the flowers. From Hawaii, five hundred minimum for twenty-five tables, it's safe to say. And that's peanuts. What about the caviar at all the bars? Prime steaks, lobster, anything you want. Did you see the other dance floor, the one they built on top of the pool?" The stout man, whose enthusiasm had begun to border on awe, was not about to wait for an answer. "Walk around. Take a look. Tell you something confidential. Later, when they're sure the kids are in bed, nobody prowling around downstairs, they're having a couple of strippers for entertainment, so don't leave too soon."

Now the bands changed places. This one pounded. The accompanying singer bellowed. The dancers went wild. They spun, they collided, their knees and elbows worked like pistons, and they sweated.

Donald looked for Lillian, and not seeing her pass, got up to search. Still unable to find her in the jostling mob now grown to double its original size, he sat down again. Oh, let her enjoy herself! As soon as she came back in sight, he would get up and join her, although the truth was that he could do without this kind of dancing; he had been rather good at it when he was eighteen, but by twenty-five or so, he had outgrown it. And laughing a little at himself, he watched and waited for her.

As newcomers poured through the entrance, the tent was constantly losing its cooled air. The young lawyer Rick looked at his watch, and his wife covered her mouth to yawn. Half an hour had gone by since Donald's last sight of Lillian.

Puzzled, a little worried, and a little angry, too, he got up and walked away from the tent. The night air and the sudden quiet once the band was out of hearing were soft. A few stars rose above the glow of the lanterns that had been hung among the trees. Little groups were scattered upon the lawn, strolling or standing. If he had not had something else on his mind, he would have absorbed the rare beauty of the scene.

Well, she can't be far, he thought, and began to walk. Somebody must have seen her.

Two men, passing him, mentioned a name that was all too familiar. "Son of a gun, they'll never catch him. He's smarter than ten Interpols. Or top-notch law firms, or the IRS, either."

The other man chuckled. "I'm on his side. Feather your nest, is what I say."

*Chuckled!* A lump of disgust formed in Donald's throat. Enough of this. Where the devil was she? Find her, and go home.

"Looking for your wife? We saw her going down to the pond, I think." Turning, Donald saw Rick with his wife hurrying away toward the road.

The wife said, "We're leaving early. The baby-sitter, you know. But it was a lovely party."

Innocent, he thought, watching them go. She wanted to be polite about the party, which obviously they had not enjoyed. And he walked on toward the pond.

Frank Sanders and a woman whom Donald did not know were standing there. "Looking for Lillian?"

"Yes. She seems to have disappeared. I can't imagine—"

"Have you looked at the beds?"

"Beds?"

"There are three or four of them on the other side of the tent." Frank laughed. "You haven't heard about them?"

For an instant, Donald went blank. In the second instant, when recall came, he was sure his blood pressure was rising.

"Yes," he said, "I'd read something, heard something, about parties like those, but I didn't expect it here."

"Why not? Anyhow, they're over that way if you want to look."

Donald's blood pounded; he even felt its swelling pressure under the wedding band on his finger. Walking rapidly back toward the tent, passing it almost at a run, he rounded a corner of high shrubbery and came upon Lillian walking ahead, and accompanied by a man.

Hearing footsteps behind her, she turned, and seeing Donald, cried out, "Where've you been? I've been looking all over for you. Hugh—it is Hugh, isn't it?—this is my husband, Donald Wolfe."

Both men nodded. Then the other one said, "Well, now that you've found each other, I'll look for my own party, be on my way."

"Lillian, what was that about?" demanded Donald when the other man was out of hearing.

"About? I was looking for you. I met this man, and he was helping me look, that's all."

Light touched her flushed face; slanting across a bay enclosed by young spruce, it revealed a bed in the background, a proper bed with a couple lying on it.

"Don't fool with me, Lillian," he said, still very quietly.

"What are you doing to me? I didn't even know about this, did you?"

"Not till a few minutes ago."

"Then why are you accusing me? You always pick on me, Donald."

"That's not true. You know very well I don't."

Now as they walked away and drew closer to a lantern, he saw that her face was burning. She stumbled, and caught herself. There was a large, wet stain on her dress.

"What have you been drinking?" he demanded.

"Do I have to explain every breath I take? Do I?" she whimpered.

Suddenly he thought he understood. No, she would not have been going voluntarily to one of those beds. The man had been about to take advantage of her condition. It was an old, old story.

"Come this way, Lil. We're going home. We've had enough of this place."

"Maybe you have, but I haven't. The party's just begun, and I'm having a good time."

"What have you been drinking, anyway? Whatever it was, you've had far too much of it."

"I don't know what it was. What difference does it make? Somebody offered me a few drinks, they tasted good, and I drank them."

"These people are foul. Foul."

When she stumbled again, he picked her up and carried her, now almost limp, to the flashy little car, and they rolled out onto the highway. From time to time he looked over at her; she had fallen asleep, and there was something vaguely sad about a human being asleep and vulnerable, or so he always thought. Only a few hours ago they had driven to the party in such high spirits. She had been especially gaily beau-

tiful in her dress—periwinkle, was it? Now, huddled in the seat with that big stain below the
incongruous diamond necklace, she filled him
with anger.

It isn't only because she drank too much—that
can happen, he thought. Or because of what that
man might have done with her if I hadn't come
along just then. It's the whole bad atmosphere of
the place. That guy Rick felt it, too. They didn't
belong there. That's why they left so early. And
Lillian doesn't belong there, either.

They were almost home when she woke up,
tidied her hair, and checked her lipstick. Before
they entered the building, she wrapped a shawl
into a graceful curve that hid the soiled dress.

"All right? Will I do?" She spoke brightly, as
though nothing at all had happened.

She "did" very well, indeed. Two men riding up in the elevator cast meaningful glances in
her direction, and then toward each other,
glances that possibly Lillian missed, but that
Donald did not.

"Shall I make some coffee?" he asked when
they opened their door.

"Not unless you want any. I don't need it,
thanks. Did I disgrace you too badly?"

"No, nor yourself, either. I got you away before you could."

When he went into the bedroom a few

minutes later, she had already removed all her clothes except the necklace.

"Unclasp this for me, will you please? I hate to take it off. It must be worth a year's rent on this place, or more, for all I know."

He removed the necklace and laid it on the bedside table. As her hand went out to touch it, he seized the finger that bore his ring.

"I'm the man who gave you this diamond," he said roughly. "Remember that."

"You're jealous," she said, smiling at him.

"Of whom? Of whom should I be jealous?"

"Of anybody. Men at the party. Men in the elevator just now." There she stood with her head high, teasing him and smiling. Damn her! She was infuriating, she was irresistible, she made him angry, and she made him want her with every bone and every drop of his blood.

"Get into that bed," he said, "and do it now."

It is remarkable, he told himself the next day, how a night of intense love can soothe the nerves, eradicate uncertainties, and make the world seem to be a place where almost everything is manageable. He was also thinking that the less time she spent with Chloe Sanders and her restless ilk, the better.

"I was just thinking," he said, "that with all the

energy you have, it might be a good thing for you to work full time until your course begins. Why not ask Mr. Buzley? You always get along so well. He'd probably be glad."

As it turned out, he was glad. And every day Lillian came home with some new anecdote or impression with which she entertained Donald over dinner. The most amazing people came to Buzley's office, surely not the kind who came into Orton and Pratt. In one week there had been a famous rap singer accused of assault, and a woman who had come off welfare and won the lottery.

"It's fascinating! And old man Buzley is remarkable. This is his wife's fourth year of fighting Lou Gehrig's disease, waiting to die, but you'd never guess when you're with him. You wouldn't believe his sense of humor unless you heard him cracking jokes. Poor old man, I'm really crazy about him."

Yes, he had done the right thing in leading her away from the Sanders crowd. Roaming through the city as they had in their first days together, renting a rowboat in the park, picnicking with friends beneath the trees, they celebrated the lovely month of June.

Early in July there came an invitation. Roy Fox was giving a party.

"I'm really surprised they remembered us,"

said Lillian. "Why, the Foxes only had us because of the Sanders!"

"This one copied his brother's list, that's all. I'm very sure no one there really remembered you or me."

"Roy's estate is supposed to be even more fabulous than Tommy's. I'm really curious to see how that can be."

Donald shook his head. "Lil, dear, we're not going."

"Not going! Whyever not?"

"One person's 'fabulous' is another person's disgust, Lil."

"What's the matter? Those beds again? Just because some people go in for that sort of thing doesn't mean other people have to."

Her voice and her posture told him that this was not going to be over with in five minutes. At the same time, something clicked in his memory: Of course! That man whom he had overheard cheering on the very scoundrel who had fled the country with his stolen millions, that man was Roy and Tommy's father.

"Foul," he said. "Those people are foul."

"Why? Oh, because of those beds you consign them to hell?"

"No, it's larger and deeper than that."

He was not about to start a discussion about

morals, sexual, financial, or otherwise, so he answered simply.

"The whole affair was vulgar. Too much of everything. Sometimes less is more. I didn't like the atmosphere, and I don't want to go again."

"You ought to get a soapbox, Donald. You sound like a preacher. You're a puritan."

"I may have been called a lot of things behind my back, possibly I have been, but I doubt 'puritan' was ever one of them."

"Then you're some kind of radical who hates anybody richer than he is."

"You really know you're talking nonsense now. Do I hate, as you put it, do I hate Mr. Pratt? No, because he's decent in every way. He enjoys what he earns, doesn't waste, doesn't show off, and is, above all, honorable."

"All this heavy talk about a simple invitation. I can't believe it." Lillian stared at him. "You can be so boring, Donald. Have you any idea how boring you can be? I had such a different impression of you that day we met, that you were vital, and humorous, and open-minded."

Strange, he thought as he met her stare, that those are the very qualities for which I am sometimes praised. Still, he stood there looking at her blue eyes as he might have looked at the knives that had stabbed him.

"I'm curious, Donald. What did you think of me when we met?"

"I didn't think. I only felt," he said.

In the wide bed they lay without touching. Lights and shadows moved across the ceiling. Can we have made a mistake? he asked himself. Pain cold as terror ran through him. All this anger, all these words, because of some stranger's worthless invitation! Should he perhaps give in and go? Something said yes, give in, it's not worth the fuss. And something else said no. This goes much deeper than whether we spend those few hours with those particular people or not.

But how deep, and why, and where does it end?

In the morning after a few cool, civil words, each of them rushed off to work. Donald's day was a typical one, filled with meetings, papers, telephone calls, and no time for personal affairs. But by early evening when the long day ended, those affairs came flooding back, and he was shocked to realize that he did not want to go right home. So he telephoned, made an excuse, and went out for a hamburger with one of the new lawyers in the firm.

This young man was lonesome because his wife was out of town visiting somebody in her family who was ill. She was pregnant, and he missed her terribly. But she would be coming back on Tuesday, and he was counting the hours, he said, unembarrassed to speak the words or to display the happiness on his face.

He seems so innocent and so young, Donald thought as he walked home, although he isn't that many years younger than I am. Why do I feel so heavy and sad? Am I seeing a mountain when it's really only a hill? Am I?

She had been waiting for him with something to tell him; this he saw on her face when he entered. He could not read whether the news was good or bad, only that it was important.

"I'm pregnant," she said.

That night, he thought at once, the night of that party when we came home. In fact, he had even wondered about it later because he had taken no precautions; she had overwhelmed him.

"Aren't you going to say anything, Donald?"

For once he was unable to speak. He could only put his arms around her, and blink away a few tender tears.

# Chapter 5

⌒⌒⌒

Suddenly, as when fresh air sweeps through an overheated space, there was a change in the atmosphere. There was a change in the tone, as if no voice had ever been harsh and no mean words ever spoken. Donald was determined that it should be so, for did not marriage, like the start of a new career or a move to another continent—yet a far more drastic change than either of these—require a time for settling in, or getting used to the newness?

He still winced at the scorn she had flung at him, although he felt this was immature and served no end.

In her own way, she apologized. "You're physically so powerful, so strong, Donald, that to look at you nobody would guess you are so soft inside. I really should try to remember it, shouldn't I?"

"You're quite all right as you are. Let's just be glad about this news. You are glad, aren't you?"

"Well, it is a bit early and certainly unplanned, but I am. Yes. Of course I am."

At the office he heard himself being as ridiculously pleased with himself as all his friends had been when they made their big announcement. With some amusement, he saw his own future, carrying photographs in his wallet and trading the usual anecdotes about babies.

"You and Lillian really ought to go someplace," one of his friends advised. "You're going to be tied down for a good long time. People don't hop over to Europe or California with a new baby, you know."

So the idea was born. In spite of all Donald's travels from Bangkok to Helsinki and in between, he had somehow skipped Italy; Lillian had often said she would love to see Italy again; therefore, they would go to Italy.

He was glad to let her make all the arrangements for the trip, the clothes, the hotels, the itinerary, and the new luggage. Really delighted, she glowed with excitement as if, he thought, there were lighted candles behind her face. And with the thought there came an instant's recall of that day in the pocket park, of her blue eyes, and her voice, and her delicate fingers peeling an orange.

The weather was lovely, cool and sunny. In Rome they walked on cobblestones through narrow streets, past massive medieval palaces. They saw cathedrals, fountains, majestic statues, and some of the greatest art in the world. In a rented car they drove on shady roads between umbrella pines in stately rows; they wandered through Hadrian's villa one day and returned to the city for dinner at a restaurant in a garden walled by cypress trees.

"I didn't need a guidebook or a guide," he told her. "You must have been born here in another life, you know it so well."

"Wait till you see Venice," she said.

"Are you sure you haven't been walking too much?" he said, worrying. "All these hills and steps? Everywhere we go there seem to be a million steps to climb."

"I'm fine. They don't bother me. There's nothing fragile about being pregnant, you know."

Actually, he did not know anything about the condition. Of course, one sometimes did still hear those old wives' tales about women waking up in the middle of the night with a terrible craving for strawberries or whatnot. There were no signs of anything like that in Lillian. As she said, she did not feel in any way different.

Yet there did seem to be a difference. At night she had no energy left. As soon as she lay down, she fell immediately asleep. Wondering about that, he tried a few times to arouse her, but since he seemed only to be disturbing her, he concluded that this must be an effect of her condition and that he ought not bother her. Once they were home, he would ask her to speak to her doctor about it. He had never heard that a man must make exceptions for a pregnant woman, but then he had never had any reason to discuss the matter.

Venice was the next trove of treasure. Arriving by train from Rome, they took a few steps up to the Grand Canal, where they boarded a boat. Within a minute or two it passed beneath the Rialto Bridge, which brought at once to Donald's mind the ninth-grade classroom and his *Merchant of Venice* in its dark green paper jacket.

"Look, look!" cried Lillian, pointing left and right. "There's a marvelous Tintoretto in that church. We'll have to see that. And over there, the Ca' Rezzonico, it's a palace with everything you can think of—*Tiepolo,* frescoes, tapestries—oh, look now. People, terribly rich people, actually live all along here in these marvelous mansions." She was almost breathless. "We need a month in Venice, and probably that wouldn't be enough. Now we're passing the Accademia, such paintings, such precious things, Donald! We're almost at the hotel, we'll have dinner and rush out first thing in the morning."

"You seem to have traveled all over Italy," he remarked that evening. "Just you alone? Or with your friend Betty?"

"Oh, I made many friends, American students and Italians, too."

"You've picked up the language very quickly."

"Yes, it's a beautiful language, isn't it? By the way, when you meet Betty in Florence, you must call her 'Bettina.' She's become very Italian."

Donald watched her. She was loving it all, the elegant dinner table on the water's edge, the church across the canal that she had lost no time in telling him was called the Santa Maria della Salute; she was loving the way she was able to translate for him; she must surely love the woman in flowered silk whom she had seen in the mirror upstairs.

"I'm beginning to show," she said.

"Not yet, but soon you will, I guess." And then, because he thought that perhaps she had sounded a trifle petulant, he asked, "Do you mind?"

"Not if it's only temporary. I should hate to get droopy, though, or ever have stretch marks."

"If you ever have stretch marks, no one will see them except me, and I won't mind," he said gently.

"Well, let's not talk about them, anyway. Tomorrow we're going to explore. I know all the little *campi* where the people live. I'll show you the real life, not only the great sights."

She could have been a teacher, he thought, as he walked with Lillian and listened to her. Then he corrected himself: No, not a teacher, but one of those entertaining and intellectual beauties that you read about in biographies of emperors and kings.

"I've saved the best for the last," Lillian said on the final morning in Venice. "For me, at least, Florence is the best. And there's a lot to see on the way there, too, so that's why I thought we'd get a car and drive." She wanted to do the driving. "I know the roads, you see. I can't believe how much I remember. So you just look and take it all in."

It was Donald's intention to take it all in. He had a habit after seeing things memorable of testing himself to find out how much of the color, the shape, and the history would remain in his head. And on this day, by late afternoon when they reached Florence, he already knew what would remain vividly and always in his head.

They had passed a cemetery where soldiers of the Second World War lay among flags and cypress trees. His mind had leapt then to another cemetery on the coast of France where, under American flags whipping on the wind from the Atlantic, he had stood looking at his father's grave. By what curious connection his mind should take still another leap, he could not have said; he only knew that an acute sensation gripped his throat, and words burst from it. "I hope it's a boy. I really want a son."

"Do you think about this all the time, Donald? Are you going to keep it up for the next six months, for heaven's sake?"

"I don't know. Why? Are you telling me that you don't think about the baby?"

"Not if I can help it. I live for today."

He looked at her. Even though the afternoon sun was falling full upon him, he felt a wave of chill. We don't know each other. I don't know her, he thought. And it was as if these last few lovely weeks had never happened.

"We're almost there," she said. "There's just enough of the afternoon left for us to see the Duomo. It's the next-largest cathedral in Italy, you know, after the Vatican. Tomorrow morning we'll walk around the central city. It's not more than a mile wide. After that, we'll start the museums. And after that, we'll meet Bettina for dinner. I can't wait."

Like a child obediently walking with an adult, Donald examined the inside and the outside of the cathedral. He saw and listened, yet all the time his own words were beating a rhythm in his head: *I don't know her. We don't know each other.*

And then a kind of fear began to creep through him, a fear of himself. Was he to go on like this, darkening the light because she had spoken with what had seemed a flip indifference to the coming child? True, she very often said things that he, and many other people, too, would probably not say. The word "boring" had been a very hurtful thing to him, and he had still not quite forgotten it. Yet there must be many who would simply have replied in kind and then forgotten the whole business.

Yes, he was touchy. Quite tough when he was out in the world and toughness was required, he was touchy at home with Lillian. She had such great power to hurt him! Perhaps that was normal in such a close relationship. He didn't know. After all, he had never had such a close relationship before.

They walked back along the Arno to their hotel. Coming and going, a stream of walkers flowed. For six hundred years they had been crossing this river on the old bridge; plagues and wars, that terrible last one, had wrought their terror here and still, new generations kept coming to live and love and walk. He began to feel somewhat small and foolish. A foolish worrier over small things. Stop it, Donald Wolfe, stop it, he said to himself.

"That's the Pitti on the other side, Donald. I think we'll start there tomorrow. It has the most marvelous gardens on the hill behind it. You'll love it."

And so it happened. By the next day it seemed as if all his heavy spirits had completely vanished, and his normally high spirits had taken their place. Fine weather, peace, and the prospect of a good dinner at the end of the day—what else could anyone ask for?

Lillian's friend Bettina was a vivacious woman, very bright, and very much like Lillian without possessing her beauty. The young man Giorgio who was with her gave Donald a cordial handshake and cordial smile, but since he spoke only a few stumbling words of English, Donald could have no opinion of him other than that he appeared to be prosperous and that he wore a wedding band on his left hand.

Two sets of conversation, each of them three-cornered, crossed the table, one in Italian and the other in English. The Italian one was often interrupted by hilarity, so that Donald had to guess whether they were telling jokes or else recalling some shared past experiences. He thought it must be the latter because Lillian seldom told jokes and she was taking a large part in this conversation. She was, in fact, the center of it.

Since Donald had nothing else to look at unless he were to stare rudely at strangers, he began to study the little scene at his own table. He thought about the unusual contrast between Lillian as she calmly fitted herself into an evening with his friends from the law office and the Lillian who was now in motion, her eyes flashing, the diamond flashing on her gesturing hand, her head thrown back as her uninhibited loud laughter rang.

She was at home with these people. He had never seen her quite like this, and he was beginning to wonder how long it would be before her energy would be exhausted, when Bettina suddenly interrupted everything.

"We are being very impolite to your husband, letting him sit here in silence without understanding a word. I have to tell you, Donald, all of Lillian's friends, all of us here, were dying to meet you. The last thing we ever expected was to see her settled. Lillian settled! You know what I mean? And pregnant, too!"

It seemed to Donald that the remark, the question, and the facial expression that went with it were all intended as a challenge. And having no intention of meeting it, he answered calmly with a question of his own.

"Why? Is that so unusual?"

"Oh yes, for Lillian it is. But we love her all the same. Everybody loves Lillian."

"Very intelligent of them."

"Ah, but what is it about you that made her choose you? Besides your intelligence and good looks, of course."

The question, delivered with chin in hand and widened eyes, meant to be both innocent and coy, was extremely distasteful to him. What kind of a ridiculous answer did the woman expect?

"You'll have to ask Lillian," he replied.

"Well, tomorrow I'll do that. I have a car, and I'm going to take you around in it. I'll show you the outskirts, places too far to walk to, and we'll have a great day."

"That's too much trouble for you," Donald objected, since he did not want this woman's company. "We'll rent a car if we need one."

"Oh, no. Lily and I have it all arranged."

Sly, he thought. It may seem far-fetched, but

in a certain way, she reminds me of Cindy. Back at the hotel when Lillian asked him what he thought of Bettina, he told her just that.

"My God, but you can say the most absurd things, Donald. You are so judgmental. A judge, sitting in court and pronouncing sentence."

"It's you who are being absurd. That word 'judgmental'—it's the 'in' word, isn't it? Don't we make judgments every day, what to get for dinner, what shoes to buy? I'm not interfering with your friendship, am I? You asked for my opinion, and I gave it. That's all. By the way, who is Giorgio?"

"Don't tell me you don't approve of him."

"I don't know a thing about him. How can I, when I wasn't able to understand a word he said? The only thing I did notice was his wedding ring. He and Bettina aren't married, are they?"

"No, no, Giorgio has a wife and three children. But he doesn't intend to leave home. Divorce isn't the thing in Italy the way it is with us. Anyway, he doesn't want one. He seems to like things the way they are."

"So then Bettina is something like an extra wife, a spare."

Lillian laughed. "You should see your face! You really don't have to look so sarcastic. Sometimes you remind me of—"

"Of what?"

"Oh, I don't know. It's just that we do annoy each other sometimes, don't we?"

As she stood at the window, her profile was in full view, so that for the first time he became aware of a very small bulge developing below her belt. The sight of it, this evidence of the new life, was suddenly confusing and very moving to him. So he replied very gently, "All of us annoy all of us sometimes. It's only natural. Listen. Let's rent a car for tomorrow and keep the day for ourselves, shall we? Call off your friend."

"How can I possibly do that? She's planned the whole thing. Oh, do be nice to her, Donald."

He was silent. When was he ever not nice to anybody? And yes, they did annoy each other. His mind, his mood, and his very heart kept switching back and forth between bleak disappointment and cheer. But he *must* try to make cheer triumph! He must make these last few days, this end of the vacation, as pleasing as the first days had been.

In the front seat of the car the next morning, the women chatted. He understood that these two friends had a few years of separation to make up for, but at the same time, he felt keenly what was unmistakably Lillian's indifference. And he watched her as he might never have watched her before.

In the churches and on the village streets near the city, he walked with the women, and yet he was not with them. He knew that men here in this country were more frank in their approach to women than they were at home; it was the custom. He also knew through observation that most women seemed not to pay attention. But these two, Lillian and Bettina, returned each frank stare with an inviting smile. They *preened.* They were two birds ruffling their feathers. They were a pair of pretty cats grooming themselves. And as they walked, he fell farther and farther behind them, thinking and trying not to think.

At noon they drove downhill and stopped for a lunch at a piazza on a hill above the city. Here Lillian resumed her role as Donald's guide.

"You can see the whole of Florence from here. There's the Arno, curving down from the hills. That soft green, those patches over there, are olive trees. I always think it's such a superb shade of green. There's nothing quite like it. Look there; you can see the old city wall, or what's left of it. Isn't it superb?"

"Yes. Yes, it is."

But Donald was only half aware of it all. Fear was what he felt, as if some crisis were approaching, a thing enormous yet unknown, so that he could make no preparation for it. Like a living thing, its fingers went running all over him. Never in his life had he felt anything quite like it. And while he pretended to be overlooking the marvelous view, he tried to control and account for this fear: his feelings about his wife and hers for him? The coming child? The spurious calm?

"Oh, I adore it." That was Lillian's voice, a musical chime. "What I want is a villa here, to live among all this for six months every year."

She was talking nonsense. How could he have failed to notice before now how often she did, and how often in the midst of a present for which any sensible person would be grateful, she looked toward some unrealistic, grandiose future?

He was breaking off a piece of bread, eating without appetite, when suddenly, with no warning, she jumped out of her chair and cried out.

"Oh my God, Betty, look who's in that car— over there—is he coming in? Quick, I'll hide in the ladies' room, come get me when it's safe, oh my God, I'm shaking—"

Donald stood up to look where she had pointed. "What's wrong? Who is that?"

"Just a man she used to know. Don't worry," Bettina said. "Sit down, she'll be all right. It's nothing."

"But what scared her? Who is he?"

"Please, Donald, sit down, don't attract attention. He knows me, too."

"Look, Bettina. You're talking to Lillian's husband. I need to know what this is all about."

"Much ado about nothing. They went around together for quite a while, then they broke up and he was furious. It's an old story."

"There's something you're not telling me."

"I forgot you're a lawyer! You'll dig till you find out something, won't you? But I guarantee that you won't like it when you do. Poor Lillian, she's in for a hard night, I see."

There was the faintest twinkle in Bettina's eyes. They're not real friends, he thought. They never were. A woman as beautiful as Lillian rarely has real friends.

"You want to tell me," he said, "but you're waiting for me to beg you. Never mind. Lillian will tell me."

"Maybe she won't give you the whole story. It's a rather unusual one. You see, there was another woman studying in our group here, a very rich one from Texas, and Lillian stole her passport. Then there were other things, a little medical problem—"

Donald interrupted her. "That man is driving away, so please get Lillian now. Here's the money for the lunch."

A rat, he thought, despising the disloyalty and

the pleasure that this so-called friend was taking in what she no doubt now saw as a mounting, very interesting drama. And he got up to wait on the outer step for Lillian.

"Donald, where are you going? We haven't had lunch yet."

"We're not having it here. We need to do some talking before we think about eating."

"Oh, I'm sure she told you, but I'll repeat it. He's a man I knew for a while. He's rather nasty, and I didn't want to see him again. That's the whole story."

"No, not the whole. What about the passport you stole?"

"Stole? She said that about me? Why, damn her, she knows I didn't steal it. I haven't stooped to thievery, for God's sake. I borrowed it for one afternoon to show somebody—oh, all right, to show it to that man. It was fun. A game. A trick, pretending I was somebody else."

"But you were afraid of him just now. You were terrified."

"He has an awful temper, and I didn't want a scene here."

"And the little medical problem?"

"She said that?"

"She did. What was it?"

"Oh, Donald, do I have to rake up every rotten memory in my life? I notice you don't rake up yours."

"I've told you everything about myself. Everything, so help me."

"Either you're not telling the truth, or you have no rotten memories, which I find hard to believe."

"No, I would have told you if there had been any. I've had some sadness, but nothing rotten. Nothing I'm ashamed to talk about."

"Lucky you."

"There's too much secrecy between us. Come to think of it, there always has been. I'm going to persist until you tell me about the medical problem. I have a right to know."

When she began to run, he caught her. "Be careful on those steps. Take my arm before you fall. In your condition—"

She turned then to face him. "All right. You won't be satisfied until you hear. I had an abortion. So?" And she waited.

They were following the river. Ahead of them a woman pushed a baby carriage, a pair of lovers paused to embrace, and tourists aimed their cameras. Timeless river, he thought again.

"Why?" he asked.

"It's a long story, and I'm terribly tired. I want to go back to the room and sit down."

In silence they walked and went up to the room. Then she spoke.

"I met this man. We were in a group. He was Italian, very handsome, and he liked me. Somebody said he came from a distinguished family. And then there was a girl from Texas who was studying here, a rich girl with a well-known family name. Oil, I think it was. So I thought it would be fun to pretend I too was distinguished. And I showed him her passport. I took her name, Jean. She didn't mind. She was going back to Texas that week to be married."

The room was still. On the floor there was a carpet printed in squares with a circle of flowers inside each square. When Donald looked down, he saw that his feet were neatly placed at the center of a square. When he looked up, he saw that Lillian, turned away from him, was staring out into the yellow afternoon. Then he looked back down at his feet.

"The man, this man, was impressed. We made love and were very happy. He took me to see his family, to meet his parents. They lived in a house, a small palace, that they'd owned for five generations. He gave me jewelry, heavy gold, beautiful pieces, the watch I always wear. He drove a Lamborghini."

"What about him? Him? Do you think I give a damn what he drove, what he owned?"

"There's nothing else. Somebody told him the truth about me—I don't know who did—and he was furious. So violently furious that I thought he was going to kill me. So I flew home, went to work for Howard Buzley. And that's the story."

Now they faced each other. There she sat waiting for him to say something while she smoothed her hands. He had always disliked the gesture, but now it roused an unreasonable anger that he fought to control.

"The whole story, except for the small matter of pregnancy and the abortion?"

"I had no money. At least not enough. What was I to do? Answer me that."

"I don't know. . . . You had no right in the first place. . . ."

"It was a joke. The whole thing was a harmless joke."

"Harmless? You fool with people, you lie. . . . Don't you believe in anything?"

"Oh yes, I believe in beauty, and freedom, and pleasure. It's a short, short life."

"You lie," he repeated. "You conceal. God only knows what more I shall learn about you tomorrow, or next week, or next year. God knows."

"Perhaps there shouldn't be any next year."

"Talk sense, will you? And please stop caressing your hands. I hate it."

"I can't help doing it. I'm nervous when I'm with you."

"Nervous with me? What have I ever done to you but love you?"

"You've been very, very good to me, Donald. That's what makes it so sad, don't you see? Because we started to go downhill after the first few months. We couldn't help it."

Downhill? he thought. Our summer days on the boat in Central Park? in Venice last week?

*But you're forgetting, Donald, because you want to forget. What of the night your were too despondent even to go home? And that awful party? You will never really know whether she was on her way to bed with that man. Very likely she was. And she has not let you touch her since we left home on this trip. Why, Donald? She is full of secrets. She has been from the start.*

Lillian continued, "The zest has gone out of it for us. Oh, don't look like that! I'm not impugning your manhood. Some passionate loves last longer than others, that's all, and ours hasn't."

"You have someone else," he said.

"I could have very easily, but it happens that I do not. Oh, it's you, it's us! I wasn't going to say all this while we were here, I dreaded having to say it, but then things happened today and maybe it's all to the good that we're out in the open."

"You told me once that it's easy to get along

with anybody as long as he's truthful, so I'm asking you to tell me truthfully what's wrong with me."

"There's nothing wrong with you, Donald. You're kind, you're honest, and you have a brilliant mind. But life is heavy for you, dead serious, while I want—"

He interrupted. "You're telling me that I never laugh?"

"Oh, you do but—well, it's just that you and I laugh at different things. I say again, we're too different from each other. The atmosphere, the friends, the people we like to be with—all opposite. You're disgusted with what you think was a cheap affair, with my trick, with the abortion, with the whole business."

"I certainly won't deny that."

"And anyway, you don't really *like* me, Donald. You only like to make love to me, which is not the same thing."

"I don't believe what I'm hearing. You might as well be speaking Eskimo, or Bulgarian, to me."

Yet always, he thought then, there are two sides. No, there are three—his, hers, and the truth. She thought him straitlaced, and he was. He thought her loose, and she was. So perhaps after all the storm, the fever, the truth was somewhere in the middle place where they could not meet?

He looked again at the swelling beneath her belt. There was another life to be considered here beside theirs. Order, peace, and common sense were slipping away. The future was slipping out of his hands, and he must retrieve it if only for the sake of that other life.

"Come on," he said. "The afternoon's half over and we haven't gone to the museum."

Lillian shook her head. "It's too late today. It's almost time to meet for Giorgio's dinner. He's invited a lot of our old friends, people I want to see again."

"You should be thinking about what we're going to do about ourselves. We have a lot to straighten out before that baby arrives and we have to take care of it. Let's have a good dinner by ourselves at the best place in Florence. You choose it."

"But I want to see my old friends. This has been a bad day, Donald, and I need a pickup."

"I don't think you do. I think you and I need to be together."

"We can be together at the party and talk later. Come on, you're invited."

"I assume I would be, since I'm your husband," Donald said, stiff with anger.

"Donald, I want to go." She stood up and put on her jacket. "Will you come?"

He had gone as far as he would. "Do as you please," he said. "So be it."

When the door closed behind her, it left an echo in the room. Whatever way all this should end, he would remember the sound of that closing door. Where would he be, remembering?

Now he, too, had to get out of this room. After consulting the city map, he found his way to the Uffizi Gallery, and there spent a weary hour standing before the masterpieces that in his present state of mind were merely a blur of colors. Afterward he walked slowly back to the hotel and ordered dinner, not because he was hungry, but because it was routine to eat at the end of the day. Back again in the room, he idled over a stack of magazines, and at midnight, went to bed, where he lay staring into the dark.

At some point he must have fallen into a doze, for suddenly he was startled to feel that the other half of the bed was vacant. It was after six by the clock. He got up and went to look out the window, where a hard rain was falling under a pale gray dawn.

Where was she? Fear like an arrow shot through his chest. He thought of calling the police, but had no idea what to tell them or even how to describe Lillian. The city was full of tourists and he had not noticed what she was

wearing. He did not even know that man Giorgio's last name. The best he could do would be
to wait another hour or two, then go down to
the desk and ask for help. Back and forth he
walked, watching at the window for full day-
light, and then put on his clothes to be ready for
it. Because there was nothing else to do, he lay
down again on the bed; sleep came, and although he felt its coming, he was too exhausted
to fight it.

When he awoke, he looked at the clock and
was horrified to find that he had slept until half-
past eight. He leapt up and ran to the outer
room of the suite on his way to the elevator and
the front desk. And there she lay, crumpled in
disarray upon the ornate sofa, her jacket, soaking
wet, tossed on the floor, along with the delicate
shoes they had bought in Rome. Beside them on
the floor was her handbag with a pile of paper
money, coins, and cosmetics.

Donald stood, simply stood, as if unable to
move, and stared at the mess, at the open mouth
and sodden hair.

Then he must have made a sound because she
wriggled up to a sitting position and smiled.
Once in a while before now he had seen that
smile. It was ugly; it was a flat row of white teeth
with no welcome in her eyes or anywhere but

on the flat lips; for an instant they opened, and then as quickly closed. It was in fact a mechanical movement, no smile at all.

"Well, I guess I'm in for it," she said.

"Where were you?"

"You know. At a party. You could have come, but it's just as well you didn't, you wouldn't have liked it."

"But you liked it."

"Very much."

"You stayed all night at Bettina's or Giorgio's?"

"Oh no, there were too many of us. We split up."

Steady, Donald said to himself. Cautious and steady.

"Who was he, Lillian, the man you slept with?"

"What's the difference? If I should ever see him again, I probably wouldn't recognize him."

"My lady wife. Why don't you stick a knife in me?"

"It was a party, Donald! People do these things. People have fun. Husbands do these things, but you're not that kind of husband. That's what this is all about, what I've been trying to tell you. Listen to me. Let's end this without anger, do things in a civilized way, as you

always say. I don't want any money from you,
honestly I don't, not a penny. I'll have an abortion and—"

"You!" he cried trembling. "There are no
words for you except filthy ones." And grasping
her by the shoulders, he shook her. "Over my
dead body will you dare touch that child. It belongs to me, too. Remember that."

"Be reasonable. You can't very well stop me,
Donald."

"Can't I? An abortion now wouldn't even be
legal! I'll have you followed every time you go
out the door. I'll threaten any doctor who does
it against my wishes, I'll threaten him with a
lawsuit. The minute you walk into a doctor's office, you'll be followed, and no doctor will want
to touch you."

"Do you really care that much? Yes, I suppose
you do. It's your family, your parents, isn't it?
You want to continue the line. Yes," she said
rather gently, "I remember, you want a son."

Her hand was dangling over the arm of the
sofa. On her finger there glittered the ring that
he had bought on that radiant day in London.
Which the illusion, which the reality?

"I'm sorry. I wish it was different, Donald.
You must know that I never meant to hurt you."

He knew that. There was no meanness in
Lillian.

"It's better now than next year or the year after that. It's bound to happen sometime. You do see that, don't you, Donald?"

He walked across the room to the window and looked out at the rain. Minutes passed, during which he was well aware that she was still sitting there watching his back, and that her eyes were filled with tears. He was aware that his thoughts were only mad, blind fragments rushing about in his head. She wanted to end it! A few short weeks into their second year, and she wanted to end it.

*When, when is the instant when a flash of certainty, a harsh, cruel light, pierces through your darkness and brings you to a halt? You may be walking across a room, or watching the rain in your despair when it stabs you.*

So it came, that instant in which he accepted the end. As Lillian said, it was bound to come. Better sooner than later.

"I'm going for a walk," he said, turning about to face her.

"In the rain?"

"It doesn't matter."

He had a plastic raincoat, but no hat. That didn't matter, either. Squalls of cold rain billowed the coat when he went outside, and beat his bare head as he walked along the river to the old bridge. In his ears, from every direction, there rang a clamor of church bells, the sounds of a European Sunday, of tradition, of habit and ordinary lives.

But now he knew better. Of course he had always known that people and things are so often not what they seem; a child knows that. Still, he had never had to apply that knowledge to himself. And he thought again, as he had once before when first there had been a serious difference between his wife and himself, of the book that you open and find within it what you had never expected to find.

There were so many questions he wanted to ask! Filled as he was with a conflict of anger and grief, he found room for pity. Lillian had so much to offer, so much intellect, charm, oh so much charm; why then, and from where, had come that other streak? What had made her so? He did not know. He only knew that he wanted and needed to fly home.

❦

They went downstairs into the lobby and ordered a taxi to the airport. Lillian, in dark blue travel clothes with a glimpse of pearls at her neck and her fine matched luggage at her feet, was the elegant young woman whom Donald had seen on that first April day so long ago. Men glanced at her as they passed. Men glanced at her in the airport.

He had only been able, at the last minute, to get two separate seats, one in first class, which he gave to Lillian, and the other in tourist. They were separate now, as they had never expected to be. And alone, in silence, each bore his burden of regret, while the engines roared to the west, and home.

# Chapter 6

"May I ask you something? What did you see that you really didn't like when I brought her here?"

It was the second time that Donald had asked this question during the last quarter of an hour. It had been an especially painful quarter of an hour, not because it was painful to talk to Augustus Pratt, who of all people would give wise support—indeed, Donald had been home for two weeks now, and had found it too difficult to tell even the closest of his contemporaries what was happening—but because whenever he looked beyond Pratt's face, his eyes met that old photograph of the united family, the wife, the children, and the cozy dog sitting on a sofa.

"Why? Did I say anything to make you think I—"

"It was what you didn't say."

Pratt made a small gesture with his hands, palms turned up. "I don't know, I can't give you an intelligent reason, it was just something. It was just an impression. I'm awfully sorry, Donald. You don't deserve it."

"Does anyone, ever?"

"Oh, you know better than that. Of course some do. Tell me, are there going to be any problems with the divorce?"

"I'm told not. It can be done in no time at all, since there's no argument about anything, certainly not about money. She's the strangest person. I don't understand why she accepts my verbal promise to take care of her and the baby. She has no lawyer and doesn't want one."

"Strange, indeed. Nevertheless, I would insist on doing this the usual way. You'll have a lawyer, and he'll insist that she have one. You could be ruined, Donald. To you, I hardly need explain how or why. By the way, where are you living now?"

"In the apartment. She doesn't want it."

"Stranger, yet."

Yes, it was very odd. They had gone by taxi from the airport to the apartment, where he had begun to pack a few clothes to take to a hotel. And Lillian had stopped him, saying that it was she, not he, who was to leave.

"She went to live, at least for a while, with Cindy, a friend she has."

Pratt frowned. "You say there's no money and no family? Be careful, Donald. I know you're a private person, and since I am the same, I understand perfectly. I only want to say that I'm here for you whenever you want a pair of ears to listen."

"Do you know what I keep asking myself? Where has the magic gone? And my strength, too. I feel as weary as if I had been running without rest or sleep, just running."

Pratt stood up and placed a hand on Donald's shoulder. "You'll be better when you get back to work. Fill your head with other things, so you won't have as much time to think about this shock. A case came in while you were away that calls for a few trips to Florida. How does that sound to you?"

The touch and the words were fatherly, so that Donald felt a surge of emotion that he fought to control. Somehow, he straightened up and got out of the room.

One evening a week later, there was a message from Lillian on the answering machine at home. Would it be all right for her to come for a talk about eight o'clock tonight? Unless she were to hear to the contrary, he could expect her.

He had not only no idea what she might have to say, but also no idea which version of Lillian to expect, the considerate, quiet lady, or the brash destroyer with the sardonic smile.

When he opened the door, he saw at once that she had not come prepared for confrontation, or at least not right away. He also saw that she was dressed for the cold in a heavy coat of the blue that she so often chose because it matched her eyes. This one, however, had collar and cuffs of mink; it was extremely expensive, and it gave him some serious thoughts about his finances. She took it off and laid it over a straight-backed chair, remarked that she would not be staying long enough to bother hanging it in the closet.

"You're thinking it cost too much," she said gaily. "Oh, don't I read your mind? Well, it did cost an arm and a leg, but don't worry, I didn't charge it to you."

"I wasn't worried," he said somewhat stiffly.

"Oh, I think you must have been in spite of what you said the last time we spoke. You must have been wondering how in the world I ever expected to take full care of myself and a baby."

Nature's jokes! He glanced at her waist. All those couples who try for years with no success, those people traipsing all over the world to adopt a baby, all those artificial inseminations, all those, and now this. Poor little thing! From wanting it so much, he had now come to fear for it. Oh God, the poor little thing!

He collected himself. "No, I wasn't worrying. We will let our lawyers work it out decently, fair and square."

"Donald, I really meant it when I said I don't want anything from you, no money, none of the usual revenge. This crash isn't your fault, nor really mine, either. We both made an unthinking mistake, that's all it was."

"And how, may I ask, without money, how do you propose to eat?"

"Ah, therein lies my story. First, get me a cup of tea, and I'll tell you. It's windy out. I walked over, and I'm cold."

Had she no nerves, no emotion? Here she sat in the very room where their wedding party had begun the voyage that was now ending; past the open door, the bed was in full sight. And she was cheerfully fussing with her windblown hair while he—he was empty inside; when he was not dragged down with a weight too heavy to hold, he was empty.

He got up, made tea, and brought it to her. It was then, when she extended her hand to take the cup, that he saw it was devoid of rings.

"I've brought it here for you," she said.

"Brought what?"

"The ring. That's what you're missing, aren't you? You were looking at my finger."

"Missing." It was she who never missed anything. In other circumstances, one could be amused.

Setting the cup down with care, then reaching into her handbag, she took out the velvet box.

"I don't want it, Lillian," he said, drawing back.

"Don't be foolish. You can get a good price for it if you don't want to keep it for somebody else."

She had no imagination. If ever there were to be somebody else—and he could hardly imagine it—that somebody else would surely not want this particular ring.

"I said I don't want it, Lillian."

"Well, I'll simply leave it on the table when I go."

"Why are we arguing about a stupid thing like a ring?"

"I don't want to argue. I came to tell you something. As soon as the divorce comes through, and I hope it comes fast, I'm going to marry Howard Buzley."

Howard Buzley! *Fat, old, and ugly.* A gust of laughter almost burst out of Donald's throat as he managed to turn it into an exclamation.

"What? Surely you're joking?"

"No, no, I'm not. He's been saying from the time I went to work for him that he'd like to marry me someday."

"But his wife?"

"She died while we were in Italy. You see what a decent man he is? She was sick for so many years. A lot of men would have left, you know that. He's a very kind man. He's been very kind to me, I can tell you. He's crazy about me."

So that was the source of the rent for her and Cindy, the spa vacations, and the fine clothes! For all that, of course, Buzley got his pay. He must have gotten plenty of it. And strangely now, the picture of Buzley and Lillian in bed together aroused not jealousy, but only disgust.

"You wouldn't believe how generous he is, always giving to people. Not only to me. I could tell you stories—we were walking past a shop one day and he went in and bought this watch for me. I hadn't even noticed it in the window."

"Wait a minute. You said that the Italian aristocrat gave it to you."

"That must have been another watch, not this one. Don't you remember seeing the other one?"

She has told so many lies, he thought, that they've become second nature to her. "No," he said, "but it doesn't matter. Tell me, why should he marry you? I'm curious. Can't you simply live together?"

"We could, but I'm not sure I'd do that. With him, I want everything safe, according to law." Lillian smiled. "He's not like you, you see. Not your type. Not what they call the 'old school' honorable gentleman."

In spite of himself, Donald was fascinated. "And you think you'll be happy?"

"Yes, I know him so much better than I knew you. Howard and I have a lot of fun together. I didn't know you at all, did I? It was pure infatuation for you and me. And admiration, too. I admired your intellect. I think I can say that we had a good many of the same intellectual interests, or am I being too immodest?"

"Not at all. But intellect is not enough, Lillian. You have to know how to use it."

Lillian shrugged. "We like all the same things, Howard and I. He knows everybody, all the New York celebrities, Hollywood entertainers, theater, everybody. I feel much more free when I'm with him than I did with you. I'm not trying to hurt you by saying this, Donald. I never would hurt you because I still care for you and I'm still fond of you. I'm just telling the truth."

This time she probably is, he thought.

"I want us to end in a friendly way. I want you

to find somebody who will make you happy, who has your tastes and your moral outlook."

There was a silence, during which Lillian was taking a last look around what had been her home, and he was wondering what she might be feeling, if anything.

"Howard has ordered a spectacular engagement ring for me. So you really must take this one back."

"An engagement ring? Of course he knows you're pregnant?"

"Well, what do you think?" she responded indignantly. "Of course he does. Even if he couldn't see it, wouldn't I tell him?"

"And it doesn't matter to him?"

"Good heavens, he has grandchildren from here to California. He's used to children, so one more won't matter. Anyway, we'll have a nurse. And the apartment is enormous, twelve rooms with a view all over the city, from the East River to the Hudson. It reminds me of the Sanders' place."

Ah, yes, the view. She had wanted a view. And ah, yes, the Sanders. At first he had blamed them for corrupting her, but that had been thoroughly stupid of him. Lillian had been what she was long before she ever laid eyes on the Sanders.

"By the way, Howard knows Chloe and Frank. Or at least he's met them. Yes," Lillian repeated, "he goes everywhere and everybody knows him." She paused to look around the room. "That painting—you were very nice about it. A lot of men would have raised hell about my spending so much money without asking first."

"Well, you loved it. I understood that. Take it with you."

"Thanks, but I wouldn't think of taking it. I'll be able to buy more if I want to. One thing I'll miss, though, going to the galleries and exhibits with you. Howard doesn't know the first thing about art and doesn't want to. But you can't have everything, can you?"

Once, he thought, for a short time, I believed you could. I believed, in fact, that we did have everything. But he did not speak as Lillian rose and put on her coat.

"I suppose we'll meet soon with our lawyers, Donald, since you insist on having them. I'm sure it won't be complicated, since we're not fighting each other."

"I have only one demand: open and generous visitation when the child is born."

How much he really would want or use that, he did not know. Perhaps if it should be a boy, he would want it. . . . At any rate, it was of his flesh and blood, and he would provide for it.

"Oh, I want to remind you about the silver.

It's worth a small fortune, so don't forget to pay the insurance."

"The silver?"

"The Danish silver that Howard gave us."

"Take it. Take it with you now. I don't want it."

"For goodness sake, Donald, don't be foolish. You may want to use it someday. One never knows. And I don't need it. Howard's got enough silver to equip a hotel." With a hand on the doorknob, Lillian paused. "Don't be angry at me, will you?"

He looked at her. Beauty incarnate, she was. Those eyes. That heavy, bright hair. The classic face—beauty incarnate.

"For a while, at least, we loved each other," he said.

"Loved? I'll tell you something that I read. I think some Frenchman wrote it. 'There are people who, if they had not heard about it, would never fall in love.' Good night, Donald."

# Chapter 7

It had begun to drizzle, and the April air was soft on Donald's face as he walked toward the hospital. On the corner of the street, he stopped to reconsider whether or not he should continue.

The early morning's telephone call at home had surprised him, although it really should not have done so because he could hardly have expected Lillian to send him a formal birth announcement. In high spirits she had urged him to visit the nursery for a look at the prettiest seven-pound, three-ounce baby girl that anyone could imagine.

"Just ask for the Wolfe baby, and they'll pick her up to show you."

*Wolfe.* Well, of course. What else should it be? He was, after all, the father, soon to be in three or four months the divorced father, but still, the father.

There was such emotional turmoil inside him! During the fall and winter just past, he had been settling down. Mr. Pratt had been right about work as a restorer of mental health; he had provided Donald with so much activity, two trips abroad and a full load at home, that there had been neither time nor energy left for personal grief. But now, as he hesitated on the street, anxiety surged back as if to engulf him again.

What was the point of going in to see this baby? For one thing, it was a girl, and even though he knew he wasn't supposed to feel this way, he believed that he would have a different kind of companionship with a boy than with a girl. So this child would belong to Lillian, and he would be reduced to the kind of pathetic father who had lunch on a Saturday or Sunday with a child who hardly knew him.

He was still standing, undecided, when he caught sight of Lillian's friend Cindy coming out of the hospital. He had not seen her since the day of the wedding, yet she was unmistakable in her slipshod clothes and long, unkempt hair. It was the sight of her that abruptly made his decision; if *she* thinks enough of a friend's baby to come here, then surely *I* have a greater obligation.

The truth was that he was also dreading what

he might feel when he beheld this child of divided parents, this child who was to be reared in another man's house.

He went inside, took the elevator, and following directions to the nursery, came face-to-face with Lillian.

"Oh—I didn't think," he stammered. "How are you?"

"Didn't think I'd be walking around? It's over twenty-four hours, and they want you to walk. This is my second trip to the nursery."

For a moment he wondered whether she felt as awkward as he did, and in the second moment, knew very well that she did not. For her there would be no embarrassment in remembering how intimate they had once been. He knew every inch of the body underneath the quilted silk robe. If he had known what he later learned, there would be no child now. He would never have touched her.

*I wouldn't even recognize him the next morning.*

"I'm so glad I didn't—didn't do that, Donald. She's absolutely adorable, the sweetest little thing. See, right here in the second bassinet? She's asleep."

A small, pink heap had a thatch of dark hair on its head. With surprise, he realized that he had lived all these years without ever having seen a newborn baby.

"Most of them are bald. Isn't it cute, all that hair? She'll probably lose it, they tell me, and be bald until the permanent hair comes in."

There was a card on the bassinet. *Wolfe,* it said. He didn't know what he felt. Perhaps he just felt *strange.* Wolfe. His name. This *person* asleep there had his name. This *person* was attached to him and would be all her life, even if they should never meet again. And he stood there looking at the small heap of pink with the thatch of hair.

"We have the most gorgeous room for her. This decorator got somebody who painted the walls with Mother Goose murals." Lillian was in an excited mood, full of chat. "And the nanny's room adjoins. Really, really lovely, the whole business. I want you to see it, Donald. Feel free to visit. Just call up first, that's all you have to do. I want everything to be friendly, Donald, and Howard agrees."

His eyes went back to the name on the card: Wolfe. And a stranger in his generosity was providing all this "lovely business!" Anger that he knew to be unreasonable rose, lumped in his throat, and was brought under control.

"It's I who will provide for her future," he said quietly. "Tomorrow morning I will open an account for her education. What are your thoughts about her name?"

"Oh, I'm having the worst time trying to decide! I thought for a while of *Bettina,* like my friend in Florence. She'd be *Tina* for short. Then I thought of *Antonia,* Toni for short. What do you think?"

"To tell you the truth, I don't like either one."

"Then give me a suggestion."

"I've never thought much about girls' names. But maybe something more everyday, not so different."

"What? Like Cathy or Jennifer? Every other American girl has a name like those."

"Well, she's an American girl." Then he thought of something. "Perhaps we could name her after my mother. I would like that, if you don't mind it. Her name was Jane."

"Jane! Oh, for heaven's sake, *Jane!*"

"Well then, after your mother. It's a nice custom, I think."

"That's the last thing I'd do. I never liked my mother."

Something about the way she said it, something even beyond the meaning of the words, her defiant stance, and the ugly challenge in her tone, affected Donald so that he could not help but respond.

"I have thought sometimes that you would be a happier person if you would learn to forgive whatever it is that—"

"Forgive us our trespasses?" she mocked, her voice rising so sharply that a nurse passing in the corridor turned to look. "Heavy, heavy. Somber, straitlaced, and serious. That's why we couldn't get along, Donald. Lighten up, will you? No, you never will. You're made this way."

He should have minded his own business. There they were, quarreling again in a public hall alongside the innocent baby they had conceived together. It was hopeless.

"Name her whatever you like," he said. "It's not worth an argument."

"Fine. It's Bettina. Tina."

Again he looked at the baby, who was still asleep. The little thing unaware of any future that might come her way. Bettina Wolfe. God bless you, Bettina Wolfe.

"I'm sorry, Donald. I certainly didn't plan to yell at you today." Lillian laughed. "But you know me by now, so you won't mind. I'm starting to feel tired. Guess I'll go back to my room."

"I'll be going, too. Take care."

For a moment he watched her walk away down the hall. Not exactly sure what he was feeling, whether pity or anger or some of each, he knew only that even if it were possible to have her back, he would never, never want her.

That great case, the one that had sent so many lawyers rushing around the globe, was coming to an end with the unmasking of the brilliant scoundrel at the center of it. How many air miles Donald had flown, he had not counted; how many documents that, by patient digging and delving had been analyzed, he had not counted, either; it was even a task to keep straight in his head all the names of the empty corporations and fake holding companies that the fugitive had concocted.

Curiously, one thing did keep its hold in a corner of his memory, and that was the overheard conversation in which two men had chuckled over and rooted for the scoundrel who was so cleverly eluding the law. Then, with this memory, there followed the rest of that painful night with all its consequences.

At the hotel bar in Switzerland a few days before they were all to go home, his partners rejoiced.

"I've had enough traveling to last the rest of my life. If I never leave my little roost on Madison Avenue at Orton and Pratt, that'll be okay with me."

"I know what you mean. I hope my wife and kids will recognize me when I go home."

These men would find it hard to believe me, Donald said to himself, if I were to say that I don't want to go home. And he thought of that play in which somebody is sitting on a bench waiting for somebody else who never comes. But he, Donald Wolfe, didn't even know what or whom he was waiting for!

Work was good. Augustus Pratt had telephoned him yesterday in his hotel room with unusual praise for his accomplishments in this difficult, complex case. Friends were good; when finally he had told them about the end of his marriage, they had supported him in every possible way.

But it was not enough. Guilt, like an unwelcome beggar, filled and harrassed him. He almost heard himself crying out: Get away from me! I have nothing to give you.

*It's true that I haven't seen it for more than three months since it was born.* Do stop saying 'it.' Her name is Bettina, Bettina Wolfe. *But what am I expected to do? Ring the doorbell—after an invitation, to be sure—at the home of my former wife, now become the legal wife of Mr. Howard Buzley? (They wasted no time, did they?) Ring the bell, walk in, and stand there gazing at the little pink stranger who bears my name and has my genes?*

Back home again in the apartment, he put down the excellent book that was unable to hold his attention and gazed about at the rooms he had so carefully planned. They would have had to move to a larger place with an added room for the baby, but all these nice things would have gone with them and been rearranged. New bookshelves were no problem; a carpenter could do that in two days, including a couple of hours to put shelves in the baby's room; a child should grow up with books. . . . So went his fantasy.

He went to the window and looked down at the street, but there was nothing to see except shifting lights, and nothing to feel except the loneliness that is so peculiarly urban. He showered, laid out his clothes for the morning's appearance in court, and went to bed.

Around three o'clock a dream awakened him. It was said that dreams only last for a few seconds, yet this one seemed to have been going on for hours. He had been lost in some cold, far-off place. Kyrgystan? Was there such a place? He had been standing in a brutal wind, while indifferent people hurried past him. No one would even pause to listen to his pleas, although it would have been of no use if they had, because he did not speak their language. Darkness was falling and he was in a panic.

"Idiot!" he said aloud. "Something I ate, no doubt. Perhaps the fish."

After that he lay awake thinking. He had done nothing about or for the child except to make some inquiries about Howard Buzley, as a result of which he had learned that Buzley was very rich, shrewd, and known for his kindly generosity. These qualities might well add up to one hundred percent safety, especially now that he was married to Lillian and could not easily abandon her without providing for her.

Nevertheless, it was Donald Wolfe, not Howard Buzley, who was responsible for that baby. It was Donald Wolfe who must at once take out a policy on his own life with the baby as beneficiary and a bank as trustee. It was he who would start a bank fund for her education. It was he who must begin to make some contact with her. All of these decisions came out of his head, but what was in his heart—well, he didn't know. He couldn't say.

Accordingly, Donald rang the bell of the "fabulous apartment with a view from the East River to the Hudson." Inwardly, he was resentful because he did not want to be here, but if he wanted to see the baby, this was the only place to see her. Simple as that.

"I was just on the way out," said Lillian when she opened the door. "You're late."

"Sorry. I had to get these papers for you. Everything that I described to you over the phone is here in writing, a list with the bank, the trust, the insurance, everything. The originals are with Orton and Pratt."

"Lucky little girl." And she gave him the false, flat-lipped smile that came and went in the same instant.

*Lucky? This child was lucky?*

"Oh, Tina's absolutely adorable. You'll see. She's grown so much since you saw her, you'll be amazed. I can't tell yet whom she looks like, but she's certainly going to be very pretty, that I know. Howard says so, too. He's wonderful with children. He's had so much experience, after all. Come follow me to the nursery."

Lillian, in a chatty mood, was the confident mistress of the house, dressed for the city summer in simple black linen with gold earrings and one wide gold bracelet. She was the woman he had seen for the first time that afternoon a thousand years ago. But no, he thought as he followed her through an elaborate sunken living room and library, whose shelves were filled with antique knickknacks and a handful of books, no. There's a change. She's climbing all around on the ladder, she's feeling glory, and she wants to show me how she lives now.

The nursery was large and sunny. The walls were bright with the Mother Goose murals that had been promised, but the canopied crib was empty.

Lillian, following his glance, explained that Tina was in the park getting fresh air.

"We have the most wonderful nanny. Her name is Maria, she doesn't speak English very well, but she's experienced, and she adores the baby."

"In the park? Where can I find her?"

"Wait. I'll draw a map for you. Maria's wearing a green hat, and they'll be sitting near the museum. It's easy to find. But of course you know your way around the park."

Oh yes, he did. All those Saturdays and Sundays, walking on top of the world . . . Let me get out of here, he thought, and never come back. When I want to see the baby, and I'll surely have to see her every now and then so she won't grow up not knowing she has a father, I'll see her in the park.

"Before you go, let me show you something. Look what Howard just bought for Tina. He's a great window-shopper, and when he passed a children's store, he couldn't resist this."

She held up a white velvet coat made for a child barely old enough to walk. The price tag was still on it: three hundred fifty dollars. He made no comment for the simple reason that there was no polite comment he could make. Let me get out of here, he thought again. He accepted Lillian's written directions, and left.

On the avenue, on the shady side edged with trees, he walked, his legs propelling him forward, while his mind was still back in that apartment. It had been one thing to imagine her in her new abode, but quite another to see her there.

This strange phenomenon that for lack of a better name was called "chemistry"—what was it? It seized you, it mesmerized you so that you became its prisoner, and then, if it wanted to, it vanished, leaving behind a debris of anger, shame, and nasty thoughts. There in the nursery he had had an awareness of the nearby bedroom in which Lillian must now spend her nights. Did she not find it queer to be standing outside its door beside the man whose bed she had been sharing so short a time ago? It seemed to Donald that most women in these circumstances would have accepted his papers when he rang the bell and politely gotten rid of him, but then he reminded himself that of course she was not like most women.

Nearing the place where he expected to find the nanny and carriage, he felt a disheartening reluctance. The situation bordered on absurdity. He would identify himself to the nanny, glance into the carriage where the sleeping bundle would no doubt be covered in something pink, say a few cordial words to the woman, and go away. Had he not just fulfilled his legal and moral obligation as a parent? He did not feel like a parent, but he had done what the world considered right and would continue to do so. Was that not enough?

Still he kept going, watched for a green straw hat, found it on the head of a neat little woman, and identified himself.

"Hello. I'm the baby's father."

"*Sí, sí,* I know. You Mr. Wolfe. She tell me. I'm Maria."

Propped against Maria's chest sat a *person* sucking milk from a bottle. This was no nondescript bundle anymore, but a *person* who actually acknowledged Donald's presence by turning her large blue eyes in his direction. He had had no idea that a human being could change that much in such a few months.

"Pretty, you think? No?" Maria asked.

From under the ruffled cap came wisps of dark hair that seemed to be wavy. The face was already feminine, he thought, although he might be wrong about that. At any rate, it was appealing, as young creatures all were, puppies or calves, all of them whose trustful dependence touched one's heart.

"Yes, very pretty," he replied.

The innocence! Someday this child would

want to know about her father and mother; she would ask what and why. It would be easier for her then if there were to be no close attachment to this father, but simply the attachment one feels toward a good friend or nice uncle who sends presents and takes one out for a treat two or three times a year. All this flashed through his mind as he regarded her.

"You want hold her, please? I fix carriage cover."

He drew back in refusal. "She won't like it. She'll cry."

"No, no." Maria smiled. "You scared? Here, take."

When he held her against his shoulder, she felt heavier than he had expected. By twisting her neck, she was able to stare directly into his face, and he wondered whether she was wondering about him, whether she knew that he was a stranger.

"What do they call her, Maria? Tina? Or Bettina?"

Maria shook her head, not understanding. "Call? Call?"

Having had three years of Spanish in high school, Donald thought he might try it out again, and he repeated his question.

Now Maria spoke freely. "They mostly call

her Cookie, Mr. Wolfe. Everybody loves her. There's something special about this baby. They aren't all alike, you know. Some of them aren't very interesting. I've cared for so many of them, so I know. Sometimes on the street with Cookie, people stop to look at her and say how beautiful she is. And so good-natured. She doesn't cry much at all. Let me take her from you and lay her down to sleep. Now that her stomach's full, she'll sleep. That's a baby's life, you know, eat and sleep."

"Then I'll be going. I'm glad to have met you, Maria." In Spanish the compliment had a special formal grace. "I'll see you again."

"You will be coming to the house, Mr. Wolfe?"

He looked at the woman, and seeing the kindness in her eyes, spoke frankly, "No, I can't—don't want to go there. Do you understand?"

She nodded. "After September, when we come back from the beach house, we'll be here every day. There'll be crowds of baby carriages here, you'll see."

"Well, it'll be a while anyway, because I'm out of the city on business. I'm out of the city on business a good deal of the time."

"You, too? Mr. Buzley has business all the time, and they take vacations all the time. When they're not on vacation, Mrs. Buzley is never home. She's a very busy, busy lady." And Maria shook her head.

She doesn't like Lillian, Donald thought as he walked away, otherwise she wouldn't treat me so warmly. To be fair, though, who knows why she doesn't like Lillian? It might be only for the perfectly natural resentment a woman could feel toward a younger employer who had everything.

Retracing the morning's steps while reviewing the morning's events, he re-passed the limestone front of Lillian's building on the other side of the avenue. There beneath the green awning, she stood, beside her a man who was obviously Howard Buzley. Elderly, gray, round-shouldered, and no taller than she, he was linking arms with his trophy wife in her summer dress.

Donald went on down the avenue and turned toward home. This day had been, to say the least, unsettling. The baby had confused him. He wouldn't know how to describe his feelings if anyone were to ask him to describe them. She was his, but she wouldn't be growing up with him, so she really wasn't his. She would always be a charge on his conscience, but little more. And if he had to have such a charge, why couldn't she at least have been a boy?

At home again, there were messages on the answering machine. Ed Wills had a windfall for him, a ticket to a Broadway hit tonight. Another friend had a girl for him, one he'd be sure to like. Actually, he was too dispirited to do anything. But on second thought he ought to call Ed and accept the extra ticket. It wasn't healthy when in this frame of mind to shut oneself up at home like a hermit, and he wasn't going to do it. It wasn't healthy.

In his tentative, diplomatic way, Augustus Pratt inquired now and then about what was going on in Donald's life. He was not one of the kind who gave cheery predictions that, meant to comfort, only made the recipient feel worse.

Yet on this morning when he summoned Donald to his office, it was to give him two pleasant pieces of news.

"You've been home for three months now, Donald. Are you by any chance itching to hop onto a plane again?"

"It would be just what I need right now, Mr. Pratt."

"Good. I'd like you to see to a matter in the San Francisco office. Hugh McQueen is waiting for you. I didn't think you'd try to beg off, you see. Not that you ever do." There went that rare, benign twinkle. "It's highly likely that you'll both be flying to Anchorage, because one of our clients is in the hospital there. You haven't ever seen Alaska, have you? No? Well, you'll have a thrill. Take a few extra days to get beyond Anchorage and look around."

"I can't tell you how much I appreciate that."

The San Francisco office didn't need Donald, he knew. This trip was purely a thoughtful gift.

"The next thing I want to mention is the bonus. The firm has had a remarkable year, and the bonus reflects it. I'll keep you waiting in suspense until you see it next week."

"All I can say besides thank you is that I'm very lucky."

"Well, in some ways, Donald, you are."

He was already thinking about how he would invest the bonus for the baby. He had more than enough for his own wants. All he spent very much on were books and good luggage to take wherever he was going, to the Moscow office, or now, to Alaska.

"Oh, before you leave," said Pratt, "I want to tell you that I'm fairly sure you'll need to be in Italy for a few days in the late fall. After that, you'll be glad to stay home for a year or so. Let some of our new people see the world."

"Is it the bank in Rome again?"

"No, a corporation in Florence that wants to

buy property here in New York. Our sellers here want us to look them up on their home ground. It'll only take a few days."

"I understand," Donald said automatically.

Florence. He had hoped never to see that beautiful city again.

# Chapter 8

In an old house near the medieval wall, a family was gathered for a typically Italian Sunday dinner, the father at one end of the long table, the mother opposite, with all the numerous rest of them, including Donald as guest, in between. Directly across from him was the grandmother, holding a six-month-old baby girl.

He could have been listening more carefully to his host, the accountant who, on the next-to-last-day before Donald's return to New York had kindly saved him from a solitary dinner at the hotel. He could have looked out the window toward the wintry garden, at the silver candelabra, or at the fine wainscot on the wall. But he was only seeing the baby.

"You have children?" asked the hostess in halting English.

"No," he replied.

It was better that way, less complicated, less painful. This sudden pain had surprised him. The baby in her lacy dress, no doubt put on because it was Sunday, had hurt him as he would never have expected to be hurt. There she sat, a queen gurgling over her milk, waving her fat little hands and smiling around the table at the people assembled there to honor her on her throne.

"Six months," Donald said. "I had no idea they came so far in six months."

"Ah, yes," responded the father, nodding wisely. "You'll find out when you have your first one. In another six months, and maybe before then, she'll take a few steps, and then before you know it, she'll talk and go to school and argue with us."

Bettina Wolfe was already seven months old. . . .

He turned politely to his host. "You were telling me about that fund to keep Venice from sinking. How do they expect to prevent it? I know almost nothing about engineering."

❧

Love grows like a weed. It is often said that a weed is only a plant that is growing where it is not wanted; some of the loveliest, the daisy, the honeysuckle, and the black-eyed Susan, are weeds. Such were Donald's thoughts. He did not want this love to grow. Most definitely had he made up his mind that financial responsibility was all he would undertake. He knew his flaw: wanting all or nothing. If he had not been an A student at law school, the chances are he would have quit. If he couldn't be a father like that one in Florence, what was the use?

But try to get rid of honeysuckle where it has already fastened its strong vines, or of daisies that have already spread their seeds.

∽◦∽

I suppose, thought Donald, it really began on the day I first saw her smile. If it had not been for the mutual recognition between Maria and me, I would have walked right past that row of benches and baby carriages. There was no resemblance between the baby I remembered from four months ago and the tiny person who was standing, actually standing, at Maria's knees while clutching her hands.

Maria called out my name. It must have been the startling cry that made the baby turn her head toward me, he thought. She must already have had a smile on her lips because she was pleased with the new experience of standing, for the smile was certainly not for me. Even I in my ignorance knew enough to understand that I was merely getting the tail end of it.

And yet he was to carry that expression home and keep it with him.

"Changed, hasn't she?" Maria said, speaking in Spanish. "You hardly know her, do you? Yes, she wants to walk. See how she's hoisting herself on my lap? And you should see her crawl. I could put her on the grass to show you, but it's dirty. We haven't seen you in a long time, Mr. Wolfe."

*They walk, they go to school, and soon they are arguing with you.*

"I've been very busy working out of the country, otherwise I would have come."

"Ah, yes, work. That's true. Come, Cookie. We'll get back into the carriage and have our lunch. Sit down, Mr. Wolfe, and watch your girl eat lunch."

*Your girl. Bettina Wolfe.*

"You called her Cookie?"

"That's what they call her. Her mother hugs her and calls her Cookie, so I do, too."

As he had been invited, Donald sat. If he had been asked to describe his feelings, he would very likely have fumbled with words. He was outside himself, observing himself as he observed his child.

"She can drink from a cup, but she likes the

bottle better sometimes," Maria explained. "I give her the cup at night when she's in her pajamas. Her mother doesn't like to have milk stains on these good clothes. Not that you can't wash them out easily enough, but—" Maria did not finish.

Something annoys her, Donald said to himself. And he asked her whether she always had to work on Sunday.

"Yes, because I need the money. I have a family in Mexico. But I don't mind. What else would I do? Mr. Buzley pays me so much. He's a nice man, very, very nice, and I don't say it only because he pays me so much extra. No. It's too bad you can't see how he plays with Cookie. He gets down on the floor with her and plays. Yes, he's a very nice old man. You want to see a picture? I cut it out of the paper to show it here in the park. Nannies all like to ask you who your boss is, so I show them this."

There on a page of photographs taken at various social events were Mr. and Mrs. Howard Buzley at a charity dinner, he looking just as Donald recalled having seen him, and she superb with elaborate pendant earrings and naked shoulders. His eyes glanced over a gushing paragraph about "Mr. Howard Buzley with his lovely wife Lillian," and glanced away.

And wasn't that a great step upward in the

world, to be in the Sunday newspaper, and mustn't she be thrilled!

Maria kept talking. Understandably, she was feeling a certain drama, a bit of excitement in this situation. She must be wondering what he, the former husband, was thinking. It was only natural. Tomorrow she would be telling the other nannies about the father who meets the baby in the park.

Cookie, with something in her mouth that looked like a cracker, but was, as Maria explained, a teething biscuit, was staring at him. Was she curious about him? How much thought was possible at eight months?

For his part, he was thinking that he did not care about the name "Cookie" when two women passed, and he heard one say, "Isn't she adorable? It's the Buzleys' baby." They walked on and he heard no more.

But Maria had heard. He was convinced of it when suddenly she said, "If I'm still here when she starts to say some words, I'm going to teach her right away to say 'Daddy.' "

He looked at her. She, returning the look, gave him the feeling that she wanted to tell him something, but was unsure about it.

"What did you mean by 'if I'm still here'?" he asked. "I thought you liked the job."

Maria shrugged. "I do like it. But you never

know, do you? Oh, now she's sleepy. Do you want to rock her? Push the carriage back and forth a little."

The gentle, rocking motion began to soothe Donald. Before him passed a parade of children in bright clothes, a tiny redhead riding her three-wheeler and a troop of boys kicking fallen leaves. An autumn peace settled over the afternoon and, the better to feel it, he closed his eyes while the sun warmed his shoulders.

Suddenly Maria's voice cut through the peace. "I don't understand. Have baby, go out all the time. All the time. Sleep and go."

"Were you speaking to me?" he asked, not sure whether he had correctly heard the murmured Spanish.

"I'm sorry! I was talking to myself. I get angry sometimes. Excuse me."

"Excuse you for what, Maria?"

"I didn't mean it for you, Mr. Wolfe. I'm sorry."

But of course she had meant it for him. And rather firmly he said to her, "Look at me, Maria. If there's anything wrong, you should tell me."

There was a silence. Perhaps she had spoken out of pique, or for some simple reason, such as resentment over having had a scolding from Lillian, and was now sorry she had revealed her feelings.

Very quietly, Donald commanded her, "You started to say something about the baby's mother. You don't have to be afraid that I will repeat it. We are not friends, Mrs. Buzley and I, but I need to know, Maria. I need to know, and you must tell me."

"She's never home! She buys things for Cookie and kisses her, but that's not being a mother."

Very true, he had to agree, but not what you would call child abuse. Sighing, he gave Maria a compliment, thinking it better to drop the subject for the time being.

"I'm glad the baby has you for a nanny, Maria."

"I'm glad, too."

"I'm going to give you my telephone number," he said, producing a card. "Here's where you can reach me during the day. On the other side I'll write my home number."

"Will you come back next Sunday, Mr. Wolfe?"

"Yes, I'm going to come every Sunday unless I have to be away from the city. Telephone me on Sunday in the morning, and if I don't answer, you'll know I'm away."

Maria nodded. "I will call you, Mr. Wolfe. Now I think we'll go home. The sun's gone in."

For a short distance Donald accompanied

them. Then at parting, he took one more look at the sleeping baby, watched the carriage safely across the avenue, and went on his way.

He was a person who especially disliked uncertainties, who would gladly undertake a mountain of hardships, as long as he could look ahead. But the future now was hidden in cloud; he had a very uneasy feeling that everything was not as right as it should be. The only sure thing was this newborn love for his child. And filled with these inconclusive thoughts, he walked rapidly toward home.

If it had not been for Bettina, or Cookie—and how he disliked both names!—Donald would have most easily been able to put Lillian back in his past along with other things anybody would want to forget. But as the months passed, she kept reappearing in one way or another. It was amazing to him that these vignettes on the social page of the newspaper, if often enough repeated, could make a *personage* out of a *person*. Once you got started—and often it only took a hired publicist to make the start—you simply kept going because you were a *name*. He didn't put it past Lillian to have done just that.

It was Maria who brought him these clippings, which Lillian must have displayed to her with pride. She also brought tattle, as harmless as those first reports about Lillian's being out all the time. Tattle of this sort embarrassed him; it was lowering to listen to it.

Yet, occasionally there were certain reports that worried him, an account, for instance, of a furious quarrel between the Buzleys that had awakened Maria in the middle of the night. He had come to know Maria very well. One had only to use some common sense, plus a bit of intuition, to see her whole. She was an honest, canny little woman, no longer young, who had learned a great many things about humanity during the course of her hard years. In a miserable, hungry village, she had struggled to survive, and it would not be easy to fool her.

Strange as it might seem to an outsider, what he most wanted to hear was that the Buzley home was a good one, a peaceful one; since Lillian's house was to be the child's primary home, let it be sound and solid. One particular argument, he found out, had been over Lillian's going out alone to a late-night party when Buzley had been detained at a meeting. I don't like that at all, Donald thought, not at all.

"Cookie is lucky to have you for a father," she said one day.

"But you don't know anything about me," he

answered, "except that I am the divorced husband. I could have been a terrible man, it could
have been all my fault."

"No, no, not your fault. I have eyes. I can see.
She needs to have somebody talk to her. Look,
Cookie, what's that?" she cried, changing the
subject.

"A wow–wow."

"Good. And who's that?"

"Daddy."

"I have to talk English to Cookie," Maria explained. "It is her language. We play games. She's
very smart. We say 'peekaboo' and 'where's
Cookie?' She thinks it's funny when I say
'where's Cookie?' Look, Mr. Wolfe. Two more
teeth coming. Six teeth already. Show her your
watch. What's that, Cookie?"

"Tick tock."

Something was bothering Maria. He felt like
telling her to come out with it, to stop dangling
it in the air between them. Instead, he lifted
the baby out of the carriage, and taking her by
the hand, set off on a walk.

There is something, he thought, about the
sight of a tall man leading a doll-sized creature
that makes people turn and smile. A man passing
by with an active boy about two years old gave
Donald just such a smile with an added twinkle.

They recognized each other, these Sunday fathers. He wondered what their stories were, each one surely being unique, since no two people are alike. Yet how different were theirs from his?

And so when the very short walk was over and the baby back in the carriage, he spoke bluntly to Maria.

"Tell me what you meant when you said that she needs to be talked to. What's going on in the family? If you trust me, you will answer me, Maria."

"It's the same, Mr. Wolfe. We live alone, just baby and I, Mr. and Mrs. go out, the cook goes home every night, and we are alone." She stopped.

"You've told me that many times," Donald said patiently. "There's something else you haven't told me. What is it?"

There was a long, long pause. And then Maria said, "I hate to say it. . . . I think she has another man, Mr. Wolfe."

"Another man? Mrs. Buzley has another man?"

"I think so. He telephones in the morning when Mr. Buzley is gone. I heard a few times. And I saw once. She came home in a taxi. Yes, I think so, I do."

It seemed to Donald that he was looking at

the approach of disaster, a speeding car in the wrong lane, and he sighed. "A young man, Maria?"

"Younger than Mr. Buzley."

"But you could be making a terrible mistake."

"I could, but I don't think so."

So he left it at that and went away. What, after all, could he do?

Sometimes he almost wished that his baby would remain a baby. Time raced; she was almost two. Life was only going to be more complicated with the years, when unanswerable questions would be asked. They plagued him now, and would have plagued him even more if he had not put up some sort of resistance against them. Who is the man whom Maria suspects? Or is there such a man? And why those night-time arguments? Are Lillian and Buzley going to stay together?

One morning as Donald was prepared to leave for the office, Maria telephoned with news: Cookie was sick. She had been up all night, hot with fever. The woman at the doctor's office had not understood her, and what should she do?

"Where is her mother?" Donald asked.

"They went away, someplace far away, to ski."

"Can't you reach them?"

"They left the telephone number, but maybe I wrote the wrong one down, I don't know. I don't think so, but nobody can find them."

Donald looked at the clock. There was on his desk a pile of documents that had to be checked before a noon conference. "There's something to be said for a two-parent family," he muttered, "with parents who pay a little more attention to their children, too." Then, after instructing Maria to wrap the baby very warmly and expect him in fifteen minutes, he threw on an overcoat to ward off the snow, rushed downstairs, and hailed a taxi.

Cookie's tear-wet face was so painfully red that it terrified him. Maria's ominous silence terrified him. The taxi, whose driver Donald had urged to hurry, also terrified him as it skidded through the slippery streets.

I don't know anything about children, he was thinking in his fear. If I were living with her mother, I would know things, would know what to do. What if she's dying? Damn the driver! Is he going to take all day? Hurry, hurry, Donald wanted to cry as the man fumbled with the fare, as the elevator took forever to arrive, and as the receptionist wasted time on the telephone before acknowledging their presence.

"You look scared to death," remarked the doctor. "Take it easy, Mr. Buzley. My guess is strep throat. There's an awful lot of it around this season. We're going to take a culture and by tomorrow we'll know whether it is or not. In the meantime we'll start the young lady on some antibiotics right now. Is she allergic to penicillin?"

Donald said helplessly that he did not know. Neither did Maria.

"No matter. We'll give her something else to make sure. Here, Maria—that is your name, isn't it? I'm writing down all the instructions for you. Maria takes wonderful care of Bettina," the doctor said, turning to Donald. "We're old friends by now. How is Mrs. Buzley? I haven't seen her in so long, I thought perhaps she had been ill."

You talk too much, but you mean no harm, thought Donald as he replied, "No, she's all right."

"That's good. Well, take this lady home and expect our call in the morning."

Back home, Donald tried to cope with his fury. Fine, he thought, fine mother! Buy an absurd mink blanket for the child's stroller—to match Mrs. Buzley's new coat, Maria said—and then go a thousand miles away after leaving the child in the sole care of a frightened woman who scarcely knows her way around the city.

So, because a week later the anger was still hot inside him, Donald went to the telephone and called Lillian.

"Who?" she said. "Oh, Donald? I didn't rec-ognize your voice. I'm half-asleep."

"Well, wake up. It's time you did." He spoke roughly. "Wake up and pay attention to your child."

"Got out of the wrong side of the bed this morning, did you?"

"Do you by any chance know, did Maria tell you what happened while you were away on your ski trip?"

"Cookie had a bad cold. What are you fussing about?"

"For your information, she did not have a cold. She had a strep throat. Maria did her best, but she was terrified. Who knows what might have developed if I hadn't been here in the city to take charge?"

"Well, that's always your function in life, isn't it—to preach and to take charge? Listen, Don-ald, you're all wrought up. But I don't want to argue with you because I don't dislike you and because I'm a really nice person. Try to remem-ber that."

"I'm not wrought up," he said, dropping his voice. "I'm only concerned because you don't pay enough attention to Bettina. I'm justifiably concerned. You went away and left a useless phone number. You left this woman here help-less."

"It wasn't a useless number. What happened was that people we know were giving a house-warming at their new place on the mountain. We stayed an extra day to talk to their builder because we're thinking maybe we'll build something for ourselves."

"Don't quibble with me, Lillian. You're a skill-ful manipulator of language, but it won't work with me."

"I really thought we had decided to end things finally in a friendly, civilized way, Donald."

"Unfortunately, you and I will never have a final ending. Our child is the reason it can't be as final as we'd like. You are neglecting her, and I won't keep quiet about it."

"Neglecting her? You're making a fool of yourself. Have you seen this home? Yes, you have, and you can still use the word 'neglect'? You're an idiot. Do hang up and let me alone."

"I'm not finished. I want you to listen to me—"

"No. Sorry. Don't bother me." The receiver slammed in Donald's ear.

Well might he use the word "neglect," but it would be difficult to prove in the face of every luxury, the Fifth Avenue apartment, the nanny, the summers at the beach house—and even a blond mink blanket for the stroller! Imagine that! Besides, everyone knows that she hugs and kisses

Cookie, doesn't she? Would anyone believe that the child is neglected?

He was late for an early conference with Mr. Pratt, and if there was anything that Augustus Pratt despised, it was lateness. In addition, the snow that had been falling all night showed no signs of stopping, so that his noon flight to the meeting in Washington, which was the subject of the morning's conference, might well be delayed or canceled. He'd have to settle for the train. Donald Wolfe was in a bad mood.

Still frazzled, he boarded the train. Red-faced passengers, people with wet coats and wind-blown hair, came in stamping their feet and rubbing their cold hands, even as he was doing. He was resenting his own bad mood and the long ride ahead. The morning's telephone call still rankled. He was too disturbed even to open the book he had bought for the journey, and lost in a welter of indeterminate, useless thoughts, he rested his eyes on the incessant, whirling snow beyond the tracks.

"That's a wonderful book," someone said.

He had barely noticed the person in the next seat except to see that she was a young woman, and breathless, because the train had already been about to start when she came rushing in.

"Oh yes, *Bleak House*. I haven't read it since high school."

"Look." And opening an overstuffed tote bag, she took out a copy of *Bleak House*.

"I tutor high school kids sometimes, so I'm reading it for the second time, too."

Now Donald looked at her. She was freckled and neat-featured, with reddish hair. She could have been Augustus Pratt's daughter.

"You're a full-time teacher?" he asked politely.

"No, I'm a farmer, a farmer's wife. I love books, and since where we live there aren't that many families who do love books, I like to help kids who don't get help at home."

"Where is that? Where do you live?"

"Well, if you look at the map, you'll see that there's a corner of Georgia where three states meet. It's where the Great Smokies end, or begin, depending on your point of view. But I'm keeping you from your book."

He was truly not feeling sociable, so taking advantage of the remark, he turned to the window and the flatlands of New Jersey. His thoughts were tossed between the morning's nastiness and the negotiations forthcoming in Washington.

After a while he heard and felt a stir in the adjacent seat. The young woman, rummaging in the tote bag, withdrew what looked like a tin of cookies.

"Want some?" she asked. "They're delicious, left over from my girlfriend's wedding. She made me take them home, and I'm glad she did because I'm starved. I didn't have time to eat or I would have missed the train in Boston. Oh, do," she went on when he hesitated, "otherwise I might eat them all myself and I can't afford to do that."

The cookies, as might be expected, led to further conversation, Donald remarking that he hoped all the food at the wedding was as good as this.

"Oh, it was! It was a country wedding at home. The bride and her mother did all the baking. Have another."

He would have liked to accept another, but since it would not have been appropriate, he declined and remarked instead that weddings were always fun—which was not necessarily true.

"Yes, aren't they? This wedding was in New Hampshire in a beautiful little town, something like one of ours at home except for the climate. I'd never seen that much snow in my life. Amy and I met at college in Georgia, you see, and we've been friends ever since, but I never visited her at home. We hadn't seen each other in ages, and I simply couldn't see myself missing her wedding."

Donald was thinking that once a conversation gets rolling, it is almost impossible to stop it.

"So it was a real event for you, a reunion, a great time," he said.

"Yes it was, except that I had to come without my husband. We have six hundred acres, fifty head of milkers, and a farm manager who's petering out, so Clarence didn't feel secure about going away. People don't have any idea of the work there is on a farm."

He could have said that, having hired out during many a summer vacation, he had a very good idea about the work. But not wanting to prolong the talk, he did not say so.

"You're a city man, I see by your briefcase. Would you like to see a picture of our place, or would it bore you?"

Now, how on earth could a person admit that it would bore him?

"Not at all. I'd like to see it."

So, out of the tote bag came a small cardboard album; undoubtedly it had been brought along for exhibition to the wedding guests. The photographs on the cover showed a tidy frame house with a porch across the front. Two handsome collies lay on the steps.

"These are Mutt and Jeff. 'Mutt' is kind of an insult, isn't it, because he's a border collie with a royal pedigree. A real extravagance, Clarence said. He bought him at a show—he couldn't resist. Now here's Clarence."

A tall man in neat shirt and jeans stood against a board fence. The corner of a barn roof and part of a cow were visible in the background.

"Now here's Ricky. He's six, but this was taken two years ago."

Between his parents on the same front steps where the dogs had lain now sat a little boy with curly hair and a serious face. Below the picture was a penciled caption: *Clarence, Ricky, and Kate*, with the date, Fourth of July, and the year.

*There would be a band in the morning when the veterans marched down the Main Street. There would be little flags in the cemeteries and big ones sagging in the hot, still air over the front door, or sometimes on a pole in the front yard. There would be picnics, fried chicken maybe, and ice cream and blueberry pie.*

Suddenly something touched Donald's heart, and he turned, not too obviously, sliding his eyes toward the woman beside him, a person naive in her certainty that he would care about these pictures. His quick glance encompassed her and registered itself in his head: slender figure, hair curly like her son's, facial features undistinguished except for the tender smile, and hands strong with nails unvarnished, clasping the book.

"He's a beautiful little boy," Donald said.

She sighed. "Yes, he's precious. We would love to have more, but nothing happens. Do you have any children?"

"Just one. A girl. She's two."

"Ah, well, you'll have more. Most people do. Clarence and I made up our minds almost from the time we met that we'd have a big family. That's the way we were, right from the beginning." She laughed.

"You were in a big hurry, weren't you?" Donald responded, taking the lighthearted cue from the laugh.

"But anyway, we've been happy together from the day we met."

He could not have explained why he was curious enough to ask this talkative stranger how they had met, but he asked.

"It was at the university in Atlanta. He was in agriculture, and I was in history, and we hadn't even noticed each other until one day when it was raining cats and dogs and he let me walk with him under his umbrella."

So that's how it happens. A woman rescues some papers from falling off a man's lap, or a man lends his umbrella.

"I never thought I'd live on a farm. Of course, it isn't just any old farm, it's what you might call an 'establishment.' It's been in the family for maybe six generations, maybe more. From right after the Revolution, anyway. That's two hundred years ago, at least. I think he loves every tree on the land. And do you know, I admit it did take quite a while, but now I've come to love them all, too."

Lucky Clarence, Donald thought. You'll take care of Kate if you're wise. She's honest, she's good, and she spreads cheer. In an entirely different way, she reminds me of Maria, except that Maria, even though she was born in a village, is naturally streetwise. This young woman is too trusting to be let out in the world without having somebody take care of her. Of course I might be all wrong, I've been fooled before, but I don't think I am all wrong.

"Well, I believe I'll get back to my book," she said.

So Donald opened his book, too. But his mind was too full to absorb it, and the reading didn't go very well. The incessant snow fled past the windows, turning white the fields, the housing developments, the factories, the city of Philadelphia, and more. If Cookie could have a mother like this, he was thinking, and closing his eyes, he saw his little girl standing in front of him glowing with joy over the fluffy bear in her arms. If only she had a mother. . . . Then suddenly Washington was announced.

He stood up to take his suitcase from the rack

and said good-bye to his neighbor. "It was nice talking to you."

"Yes, it was. Let me scribble our address for you. I always do this when I meet somebody I like. If you and your wife ever travel south, come see us."

∽◠

Two days later Donald left Washington by train. It would take a bit longer than the shuttle flight, but at least he would arrive in the heart of the city, near enough to reach his home after a brisk walk that would be welcome after two days of sitting in chairs.

As it happened, his seat on this return trip was in the middle of the car, most likely the same one he had occupied on the way down. No doubt it was this fact that brought to mind the talkative young woman who had sat next to him. My Lord, he thought, she gave me her address, me, a total stranger, and invited me—and my wife— to visit her and her husband if we should ever "come south!" Poor innocent, she had no guile, not at all. Why, he hadn't even given her his name, much less any means of identification!

They had looked so *sweet,* the three of them, seated there on the porch steps; they reminded him of one of those old illustrations by Norman Rockwell. And reflecting then on the incredible variety of human types, his mind made a natural jump back to the events of this rotten week.

He must, he absolutely must, learn something about child care, so as to be better prepared for the next time, heaven forbid, when Cookie should need more attention while Lillian was away on a safari or someplace. A simple medical guidebook for parents, as well as a couple of books on child psychology and general development, were essential. With these in mind, he already began to feel less helpless.

Accordingly, a few hours later, he emerged from a bookstore with four volumes in a bag, trudged through gray slush toward home, and turning a corner near his house, came face-to-face with the man whom he recognized only as Cindy's boyfriend.

Identification was not difficult; he had no friends or even an acquaintance whose matted beard reached up to the eyes and down to the waist.

"Hey, Donald, long time, no see."

No, not since the wedding party. "That's right. How've you been? How's Cindy?"

"Cindy? You didn't know? Lillian didn't tell you?"

"I don't see Lillian. Hasn't Cindy told you that?"

"Yeah, I heard something. Anyway, Cindy's dead."

"Oh, I'm sorry. What happened?"

"She got sick. Too much booze, or other stuff. I don't know exactly. She died in the hospital."

An instant's recollection of a young woman with a raucous voice and gaudy makeup came to Donald; then, even though he hadn't liked her, there came a rush of pity because there was no sense at all in dying so young. She couldn't have been much older than twenty-five.

"I'm sorry," he said again, meaning it. "I used to wonder about her, even though it wasn't any of my business. Frankly, I used to wonder about Lillian and Cindy being friends. They were so different. But Lillian was really very good to her. She practically supported her, I think."

"Friends?" The tone was almost mocking. "They were sisters, man. Cindy was her sister."

As if a stone had struck him, Donald went into shock. "A foster child? Adopted?"

"No, no. Same father, same mother."

"I don't understand it. It doesn't seem to make sense. Who were the parents? What were they? I mean . . . what were they like?"

"Like? Like nothing. Just people."

Donald shook his head. "I tried . . . I never could get her to talk about anything."

"What's talk? Chewing the fat. Gets you nowhere."

"But do you know anything at all? Did you know the family very well?"

"Sure. Lived across the street. I'm sort of a third cousin or something. That's why I stuck around."

"I don't understand," Donald repeated, and stared at the man as if some answer might lie hidden behind the outlandish face.

"What's to understand? I told you. Just people, you know? People like you. Like me. Anyway, I'll be going. Take care. Keep the faith."

Donald stood watching Cindy's boyfriend saunter away out of sight. What was the secret? he asked himself. But no answer came. Then he went upstairs into his apartment, and foraging in the refrigerator, made up a plate with a sandwich and a pear, after which he sat down with one of his new books on child care.

But the astonishing facts he had just learned went whirling through his mind instead. So many conjectures had come to that mind during his brief marriage: that there was something dishonorable in her family's past that she was ashamed to reveal, or that they had been cruel to her, so that she was unable to forgive them. All of that could be true, or none of it could be. Perhaps there wasn't any secret at all other than a desire, grown out of all proportion, to escape into another personality, into another environment and another world. It was not uncommon.

More than once, when he had been living with Lillian, he had thought about making a quiet investigation with the ultimate purpose of helping her to understand whatever it was that she was hiding. But he had hesitated, and in the end had come to realize that it would have been useless. For whatever damage, real or imagined, had been done to her, or not been done—unless you wanted to count one of nature's devilish jokes that had caused her to be born the way she was—it was too late to change anything. He had lived with her long enough and had experienced enough with her to be certain of that. It was too late.

# Chapter 9

Donald began to have a strange sensation of speed, as if everything were moving too fast for him. Things piled up: conferences, depositions, telephone calls to be returned at once, letters to be answered at once, invitations that were half social and half business, the funeral of a senior partner's brother, and never, never enough time. At the end of each day he felt a weariness that he had never felt before. A vigorous young man, not supposed to tire like this, he knew very well that the tiredness was not only of the body, but of the troubled spirit.

Maria said: "They had a terrible fight after dinner yesterday. Cookie heard it, and it scared her, so I took her out of the room." Another time she reported: "Mrs. Buzley went away for the weekend on somebody's big boat. Mr. didn't go."

There was a cheapness, a shabbiness, in listening to what was after all gossip. And yet Donald had no other means of knowing anything about what he thought of as his child's home. Odd it was that he should be on the side of Howard Buzley, the man to whom Lillian had been mistress before she married him. Yet Buzley was apparently the steady force in that household and the one who gave the most attention to Donald's child.

One day at a quick lunch down the street from the office, Ed Wills set down his coffee cup and asked a question. "Will you object if I should ever mention Lillian? Please answer honestly. I hesitated even to say this much, but June said I should. She and I both know how you worry about your little girl, and so—"

"Please tell me anything and everything. I need to know."

"Well, it isn't much this time. Or maybe it is, but we've been seeing Lillian at the beach near that cottage we rented for the summer. It's rather remote, not in a fashionable neighborhood, not Lillian's style at all. But we've seen her way down at the deserted end of the beach a few times, and not with Mr. Buzley. At least, we didn't think he was."

"A man over sixty? Short and gray?"

"No, not at all. Far, far from it."

Donald sighed. "I worry, Ed. If that marriage breaks up, where's she going to go with the baby? Yes, I could find a larger apartment, go to court and get alternate weeks or something, but is that a way to bring up a child, back and forth between parents who don't like each other?" And his thoughts returned to the book on child psychology. "So where are we going? Where's Lillian going?"

"According to my wife, she's flying up and up. June likes the society columns, out of sheer curiosity, I suppose, because as you well know, she's not like that. But she's been fascinated by Lillian's career, if you want to call it a career. Did you see the photo last week?"

"I only saw a couple that the nanny showed me, but that was more than a year ago."

"Well, there've been plenty since then. The latest was in one of those fashion layouts, a group of women at a bazaar in somebody's garden. June says Lillian's a meteor, a bit too old to start out as a model, otherwise she'd be on every front cover."

*People. Just people like you and me.*

But that was far too simple. She needs to know who she is, only God can tell why. No, that's not true either. She must know very well why she has that need to reinvent herself, to show she can reach the top or whatever she believes to be the top, where you can have everything you want and can do everything you want.

"We really liked her in the beginning," Ed said. "June tried to be her friend after you were married, but suddenly she didn't seem to want June anymore."

Donald remembered: That was when she met Chloe Sanders.

"I hope she's not going to break up with Buzley," he said as he stood, paid the bill, and went back to work.

Now propelled by his worry and a small spice of curiosity, Donald began to follow the Sunday social pages and even, whenever June Wills, via Ed, sent news of an item in a magazine, read that, too. He made mental note of every detail: She was magnificently dressed; most often she was with Buzley, yet many times not; she started to be seen not as often with entertainers and others on Buzley's level, but even with European celebrities here on behalf of cultural monuments and events; she was recently photographed in a group standing next to a count and countess.

She was leaving Buzley behind. Counts and countesses, no less! Oh, he said to himself, she will hold on to Buzley until she gets someone better. He saw it clearly, even though Buzley might not see it yet. But he would, poor man, and possibly sooner than later.

❧

One Sunday morning the telephone rang.

"I hope I didn't wake you," Ed Wills said, "but I wanted to reach you before you got to the newspaper."

"Why? What's happened?"

"An accident. I'm going to tell you the end first: Your baby's fine. Not a scratch. It's a miracle. I'm telling you the one hundred percent truth, so stay calm. I wouldn't fool you, Donald."

He breathed in and breathed out, that being the instruction for staying calm in an emergency. Stay calm. Calm.

"Go on," he said.

"It happened last evening around ten o'clock, a collision on the highway. A car going fast, or maybe both cars, were changing lanes, swerved into each other, and sent one of them spinning into a tree. Lillian was in the front seat with the driver. He's in the hospital, in critical condition, it says. He didn't have a seat belt on, so he was thrown out. Lillian has a broken shoulder. Your little girl was untouched, thank God. It's incredible. You'll read it in the paper."

Donald's right hand was shaking, and to steady it, he placed his left hand over it. "Where is she?" he asked. "Where did it happen?"

"Out on Long Island. Some friends took care of Lillian and the baby, took them home after the doctors had seen Lillian. They're people who live here all year round. I don't know them, but I'll find out. June and I would have taken them if we'd known in time. We're in the middle of packing, end of summer, start of school."

Donald understood that Ed was talking to make the call seem ordinary, prolonging it so as not to end on a downbeat. "I'll call you back as soon as I make some calls in the village. I won't be long."

The Sunday paper was maddening, page after page of politics, international news, business news, and the rest, when all he wanted was one small item. Frantically his hands raced through the pages. Finding it, his eyes raced through it.

**Man killed in highway crash. Leo Simmons, 37, of Jefferson Township, was killed in a two-car collision at the intersection of Jefferson Avenue. Phillip Ferrier, 32, of New York City, is in critical condition at Jefferson Memorial Hospital. One passenger, Lillian Buzley, 29, of**

New York City, sustained a broken arm and shoulder, while her child, Bettina Wolfe, age 2, escaped injury.

Flinging the paper to the floor, Donald cursed aloud. "On her way to New York! On her way! Where the hell had she been, and why, out with the baby—my God, I knew, I knew something was bound to happen. For weeks I've felt it whirling in my head, damn her. Damn her to eternal hell."

And he sat there with his head in his hands, trying to think. What to do? What to do? After a while he got up, washed his few dishes, and went to stand at the window looking down upon the Sunday morning quiet in the street. Why? Why, when it could have been so blessedly good with productive work, a wife, a child or children, and more than enough to feed them all?

When the phone rang again, he sprang to it. "Ed? Ed? Where are they? I'll borrow a car from somebody and go for them."

"You won't have to. The people who gave the party are driving them home. They're leaving now. Their name is Carter. Lillian's all bandaged up, but the baby's happy, they said. I asked especially about her."

"Thanks, Ed. Thank you very much."

"Thanks for nothing, Don. You must be pretty washed out."

"I guess so. But I'll see you in the morning, same time, same place."

Too distressed to sit still, he walked around his rooms as if in search of something to do. He rearranged some books on the shelves and watered the fern that Lillian had bought and cherished. The fern was a fountain of healthy greenery, whereas Lillian—

The telephone rang again. This time it was the agitated voice of Maria that he heard.

"Mr. Wolfe, Mr. Wolfe, what happened? I just came home from my cousin, and Mrs. Buzley called up, and she said there was an accident, and Cookie was fine, and she has a broken shoulder, and they'll be home by one o'clock—where are they?"

"I don't know anything more than you've just told me. But where have you been, Maria?"

"I told Mrs. Buzley on Thursday that my cousin come to New York this week and I want to have two days to see her. She was angry with me, no, not really talking angry, but I see she was. She wanted to go to a party Saturday, but I thought my turn. I need to see my cousin. Mrs. Buzley goes to parties all the time. I said I'd come back Sunday morning, and here I am, but where is Cookie? Where did they go?"

"Someplace on Long Island. That's all I know. You'll find out when she gets home. Please phone me then right away. I need to know. But where's Mr. Buzley?"

"He went to California. His work. He's coming back now. There was a message on the machine. Sunday early, it said. I thought she say not until Tuesday. Yes, she say Tuesday. I don't know what—all right. I'll call you, Mr. Wolfe."

He walked back and forth again through his three rooms, thinking. There was dirty business going on here. No question of it. It was no business of Donald Wolfe's, or would have been no business if it had not been for Donald Wolfe's little girl.

After a while he went downstairs and outside. The day was balmy, and people had come out to enjoy the afternoon, strolling with their beautiful babies in carriages and their beautiful dogs on leashes. It seemed to him that the atmosphere was filled with a friendly peace. With terrible anger, he thought about Lillian, destroyer of peace. Then he turned about and went home to walk back and forth again like a prisoner measuring his steps, trying to think of something sensible that he might do.

When the phone rang, it was Maria speaking in nervous haste. "I'm in the kitchen. They can't hear me, but I'll be quick. Mr. Buzley's here. They're in their room, she's all bandaged, he's yelling at her, it's awful, Mr. Wolfe, Cookie's all right, I have her in the playpen, I have to go."

"Come to my apartment instead of going to the park on Saturday afternoon. If it should rain so you can't go to the park, I'll come to your place whether anybody likes it or not."

"Oh, don't come here, Mr. Wolfe. Don't do that."

"Then you must promise to call me every day so I'll know what's happening."

Thank heaven for Maria, for her loyalty and her common sense. You didn't find Marias on every street corner. Then it occurred to him that he was hungry, so he made a sandwich, and then had no appetite for it. He looked out of the window again; an ambulance passed below, shrieking along the street, and he imagined the accident. By what marvel had his little girl been spared?

When evening came, he went to bed, for it seemed that he had been awake for days and was dying to sleep. But the sleep that came was only fitful, interrupted by frustration dreams. He was being pursued by some unidentifiable horror, was running with every muscle strained to the fullest, yet he was unable to advance an inch. The horror was coming nearer . . .

He awoke and fell asleep and dreamed again. So the night passed.

∽

Everyone at the office had heard about Donald's baby and the accident. It was surprising that so many people had read that tiny item on an inside page. If some hadn't seen it, they had been informed about it as soon as they came to work. By the way people spoke to him or by their facial expressions alone, he knew that they were aware of his pain, and he was grateful for their sympathy.

Mr. Pratt said little, and by doing so, said it all with the pressure of his hand on Donald's shoulder and one sentence: "Your baby's not hurt, which is all that matters. Remember that."

On Donald's desk lay a small stack of important mail, which was probably a good thing because it made the morning pass quickly. Then at one o'clock, when Ed Wills came in to suggest going down the street to lunch, all yesterday's trouble erupted again.

Ed began it. "I had somebody look up the police report in Jefferson. That driver was not in the best of shape. He was over the white line when it happened. He seems to be some kind of good-time guy-about-town with a reputation for drinking too much, and maybe having a cocaine habit, too, although they haven't checked that. Anyway, it doesn't matter, except to his heirs, if he has any. If he has, they had better hope he had plenty of car insurance. According to the hospital's report an hour ago, he's not going to make it through. Landed on his head when he was thrown out of the car."

Donald shuddered and listened.

"I'm wondering how much of all this stuff you want to hear," Ed said, fingering a stray fork. "Yes, I'm uncomfortable," and putting the fork down deliberately, he continued, "I hate this kind of talk, sounding like a gossip columnist, but for your sake, I should do it, so—"

"What is it, Ed? Come on. This fellow, was he the one you've told me about, the one on the beach near you?"

"No, no, that's another story."

"Excuse me if I sound confused," Donald said, not disguising his bitterness, "then who is the mysterious stranger on the beach? Not that I give a damn."

But thinking of permanence, of stability, and of Howard Buzley, he did very much give a damn.

"June doesn't run with the gossiping set," Ed began, "but she knows a lot of women who do, so she got on the phone last night when I asked her to and she found out. The man is Storm,

Arthur Storm, some sort of tycoon who has a showplace about ten miles east of our beach. I've seen it, or at least as much of it as you can see from the road. Big trees, lawns, acreage, long, low white house—you get the picture."

"Yes. What else?"

"Does it matter?" Ed asked gently.

There was really no point in hiding one's fears any longer, especially from a friend, from one's closest friend. So Donald spoke out.

"I am afraid Buzley will leave her if she doesn't behave herself. In this short time, I've come to rely on his steadiness, and isn't that strange? He's given Bettina a home, he's fond of the child, and the arrangement is a lot better than having the child's mother go adrift. That's why I'm worried and that's why I need to hear anything you can tell me."

"Okay. Arthur Storm is a good-looking guy, about forty, they say, or maybe not even that. He has a wife and four young sons, thirteen or fourteen and younger. When he met Lillian, he went wild over her."

"I understand."

Neither spoke until Donald asked whether Storm's wife knew about it.

"Yes. She's left him."

"Was it Storm's party that she went to last Saturday?"

"No, Storm's gone to France temporarily to see to the house that he owns there."

"I see." This was a perfunctory remark, since he was not seeing anything at all other than an ugly muddle.

"If only I could get total custody . . ."

"Very, very difficult," Ed replied, shaking his head. "That you know."

Yes, that he knew.

On the following Saturday afternoon, Maria arrived at the apartment with Bettina all dressed up in something yellow that, when it was removed, revealed a prestigious Paris label. Lillian had taste; you certainly had to give her credit for that.

Donald had prepared for the visit by removing whatever was reachable and breakable. He had provided a fluffy cat that meowed when it was squeezed, a wooden game with wooden balls that rattled through a maze when it was shaken, a large, plush ball to be rolled around the floor, and vanilla ice cream for refreshment.

"And for you and me, Maria, a cup of coffee and cake from the French bakery. Wait till you taste it."

The day was cloudy, so that the light that lay upon the little table at the window was a gentle one, muting the lovely colors in the room and on the carpet, where Bettina sat concentrating on the wooden balls.

"So nice, so quiet here," Maria murmured. "I'd like to stay."

"Not quiet at your place?"

"Oh yes, sometimes. A lot of times. But you never know. Mr. Buzley was so—oh, oh, so oh, oh angry, Mr. Wolfe! The accident, you know, with Cookie in the car, and why she went to the party. Sneaked out, you know. But he found out. Oh yes, he found out!"

It seemed then, as Maria continued, that Lillian, upon learning that Buzley was coming back two days earlier than planned, had been in a rush to get home before he did. Apparently, the couple who had driven her to the party were in no hurry to leave it, so that she had accepted a ride from this young man whom she had never met before.

Maria became emotional. "It was terrible, so sad. I wanted to cry. Mrs. Buzley cried. Her arm hurts, I think. Then he felt sorry. First he yelled, then he felt sorry, and yesterday he was very nice to her, bought her a present, some jewelry, I think. I saw the box, and she was nice to him then, too."

He doesn't yet know about Arthur Storm, thought Donald.

"You know, Mr. Wolfe, she is a funny woman. Always nice to me, laughs all the time, is nice. At the party she says people played with baby, and she was very glad because Cookie is so beautiful."

*Because Cookie is so beautiful.*

He was outraged. So beautiful, she says. Yes, and so close to death, literally by inches, in a car driven by an irresponsible stranger when she should have been home in bed. Suddenly Donald stood and picked up his child, along with a toy which he set on the table before her.

"Daddy!" Squealing in delight, she reached down to his plate. "Cake! Cake!"

Apologizing with a laugh to Maria, he gave it to her. "I know she's not supposed to have it. But a little chocolate whipped cream once in a while won't hurt."

"You never will hurt her, Mr. Wolfe. Not you. But Mrs. Buzley, yes, she is a funny woman. Very nice—but still not *good* for child. You understand?" And sadly, Maria shook her head. "Very smart, but foolish too. Not *good* for child."

Oversimplified, Donald thought. "Mixed up" would be more accurate. Damaged goods, either born or made that way. But what difference? She was what she was, no matter why. He looked down at the little hands, now smudged with chocolate. Those hands, their future, were everything.

Maria said soon, "She needs her nap. I'll put her on your bed in there, all right?"

"Will she go to sleep in a strange place?"

"Oh, Cookie is easy child. Easy nature. She sleeps a little, then we go back."

In the living room, he sat where he could see the bed. Maria had picked up a magazine. With obvious difficulty, she read, her lips shaping each word. This woman, Donald thought as he observed her, this kindly stranger, was his only link with the child asleep on that bed. If ever he wanted the truth, she was the only one who would give it. This was his situation.

His impulse was to pick up the telephone and give Lillian a piece of his mind. But the reasonable part of that mind knew better. How often had he not done that before and received nothing more than a slammed receiver?

"Maria," he blurted, "will you always stay with Cookie? Always?"

"Always, Mr. Wolfe?"

"Yes, because—" There was no dignity, no decency even in saying what he wanted to say about a woman who had once been his wife and always would be his child's mother; everything in him rebelled against washing this particular linen, so he said only, "There is no one like you, Maria. Cookie needs you. Do you understand?"

"I love Cookie, Mr. Wolfe. I carry her home from the hospital, two days old. And Cookie loves me, more than mother, that's true, you know?"

"I'll give you more money, Maria. Whatever Mr. Buzley gives you, I'll give you more."

"No, no, I think you're not rich like Mr. Buzley. I don't want that, Mr. Wolfe."

"You won't go soon, will you, Maria? Not without telling me?"

"No, no. Maybe sometime. Not soon. I tell you everything, Mr. Wolfe."

Later, when Donald closed the door upon Maria and on Cookie, in her yellow coat with the white plush cat in her arms, he stood for a moment quite still. *Maybe sometime.* A kind of sadness crept through the quiet rooms, heavy and gray as a fog on a winter night.

Donald's friends at the office told him what he, as a litigator, already knew, that he would never get sole custody of his child. The divorce was past and agreed upon. And once the child was in a foreign country? It didn't bear thinking about.

*I wouldn't even recognize the man the next morning . . .* Anyway, would that be grounds enough for removal of the child? One never knew.

His friends, chiefly Ed Wills, also told him some things he did not know: that Arthur Storm's wife had filed last week for divorce, that Arthur Storm was famed for his collection of modern art, chiefly kept at his house in France.

*When I am rich, I shall collect great art.* Ah yes, it all fits. . . .

One evening Maria came back. Her familiar green hat was lopsided, and she was gasping, out of breath.

"Mr. Buzley gone! Took his clothes, everything, closets empty, all his things gone. He was so angry, I never saw, Mr. Wolfe. Terrible, terrible! Said to me, 'Take care of baby.' He kiss baby, and go."

"Where is the baby?" Donald cried.

"Home, sleeping. You think I leave her? Cook is there tonight. Mrs. is out. Some friends come for her, I don't know. It's terrible, Mr. Wolfe."

Before Donald's eyes, there appeared an instant picture of that apartment, seen once so briefly, but not forgotten: the vista of great rooms, things now heaped and jumbled, the faces of curious, astonished onlookers, and again, Lillian's face as it must be now, her pale skin red with tears or rage.

He looked at the trembling woman, the innocent bystander, and gently removing her coat, made her sit down.

"Have you had any dinner, Maria? Can I get you something to eat or drink?"

"I'm not hungry. Nothing, please."

So Buzley had left! Now possibilities, or probabilities, must be considered, questions about the apartment, whether owned or leased; if leased, the term of the lease. If divorce was to follow this upheaval, where was Lillian—meaning of course the baby—going to go? And then there was that other man, the likely cause of this mess.

"Took furniture, too," Maria said. "His desk. Big desk he loved. Big chairs and pictures, his family, children, that's all."

Then it was to be permanent, this upheaval. An angry man may take his clothes, but he doesn't move his favorite furniture without knowing that he's not coming back.

Maria reflected for a few minutes as if to make sure of her conclusions and continued, "You know, Mr. Wolfe, I think she has different man, no boy—big man this time. Yes, yes, she has. She ask me to go with her to France, because Cookie love me. Beautiful house in France, beautiful picture. Me! I just come to New York. I say no. Sorry, Mrs. Buzley, no."

It was an enormous effort over the leaping of Donald's heart to speak quietly. "Did she say when?"

"Soon. A couple of months. He have business here first, then they go."

He had business indeed, did Arthur Storm: the divorce and the four young sons, whom he was trading in for Lillian Buzley, formerly Lillian Wolfe, formerly— And so forcibly did Donald strike his fist on the table beside his chair that Maria jumped.

"Mr. Wolfe, don't worry! I stay with Cookie until she go. Maybe they will not go. Maybe she just talk. Mrs. Buzley, she like to talk."

Donald knew better than to believe "just talk." To begin with, he knew Lillian, her drive, her impatience, and her successes. Second, he had his contacts, the chief of them being Ed Wills, who through June made a helpful effort to learn what was going on in the Arthur Storm situation. Maria, of course, was his other contact; through her, he kept track of the French connection.

As one tense week followed the other, it became clear that Lillian was not even trying to conceal her plans from Donald. Surely she was not relying on Maria to keep silent on those Sunday afternoons in the park! No, she was only too aware that Donald had no real power to stop her from taking her child anywhere she pleased.

He berated himself for having had no fore-sight. It was true that on the day he willingly signed those papers he had seen the baby only twice. His feelings, now hard to describe, had been a mixture of sadness, rage at Lillian, bewil-derment, a certain odd sense of detachment, along with a sense of moral obligation—all of these, and nothing yet of real love.

Yes, that was true. But still, no excuse for hav-ing been a fool, he a lawyer with a distinguished reputation. For love had come, as he should have known it would, when at the age of four months, his child had smiled at him. And what beside his love could he give back to her other than the considerable sums of money he had in-vested in her name? Could he give her a home or any life apart from the kind of life that Lillian had to offer?

Never mind what had made or not made Lil-lian what she was. This baby has a right, he told himself again and again, a right to be molded and become somebody whole and good.

Sometimes, as he sat at work, he caught himself muttering as if Lillian were sitting op-posite: You are not fit to mother a child! You

destroy whatever you touch. No, that's not altogether true. You were kind to Cindy. Perhaps
she was Dr. Jekyll to your Mr. Hyde? But I'm
no psychologist. I can't fathom it. And in any
case, it doesn't matter now.

One day he remembered what Maria had told
him about Buzley's departure, that he had kissed
Bettina before he left. And suddenly Donald felt
sorry for Buzley, the generous, foolish old man.
For all his shrewd New York-Hollywood so-
phistication, he had been deluded and tricked.
Was there a moral in this? he asked himself. And
with bitter irony replied: Yes. Be lucky.

For the past two years, or even longer, ever
since Lillian had been making an appearance in
some social column or other, he had been reading these announcements. So it was that he came
across a mention in connection with a report on
an art exhibit of Arthur Storm's decision to
move permanently to France. "In order," it read,
"to take care of his business concerns there." Six
weeks had already gone by since Maria's revelations, six weeks during which Donald ought to
have been taking some action. But what action?
Asking his friends, asking Augustus Pratt, he received no helpful advice, for the simple reason
that they had none to give.

*Despair,* he told himself, is a fearful word. He
went about his days—how many days were

left?—with a picture of an airplane bearing Bettina-Cookie away over the Atlantic. To whom, to what? he cried to himself, and lost his appetite and did not sleep.

Through his mind there flitted odd recollections of crises from his past: the day he read the War Department telegram that had been sent to his mother in 1944, the morning when his dog was run over, and the day of the cyclone when on the farm where he worked the horses all went berserk.

*Hurry, hurry, hurry! There is no time. It may already be too late.* On Sunday afternoon, he took his baby's hand, and they walked, her small, soft hand secure in his. Secure for now, it was, but what of tomorrow?

More days passed. The strain was visible on his face. He knew it because of the way people looked at him. His dreams were hideous: One night he was in a courtroom with his argument perfectly prepared; yet when he rose to speak, the argument fled from him, so that he stood with nothing to say while the entire courtroom stared in horrified amazement. He woke up sweating. And more weeks passed.

Then on another day, and for no real reason, something occurred to him on his way to work:

People, if they will it, can make a fresh start.
They can turn their lives around. Hadn't he
done so once when he came to this place, New
York? There were so many, many places . . . And
he was free! He owed no man. He had wronged
no man. Yes, he was free. I can go anywhere, he
thought, repeating the words and surprising
himself.

That night he went to bed without fear. It was
as if some miraculous transformation had taken
place, as if he had drunk some magic potion. It
was as if a door had been opened, admitting light
where there had been none. He had not yet
stepped through that door, but it was there. The
sight of it was in some way reassuring. For the
first time in a long while, he fell into a comforting, easy sleep.

In the morning he got up cheerfully and made
ready to go to work. He could not have explained how or why it came when it did, but
suddenly as he walked across the room, as he
reached the center of it, something struck him,
hard. Something came ringing into his ears,
commanding him.

*Do it! Do it! Yes.*

# Chapter 10

First of all, he had to accept that Donald Wolfe had no confidant. Except for those remote cousins in Wyoming, who would not recognize him if they were to bump into him, there was no one of his blood to whom he might appeal for shelter or advice. Nor could he confide in any good friend, such as Ed Wills, and involve him by even the slightest hint in an illegal act.

How to get away? Where to hide? It had to be someplace remote and untraveled by tourists or by any acquaintances whom he might accidentally encounter. The world was large, yet small enough for him to have once met on a windy, hilly corner in Edinburgh a client from Chicago whom he had not seen in four years.

In the corner of the den there stood a large globe on which he had liked to retrace his travels; it had been fascinating also to track the wanderings of that famous scoundrel with whose case the firm had for so long been connected. A man like him had had to have many contacts with criminals, several false passports, and a phenomenal memory to keep all these things in order. Donald had none of these, nor did he want to have them. So that far, empty corner of Canada that had first come to his mind was out of the question.

Next, then, he spread out on the table a folding map of the United States and studied it. Alaska was as far away as you could get, except for Hawaii. Hawaii involved an airplane, where notice would be taken and a record would be on file of a man traveling with a two-year-old girl. Alaska? It was too sparsely populated, even in its few cities, for the man and the child to melt away in a crowd. Where to go to find a place that was neither too crowded nor too empty, that could be reached without a journey of two or three thousand miles? It should be a rural area, perhaps with a little town tucked into a pocket between mountains, away from the stream of modern life. The obvious answer was somewhere in the mid-South, exactly where, he had no idea.

But wherever he might go, how was he to

make a living? The only dollars he had ever
earned had come to him from working on
somebody's farm and from working as a lawyer.
Impatiently, he thrust the map aside and went to
the mirror that hung in the coat closet, there to
stare at his reflection and demand aloud: "Can
you possibly be crazy? Here you are in the midst
of a case that Augustus Pratt has assigned to
you—to you, Donald Wolfe, rather than to any
of the others who have been in the firm twice as
long as you have."

Then, as he turned from the mirror, the first
thing he saw was the framed photograph of his
baby. She was sitting in the stroller with a half-
eaten graham cracker in her hand and a merry
grin on her face. All of his stalwart resolution
came flooding back.

*Do it! Do it!*

On Sunday in the park, Maria reported that
"the man come from France. She see him every
day. Come every day, Mr. Wolfe. Big man.
Good-looking. Mrs. Buzley very happy with
him."

No doubt she was, for however long that happiness might last. Scenes as on a reel of film flickered past Donald's eyes: the beds at that party—so
long ago now—oh, she had been on her way
to them, no doubt of that. Those people in

Florence, Lillian lying rumpled on the sofa that
terrible morning; all of these and so much more
came flickering back.

"Daddy. Walk. Cookie wants to walk."

She did not walk, she scampered, and he had
to hold fast to her lest she get away. The "terrible twos" it said in one of Donald's books.

One of the first things he would do was to
change her name because both "Cookie" or
"Bettina" grated on his ears. They did not suit
her, although he could not have given any reason other than that they represented the world
from which he was about to take her.

~

From someplace in his mental storage room,
Donald remembered having once come across a
magazine with advertisements for books on
changing one's identity. Number-one task, then,
was to track down the magazine. This he did by
inquiring for it in several neighborhoods where
he thought it might most likely be found. Having done this, he ordered a book in which he
learned what common sense alone should have
taught him: He needed a birth certificate. With
that he would turn himself into another man.
And a child starting school would need one, too.

This sort of thing did not always work, he
knew. It probably did work very, very seldom—

and it certainly *should* work very, very seldom, or else what kind of world would we have? Yet sometimes, in desperate circumstances, might not one be forgiven?

Cash was his first need, cash that usually leaves no trace. He began to withdraw it from his various accounts, occasionally giving a casual explanation that he was traveling to Indonesia. He owned no valuables other than the silver tea set that Lillian had left behind because Buzley already owned two of them. To his surprise, he received ten thousand dollars for it, which he took in cash. Lillian had surely wound poor Buzley around her little finger! He sold for a very fair amount the engagement ring that she had no longer wanted because poor, foolish Buzley had given her a better one. Poor, foolish Donald, too, he thought, remembering that afternoon in London when he had been in such a panic that he might lose her.

He got a money belt and wore it every day. This alone made him feel like a hunted person, skulking with his secret along the familiar corridors of the splendid offices where he was known as Donald Wolfe, a highly respected citizen in the heart of Manhattan. Every once in a while, he had a frightening sense of hallucination, from which he had to bring himself up short and confront reality; soon he was to be an unknown,

temporarily unemployed person in a place that
was also as yet unknown.

What was to be his name? he asked himself.
Where should he have been born? He must have
been living in a city large enough for him to
have gotten lost in the crowd. It must also be
near enough for him to spend a few days there
now to acquaint himself with it, if heaven forbid,
he should ever have to undergo any serious
questioning, such as where did you go to school,
or church, or the neighborhood movies?

He decided on Philadelphia. In that case he
could probably have been born in some nearby
town where he might easily search the cemeteries for the name of someone his own age who,
dying in early childhood, would probably be
forgotten by now. With this information, he
would be able to go to the registry of births and
ask for a duplicate birth certificate to replace the
one he had somehow lost. So, for three Saturdays in a row, he rented a car, toured through
five cemeteries in scattered towns, and ultimately came up with a name: Laura Fuller,
beloved daughter of James and Laura.

For a few minutes, he stood there looking
down at the unkempt grass on the grave. Died at
the age of two! Poor little thing. What would
her life have been if she had lived?

Yet, her name might be the means of giving a

better life to that little girl in New York. And her father's name, Donald's middle name, might be an omen of luck (since when did I believe in omens?). Nevertheless, it was a good, plain name, drawing no attention to itself, and "Laura" would be a pretty one for James Fuller's little girl.

Through all this mental and physical turmoil, fitting the project into his crowded days, Donald managed to have one amusing thought: Howard Buzley, through his contacts, experience, and style of life, would very likely have possessed in this field all the expertise that Donald lacked.

"They ready soon." Maria's voice was tearful. "Mrs. Buzley tell me they going soon. Her man taking her and Cookie. In France they have nice nurse for Cookie, so don't worry, Mr. Wolfe. But I am sad," she wept, "sad, Mr. Wolfe."

"When, Maria? When?"

"Next month maybe, I think."

"But you'll stay till then, Maria?"

"Yes, yes, I stay. I miss Cookie. Like my own baby, she is."

Next month. He had to get a little notebook right away and write down facts too important to leave to memory, details about clothes, toilet training, naps, and other things that he thought he already knew, but perhaps did not really know.

Most important, he had to buy a car. Accordingly, he called in sick for a few days, boarded a train to Philadelphia, and at the terminal asked a cab driver to take him to a used car lot. Instantly, he regretted the question. What if a countrywide search were to be made and this cab man should remember him? Then he scolded himself: You're ridiculous, you're as nervous as a cat on a rooftop. Stop it. You're just a citizen looking for a car.

The salesman was young and very eager. "Tell me what you need, and I'll find it. We've got some of everything."

This much Donald knew: The car must be as inconspicuous as the jeans and sneakers he was wearing, not likely to stick in anyone's memory, therefore not shiny or smart, or shabby-sad either, or white, or red.

"No particular make," he explained, "but low mileage and dependable. I'm taking it to western Canada, rough country." He must leave a misleading trail. "And I'll need a big trunk, really big. I'm moving a lot of stuff."

They were walking side by side through the rows. "That looks nice," Donald said, stopping to look at a clean black sedan. "Let's see the trunk. What's the mileage?"

While appearing to hear all the facts and figures, his mind was spinning a story. Let it sound so distinctive that there would be no way in which this young fellow would ever associate him with Lillian's lost baby.

*But it will happen, it's bound to happen. No it isn't, and you'd better get hold of your imagination, James Fuller.*

"My wife just died, you see, and I'm taking a lot of her things back to her parents."

"Sorry to hear that."

"I'm not flying because they live out in the country, seventy miles from the airport, so this is easier. I could ship the stuff, but I really ought to visit them. She was their only child. Died suddenly."

"Tough break."

There was appropriate sympathy in the young fellow's eyes. How easy it was, after all, to lie and get away with it! He had passed the first test.

He explained that he would be paying with the cash he had received from selling his furniture.

"Sold your furniture? You moving?"

"Moving to a smaller place right off Spruce Street. Listen, I'll call you in a couple of days when you've made the transfer, got the plates and stuff. I had my phone pulled out right after the last bill, and the new one isn't in yet."

"Tough breaks, mister."

"Well, that's life. Thanks a lot. You've been a big help."

He was a fraud now, sick with shame. But he was pursuing a greater cause than his self-esteem, so having planned to spend the next few days in Philadelphia, he took a hotel room, and armed with notebook and pen, set about on a walking tour to familiarize himself with the city. After that, with its map and a couple of pamphlets about its history and its historic places, he called for his car, the first he had owned since selling the jalopy in North Dakota, and drove back to New York.

~~∽∾~~

He began to dismantle the apartment, destroying any object that might disclose his identity, such as a snapshot of Cookie—of Laura—in Central Park with apartment buildings in the background, or an album containing a picture of himself in law school with cap and gown. He tore up extra copies of the United States map, saving one for his pocket to be pored over again and again.

~~∽∾~~

"Mrs. Buzley has great big trunk now," Maria reported. "She put in front hall. I think they go very soon, Mr. Wolfe."

Donald's heart was an engine, straining up the

side of a mountain. There was still so much to be
done! On the list were things still to be bought,
a large suitcase for the baby's clothes and the
clothes themselves. Every day after work he got
into his car and visited small shops in distant parts
of the city, buying a few items in each, so that no
salesperson might remember a man who had
bought a suspiciously large quantity of garments
for a little girl. He bought a child-sized mattress
to put on the floor at night, a proper car seat for
Laura's safety, a cooler for food, and a variety of
toys. Having done all these things, he prayed that
no sickness, however mild, would befall his
Laura, for might not a doctor sense something
amiss?

The days came and went too fast. He felt like
one who, pursued, was afraid to look back and
gauge his distance from the pursuer, or like one
afraid to look at a calendar and face the shrink-
ing time that was left to do anything that still
needed to be done.

At last only two days remained, this one and
tomorrow, the Sunday on which he would take
Laura away. His walk back and forth was a
nervous habit that he knew he must get over.
But it was only a recent habit and understand-
able, this constant rehearsal of things to come.
The name being one of them, he would pause

before a mirror to act out his part in a dialogue: *Hello, I'm James Fuller and this is my daughter Laura.* Up and down, up and down. Check the refrigerator for tomorrow's food: a chicken sandwich, bananas, her favorite graham crackers. Pack his own two largest suitcases; the doorman would assume he was off across the oceans again.

In the den he looked around at the shelves. Here were his luxuries, every book a precious object to be kept forever. On the topmost shelf, the red leather *Jefferson* glowed like the special jewel it was, the first book he had ever really afforded to buy. On the bottom shelf were his latest acquisitions, the guidebooks on rearing a child. These must go into his suitcase. And the *Jefferson,* too? Donald asked himself, and answered yes, that too. Say good-bye to the rest.

On the wall hung the lovely prints of eighteenth-century Paris. Between the windows hung the landscape that Lillian had bought when their troubles had barely begun. Would it go back to her now? he wondered.

Then he could think of nothing more to do, he went to bed, slept restlessly, and woke to a warm, windy Sunday morning. Shortly after noon, having for the third or fourth time checked the apartment, he went downstairs carrying a lunch box concealed in a paper bag and his own two suitcases with his clothes.

"Off again, Mr. Wolfe?" inquired the door-man, as Donald had expected he would.

"Yes, see you in a couple of weeks. Can you get me a taxi? I'm meeting a friend at his house and riding with him to the airport."

After riding in the taxi as far as an apartment building near the garage where he kept his packed-up car, he got out and stood with his luggage as if he were waiting for someone. When the taxi had left and was out of sight, he walked to a barbershop where he had his thick, somewhat unruly hair reshaped into a crew cut. In his pocket were the eyeglasses that would soon replace his contacts. Then he walked to the garage, drove to a street not far from Central Park, and left the car.

His plan had been to work the conversation around to a suggestion that he take Cookie in the stroller to see the lake, thus giving Maria a rest. But unexpectedly, she made things easier by having a very obvious head cold.

"Everybody out for the afternoon?" he asked.

"Out? Gone. Mrs. Buzley and Mr. Storm gone visit his brother someplace. Back late tonight. Maybe they stay till tomorrow, too."

"Well, why don't you go home and take a

long nap, Maria? Take care of your cold. I'll be at the front door with Cookie by five o'clock. The doorman will call upstairs for you to come down."

"Oh, I do need to lie down. You're a good man, Mr. Wolfe, you are."

He thought as she walked away that this was the last time, barring any disaster, that anybody would address him as "Mr. Wolfe." *This is the moment I leap off the bridge. I swim, or I sink.*

When he had collapsed the stroller and put it into the car—for leaving it on the sidewalk would seem very, very strange to anybody who might be looking out of a window—he settled Laura in the car seat with a pink teddy bear and started the engine. The journey had officially begun.

"Where's Mia?" She was dangerously close to tears. "Where's Mia?"

"Mia's taking a nap. You and I are having a nice ride."

"No! I want Mia!"

"Mia's taking a nap. Be a good girl," Donald soothed. "You're such a good girl."

"No."

How on earth was he going to manage if this were to keep up for the next thousand miles? Against all the rules, he reached into the glove compartment, broke a chocolate bar in two, and handed it back over his shoulder. Immediate silence followed; now he could concentrate on getting out of the city.

Heading west toward the Hudson River, he took a last glance at what he was leaving. Behind him, when at a red light he turned to look, was the standard postcard scene of Central Park surrounded by towers. In one of the towers were the offices of Orton and Pratt, of Mr. Pratt, who was expecting him early on Monday morning to discuss the new case, of Mr. Pratt to whom he owed so much, of Mr. Pratt whom Mr. Wolfe was now rewarding for all the goodness he had bestowed by—doing what Mr. Wolfe had to do. Would Mr. Pratt perhaps understand?

The car rolled northward along the river. Since his destination was in the South, it made sense to head north and mislead the searchers. An eerie feeling that they were being followed sent a chill through Donald. But that was absurd; Maria must still be asleep, so he had two or even three hours leeway before she would give an alarm. In the windshield before him he saw her plain, puzzled face when he failed to appear. . . . He must steady himself.

Laura, having smeared her cheeks and hands with chocolate, was drowsing. Maybe it wouldn't be so difficult to get through this journey if a piece of chocolate was enough to keep her contented. Thinking so, his spirits, and with them his nimble wits, revived. He would cross the river at the Tappan Zee Bridge, fill the tank with gas, and ask for directions to Albany. They would naturally direct him to the Thruway, a route that he had traveled many times; he would pretend to take it and continue northward on back roads where there were no toll booth attendants who might remember a man traveling with a tiny girl.

Narrow country roads curved through the Catskill Mountains. On a flat stretch of ground he stopped the car and spread a picnic cloth, congratulating himself for having been brilliant enough to think of bringing such a thing. But he had not been brilliant enough to allow for exercise. Luckily, the car's motion had lulled the child to sleep, or she would have been miserable. Nor had he thought that she might have need of a bathroom. Indeed, she had needed one, as he soon found out when he pulled off her training pants. Having done that, he took a plush ball from the trunk and gave her twenty minutes of hearty exercise.

Then he spread out the supper of chicken sandwich, banana, and milk. It was a pleasure to him to watch her eat. At least she wasn't going to be squeamish about food, he thought. She was really adorable, munching so solemnly. And she was clever, too, the little devil, for she had noticed where the chocolate bars were kept, and now, pointing to the car, very noisily demanded another piece.

Back in the car, and aware again that he ought not to do it, he gave her a piece and drove on, seeking a place to sleep. As they passed a resort hotel, he was tempted by the thought of the comfort it would provide, but prudently chose instead a dreary-looking motel in an obscure spot.

It was, as he was later to recall, a night to be remembered. Laura—he *must* keep that name in his head—was terrified of the bed he made for her on the floor and kept calling for Mia. Nothing he said would quiet her. At midnight, the agitated proprietor knocked somewhat angrily at the door, but as soon as Donald explained that the little girl's mother had died a few weeks ago, that they were on their way to the grandparents and had been riding all day, the man's face changed on the instant to deep sympathy.

"I'll get my wife," he said. "She'll help you."

And indeed she did. A stout, warm woman, perhaps she reminded Laura of Maria when she picked her up and gave her milk in a baby's bottle.

Donald was puzzled. "But she drinks from a cup," he said.

"Two-year-olds still like their bottle now and then when they're upset," the woman explained. "Now, mister, you hold her and walk with her until she falls asleep. Poor lamb, she'll be all right."

Perhaps, he thought as he lay awake until morning, I have made a terrible mistake. How am I going to keep going from here to wherever we do end up? Have I frightened her too badly, harmed her by doing this? Have I aroused suspicion tonight?

But he reasoned that he was not, after all, a national figure, and that thousands of children, every year, are taken away from the custodial parent. He thought, too, of Arthur Storm, of France, of Buzley, and all the long train of events going back to the day he had met this child's mother. . . .

In the morning he left the motel, had breakfast at a diner next door, and made sure that he was seen traveling toward Albany. After covering five miles or more, he made a wide circle toward the south. Now having learned something from yesterday's errors, he was prepared to travel by easy stages, to stop for necessities, for exercise and games, and even a ride in a supermarket cart. If any alarm had already been given, he reasoned, no one would be looking for a father out marketing, taking the time to admire a baby in arms and passing more time chatting with a man at the checkout counter. Back in the car his spirits rose so much that he began to sing, which amused Laura and raised his spirits even higher.

Between one small town and the next, past strip malls and once a playground where he stopped to let her enjoy the swings, the day passed without event.

Then, in the late afternoon, after driving through rural New Jersey past apple orchards and dairy farms, he went in to eat at a roadside diner close to an intersection. He had barely gotten past the door when he felt he had made a mistake, walking in here with a two-year-old baby in this week of all weeks. What if there was something on television? For surely people would be watching it while they ate.

Sure enough, it was blaring the news! Three-car crash, two dead in shoot-out, four-alarm fire, eighty-year-old woman mugged, wife says ex-husband stole two-year-old girl in New York.

The waitress, paying no attention to it, brought Donald's order and even lingered.

"Got a kid myself. Three-year-old boy. What's this one, two?"

Donald nodded. "Past two. Going on middle age. I swear she reads my mind," he said, speaking with casual cheer.

"Pretty kid. What's your name, little lady?"

"She doesn't know you, so she won't talk. We're in such a rush anyway. My sister-in-law's waiting for us."

*Get out of here before she says her name is "Cookie."*

It seemed to Donald that the woman was scrutinizing him. My nerves, he thought. Just when I begin to feel a little easier this afternoon they have to spark like crossed wires.

The police must be harassing poor Maria with a thousand questions. Still, she was very smart, so she almost certainly must have surmised the truth. Mr. Pratt must have guessed it, too; why would I otherwise have failed to appear at the office today? And as for Lillian, this must be agony for her, except that she knows the baby is in loving hands. Yet it must be agony, and I'm sorry about that. I never wanted to hurt you, Lillian, yet I had to.

That evening, lying awake in another motel, he decided that he must make a record of each day on the road. Memory, especially when one is caught in conversation as he had just been caught, was not dependable, and he must be sure to remember everything in case of disaster, and not contradict himself. So he began.

***Tuesday.*** *Unseasonably warm. Still heading south, we made a detour to a beach for a little rest* *and recreation that Laura badly needed. Half a dozen local families. Nice woman, a Mrs. Day, with older children who played with Laura as if she were a puppy. Recommended a bed-and-breakfast in Maryland.*

He had told the same story, automatic by now, about the dead mother. The day had gone well, but the night in yet another motel had been a hard one, with Laura crying, not for her mother, but for "Mia."

**Wednesday.** *Crossed the river into Maryland. I am afraid and terribly tired.*

By midmorning, they arrived at Mrs. Maguire's bed-and-breakfast. The house was clean and bright; the owner, having heard from Mrs. Day, was very friendly. Although Donald was sure he had not revealed his mood, she must have sensed it, for almost at once she took charge of Laura.

"I understand that you've recently lost your wife, Mr. Fuller. My friend told me over the phone that you're driving to a relative in Ohio. It must be hard to go all that way with a baby."

"It's not exactly easy," he admitted. "I have a lot to learn about two-year-olds."

"Let me help you. She's such a darling. Let me give her a bath and a shampoo."

Laura had not had a bath since Sunday, the reason being that he had not known how to go about it, how hot the water should be and how to avoid getting soap in her eyes. Very embarrassed, and also very grateful, he handed Laura over and went out to sit in the yard.

It was so safe here, sheltered behind these trees! The open road was filled with dangers. What if he were stopped for speeding, as could happen even when you had not been speeding? What of a fender-bender, your fault or not?

But safe as it was here, they dared not stay. So after a good breakfast the next morning, they took to the road again.

The old lady, gently teasing, called after the car, "Don't forget, Ohio is west."

"West it is," Donald replied, and took the road from which he would turn off at the first intersection.

*Thursday. It happened. I don't need to write down his name because I'll never forget it: Ron Reynold, six-feet-eight, and nasty.*

Donald had driven out of a gas station just as the other man in his light delivery truck was entering it. The two vehicles touched each other in passing and left on each one's fender a scratch. Who was at fault? That could be argued, and was, or would have been if Donald had not quickly taken the blame.

Ron Reynold of Ron Reynold Heating & Cooling, strolled over, poked his face up to Donald's, and roared through the window, "Where the hell do you think you're going? Look what you've done to my truck."

All Donald wanted was to get safely out of that place with no names, addresses, or display of papers. "I'm really sorry," he said. "I'll be glad to pay for the scratch."

"You're damn right you will. It'll cost you a hundred bucks."

"No problem. Here it is."

"And I want to see your license and your address."

"Why do you need them?" Donald asked mildly.

"How do I know this here bill ain't counterfeit?"

"Hold it up to the light, and you'll see it isn't."

"Quit stalling, will you? Get out the license."

The man was a primitive thug or else a maniac, or both. You didn't hesitate with such people; you obeyed. And with trembling fingers, he complied.

At any rate, the matter was settled, and Donald

drove away toward Virginia, still trembling. Imagine if there had been real damage done, and lawyers had written to the house in Philadelphia, a house with a nonexistent number and no record of anybody named James Fuller!

In the backseat, Laura was talking. "I want wollipop. I want wollipop, Daddy."

On top of everything, he was ruining the child, giving her chocolate and lollipops on demand simply because it wasn't possible to drive and entertain her at the same time.

Was he going to spend the rest of his life in fear like this?

*Friday. This is the sixth day since we left New York. The Shenandoah Valley is said to be very beautiful, but I saw nothing because the windshield wipers could scarcely compete with the hard, driving rain. Nothing to do but stop at another dreary motel and try to entertain Laura with every toy in the box. I am going to give her a good life. I don't yet know where, but I know I will, if only our luck holds out.*

*Saturday. Wonderful weather. Heading southwest. Laura woke me at half-past five, which was all to the good, because we have a long day's ride ahead. I notice a strange thing: She hasn't cried for "Mia" since Tuesday night.*

Driving by the usual easy stages, they traveled toward the southwest, stopping once in a grove of dogwood and laurel alongside the road to eat the sandwiches bought at the restaurant near last night's motel. And in Donald's mind there rose a picture vaguely pink and white of a small house in a grove of laurels, a hidden house where no Mr. Buzleys, Storms, or anyone else could take his little girl away from him.

Then as clearly as the picture had formed itself, a huge black question mark took its place: How is this to be done? Of course the question had already filled his mind for many, many dismal days and nights before this, but now that he had actually reached the South, the hoped-for place of safety, the question needed to be answered and answered now, without delay, this minute.

Back again on the mountain roads, driving with extreme care around the curves, he reviewed the situation. In his money belt was enough to live modestly for two years, or maybe more. Still, he must look for a job. But he had no skills! Perhaps he could be a salesman in a shop? Or should he buy a small shop? And if so, what kind? He knew nothing about merchandising. . . .

At a crossroad, signs pointed in a choice of

directions, cities in North Carolina, Tennessee, and Georgia. So here he was where three states joined, states about which he knew almost nothing except that they were filled with monuments and memories of the dreadful Civil War. He had always been a history buff, and if he had been easy in his mind now, he would have felt eager. But instead a vast loneliness engulfed him; he needed to talk to somebody, to anybody whom he need not fear and who would give him a little guidance through the strange territory that he was about to enter. He turned around to look again at the little person in the backseat. There she sat, his innocent, dependent child, hugging her stuffed bear. And panic attacked him. He had taken the very life, the future of this trusting little person into his hands. She was growing sleepy, night was coming on, and her eyes and her little head were drooping; he must make up his mind, he must pull his thoughts together and take a direction. So he drove the car onto the side of the road, turned off the engine, and considered the subject with every atom of strength that he could summon to his mind.

Drawing a much-crumpled map from his pocket, he also removed a candy wrapper, a tissue, and a scrap of paper, on which in an unfamiliar hand and under dim light, he read a name and address: Clarence and Kate Benson.

The names for a moment meant nothing. In the second moment, they flashed: the woman on the train! "If you and your wife ever come by our way, stop in," he read. And he remembered thinking that it was incredibly innocent, even peculiar, for her to give a totally strange man her name and address. He also remembered that he had been on the verge of throwing the scrap away, and for no reason at all, had not done so.

No cars passed. The countryside was empty, as if abandoned. And the baby, as if she too could sense this loneliness, began to whimper. For God's sake, he *must* do something!

Ridiculous as it might seem, would it really be that ridiculous to take up the woman's offer? These Bensons, whoever they were, surely knew more about the area than he did. They might know something about jobs, where to seek one and where to live. On the other hand, they might not. They might even, in spite of the wife's invitation, be deeply offended. Still, nothing ventured, nothing gained, he told himself, taking comfort, as he often did, in proverbs.

This wavering decision of his was born of simple desperation, he knew that well. It was born of a darkening day and the baby's mounting cry. So he started the engine, and the car rolled away down the hill into Georgia.

# Chapter 11

The small parlor was furnished plainly, be-speaking no wealth, but certainly no poverty, either. One wall was covered with shelves which, although sparsely filled with books, held the promise of more books to come.

Along the opposite wall were ranged the Bensons, he a tall, brown-eyed man who reminded Jim of himself, she the lady from the train, with curly reddish hair and a prettier face than he remembered—not that he remembered very much—and a seven-year-old boy, also reddish-haired, named Richard, who looked serious for his age. Together they reminded Jim of a daguerreotype or of one of those stiff family portraits done by some itinerant artist a century or more ago.

It was a good thing, he thought, that he had

decided to wear a jacket and tie, for it was Sunday, and all three Bensons were dressed for the day. He had surprised himself by having so few qualms about stepping onto their front porch, ringing the bell, and entering into conversation. But suddenly now he had become ill at ease, and he said so.

"To tell you the truth, I feel queer about barging in on you like this. But I'm not exactly myself . . . trying to forget, to start a new life . . . take care of her . . ." And he nodded toward Laura, who fortunately was behaving well; clutching her stuffed bear, she sat quietly staring at the strangers.

Mrs. Benson said gently, "Well, it only just happened, after all. In February, did you say?"

Always when called upon for a fact, Jim felt that acceleration of the heart. He must, he absolutely must, plant these facts so firmly in his mind that there could be no chance of a mistake or a hesitant stumble.

"Yes, February tenth, when Rebecca died. It was cancer—leukemia. That kind can strike very fast sometimes."

The bravado that had been building during this last week was faltering again. And as his tale of tragedy brought forth the usual nods of understanding, he hated himself. What he ought to do was to stand up and get out of there and forget the whole thing. But then they would wonder why he had come at all. They would think he was out of his mind, even possibly a dangerous person, to walk away after having made all his explanations. Still, what difference what they thought? On the other hand, having come this far, should he not try to pursue the subject?

"So as I said," he resumed, "I'd like to look for some kind of work in town. We arrived yesterday, and got to the hotel. But it was too late for me to look around, find out what kind of businesses there are, either here or in some other town nearby. I like the area, though. Nice climate, the national park not too far away . . ."

His voice dwindled, and he was relieved when Mr. Benson spoke. "Jeff Wheeler's a friend of mine. Runs a haberdashery in town across the street from your hotel. He might need help. I don't know. You can tell him I sent you. I buy a few things there now and then. Don't need much fancy clothing on a farm, you know."

"I know. I worked on a farm every summer while I was growing up."

"That so? Where you from?"

"Maine, up near Bangor. Mostly potatoes up there. You may have heard about Maine potatoes."

"But after that," said Mrs. Benson, "you became a city person."

"Yes, Philadelphia. I sold insurance." And wanting to avoid any further specific questions, he asked one. "Did your wife tell you exactly how we got to talking on the train, Mr. Benson?"

"Something about a book," she said. "Doesn't surprise me. Look there at that wall. They all belong to Kate. And upstairs we're loaded with more, all hers. You don't usually see this in a farmhouse, do you?"

He's very proud of her. She's the stronger of the two, Jim thought. There's something about her that I didn't see on the train. Of course I didn't. I hardly looked at her. They're entirely different from each other except that they're both very straightforward, very decent people. You can tell.

"My folks used to say when I married Kate that she wouldn't last. She'd get lonesome out here and tired of it. But they were wrong."

Kate smiled. "Why should I be lonesome? The countryside gets in your blood. At least it's gotten into mine."

Jim agreed. "Yes, it's beautiful. Those hills, the hemlocks— Oops, Laura, what are you doing?"

For Laura, in reaching toward a plate filled with nuts and raisins, had spilled them over the little table beside her chair.

"Waisins!" she cried.

"No, no, Laura. I'm sorry," he apologized as he scooped them up. "She loves raisins, and—"

"Wollipops!" Gleefully, Laura was enjoying both the raisins and the attention.

"She's the cutest thing," Kate said. "Why don't we all go outside and let her run around? She must have done a lot of sitting between here and Philadelphia."

"Thank you, but I've taken enough of your time. And this is your day of rest—" he began, when Benson interrupted. "There's no day of rest on a farm. You know better than that, Mr. Fuller. Right now I'm going up to change these clothes and make my rounds. The baby can play in the sandbox. It's from Rick's baby days, but we still haven't got rid of it. Rick, go see whether you can find one of the old pails and shovels."

The child without a mother and the man without a wife had moved them all to a certain amount of pity, as they had done throughout this past week. Now again he was being asked whether he wanted a hot or a cold drink and whether Laura wanted milk or needed the bath-room. And as always, when he accepted these kindnesses, he wished they did not force him to see himself as the imposter he was.

"Would you like to have a look at the place?" asked Benson when he returned in shirt and jeans. "Since you come from a farm? Maybe it'll remind you of your potatoes in Maine. You never think of going back up there with the baby?"

"It's too cold. I'm not used to it anymore," Jim replied as they walked toward the barns, and then changed the subject by remarking that those Holsteins in the pasture beyond were a pretty sight.

"Twenty-two head, that's all. I'd like to get more milkers, but I haven't been having much luck with help. Want to see something funny? Look over there, that little tan cow. Looks like a runt among those Holsteins, doesn't she?"

"What's a Jersey doing with them?"

"Kate. A fellow we know wanted to sell it for veal. Needed money in a hurry, I guess. So Kate looked into its eyes and bought it. Named it Lucy. She gives rich milk, that I'll say."

"But much less of it."

"True, true. Wait. I just want to check on the gate here. Fellow kept it open last week and I would have lost a pregnant cow in the road if the driver hadn't stopped in time. Next I need to check on the chicken house. If you don't mind all the walking, you might like to come along and let somebody else watch the kid for a few minutes. Don't worry, Kate's a great one for little kids. Ricky's all we have."

"Those are new henhouses, aren't they? Spick-and-span."

"Built them last year. The old one was falling apart. Must have been seventy years old. Yes, it was. My grandfather had it. So I replaced it with two. Thought I could double my egg business, but seems to have taken more time to build it up than I expected it would. Besides, I had a run of bad luck. Last summer I ordered a thousand three-day-old chicks; it turned freezing cold one night and the fellow supposed to take charge left them outside, so I lost most of them. Yes, I've had problems. But what can you do?"

"Like everything else," Jim said for the sake of saying something.

"Problems, I should say so. I'm trying to build this place up, you see, and it's not easy. My dad—he died, he and my mother, in the same year, six years ago when Ricky was born. It was a family farm for I don't know how many generations. They raised fruit, vegetables, sold hay, every-thing you have on a family farm, enough for the family and a little left over to sell for cash. But I went to agricultural college, and I learned stuff my dad never heard of. I want to build up big. Well, I will. I'll get there. Never say die."

He's in over his head and worried to death, Jim thought, noting the depth of the frown lines in the man's forehead.

"Well, you've got a fine place here," he said, again for the sake of saying something. "What's that cottage up there by itself?"

"My parents built it when Kate and I married and we moved into the big house. It's nicely furnished, four rooms, nice kitchen, and empty ever since they died. Oh, you haven't seen the half of this place, Mr. Fuller, not a quarter or an eighth. I've got over six hundred acres here. I've got corn, a hay meadow, a peach orchard, I've got everything. If you feel like walking, I'll show you—but you're dressed up. You don't want to spoil those shoes."

"I'd like to see it all, thank you, but I should get Laura and take her back to town. It's quite a drive."

"Just thirteen miles. We do our errands in the village, though. That's the other direction. I almost never go to town anymore. Don't have the time, for one thing."

"Well, you've been really nice to spend so much of it with me. We've been here almost three hours, and I thank you."

"Oh, I enjoyed it. I know Kate did, too. Outside of a couple of friends from the village, we don't see many people. You can sit on our porch all day and not see more than ten cars some days. Well, good luck. I'd be interested to hear whether you get the job."

Yes, he's in over his head, Jim thought on the way back to the hotel. Cattle, chickens, orchards, flowers—for the wife had spoken about the flowers she sold to florists—it was a jack-of-all-trades situation, or so it seemed to him. Benson was very likable, almost touchingly so; you could feel something vulnerable about him, something a trifle innocent.

Smiling to himself, he reflected: He saw my handmade shoes and my London suit. That's why he recommended a job with the haberdasher. Well, we'll see in the morning. Haberdasher or no, this town would be a safe place. It's a million miles from nowhere.

❧

"I'll tell you," Jeff Wheeler said, "I'll be glad to have a helping hand here, but not for more than two or three evenings a week. Just so I could go home a little earlier to the wife and kids. This being a farming community, we get our evening trade from the farm people, after their day's work. Not that I have a big lot of their trade in my kind of store, but it pays to stay open just in case. Every dollar counts, doesn't it?"

They were standing in the walk outside the store. Jim, keeping the stroller in motion, back and forth as Maria had instructed because "it soothes her," glanced down Main Street. It was pleasant enough this morning, lined as it was on each side by a row of poplars, and behind these, a row of low buildings, almost all of them red brick. It was pleasant and yet, Jim saw, not brimming with opportunity.

His doubt must have been visible, because Wheeler continued with his advice. "I don't know where anybody's hiring much, except part time, like me. You can stand here and see most of the places where they do hire when they have to. There's the car dealer, the market, the funeral parlor, the shoe store, the bank, and the beauty parlor, and—well, you can see for yourself it's a little town and very quiet. Then off Main Street you'll see some of the nicest homes you ever laid eyes on. The best part is out toward the hospital. It's small, but it's one of the best in the state, I hear tell. Then the schools are all on Liberty Street, that runs off Main, down that way—but let me tell you what, Mr. Fuller, you'd be better off looking in a place like Chattanooga, for instance. You'd stand a good chance of finding a job in a city with people coming and going from all over the country. And you'd find plenty of nice apartments, which we don't have. Because you wouldn't want a house, would you? I mean, to get to the point, there's just you and the kid, no wife. Yes, you'd do better in a much bigger place than this."

"Well, thanks. I appreciate the advice and I'll think about it. Right now I guess I'll take a walk around and show Laura the sights."

"People coming and going" was exactly what Jim did not want. But he had only to stroll down this Main Street past its simple shops and sparse traffic, then out toward the schools and the hospital, past family-sized houses—no tiny tract houses here—to know that this kind of town, where the streets petered out and the countryside began, was not right for him, either. He had no skills to offer it, nothing it needed.

A cold, bleak sensation washed through him. It was as if he had reached a dead end—and he had only begun to look.

Well, then, he must just look further! He must study the want ads. Surely there must be something he could do. . . .

It took him a couple of seconds to become aware that Laura was crying and vomiting over the side of the stroller.

"What is it? What is it? Oh my God, you're hot, you're burning up. I didn't know—"

He had brought tissues and cloths for bibs and spills, having learned this much from Maria; with these he wiped as best he could, murmuring and comforting as he held his baby, all the while staring around the street for help and finding no one in sight.

Then, "Head over heart," he said aloud. "Think!"

Hadn't Jeff Wheeler said the hospital was out this way, near Liberty Street? I'll ask. Hold her tight. And pushing the stroller with his other hand, he began to race, out of breath, cursing his ignorance of child care, cursing the hospital for not being where it ought to be, terrified—until the sight of a doctor's sign on a house jerked him to a halt.

"What's this?" cried the doctor when he answered Jim's ring. "An accident?"

"No, no. She's sick. She's awfully sick."

"Give her to me. No, I don't care, I don't mind, that's why I wear a white coat. Annie, come help me with this young lady."

So pitiful she was, lying there on the examining table with her frail baby arms outstretched toward her father, as if asking him to protect her from these hovering strangers. He was terrified. What kind of a father was he to have done to her, or not to have done, what he should have done? And now, he could do nothing but stand and watch as this strange man poked at her poor little stomach, peered into her eyes and ears, stared down her throat, and frightened the life out of her.

Afterward, about ten minutes later by the clock although it had seemed as if an hour had gone by, Jim found himself sitting with Dr. Scofield in a small room near the examining room, from which Laura had been carried to fall asleep on a couch between them.

"A bad stomach upset, Mr. Fuller, that's all it is. It's either something she ate, or a virus. There's no fever to speak of. She was simply overheated in the sun, frightened by the vomiting, and maybe overexcited, mostly because of your excitement." The doctor smiled. "Take her home to her mother. She's probably more used to this kind of thing than you are."

"Well, she—she has no mother. Her mother died last February."

There was that expression again, the sober sympathy for the two-year-old whose mother was dead.

Faces changed when you told people something sad. Was it because they really felt for you, or because they knew they were expected to feel for you?

"You don't live in town, do you, Mr. Fuller? It seems to me I know practically everybody here, by sight if not always by name."

"No, I'm from a long way off. Philadelphia. We've been more than a week on the road."

"Just passing through, then."

"No, hoping to settle somewhere around here. Hunting for a job."

"In any special field?"

"No."

"Just looking? Just like that, without any plan?"

"That's about it, I'm afraid."

He wondered why so many doctors seemed to feel free to ask such personal questions. Did they believe that their degree entitled them to such liberty? But this man, although garrulous, was modest and had been especially gentle with Laura, so he replied with candor, "I have simply a need to forget the past and start fresh."

"I see." The doctor looked thoughtful. "Kind of hard to do with a baby, and driving all this way. Strange food, the motion, the constraint; she's an unusually strong child. Most of them would have gotten sick before this. Frankly, Mr. Fuller, I think she's had enough for a while."

"I know that only too well. We're in the hotel here in town, but it's no place for her. I was wondering, is there any nice inn nearby, a country sort of place where we can rest and play outdoors or something?"

"I'm afraid not. Tourists don't come through here very often. The hotel's never more than a quarter full, if that. When you're this close to the mountains, you keep going till you get there, I suppose."

It occurred to Jim as he sat looking out at the

quiet street, where two young women were walking together and a dog was trotting alongside an old man, that this was the first time in his life when he was without an anchor. Job, school, university, law, New York, had flowed in orderly succession, one firm step after the other. Now he was afloat. Why had he not known it would be like this? But he had only and frantically needed to get away before it should be too late to save Laura.

"Might there perhaps be some family with extra space for us for a few days or so? Until I get my bearings? I'm not hard up, Doctor. I'll pay whatever they ask."

The two men regarded each other. He is wondering about me, whether I am some sort of unreliable drifter fighting a nervous breakdown, Jim thought. He was about to say something that would show how steady a man he really was, when Dr. Scofield struck the arm of his chair with the flat of his hand.

"I just had a brainstorm. There's a family way out toward the mountains, Clarence and Kate Benson, they've got a cottage on their place. His folks lived there, but I don't think anyone's in it now. It'd be a great place for you to rest up and get your thoughts together. You look as if you need a rest, and they're the best people you could ever know."

So I look the way I feel, thought Jim, as he explained that he was already acquainted with the Bensons. He remembered the cottage that Benson had pointed out. He thought he had had an impression of hemlocks dipping under strong wind.

"They're first-rate people, and you'll be perfectly safe out there with this baby of yours. Want me to phone them and ask?"

"Yes, please do," Jim said.

The cottage was immaculate when, on the following day, Jim, with Laura and the heaped-up contents of the car, arrived at the farm. It was even welcoming. At every window hung white curtains, newly washed and starched; the bed and the yellow-painted crib left over from their boy's baby days were made up with sheets that looked new. Also left over from that time were a high chair and a playpen which Jim, with a laugh, doubted that Laura would consent to use.

"She tends to be what you might tactfully call 'independent.' No, no, Laura! Don't touch." For she had spotted a splendid gardenia in a plant stand.

"Obedient, too," observed Kate.

"Not always. Remember the raisins? Look, she's sniffing the perfume."

"Kate's flowers," Clarence said. "She hoped to supply every florist and nursery for miles around, but things just didn't work out that way. That's her greenhouse down there. See it, back of the barn?"

Following Clarence's finger, Jim looked down upon greenery, pastures, a cornfield, and forested hills.

"You'll have a beautiful sight to greet you when you wake up every morning, Mr. Fuller," Clarence said.

"Jim, please. The name's Jim."

"Okay, Jim. Some folks wouldn't appreciate all this or even like the quiet, but I have a hunch you're not that type."

"Your hunch is correct. Dr. Scofield also told me that this place would be just right. By the way, I'll pay you in cash. Naturally, I don't yet have an account at the bank here." And Jim drew some bills from his wallet.

"Jim Fuller! This is double what I asked you for."

"This is less than half what I'd pay at a resort, and it's worth more than many resorts, so let's not argue."

"It just doesn't seem right, though. It really doesn't."

One of the world's innocents, this man was. "It's right," Jim said firmly.

"Well, I won't say we can't use it. We may look well-off, but we're not. Yet, look out there! Everything between this cottage and those hills is ours."

"You could probably get a good price for it," Jim said, "rich farmland like this—"

"Good price! Over my dead body. Literally! This is Ricky's heritage, for him, and his children, and their children."

"You've touched a soft spot," Kate explained. It seemed to Jim that she looked slightly embarrassed. "This land is Clarence's life. But enough of this for now. It's almost suppertime."

"So it is," Jim agreed. "I've got to unpack these groceries and get going or Laura will be complaining. She likes her meals to be on time."

"Never mind your groceries tonight, Jim. You can start your housekeeping tomorrow. You'll have supper with us tonight."

∽⦿

The table was set in an ell off the kitchen in full view of the stove, the cupboards, potted geraniums on a windowsill, and two dogs at their dinner bowls.

As if to fill a lag in what had been an ongoing conversation, Jim made a comment about the dogs.

"I seem to remember you had two collies in that snapshot, Kate. Am I right?"

"Unfortunately, you are. We lost Jeff to diabetes. Buster the Airedale is his replacement. Quite a contrast to Mutt, isn't he?"

" 'Mutt,' " Jim observed. "Isn't that rather an odd name for a thoroughbred collie?"

"He had that name when we bought him, so we kept it because he already answered to it. Besides, 'he' is a 'she.' " Kate threw up her hands in mock dismay. "Can you believe it?"

He liked the gesture, and the way her eyes widened as if with surprise.

Ricky made an important announcement. "Buster belongs to me. I picked him out. There were five puppies, but we liked each other right away, so he's my dog."

"Wow-wow," said Laura.

Ricky corrected her. "Say 'dog.' "

"Wow-wow."

"No. Say 'dog.' "

For a moment, Laura seemed to be studying the matter. Then, "Dog," she said.

Everyone laughed and clapped for her, while Ricky said importantly, "I can teach her. Do you want me to teach her? I can read, you know."

"Wead," Laura said. "Wed light top. Geen light go."

Again everyone laughed, and Jim cried, "Now, what on earth? I never taught her that."

"She must have made the connection herself," Kate said. "She saw that you stopped and started according to the lights."

"But that's incredible!"

"Not really. It's genetic. I'll bet if you could ask your parents, they would say that you had the same grasp of words at this age. And your wife was probably the same."

"I don't know. I never asked her mother. I mean, Laura's mother."

That sounded queer. For God's sake, speak naturally. Say the name: *Rebecca.*

"Rebecca and I never got around to talking about things like that. It all happened so fast, our times together, I mean."

"Does she miss her mother very much?"

"Rebecca was so ill for a while that we had to get a nurse to take care of Laura. If she misses anyone, it would be the nurse, although she seems to be forgetting her faster than I expected."

That much was true, but the rest, the lies to these good people, would only lead to more inevitable lies. How could they not? Sitting here at their friendly table, he was tricking these good, simple people.

Simple? Who is to say what simple is?

"That next house, the one you pass down the road at the curve, belongs to a friend of mine," Kate said next. "She used to assist in a kindergarten, and she has a day care license. Maybe you'd like to send Laura there. Right now she has two children and a two-year-old of her own. Jennie's wonderful with children."

Jim had no intention of staying here any longer than he would stay at a vacation resort. This was a rest to be savored, a place in which to stop running and catch his breath. On the other hand, what was Laura going to do here all day? Perhaps this day care would be a good thing for her during the next week or two. Also, it would be a place to leave her while he gave some deadly serious thought to their next move.

❦

In the predawn chill he woke, and opening the front door, stood on the steps to watch the sun ascend the sky. The air was cool, the birds were twittering, and at the bottom of the slope, the farm was already at work. Day laborers were arriving in battered old cars; two men carried milk cans to the roadside, where obviously they would soon be collected; someone was pulling a harrow from under a shed, while someone else trundled a wheelbarrow filled with empty quart baskets in the direction of what probably was a field of blueberries.

Was it a century ago that he had been, however temporarily, a part of this mild farmyard bustle? Was it a century ago that he had checked his luggage through the world's major airports and settled himself and his fine leather attaché case in a first-class seat? He looked at his watch. A few minutes from now he would have been in Washington, assuming that the case had not yet been settled, getting dressed for the resumption of argument. A few minutes from now, allowing for the difference in time zones and if he had not taken the risk he had taken, his Laura might have been waking up in Arthur Storm's French villa.

With this thought in mind, Jim had to rush back inside to the crib as if to make sure that he was not dreaming, that Laura was still there. Yes, there she lay in the pink pajamas printed with rabbits, elephants, and turtles that he had bought. Her fashionable coat that she had been wearing that last Sunday afternoon he had dropped on the grass south of Albany, thus leaving behind the last relic of her former life.

When she stirred and turned, he moved away without making a sound. A child should be encouraged to keep regular hours. Gently and gradually, he would train her to wake up at half-past seven. Breakfast should be ready at eight, and it should consist chiefly, according to the books, of whole-grain cereal with fruit; eggs, once a week, should be scrambled or boiled, never fried.

Almost by heart, Jim knew those rules. Reading time could come at any hour; it was especially valuable between supper and bed as a way to relax. He had already begun to acquire some of the fine old storybooks, beginning now with *Peter Rabbit* and leading gradually up to *Charlotte's Web* a few years from now. It was never too soon to start building a library. . . . And with a sudden pang, before his eyes he saw the shelves he had left behind, divided by subject, history or fiction or biography, then subdivided and alphabetized by author. Who owned them now?

But, first things first. This morning he was a little worried about the day nursery. Laura had never been used to children other than those who went to and fro in Central Park. Yet last night at the supper table she had readily accepted the strange adults and the six-year-old boy. Dr. Scofield had remarked that she was a "strong" child. Had he meant her physical body or her temperament?

Now Jim had to laugh a little at himself. Never before had he been such a worrier. Never had he fretted over even the most important trials or presentations; he had been confident in

himself. Yet here he was questioning the right-
ness of the smallest matter that concerned this
tiny girl.

It was only a few hours later that he knew he
need not have fretted. At Jennie Macy's little
play school, he had lingered for an hour to make
certain that everything was in order.

"She's taking to it like a duck to water," Jennie assured him. "Look at her with those blocks.
She's collected a pile, and she's perfectly content.
You really don't need to worry about this child,
Mr. Fuller. My Tommy is just Laura's age, and
he's not as calm as she is, even though this is his
own house."

So, with a pleasant sense of relief, Jim left and
walked back to what he thought of as his vacation home.

Now he was feeling the luxury of having
nothing at all to do for the next few hours. Until
this very minute, in this sudden peace, he had
not realized just how these last days had terrified
and exhausted him. Maybe he'd take a pillow
and a book, lie down in the shade, and just loaf.

He was halfway to the cottage steps when his
attention was drawn to a woman crossing the
barnyard on horseback. The sight was striking,
the woman tall in the saddle, her reddish hair
glinting below her hat brim, and the horse, a
magnificent pinto, splashed with dark brown on

a background of white. It took him a few seconds to recognize Kate Benson, and only seconds more for her to see him.

She was dismounting as he approached. "Your first night went well, Jim, I hope?"

"It couldn't have been better. And Laura's introduction to the play school couldn't have been better, either."

"I'm so glad. I had an idea it would. Laura's a character, isn't she?"

"I'm afraid I don't know enough about children to tell."

"Well, take my word, she is. Do you ride?"

"I used to be pretty good at it, but I haven't done it in years."

"If you were good once, you haven't forgotten how. We have another horse for you, if you want. Come, I'll show you. He's in pasture, the one behind that row of chicken houses."

A light chestnut Shetland pony with a wavy mane, not much larger than a very large dog, was grazing along with a tall, dark horse.

"The Shetland is Ricky's, of course. He's Rick's treasure. His name is Rabbit, but don't ask me why. This pinto is Elf, and the big one over there is Cappy."

"A smooth high-stepper," Jim said. "Cappy is an elegant Tennessee Walker, if I remember right."

"Yes, he's handsome, isn't he? He's Clarence's horse, but Clarence doesn't ride anymore. He's had a few problems, and it's not good for him. We used to go up together every day into the hills, or sometimes just around the property. We'd squeeze in the time, no matter what. And now I have to go by myself."

"Taking turns with the horses, I suppose, because they both need exercising?"

"Exactly. But I don't enjoy the big one as much. I'm not used to his canter. Still, he needs attention, so I do it. How do you feel about trying him?"

"I feel I'd like to, very much."

"Good. I'll wait for you tomorrow morning after Laura goes to Jennie's."

"We'll take it easy, since you haven't ridden in so long," Kate proposed on the following day.

So they trotted a few miles around the perimeter of the property, which was far larger than Jim had imagined. He had expected a barrage of chatter along the way, but Kate was very quiet.

There was in fact a marked difference between yesterday's woman and today's. Something had happened. Perhaps trivial, perhaps not. But it was no business of his.

After a while they came to a halt, allowing the horses to drink at a small stream, and stood in silence. Even at this remove, the varied foliage was recognizable: white pine, dogwood that must have been a cloud early in the spring, azaleas, and rhododendrons that grew ten feet high, as Jim had noted in his travels through these hills.

"In the fall," Kate said, suddenly breaking the silence, "the sumac turn orange-red, like flame. Clarence calls this 'God's country.' "

"Yes, God's country," Jim repeated. A sense of the most intense thankfulness rose within him. In safety he had brought Laura this far, and even though he did not plan to remain in this particular place, it was a good omen. Surely the next lap of the journey would bring them to their final safety among these hills.

❧

No matter what the course of the future, this little stretch of time would be remembered as an extraordinary calm. Even the weather was moderate. In the play group, Laura was flourishing, learning to share her toys as well as to defend her rights; she had developed a genuine laugh, and before his eyes she was beginning to change from a baby to a child. Every day Jim rode Cappy for a healthy hour, soothed by the sense of space and silence.

Apparently Kate Benson had changed her hour for the early-morning ride, but he had no idea why and he did not miss her. Rarely did he see either her or Clarence, so his first impression that they wanted to be friends must have been a mistake.

One day, he passed Clarence near the stable as he was coming back from his ride.

"You're doing Cappy a world of good," Clarence said.

"He's doing me a world of good. We like each other. We almost talk to each other."

"I know, I miss him, too. Maybe sometime I'll get back to riding again."

It seemed to Jim that Clarence looked decidedly different, as if he had changed almost overnight. His healthy sunburn had turned to a sickly yellow; even the whites of his eyes and the brown irises seemed to be tinged with yellow.

"Looks as if you like it here, Jim. Didn't plan to stay three weeks, did you?"

"Three weeks. Where's the time gone? It can't be—"

"Will be, this Tuesday."

Jim shook his head. "I guess I stopped counting. All this peace and ease—I'm a kid in a toy store, or a candy store."

A tired smile crossed the other man's face and vanished.

"Are you all right, Clarence? You seem tired today."

Clarence shrugged. "Look around at the bustle. It's a hubbub on this farm, enough to make a man tired."

"Are we staying too long, Clarence? Tell me the truth. Do you need the cottage for anything and don't want to tell me to clear out?"

"No, no. Well, the truth is, we were talking, Kate and I, about how you said you were hunting for a job, and we wondered about that. It's not our business, but we were wondering about you and the baby, how long you would stay."

You block things out, things you don't want to face, just as you block out bad memories . . .

"You're right, Clarence. I'm taking too long. I ought to get down to business."

"Oh, I didn't mean that," Clarence protested. "Forget I said it. You just do what's best for you. I didn't mean you should either stay or go. I was only wondering."

A few minutes later, Jim was in the car on his way to the newspaper stand in town. Buying a local paper, he realized that he had never noticed the New York journals and magazines on the top shelf.

"Do you sell much of this stuff here?" he asked.

"Only to a couple of teachers at the high

school. Can't for the life of me fathom why
they're interested in all this, but they are, so I
order a few copies."

When he had scanned the sections where he
might find the news he had neglected during
these lovely days in never-never land, he was
both relieved at finding nothing and angry at
himself for the careless neglect. And then because of this abrupt anxiety attack, he bought
three newspapers from outlying towns, went to
the car, and read through all the help-wanted advertisements. Only one seemed to offer a possibility, a post as office supervisor in what sounded
like a prosperous shirt factory in what sounded
like a prosperous town. Of course, he knew
nothing about shirt making, but an office was an
office; it meant correspondence, records of
wages, employment, and taxes. When he
thought of the complicated puzzles he had un-
raveled at home and overseas, he certainly
should be able to manage those.

Accordingly, the next day he asked Jennie
please to keep Laura through the late afternoon
in case he should be delayed, since the round
trip amounted to sixty miles, and the length of
the interview was unknown.

Once he was down out of sight of the hills and
on the highway, the heat began to rise. It will be
an early summer, he thought. Perhaps it was

normal for this part of the country? The car's air conditioner languished into a faint, warm breeze; clouds made a dreary landscape more dreary, so that Jim had to work at keeping his spirits lively. Upon entering the town, he had to work even harder. All was old, neither quaint nor with any charm of history, but merely old and grim, a town left over from an industrial age that was about to die. It even smells dreary, he thought as he parked and walked the streets. His heart sank. This town was one of those places in which you wouldn't want to grow up. Someday it would change, but not soon enough for Laura.

Nevertheless, on the theory that you must hear the whole story before you judge, he went straight to the factory and presented himself, there to answer the questions and relate the story that was becoming easier with every telling. His wife had died, he had a young child, he had left his insurance job in Philadelphia, and he was well qualified.

As it turned out, the interviewers thought so, too. He could not help but think when they told him the salary, which was not really bad at all, that they would never believe the amount of his last year's income tax.

All right, if he had to, he would make do. Wealth was not what he was seeking now, although wealth was very enjoyable indeed. There was no real wealth back at the Benson farm, and yet it was heavenly to wake up there every morning. But the Benson farm did not belong to him.

So he asked a few practical questions. What were the rents here? Could he get a small house with a yard, or could he afford a nice apartment, perhaps close to a park, on this pay? And was there any good day care that they could recommend? One of the women in the office made a kind suggestion. If Jim would come back on Saturday, she would be glad to take him around, show him places where he might live comfortably, and make an arrangement for day care. So with his decision to accept almost made—unless of course an offer far more attractive should abruptly pop out of the air—he departed.

Driving back by another route through the town and passing a few tree-lined streets that looked more cheerful, he told himself that if the return trip on Saturday should end successfully, it might not be a bad undertaking after all. Thus did his mood veer from high to low, and from low back to high. One thing he did know: the vacation was over.

After an early breakfast and no lunch, he was hungry, and at the edge of town, approaching the highway, he stopped at a luncheonette, got hold of somebody's abandoned newspaper, and read it while he ate a sandwich. There often wasn't much news in these local papers, mostly sports and politics as you might expect, although now and then on a feature page, they printed an unusual human interest anecdote.

*My God! My God!*

The coffee spoon fell clattering on the table. The cup tipped, leaving a brown stain that circled and dropped onto Jim's knees.

A man named Wolfe in West Virginia was suing the state for false arrest. Traveling with a two-year-old girl in the backseat of his car, he had been stopped, brought to the station house, and held there for five hours until his wife, by telephone, had assured them that he was only taking their child to visit his parents for the day. It seemed, so went the account, that he had been mistaken for another man named Wolfe in New York City, who really had kidnapped his child. Arthur Storm, a spokesman for the child's mother, Lillian Buzley, was quoted as saying that "Donald Wolfe is sure to be found. He is probably hiding out in some rural area. He originally came from one, and it is likely that he has returned to a country town where he can find employment. But he should have no doubt that wherever he may be, we will find him, and it won't take very long, either. We will ferret him out."

For several minutes, Jim sat there staring at the page. He had lost the power in his legs. He had lost the power to cope with this new reality. Arthur Storm . . . retired chairman of Regulex Amalgamated . . . Matisse . . . Picasso . . . power . . . detectives . . .

*He should have no doubt that we will find him.*

Why had he told those people just now that he was traveling with his two-year-old girl? He had to get back to her without losing a moment. And stumbling to his feet, he put down a ten-dollar bill, left without waiting for change, and ran to the car.

He wanted to speed, yet fearing the risk of a ticket, he did not dare to. So it was midafternoon before he drove down the redbrick main street that, by its relative familiarity and in spite of his agony, gave him a vague feeling of ease. The only thing he had to do there before his retreat to the farm was to buy a few more newspapers.

"Mr. Fuller! Still here? I thought you'd be in Memphis or Atlanta or someplace by now."

Behind Jim stood Dr. Scofield, buying a magazine. This was the wrong time to get involved with anybody as jovial as the doctor. Once in his friendly clutches, it was almost impossible to get away.

"No, I'm still here," he said pleasantly, "but leaving soon."

"I still think of that young lady of yours. Throws up, feels better, and has the nerve to ask me for candy. Remember? Hard to resist those blue eyes, isn't it?"

"You bet. But I resist. Stern father, you know."

"You don't look stern. Say, you must get along very well with Kate and Clarence to be staying so long. They're a nice pair, those two. I've known Clarence since he was a kid."

Each having tucked his paper and magazine under an arm, they were proceeding toward Jim's parked car. But when they reached it, Scofield was still talking, and there was no way short of rudeness to stop him.

"It's a pity that they're having so much trouble."

Trouble, thought Jim. At the present moment, Doctor, I'm the wrong man to be sympathizing with anybody's troubles.

But the doctor, resting his shoulder against the car, apparently had more to say. "They're an interesting pair, don't you think? She doesn't always care to show it, but Kate is a brain. He's an innocent dreamer, a hard worker, but he can't manage anything. He's too gentle and gullible for this modern world. So it's all on Kate's shoulders, a heavy, heavy burden."

One might say that this was mere trivial gossip, the result maybe of living in a place where nothing of much greater importance ever happened. And probably that was true. Or possibly, it was the result of a genuine concern.

Still Scofield held him, although Jim wanted to walk around to the other side of the car and drive away. "Clarence is a born farmer, and he should have stayed one, like his father, instead of trying to develop himself into the CEO of some enormous corporation. Why, he's spent a small fortune on that place, about everything he owned, I guess, so now he's in debt all over town. Owes the bank, owes everybody, poor fellow. People have been patient because they've known the family forever, but there's a limit to patience. In fact, I've heard the limit now is sixty days, and then the place goes to foreclosure. You didn't know?"

"No," Jim said, adding automatically, "I'm sorry to hear it."

Perhaps that was why, after suggesting that they exercise the horses together, Kate had changed the hour. As a matter of fact, he had not even seen her on horseback, or anywhere, for at least a week.

Scofield mourned, "Yes, it's disaster. I wonder where they'll go."

Jim was thinking, I'm wondering where I'll go, then felt a twinge of shame at his selfishness. If he could help them, he gladly would.

"It was nice to see you again, Doctor," he said. "You were a lifesaver that day. But I have to get back to Laura. I'm late now."

With the bundle of newspapers lying on the seat beside him, the first thing he had to do was to go and read them. *We will ferret him out,* said Arthur Storm. She was still Mrs. Buzley. But soon, little doubt of it, she would be Mrs. Storm. *Ferret him out.* Small pains quivered in Jim's temples. Let Laura stay later at Jennie's today. If she was there, it meant she was safe. Right now he hadn't the will or the strength to take her back to the cottage. My God, how much of this terror could a man stand?

As much as he had to stand, was the answer, the only answer. So he would stand. Yes.

He had parked his car and was walking to the cottage when he saw Clarence standing alone by the fence. There was something in the man's posture, leaning there with his face turned up to the hills, that caught Jim's attention. Foreclosure, Dr. Scofield had said. Leaving all this and going—where? He with the gentle wife; anyone could see the gentleness in her, especially as Jim had seen it on that single morning when they had stopped to let the horses drink. *God's country,* she had said. And then there was the boy, a scampy little fellow, but sweet, too. Gentle folk. What was to happen to them? And his hand went to the hot, heavy money belt under the loose shirt. There was undeniably a certain comfort in having it there. Clarence, leaning on the fence, would no doubt give anything to own a small portion of this comfort, he thought. And yet, nobody's hunting Clarence down . . .

Clarence moved closer. "I promised to finish your tour of the farm, and I've never done it."

"That's all right. No rush. Another time will do."

"How about now? Come on. I'll show you around."

He wants to talk, Jim thought in sudden comprehension. He simply needs not to be alone. And he remembered how, only a few weeks ago, he had sat in his car at that crossroad, longing for somebody, for anybody at all, to warm the chill of his loneliness and fear.

"Come on," he said. Let the newspapers wait. The bad news, if any, would still be there an hour from now.

"This gate's all rotted, you see. One thing we didn't get around to fixing when we did the big overhaul two years ago. Used to raise beef cattle, you see, but I had to quit because Kate hated it. Well, it's true she hated eating beef; she kept thinking about the slaughter, but that's not the real reason I gave up. The real reason was I couldn't afford it. Short of cash. The place needed everything when my dad died, so I went ahead and gave it everything it needed. Or almost everything. Take these two barns for milkers. This one's half empty. Cost a fortune, too. But I didn't know when I bought the herd and built all this stuff that a fellow on the other side of the village has all the business sewn up. He's got about six hundred head. Maybe someday there'll be a rise in demand for milk, but right now there isn't. Sometimes I figure this milk costs me five dollars a bucket. Suppose you know how to milk a cow?"

"No, but I could have learned all those summers when I worked on a farm before—college." The sudden question had almost thrown Jim off guard. He had almost said "law school."

"Reason I ask is, you get close to a cow. It's like dogs, or almost. When you have to sell one because it's too old, it kind of makes you sick, you know?"

"I understand," Jim said gently.

A wire fence stopped the two men. Beyond it lay a fallow field, at least ten acres across, Jim estimated, on which wild grass was bending in the breeze.

"Grazing land for beef cattle, that's what it was. There's more across the creek. I don't know why I'm telling you all this, but I guess I just need somebody to talk to. Sometimes you have to bring your worries out of hiding, or they'll split your head open. I'm sorry, Jim."

"It's all right. I've had a split head in my time."

"Kate kind of thought you did, hightailing it around the country with that baby. A man doesn't do that for nothing, she says."

Jim looked at his watch. At this rate, Clarence would tie up another hour, and this last remark was too personal, anyway.

"I need to get my girl at Jennie Macy's," he said. "I'm late as it is."

"Yes, of course. I didn't mean to keep you. The children always come first. Always." There were tears in Clarence's eyes. "No one knows that better than I do."

The man was sick, very sick, in more ways than one. And heavyhearted, heavy-footed, Jim walked away. He looked again at his watch. It was almost five, and he had been away from Laura all day. She must be wondering where he was; perhaps she was crying for him. He rushed down the path, around the barn and up the hill, to find her sitting on the grass with Ricky and Kate.

"Jennie took her home when you were late," Kate said.

"I'm sorry about that. I'll thank her tomorrow. And thank you, too."

He was about to say that there had been a lot of traffic when Laura interrupted.

"See, Daddy! Duck!"

Ricky, holding a large, flat picture book, explained that it had been his "a long time ago," but now he read real books, so he was giving this to Laura.

"It's a present from me, even though it's not her birthday," he announced with some pride.

Jim was touched. "That's so nice of you, Ricky. Can you say thank you, Laura?"

Her eyes, those magical, intense blue eyes of Lillian's, were bright with excitement. She never even cried for "Mia" anymore. So soon do children forget! But somewhere Maria knows that she is happy and loved, he thought. His nerves were so delicate at that moment that he didn't know himself. It wouldn't have taken much to fill his own eyes with tears.

"Say thank you," he said again, as a proper father should.

"Sank 'oo," said Laura.

Ricky made another announcement. "I'm going to teach her to read as soon as she's three because I'm a very good reader. Did you know I'm in the fast group?"

"No, I didn't, Ricky. That's wonderful. You'd have to wait a while, though, because Laura has a few more months to go."

"Then I'll wait till she's three. Is that a long time?"

"Well, not very long," Jim said.

Without intending to, he glanced at Kate and glanced away, yet not before she caught him.

"Well, now I suppose you know all about us," she said.

"I'm not sure—" he began.

"I saw you walking with Clarence, and I'm talking about what he probably told you."

"He's heartsick. I'm terribly sorry."

Turning her face and voice away from the children, she said very low, "It is his life. His whole life is here. You'll have to leave here, too, you know, and you didn't get any job today."

Jim was astonished. "How can you know that?"

"Because you would be saying so. And it would be on your face, anyway."

She is definitely not the simple woman I believed I met on the train, he thought. She was seated with her hands around her knees. Thinking that he must look stiff as a beanpole standing tall above her, he sat down beside her.

"You won't find a job here," she said. "You need to be in a city."

"I don't want a city."

Then she asked an astonishing question, so astonishing that he stammered when he answered it.

"Who are you, Jim?"

"That's a mighty queer thing to ask a person. What can you possibly mean?"

"I mean that I see you've had more troubles than you want to talk about. You wouldn't be putting your past behind you to start fresh almost a thousand miles from home if you hadn't had them. Anyway, this isn't your kind of place—"

With a stir of anger, he interrupted her. "You don't know the first thing about me, Kate, or about my 'kind of place.' "

"The other day, as I was passing the cottage, I heard your music. Men around here don't put Strauss waltzes on their record players."

"So? It was pretty. It was happy, and I thought it would be good for Laura to hear."

"You're dodging my question."

"You haven't asked me a question."

"Yes, I have. Who are you?"

"Do you really want to know? All right, I'll tell you. I've robbed a bank in Philadelphia, and I have a couple of bombs in my car, so they're hot on my trail."

Kate smiled. "You had your little girl in the car, too. No, Jim. There's no one out hunting for you. Of your own volition, you're running away. I know you've lost your wife, but there's something else about you that makes me feel sad. And especially sad for Laura."

This woman was going much too far! Still, her expression was gentle and genuine. . . .

"Clarence is very ill, and that should be enough for you to cope with," he replied with equal gentleness.

And there came that expression again, the one he had observed, then forgotten and now remembered, when she had sat on the pinto looking out at the hills. It was the expression that gave a momentary beauty to features that were not beautiful, but merely regular and without noticeable fault. One would not turn to single her out of a crowd. Yet she caught your attention.

*There's something about you that makes me sad.*

Kate stood up. "Well, I need to make supper. Come on to your job, Ricky. The dogs are hungry, and they're waiting for you."

For a moment Jim watched the two going back to their home. Then, taking Laura's hand, he went up the hill toward the place that was, for this very brief time, their home.

"Duck, Daddy," Laura babbled, clutching the picture book. "Duck, Daddy."

"Yes, duck. That's very nice, darling," he responded, while his mind went racing. The first thing was to prepare her supper, the next to give her a bath, read a short story, and put her to bed.

And then—then the long night would come, and he'd lie awake, and his mind would keep racing.

People don't want much, he thought. When you come down to it, what we really need is a fairly simple thing, just not to be afraid of to-morrow morning.

A row of cans stood on the roadside with the milk going sour in the heat. It was half-past nine, and Jim, walking back from Jennie Macy's house where he had left Laura for her half day, met Clarence staring at the cans.

"Can you believe it?" he cried. "The bastards overslept and missed the pickup truck. It's the last straw." With a violent kick, he overturned a can. "Everything! Everything I touch goes wrong!"

Jim set the can straight and said quietly, "Let's carry them back. They'll need to be emptied and scoured. No use in upsetting yourself too much, Clarence. Things happen."

"Things *don't* just happen! People *let* them happen. Ever since Dad died, we've been going downhill. It isn't my fault, I've tried and tried, but everything I touch is jinxed. Nobody I hire will cooperate. Sometimes I think they're all against me, they want me to fail, they're envious, they soldier on the job, behind my back, they—"

Jim stared at the man's poor face, his mouth distorted as in a tear mask. He was falling apart.

"Come on. Let's start carrying this stuff back to the barn."

"I don't want to set one foot near the barn. I'll give them a piece of my mind if I see them, and then they'll quit, and then what will I do? What will I do anyway? I'm in this mess with my hands tied and a rope around my neck. Do you understand?"

"Listen to me, Clarence. I'll go send the men down to carry these back. Then you and I will take a walk."

In the barnyard, two young men were having a smoke when Jim interrupted them.

"We'll be down in a minute," one said. "What's the matter? He having a fit? Tim's clock didn't go off and the milking was late for once. So what? Old Clarence is losing his—" And with his forefinger, he made the insulting circle at his temple. "Every day he finds something else to bellyache about."

They had lost respect. They saw weakness, failure, and a sinking ship.

"I don't have time to talk about Mr. Benson." Jim gave them a cold stare. "And you don't, either. There's plenty of work to be done around here, and you'd better get started on it."

"There's all this land," Clarence began when Jim returned. "I could raise hay. As a matter of fact, I did raise hay, but there was so much of it that I wasn't able to sell it all, so there's the land, just lying there eating up tax money."

The day was one of those rare ones when the temperature is fitted to the comfort of the human anatomy, the sky is an arc of perfect blue over the flourishing land, and a human being should rejoice in simply being alive. Instead, Clarence renewed his pathetic litany of complaints.

"I know I need new machinery. Some of the stuff, unbeknownst to me, was left outside to rust. But a lot of it was old even in Dad's day. It costs a fortune to replace, and I'm already up to my ears in debt. I suppose you heard, it's all over town, but you're a stranger here, so maybe you haven't heard."

"I have heard something, yes. What are you going to do?"

"That's my trouble. I try to think, but I can't think anymore."

How well Jim knew. . . . Yet along with his wish to be compassionate, he was feeling impatience. *What if the man had my problem?*

"You need to simplify," he said abruptly. "Your

father managed here, and you can, too. The land is rich, but you don't know how to use it."

Clarence gave him a shy, chastened look. "I told you," he mumbled, "I wanted to use what I've learned, things my father never knew. I've just had bad luck, that's all."

Jim stood still. "Now look," he said, "this place is a hodgepodge. Milk cows, untended berry fields, orchards full of rotting fruit, corn, and an expensive, unused hothouse. You've got to make up your mind what you want to be and do. Then do it."

Raising his head, which had been hanging, Clarence said piteously, "I want to keep this for my boy. I need to find somebody who will tell me how I can do it."

"I don't understand. You've lived here all your life, and you mean to tell me you have no one to pull things together for you, no one to advise you? No lawyer, no accountant, nobody at your bank?"

Kicking pebbles, Clarence looked like a child who was being scolded. "I did have, but I guess they're tired of me and my troubles by now. I'm very sick, you see. I'm sure you'll understand because your wife died of cancer. I have it, too. They treated it a couple of years ago, and everybody thought I was all right. At least they said they did. I don't know. Now it's come back."

Jim was barely able to look at those eyes, only at the enormous Adam's apple, which bobbed as Clarence swallowed. So that was it: penury, and now perhaps dying, too. For a few moments he could think of nothing to say.

Then something said itself: "I could go with you for another talk at your bank, or wherever you have your loans, if that would be any help."

"You would do that for me?" And when Jim nodded, "Now all I keep thinking of is Kate. There's no one in the world like her. . . . I don't want to leave her like this, her and the boy. So maybe you can think of some way to talk to these people. . . ."

Jim turned away. I could never have been a doctor, he thought strangely. I can't stand the sight of pain.

"Whenever you want to go, I'm ready," Jim said.

# Chapter 12

With a smile, Mr. Holden remarked, "You sound like a lawyer." He was not nearly as formidable a man as Clarence had described, although that was probably, Jim had to admit, because of his own presence. And he returned the smile.

"I've had people tell me that now and then. Working in the insurance business on wills and trusts same as you do here in the bank, we get to meet a lot of lawyers."

"For an insurance man, and from Maine at that, you have a pretty good handle on farming, I have to say, especially farming in Georgia."

"Oh, the climate's different, but the backaches and the sweat are the same, Mr. Holden."

"And you did say, didn't you, that you're not a relative?"

"No, we're just friends. Both farmers."

"Well, as they say, friends often do more for you than your relatives will. Not that we haven't been very patient with Clarence's debts because we know he's an honest man doing the best he can. But you have presented us with some very new ideas, some fairly sensible arguments on Clarence's behalf. And so in conference, we have all decided to give you six months to see whether you can pull some of his irons out of the fire. What do you say about that, Clarence?"

Clarence had said barely a word the whole time, and they had been in the president's office for almost two hours. Helpless as a child he sat, listening obediently; now he merely nodded and smiled.

"I'd like to say one thing before we leave, Mr. Holden," Jim said. "I'm well aware that it's most unusual for any bank's president to give his time to a small matter like this one. And I want to express my very deep appreciation, Clarence's and my own."

"Thank you. But we, all of us here who are familiar with his situation, appreciate what you've done, too. Families in this little town know each other from one generation to the next, you see. We generally trust and try to help each other."

Jim nodded. "I see that. I've been feeling it."

"But there's something else in this case. Dr. Scofield, when we talked about the Bensons and I spoke about your help, also had something to say about you. He said that you are an unusual person. You're a good Samaritan, coming forth as you have on behalf of another human being who is almost a stranger."

Jim smiled. "You're giving me too much credit, but of course I appreciate it, and I thank you."

# Chapter 13

The six months' delay that the Bensons' creditors had given them also meant six months
of relative safety for Jim and Laura. If at the end
of that time he should have come across no
further evidence of Lillian's pursuit, he would
certainly depart, regardless of whether the mort-
gages were foreclosed or not. He would simply
have to take his chances.

*He should have no doubt that we will find him.*

Sometimes he thought about the horse farm as
a possibility for a job, having delayed on accepting the office supervisor position until the opportunity was gone. He had stumbled upon the
idea while looking through the paper and seeing
an advertisement from somebody who wanted
to lease "extensive pasture land" for his herd of
American saddle horses. And immediately he

had thought of using Clarence's idle land, where once beef cattle had grazed, as grazing land for those horses. He had had no idea what a fair price might be, and had been pleasantly surprised when he was able to tell Clarence what the people were willing to pay.

As for the Holstein milkers, it was for the best that they be sold off; his own experience, slight as it had been, told him that the dairy business was an almost twenty-four-hour responsibility, for which Clarence was no longer fit. So dispense with that, he thought. Remove the cattle stanchions from the bar, replace them with stalls, and you have bad weather accommodation for those expensive horses; the lease should cover the expense, he figured. And he went on figuring.

One day he remembered having seen an item about fir seedlings for sale. That whole flat tract of grasses on the other side of the creek where Kate and he had paused on that morning to view the hills—would that not be a natural place in which to grow trees? If the tract should turn out to be large enough, would it not be ideal for the ornamental shrubbery that Clarence had once spoken about?

Actually, Jim was enjoying this analysis of the Benson farm, pulling its pieces together and reorganizing them. It was in its way a practical, a mathematical, and a minor intellectual challenge. Yet even as he was sitting there with pencil and paper before him, he was always well aware that he was involving himself in the Bensons' problems because he was too afraid to concentrate on his own.

❧

The last of the placid Holsteins clambered into the open truck and were driven away down the lane.

"It hurts to see them go," Kate said. "Half of them were born on this farm. But at least they're not going to slaughter."

"They're going to join a herd four times the size of this one. You see," Jim explained, "it's a case of either-or: either you go into the dairy business on a great big scale these days, or you don't do it at all."

She did not reply. He could barely imagine what she might be thinking while Clarence, visibly fading away, dozed on the front porch glider with the dogs at his feet. If Jim had been free to talk, he would have said to her, "I know you are completely alone, and the nights are the worst. You are looking into a void."

Instead he spoke briskly. "We've been having a run of luck. Not a long run, but not too short, either. Now with the lease money, there's something in the bank, enough to take care of expenses like repairs and the wages for the blueberry harvest. Oh yes, the chickens. We got a good price for the lot, enough to pay for the fir seedlings."

Speak with a lift of the voice at the end of each sentence when you want to encourage. Those fir seedlings couldn't bring in much for at least five years, and even then you'd want to market only fifty percent of them, leaving the rest to bring in much more after ten years' growth. But Kate was smart. She would know all that without any need of a lilt in his voice.

"So now we're back where we once were," she said. "A few chickens for eggs, Lucy for milk, fruit and vegetables for our table, hay and corn for cash. And blueberries for market, lots of blueberries. That's the way it was when I came here."

"Well, not quite."

"I didn't mean—of course you've made great changes. It just feels more like what it used to be. More peaceful."

Jim was curious. "It must have been very different from where you grew up before you were married."

"Look how a mist is rising. It's going to rain," she said, as if she had not heard him.

" 'Autumn, season of mist,' " he quoted for no reason except that the poet's phrase had come into his head.

"But not the same as in England, I should think."

"No, not at all. What they call 'mist,' we would call 'fog.' "

"You've been there?"

"Yes."

"You've done a lot of traveling for an insurance agent. England and France—where else?"

Had he ever mentioned France? Obviously, he must have done so. He must have let it slip while talking to Clarence, surely not to her because he had had almost no conversation with her throughout the whole long summer.

"Nowhere else. I took a little vacation once," he said uncomfortably.

Suddenly Kate said, "I don't understand why you are staying here and doing all this for us."

He seemed to recall that some time ago she had once asked that question. So he paused, and weighed his reply. "Let's put it this way. It was a tangle to unravel, a business going into failure, and it was a challenge for me."

"In the beginning, you said it was because you needed a change of scene and a short rest. But now, you're almost into the second year."

Her heavy-lidded gray eyes, of the shape and

color that often seem dreamful, were bent upon him. Disconcerted, he answered with a question.

"Have you never heard of simple human kindness? Your husband has been too ill to cope with your troubles, and he's getting worse. I merely thought I could help."

"That's the whole reason?"

"It's as good a reason as any, isn't it?"

"Don't be annoyed, Jim. I am so grateful to you for what you've done. It's just that it seems so strange. People don't usually do things like this for each other."

Fencing, he thought. It's one thing I hate. It would be so much easier if he could say, "Listen, I don't like your questions! I don't like feeling puzzled, being unable to figure out whether my presence bothers you or whether you want me to stay here."

"I was wondering whether you and Laura would want to come to Ricky's birthday tomorrow," she said.

"Of course we will."

"It's not a real party because Clarence isn't up to that. I'm bringing a cake to school and making another one for our supper at home."

"What shall I get for Ricky? Is there anything special that he wants?"

"Anything at all. He hasn't had a present in a long time."

"I'm going into town now to do some errands and I'll think about what I wanted when I was his age."

Coming across the field were the two young farmhands, the ones who had so impudently jibed about Clarence that day. By offering better wages and laying down rules, Jim had pulled them both into shape. Ellis and Tom had turned out very well. A smile and a firm hand had put some sense into them. He had a feeling of such satisfaction that his mood reversed itself and he was actually able to chuckle at the thought of Augustus Pratt, Ed Wills, or any of his old associates seeing him now.

As he progressed through the day at the supermarket, the stationers, where as always he bought the New York newspaper, and the toy store, where he bought a rag doll for Laura and a book and a baseball and bat for Ricky, his thoughts enlivened him. Ultimately he would find a good place, if not the horse farm, then some other local enterprise where nobody would delve into his past as they had at the factory. Back at the cottage, still in a good mood, he walked over to Jennie Macy's, brought Laura home, went through the usual cheerful routine, put her to bed, and entered the kitchen to clean up.

On the counter lay mail that, in his hurry, he had tossed there unread. It still surprised him to be receiving mail here, although it should not have done so, because when you start a magazine subscription, you can expect a stream of advertisements. He was about to throw away a handful of them, when two photographs jumped up from a card and struck him between the eyes.

Side by side, each was accompanied by a succinct paragraph: Bettina Wolfe, age, description, date missing from New York City; then Donald Wolfe, along with the same facts. Beneath was a telephone number to be used by anyone who recognized them.

*"Have you seen them?"*

He fell onto a chair. For a few seconds, the room reeled around him; he was going to be sick. There was a pounding in his ears, as though his protesting heart had sent his blood careening crazily through all his arteries. He clenched his hands and clung to the tabletop, where the two faces stared back at him.

After long minutes, when he had managed to collect his wits, he studied the faces. A two-year-old—three by now—child did not look too different from millions of others, did it? You wouldn't, for instance, remember Laura if you had seen her somewhere last week, would you? As for himself: Would a stranger remember him or, from a crowd of men, select him, medium to tall, of indeterminate age somewhere between twenty-five and thirty-five, neither fat nor thin, with hair and eyes a medium brown? Did he not, if one were to give a quick glance, look almost like everybody else in a crowd? It was not as if he owned, for instance, a crown of white hair, or measured six feet nine, or four feet nine, or was sixty pounds overweight, or had a scar on his cheek, or— There are, of course, distinctive people who have unusual features, such as a prominent nose, or very large eyes, or thick glasses. He had none of these. He thought of himself as one of those faceless people you see in crowds.

He got up to stand in front of the bathroom mirror and study himself. He had large, very regular teeth. But this photograph did not show teeth. Actually, this photograph was not a very good one. It was blurred. Lillian had apparently, and quite naturally, not bothered to keep any good ones, which was a help. Perhaps he should grow a beard? No, that would be too obvious an attempt to disguise himself.

He was arrested between fright and a need to reason it away. Could anybody in town, having received this advertisement today, have noticed a resemblance to him? Might it not perhaps be smart to spend more time in town, walking boldly and normally among people?

After a while, on the unproven theory that a

glass of warm milk can induce sleep, Jim drank
one and slept, but poorly, beset with bad dreams.

He was of two minds. One mind was frozen in
terror. The other roved around the little birthday party, produced the right comments at the
right moment, and roved again without aim.

The nice little boy, elated at being the center
of attention as he sat with the cake before him,
was a reminder of the jolly, vigorous son he had
once expected to father. Clarence, at the foot of
the small table, was livid; if you allowed your
imagination to go free, you could see death hovering behind his chair. Across from Clarence,
Kate was making an effort to keep the atmosphere cheerful. The little girl next to him was
the reason Jim was in this room tonight.

As always, his thoughts came back to her, and
stayed there. Day by day, he was a witness to an
unfolding, those tiny revelations of the person
she would become. Yesterday she had shown
him how she could count to ten on her fingers;
she had named her nose, and her teeth, and her
toes. She had waved to him when he left her at
Jennie's. And today when he was dressing her for
this birthday party, she had selected most definitely what she wanted to wear.

Oh, what is to become of her! he cried out

within himself. His hand was trembling. I need to do something with my life that will keep her safe, and I am so afraid.

Ricky was talking. "When I am ten, I can have a horse like Dad's."

"That's nice," Kate said. "But right now you have your own pony, and you love him."

"I know. But Dad promised me a horse like Cappy for my birthday when I'm ten. He promised."

None of the three adults at the table looked at the others.

"Dad can't go riding just now," Ricky explained in his loud, innocent voice, "but soon he will. Maybe you could ride up in the hills with me sometimes, Mr. Fuller, until Dad gets better? Mom's too busy staying with Dad."

"Sure. Sure I will," Jim said.

"In the meantime," Kate quickly reminded Ricky, "Jennie has an errand in the village and she said she'll drive you there, since you wanted to visit your friends tonight, didn't you? I'll pick you up later. Okay?"

"Okay, Mom. Okay, Dad."

"Did you mean that about going to ride with him?" Clarence asked when Ricky had left.

What could Jim answer? God alone knew where he himself would be this time tomorrow.

"As long as I'm still here, I'll be glad to," he said. "He's a great little boy, especially nice."

"I was wondering—you said, 'As long as I'm still here.' Does that mean you are getting ready to leave us?"

Kate stood up and excused herself, while Clarence, in a low voice, went on, "I wanted to say . . . this is hard for me . . . could you, will you stay until this is over for me? Or maybe longer, if she needs help? You know what's the matter. It won't take very long, at least they don't think it will. If you would stay until she gets straightened out . . . You've already done so much. Will you take a salary to stay awhile? Or just not pay any rent? That would even out, wouldn't it?"

Jim was looking for a way to say something painless, something that would neither refuse nor imply a promise that he could not keep, when Kate returned.

"Clarence, you ought to go to bed," she said softly.

With relief, Jim agreed. "And my Laura is tired, too. It's past her bedtime."

From the front hall as he left, he watched Kate help her husband up the stairs. Something is different, he thought. Why of course, it was her hair. She had been letting it grow, and the weight of its length had straightened the curls.

Now past her shoulders there fell a glossy length of living red. Remarkable that he hadn't even noticed it before this!

And he had a sudden crazy thought that had nothing to do with her hair: *They don't fit together, those two.* They never could have done so, not really. He adores her, but for her it is the child who unites them. She's far too alert, too quick, for him.

Then as he took Laura's hand and went outside into the night, he said to himself, good Lord, what business is it of mine whether she ever loved him—in the way I think of love—or not?

In the morning his hand began to tremble again, so that while slicing an orange for breakfast, the knife slipped and sliced his arm instead.

"Damn fool," he muttered when the blood, an astounding amount of it, spilled onto the counter. Then he sighed, for still in sight was that torn-up piece of paper with the question: *Have you seen them?* It was no small task to bind up the cut with his left hand, then to zip Laura's clothes and tie her sneakers, still with his clumsy left hand and that question leering up at him: *Have you seen them?*

"Boo boo," Laura remarked with some interest. "Does it hurt?"

It did indeed, and so much so that it very obviously needed care. After leaving her at Jennie's house, he walked back to his car and stood there hesitating.

There was no possible way to avoid going into town. They had to eat, didn't they? And buy a paper, get a haircut, and—and *live*. If it was destined to happen (since when did he believe in predestination?), nothing would stop it. He got into the car, and driving slowly with his left hand on the wheel, arrived at Dr. Scofield's house.

"Some nasty cut there, Jim. You must have had your mind on something else when you did that."

"I guess I did. It happens."

"By the way, when did you have your last physical?"

He wanted to get out of there, do a few chores, and leave town as fast as he could. Now this talkative old man was trying to keep him.

"A couple of years ago. I don't remember. Maybe last year. I've had a lot—"

"I know, I know. A lot on your mind. That's no excuse for neglecting yourself."

Jim forced a smile. "I don't neglect myself. I'm strong as an ox."

"Right now, you're not. You're shaking. Do you realize you came close to cutting an artery? And then what would have become of Laura? Never mind yourself, but what about her? Now go in there, put on a robe, and let me take a look at a cardiogram, blood pressure, the whole works."

The words had an instant effect. Her father's health was indeed Laura's only safeguard. What if he were to be injured in an accident, or die of pneumonia, or— Fool! He had been taking his health too much for granted.

Back at the doctor's desk an hour later, he learned that although he had no serious organic problems, he was for some reason under too much tension and should try to do something about it.

"I know it's easy to tell a person that he ought to stop worrying, easy and rather ridiculous. I know, too, that you've taken the loss of your wife very hard, as is only natural. But apparently running away hasn't helped you enough. Perhaps you should go back to your friends and your familiar environment."

This man is clever, Jim was thinking. There are no physical symptoms, and yet he has unearthed what's hidden. And he answered lightly, evasively, "Americans like to make fresh starts, Doctor. They like to go west. And I'm slightly west of where I began, you see."

"All right, so you've made a fresh start. Maybe then you need some social life. Maybe you need to be with somebody else beside your tiny girl."

"Not so tiny anymore."

"Even so. You should join some kind of a group. You need to belong. I'm no psychiatrist, but I do know a thing or two."

"You're forgetting that I'm only passing through. I'm not staying here."

"It still wouldn't hurt you to make some acquaintances. Sunday afternoons we always have a pack of relatives at our house, mostly children and grandchildren. It's an open house. Come on down with Laura. Join the crowd."

"That's awfully nice of you. I'll try to do that," Jim said, wanting only to get away.

"I hear talk about you everywhere, even at the hospital. Coming here as a stranger and taking up Clarence's cause—what a splendid act of charity! People have long been worried about the Bensons. Well, of course you know all about that."

Of course Jim didn't, not really. Things didn't just happen. There had to be so much more, so many unknowns, questions of character, of two characters, of Clarence and Kate, and what had made them what they were. It was all too complex, as it always is, as he himself so well knew, and it made his head ache. Besides, it was none of his business.

But Scofield, in his harmless way, continued. "Clarence is the best there is. Honest, I mean, steady. Yes, the best there is. Trouble is—well, he isn't the smartest there is. Kate was only nineteen when she married him, too young in my opinion. You're so infatuated, you don't really see what you're getting, whether it's the right choice for you. Then afterward the babies come, although they waited a long time for one, and the way it looks, he'll be their only one."

The good doctor certainly meant no harm, but these intimacies about Kate Benson were for some reason very distasteful to Jim. He rushed to leave before he had to hear any more of them.

Outside on the street he was hailed by Mr. Holden, who crossed it to join him.

"Can I give you a lift to the bank?" Jim asked.

"No, thanks. I live a mile out, and I make it my business to walk both ways every day. But first I have to tell you the craziest thing. You'll laugh. Did you get an ad that came in yesterday's mail, the one with the missing child?"

"No, what about it?"

"Oh, the usual thing, except that the man, the father who apparently kidnapped her, looks a little bit like you. I thought you'd get a laugh out of it, although of course it's not funny."

*A little bit. The hair and the glasses instead of the contacts. Only a little bit. Dear God, please.*

"I guess a couple of million guys must look like me."

"Of course. Like me, too. You know, I have

to tell you again that you've surprised us all, coming in with a profit last month. Nobody expected it so soon."

"It wasn't much of a profit," Jim said, breathing a trifle more easily.

"You have to remember that they haven't been out of the red for the last five years on that farm, so this is quite some accomplishment. Let me ask you something frankly. Are you planning to stay out there? Scofield tells me you only intended to take a rest in the country. But he says Clarence plans to ask you to stay awhile and help out."

"He already has asked me. I don't know how to answer."

"Well, you've been here this long, so a little longer . . ." Holden did not finish.

"I know what you're saying. You're saying that he's watching his own death."

"Well, you are doing a lot of good there. You've got an eye for business, and that's what they need right now. The wife and the kid, I mean."

Talk lightly again, as if you had nothing heavy on your mind. "Business is a kind of game, isn't it? Sharpens your wits."

It occurred to Jim while the two men talked that the two conversations this morning were the

first he had held with any man, except for poor
Clarence, in many, many weeks. The company of
men was, after all, the normal way of life, yet so
fraught with fear had he been that he had not
even realized how much he missed it. So even
now, and in spite of all the fear that beset him, a
friendly warmth spread over him, a sense of
being liked and welcomed.

"If you really want to sharpen your wits,"
Holden said, "I've got a volunteer job for you.
The woman who practically ran the Red Cross
drive in town for the last few years has moved
away. And now, since everybody depended on
her, there's no direction for this year's drive. It
looks like the kind of thing you could do, Mr.
Fuller, if you wanted to. And it would be a big
help if you'd step in for a couple of months at
least."

Jim thought rapidly: If because of that ad any
question about me should ever arise, this Red
Cross business should help quash suspicions. A
fearful man with reason to hide doesn't usually
take a public position.

"Yes, I can do it," he said promptly. "I've always supported the Red Cross, and I'm honored
that you asked me. After all, I'm a stranger here."

"I told you this is a friendly place, didn't I?"

He was sitting on the front steps of the cottage going over accounts when Kate came walking toward him up the hill.

"I didn't know about your arm, Jim, or I would have driven you to the doctor," she said. "Jennie told me it was awful, and she didn't know how you ever managed to drive, but you insisted."

"Fortunately, it's my left arm, so I'm able to manage pen and paper all right."

Remembering his own thoughts last night as he had left her house, he felt uncomfortable and wished she would go away.

But instead, she remarked about the blueberry crop that was even now being loaded onto a pair of trucks parked just within sight below them at the curve of the road. "Clarence says we've never raised a crop this size. It's a record for us."

"That's only because we ripped out all the market vegetables and concentrated on it. Anyway, if you can't raise rabbit-eye blueberries in Georgia, you can't raise them anywhere."

"Clarence still can't get over all you're doing here. He can't thank you enough."

This repeated thanks had begun to grate on Jim's ears. Always a flush of shame went through him because they who thanked and felt indebted to him had no idea that he, too, desperately needed them. Changing the subject, he inquired about Clarence.

"He's growing weaker. That's why he doesn't like going downstairs anymore. I think he only does it at all because he doesn't want to frighten Ricky."

It won't be long, Jim thought.

"You'll laugh. He says such funny things sometimes. He misses the rooster's crow in the morning."

"I won't laugh," Jim said gravely.

"I didn't say that right. What I meant was, it's strange what little things a person in his condition will seize upon. Some of them are happy, like remembering how it rained on our way to the hospital to have Ricky, and then how the sun broke through the minute he was born."

She had sat down on the step below Jim. He had a feeling that she had done so unconsciously, for she was otherwise too courteous to have interrupted him at his work.

"And then he reminisces about hard things, the time for instance when we lost a thousand three-day-old chicks because somebody left the chicken house door open. I always believed that he himself left it open. His mind wanders sometimes."

Jim stirred, crossed and uncrossed his feet, wishing again that she would go away and leave him alone. But he saw also that she needed to talk, and there was no one else right then but himself.

"I was wondering," she said, "whether, now that so much has changed here, it would make sense for me to—well, to do my own thing. There's that wonderful greenhouse that Clarence had built for me, and it's never been used because we couldn't stock it. Have you ever been inside?"

Jim had been over every square foot of this land and every building in it.

"Yes," he replied.

"I've taken two courses on bulbs and perennials, and I believe I could make a success if I had some advice on the business end. I never got any advice, and so I never started." She smiled ruefully. "I don't even know what kind of demand there might be. All I know is, I'd love to do it."

"There was a four-page feature about that last month in my paper. I'll send for a copy," he offered.

"I've wondered why you got all those papers from New York when you come from Philadelphia."

"The international news seems more complete, and I'm interested in it. I used to get the New York papers even when I was in Maine. There's nothing unusual about that."

The last sentence was barely out of his mouth when he heard its curt echo. She, too, might have heard a subtle defensiveness, because she stood up and gave him her formal thanks.

"I will be very glad if you'd do that for me, Jim. And thank you. Thank you for everything."

He pushed his papers away and watched her. It was queer that whenever he did pause a moment to consider, she was always walking away. Suddenly he embarrassed himself by seeing her with jeans and shirt removed, seeing most vividly her long-legged, supple body and the heavy sway of her red-bronze hair. Then he turned her around to imagine her coming toward him with arms outstretched.

And as suddenly, embarrassment turned to anger. Ridiculous! Impossible! It was not that there was anything unusual for a man to undress a woman in his mind. In fact, it was more unusual for a man not to do it. But this woman and this tragic' situation were exceptional. Her sad husband was dying in that house down there. And he, he himself, known now as Jim Fuller, had no rights anyway under the law, not even to the stolen name he bore.

The earth was peaceful that year. The crops throve, and the business of the farm began to run so smoothly that there was each month a steady, modest gain to show to the creditors. And Jim, who had undertaken his commitments in the town only to seem like an ordinary sociable citizen, had even begun to look like one. The Red Cross effort in a town this size was no burden; he could, as poor Clarence would say, have done it with one hand tied behind his back. From there, he took to helping the Policemen's Benevolent Association, starting with a gift that was generous, but not so generous as to be remarkable. These efforts brought him to a membership, sponsored by Mr. Holden and Dr. Scofield, in a men's club that met once a month at a local restaurant. One of the members asked him to volunteer at a blood drive at the hospital, and he did that, too. After the long flight in terror of pursuit, he even began to have a few brief moments in which he allowed himself to believe that he was on his way back to the world again.

One afternoon, coming up from the outer fields where he had been overseeing the planting of hemlocks on what had been fallow acres, he was arrested by a living picture. Partway up the low hill that separated the Bensons' house from the cottage, there was a leveling, a grassy seat with an outcropping of rock for a back. There, in mingled sun and shade, was a portrait clearly

titled *Woman and Children, Summer Afternoon.*
The three had stepped back a century in time;
the woman wore not her usual jeans, but a wide
cotton skirt striped in pink and green; the little
girl had a ribbon in her hair and a floppy book
on her lap. The boy was leaning over her shoulder, and Jim had to chuckle at him, displaying as
always the authority of his age.

"Daddy! I can read!" Laura cried out. And
Ricky cried out, "I'm teaching her. Didn't I tell
you I would?"

"You did. I remember it exactly. It was on
your birthday."

"Mom said I can read," Laura said.

" 'Mom'?" Jim repeated. "You mean Ricky's
mom."

Kate said quickly, "It's only a name to her. It
means nothing. It could just as easily be 'Annie'
or anything. She's simply imitating Ricky."

He understood. She was assuring him that his
child was too young to know what she was saying, and that in time, he would be able to talk to
her about her mother.

Pricks of a cold needle went down Jim's back.
He was about to say something, to say anything,
when Kate added, "I've tried to correct her, but
it hasn't worked. It must be painful for you, and
I'm sorry."

With a clumsy wave of a hand, he dismissed

the subject. "You never mentioned that article about the woman who started a nursery, the shrubs and perennials."

"Oh, I read it. And it whetted my appetite. Well, maybe someday I'll do it, too. I hope so." She stood up. "I never leave Clarence this long, but he wanted a nap. I'd better go and check on him."

He watched her go down the hill. How could he ever have thought that she was not beautiful? Hers was a classic beauty, calm and strong. It did not invite. It did not twinkle or sparkle. Oh, he had had his fill and more of sparkle!

⁂

He had always been a light sleeper, as well as one whose dreams are so vivid that he does not forget them the next morning. That night he had an erotic dream about Kate Benson.

⁂

So it happened that he knew he must really leave this place. *Somewhere there is a woman who is going to give you great joy,* Pratt had said. Great joy for me? With an invisible sword above my head and over Laura's? Not that it would be this woman, this Kate, who would ever have me, she with her quick, disturbing glances and her avoidance. If it were not that her husband is dying and that I am helpfully here, she would—oh, ever so kindly and courteously—ask me to leave.

"Mom," Laura said, wanting attention, "Mom said I can read."

"Soon you will, and you'll read to me, darling."

So quick and bright, my little girl! Tiny thing, if you had a mother, somebody like Kate—

The minute that poor man dies, I must go. There's too much guilt here with these thoughts that I have. It can't be more than a few months, if that, Scofield said. The longer it takes, the harder it will be to go away. It's been so good for Laura, this safe haven, and for me, too.

But I've been playing a role, and that's bad. Country gentleman, I am, supervising my estate and tinkering with the life of a pleasant, small town. Country gentleman? Get real, Donald Wolfe. You're a wanted man.

# Chapter 14

Winter, or what passed for it this far south, came abruptly on the day Clarence died, not in the hospital where he could well have been, but in his own bed.

"He died as he wished," Kate said. "He wanted to die in his home."

Jim offered, some weeks after the death, to sort through Clarence's possessions and take them to a charity in town.

"I suppose you'll be going soon, you and Laura?"

"Well—yes. Is there any special time that you want us to?"

"Whenever it's convenient for you. I know he asked you to stay awhile to help us, but we'll be fine."

"The important thing is when it will be best

for you. You have a big responsibility here, bigger than ever."

"Yes, thanks to your work, but I'll manage."

It would not be so easy for her to manage this huge farm alone. He was also thinking about Ricky's tears.

"Mr. Fuller," Ricky had asked that night after the funeral when the neighbors had crowded the house and heaped the table with food, "will you be umpire sometimes? Dad always was before he got sick. Will you, Mr. Fuller?"

The father, so loving and so childish himself, would be deeply missed. Nothing would be easy for either woman or boy.

"You can really build this place up," Jim said now, briskly and cheerfully. "We've only started. The tree seedlings are a great investment for the future. I've an order in for more seedlings, tulip trees. They're very desirable on large estates up north."

"We call them 'yellow poplars' in this part of the country."

"I see you've been studying."

"I took your advice."

She was folding sweaters into a grocery carton. Boots, old shoes, and a worn raincoat lay on chairs, ready to be sent away. He wondered about her thoughts, the ones that might lie below and behind the natural sorrow after death.

Why there should be anything hidden, he did not know. He only sensed that there was.

"Look over there at the window," she said. "I suppose he told you about that row of arborvitae? His grandfather put them there to shelter the gardens from the wind off the hills. They meant a lot to Clarence, those trees did."

Jim could understand that. The hands of a grandfather long dead had planted those seedlings, now grown to three times the height of the grandson. And he looked out at the living green, at this row of Gothic arches serrated against the gray, hazy sky. He the newcomer, the stranger, had foreknowledge of himself: These trees, these hills, this woman were indelibly written, were in fact engraved upon his most secret heart.

Toward spring, there came a change. They were in the greenhouse, where a carpenter had been building shelves. When he left and Jim was about to follow, Kate stopped him with an odd, blunt question.

"Why do we never talk to each other?"

Once, a long time ago, she had asked another strange question: "Who are you?" And he had been unable to answer. Now, unable again, he said the first thing that came into his head.

"About what?"

"I don't know. But people talk, and you avoid me."

He was so tempted! That flowing hair, the pure face, the warm, curved shape under the T-shirt, and the perfume of the gardenias in the flowerpots . . .

Speak kindly, he admonished himself. Be friendly, but no more than that. You have nothing substantial to give, not to her, not to any woman.

"I haven't meant to avoid you, Kate. I'm sorry. It's a misunderstanding. I will talk about anything you want or answer any question if I can."

"All right, then. When are you leaving here?"

*Storm said: If the child is on this planet, I will find her.*

"I have a tentative offer from the horse people. For the spring."

"It's already spring."

"Within the next week or two, we will leave. Is that satisfactory?"

"I'm not pushing you out! I only asked when."

"I know you're not pushing us," he said. "You wouldn't do that. But it will be soon, I promise."

"You haven't had a day away since you arrived here. Why don't you go down to Atlanta for a couple of concerts before you leave? You love music so much. I can easily keep Laura. We've two extra bedrooms."

"That's very good of you. You've been wonderful to her, and I appreciate it. I appreciate the offer, but I need to see the people at the horse breeders' place to make arrangements."

"I don't think much of that area. It's very isolated. Have you checked into schools over there? Laura will be ready for kindergarten before you know it, and she needs a first-rate school. She's a rare little person. I've tutored children, and I know."

They were standing face-to-face. Hers was flushed. The gold locket that lay between her breasts seemed to rise and fall, as if she were breathing hard. And she spoke so softly that he strained to hear.

"You don't have to leave, Jim. I'm sorry I've been talking so much about your leaving. I apologize. I don't know why I did. I've been giving you the wrong impression."

"I gave the impression myself. I have to leave. I have to find a job."

That was true for more reasons than one. The money that had traveled south on his money belt wasn't going to last forever.

"But you already have one here."

When he did not answer at once, she continued, "I don't know what to say. It's all so complicated."

"I don't know anything in the world that isn't
complicated, Kate."

They were still standing face-to-face. And
suddenly, as if a terrible, fierce light had been
thrust upon him, Jim understood everything.
That which had taken all these months to root
and flourish within him had done the same
within her. The terse replies, the glances, the
avoidance—all these had been only an attempt
to cover a struggle.

And with an equal shock, he was aware that
he had never before felt such tenderness. Let
nothing, let no one, and surely not I, ever hurt
this woman.

Later he wondered what more he would have
said at that moment if Ricky had not come into
the room and interrupted the agony.

Certainly he could not even think of continuing
to live so close to Kate. His tension mounted so
that he was sure he was hearing the blood pound
in his ears. Even though he despised self-pity, he
had to wonder whether the fates had decreed
that he should from now on stand between the
devil and the deep blue sea. And early one

evening after Laura had fallen asleep, he went outside to calm himself with a walk in the foothills. The light of the lengthening spring day lingered over the dirt path, while through the streaked sky in a gigantic V-formation, wild geese honked and raced toward the north. Complicated, she had said, without having the least idea how much so. At random, his thoughts spun as he walked. He saw his office at Orton and Pratt with its view of the avenue below; cars glistened like beetles as they crawled through traffic. He heard Ed Wills's distinctive nasal voice. He saw Pratt's family photograph on his desk. He saw Lillian lying on the sofa that morning in Florence. He imagined himself saying good-bye to Kate for the last time, then driving away with Laura and her rag dolls in the backseat, while his whole being yearned to stay.

How could he have failed to understand what was happening to Kate?

The path narrowed enough to let a single horse go through the underbrush. Then it was blocked by a fallen tree, struck by lightning in last week's storm. Exhausted now, he sat down on a stump and tried to collect himself.

How could he have failed to hear her unspoken words? He should have left long ago. He had waited too long. The man at the horse farm had changed his mind about retiring, so that job had fallen through. There remained only one choice: Make some move and trust to fortune that Storm's private detectives will not get wind of him. No, nothing but danger and pain to offer—danger, shame, and pain. He groaned, startling a rabbit who had been quietly feeding near where he sat as still as a stone.

Above him as he walked back, the evening star appeared on the rim of the hills. If only, like a sailor, he could fasten his eyes upon it and know his direction!

Upstairs at the cottage the night-light glowed pink. In the nest of stuffed animals, Laura lay so sweetly asleep that he wanted to pick her up and tell her how much he loved her.

Out on the steps again, he stared toward the house below, when a light came on in the downstairs room where Kate liked to read. As if compelled, he walked down the slope and knocked at the door. When she opened it, he had no idea why he had come or what he wanted to say. All he had was a flashing memory of the first time he had knocked at that door; it could have been yesterday, or a dark age ago.

For an instant, they both stood still in the hallway and looked at each other. Then with some sort of sounds, cries, or maybe questions, they came together and clung.

When he opened his eyes again, the first thing he saw was the clock on the wall between the windows. The minute hand made a stiff little jump from 7:20 to 7:21. She was still in his arms when it jumped to 25. The day was Friday, the time was 7:25 on an evening in April, when he found her, and lost her.

*Somewhere there is a woman who will bring you great joy,* said Augustus Pratt.

They broke apart and stood looking again, deeply now, searching each other. Her eyes were shining, and then she began to cry.

"I thought . . . oh, Jim, I thought you would never . . . I hoped."

What had he just done? Reality, in full force, had struck him. "I wasn't able to," he said, almost whispering.

"Because of Clarence? I would never have hurt him. You know that. But he's been dead for months, and we're alive! Oh, Jim, we'll be so good together."

*My God, what had he done?* And struggling to bring some order out of the chaos in his head, he sat down on the sofa with that poor head between his hands.

"What is it? What's wrong?"

"It's my fault. Oh, Kate, it's all my fault."

"Your fault? What fault?"

"Because I have to go away."

"Will you, for God's sake, say what this means?"

"Kate, you don't understand. How could you? I can't stay with you. Believe me, oh my dear, my dearest, I can't. I would give anything if I could—"

"Go away! What are you saying?"

She was quivering. When he got up and reached for both her hands to hold them in his and try, somehow try to explain, to console, to reason, she pulled them away.

"How can I find the right words? There are none. I can't stay. I can't."

"What are you trying to do to me?" She was sobbing, beside herself. "What crazy, cruel trick is this? You have never talked! Do it now. You can't go away and leave me like this after— after—"

She fell into a chair across from him. Her mouth twisted in the ancient mask of grief, her hands twisted together on her lap, she stared and waited.

A thought came to Jim, vanished, and came back, insisting: This pressure is more than human beings should have to bear. There has to be a limit. . . . And looking fully into Kate's anguished face, he began to speak.

"My name is Donald Wolfe. A few years ago,

I met and married a woman who shone like a diamond. After a while, I found that she was only a glittering imitation. I suppose I should not fault her too much because we are all what we are, and mostly we do not know why. But I did not want our child to become like her, and so I took Laura away."

When he had finished, he looked at the clock just as the minute hand moved to 7:45. Twenty minutes it had taken to unfold the facts, the hopeful, the pleasing, the disappointing, the sordid, the unbearable—all of them. At the end, overcome, he buried his face in his hands and turned his back upon Kate so that she would not witness his tears.

After a while, he heard light footsteps on the rug and felt a hand on his shoulder.

"Jim, Jim, it's okay to cry. I'm crying for you."

He whispered, "Now you see why I can't stay with you."

"No. No, I don't see."

"There've been things in the newspapers and one of those advertisements with photos. They're searching everywhere."

"They won't find you! You've earned a reputation here. It was very clever of you to come out so boldly in town."

He smiled weakly. "And clever of you to see why I did it. Not that that's the whole reason. I've made friends here, too."

"You're safe, Jim. They'll never find you."

" 'Never' is a big word. Suppose they do? Think what that would mean for you and Ricky. You'd be an accomplice. That's why I can't stay with you."

"If they find you, they're welcome to find me, too. I love you, Jim. And love means being loyal."

As you were to Clarence, he thought, and said so.

"Yes, he was a good man, very kind to me, although he and I—well, no matter. If he were living, do you think I would be telling you that I love you? He never knew it, and never would have known, that on the very first day when you came here with Laura, something happened to me. You made me feel guilty, and that's why I wanted you to go away."

He was so tempted! But it would be wrong.

"You don't want me to be harmed if things should go bad. But you'll do more harm if you leave me now."

Between love and danger, he thought, and could not speak.

"Once or twice I asked, 'Who are you?' and was sorry afterward because I felt that you were hiding something, and that I shouldn't have asked. But still I knew it was nothing evil because there is no evil in you. It is a frightful thing to take a child away from its mother, and a good human being who does it must have an overwhelming reason. You are the soul of goodness, Jim, and I believe you."

Still Jim was silent. Within heart and mind, his fear and his yearning fought each other. Long minutes passed as he sat. The dogs came into the room from wherever they had been sleeping, flopped thumping onto the floor, and went to sleep again. The screen door creaked when Ricky came home with a friend and they went upstairs. Silent, too, Kate went to the window and looked out into the fallen night.

*Decide.*

One way or the other, Jim thought. When he turned to where she was standing, the evening star was framed in the topmost pane above her head. And suddenly it spoke to him.

"Choose love," it said. "Choose love."

Yes. He went to her then and took her back into his arms.

# PART
# TWO

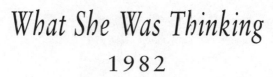

## *What She Was Thinking*
## 1982

# Chapter 15

At lunch one Saturday in the spring, Laura made an announcement. "Hansel pushed the witch into the stove so she wouldn't eat him and Gretel. Did you know that?" she demanded.

Rick scoffed, "Dope! Everybody knows that baby stuff."

Now that he was only a few months away from the fifth grade while Laura, already in first grade, was no longer a cute baby, he had lost his sweet, amused protectiveness of her.

The parents were enjoying themselves. These weekend lunches were the only ones at which the four were together at the table.

"I'm going to Jessica's house to play," Laura said, looking straight at her father.

"You haven't asked me whether you may," he responded.

"Can I? I want to. I finished my milk, so can I?"

"If you mean 'may I,' the answer is yes, you may. And have fun, honey."

Kate gave instructions to Rick. "Since you're going that way, too, take Laura. I don't want her walking alone on the road. There's that curve where drivers can't see very well."

"Come on, dope," Rick said, and the two went out, he in the rear holding Laura by her collar.

"Shall we take Cappy and Pinto out for some exercise?" Kate suggested.

"No, it's going to pour soon. Look at the sky. It's a good day to tackle some paperwork, anyway. There are accounts outstanding and first-of-the-month bills."

As business had burgeoned, the living room had been more or less turned into an office, which itself was becoming too small to accommodate two desks overflowing with papers. At the one that belonged to him, Jim sat down, took a ledger out of a drawer, and stared outside at the afternoon.

It was a lazy day, he reflected. The satisfying view of the well-kept grounds outside, the bottom line in the ledger, the sounds that Kate made as she moved about the house, the thriving children—the manly little boy and that funny little person, his Laura—all were cozy. And as his pen hovered over the page, his mind wandered through some of the past worries that could now be so thankfully dismissed.

He had worried about being a stepfather to Rick; even though he had not yet married Rick's mother, he was in fact the substitute for Clarence; to his shelves he had added books about stepfatherhood, books that brought a smile to Kate. "Because," she said, "you are a model father to my son, as much as to your daughter. You're the last man to need a book." He had hoped, as he watched the little boy mourn, that that was so. The boy, like Clarence, was already wedded to the farm, but unlike his father, there was nothing timid or hesitant about him, and Jim, on long rides and in long conversations, had been trying to foster his good qualities. He had worried much about giving the right companionship to a daughter, but she and he were, as Kate said, "as close as two fingers on a hand."

Yet beneath all this, there was something else, a dark and sinister reality.

"Stop reading that newspaper," Kate commanded from the doorway.

"I wasn't reading it. I'm figuring sales taxes, if you want to know."

"I don't believe you. What's it doing on the

desk? Jim Fuller, I wish you'd stop bringing that paper home and reading all that foul stuff."

"You haven't read it yet, so how do you know what's in it?"

"I can tell by looking at you, so I don't want to read it." For a moment Kate frowned. "Well, maybe I do. Maybe I should. Spread it out."

**This week in Paris, a private jet arrived delivering their socialite friends to Arthur Storm and the former Lillian Buzley. After a hard-fought divorce and an idyllic honeymoon on a yacht cruise among the Greek islands, there was a celebration, a housewarming party at their magnificent new house near the Bois de Boulogne.**

**The new Mrs. Storm was radiantly beautiful in the blue that she so often wears, her friends say, because it matches her remarkable eyes.**

**"Lillian is one of a kind," said Chloe Sanders. "I've known her forever, and I can swear she never changes. Her energy can positively lift a roomful of people. It's like oxygen. People adore her. She's smart, and lovable, and funny. It's amazing how she can still be funny after all**

she's gone through, and is still going through."

Lillian Storm, as everyone remembers, is the woman whose former husband, four years ago, absconded with their two-year-old daughter, Bettina.

In response to compliments about the new house, a gift to his bride, Mr. Storm explained that his real gift to her would be the return of her child. In praising what he called her "inimitable courage," he promised to use all his resources—of which there are many—to find Bettina and bring her back.

In the meanwhile, the new Mrs. Storm plans to go on with life in as normal a way as possible. "At least," she says, "I know Bettina is not with some stranger who might harm her."

Very complimentary, Jim thought. Fine words. And "normal," also a very fine word. Let's see what Storm finds out about his new wife. Still, with a mansion and a few million dollars' worth of museum-quality art—how she loved to sound those words—she may be satisfied to leave well enough alone. Or she may not be.

"She's very, very pretty, Jim. Does she really look like the photograph?"

"I guess so."

Buzley, the poor old man who had been so good to her and her pathetic sister, had thought she did.

"She's holding flowers, a sheaf of lilies. This must be a wedding picture."

"Kate, I couldn't care less. Better bring the dogs and the cat in. It's starting to rain."

The sky had opened. A cloudburst poured water as if from a spigot. Restlessly, Jim got up to stand by the window and watch the drenching, furious rain.

Would he ever forget that room in Florence? The sodden woman sprawled on the sofa? *You're such a puritan, Donald. People need to have some fun.* And that is the woman who wants to take my Laura away.

Kate broke the silence. "You need to stop worrying, Jim. You really do."

"You're not making sense. How can I stop when I read something like this?"

"I keep telling you not to search through all these papers and magazines. It's been four years, and in spite of all this stuff, nothing's happened. And nothing will happen if it hasn't by now."

Just then came a pounding at the front door,

so that both of them ran to it. There stood Laura in a state of high excitement, and soaking wet.

"Mom! Mom! I told Jessica you're not dead. She keeps saying, 'Your mother's dead,' and I hit her because you're not dead, and I said I have a mom. And she said, 'You don't even live with that mom. You have a different house.' I hate Jessica."

When Kate had suggested that they should honestly explain some facts to Laura, Jim had argued that she was still too young to understand anything. Now he looked in helplessness to Kate, who spoke boldly.

"You call me 'Mom,' Laura, and that's fine because I love you. But a long time ago, you had another mom, who went away like Rick's daddy. You remember Rick's daddy. I tried to tell you this once, but you forgot."

"Dead is living where all those stones are, where people put flowers?"

Kate, as she stroked Laura's hair, was cheerful. "Yes, that's what it is."

"Rick says his daddy is never going to come back."

"That's true."

"Is that other mom coming back?"

"No. Listen, honey, I'm going to take you upstairs, and I'm going to wrap you in a big towel while I put your clothes in the dryer. Then how about a nice cup of cocoa and cookie while they're drying. Okay?"

So easily had Kate met the crisis, Jim thought, while I almost had a cardiac arrest. She was right, and it is time to think about how I'm going to answer when more questions are asked, as they will be.

"The first thing we have to do is give her a picture of her mother," Kate began one day not long after this event. "I understand that the subject is horrible for you, but, Jim, you have to face facts. It's too queer, too unnatural, for anybody to accept that you have no photograph, no mementos at all of your dead wife, nothing. Prepare yourself as Laura gets older for all sorts of questions: Rebecca's maiden name, her family, where they came from and where they lived, and where Rebecca went to school. Had she any brothers or sisters? Does Laura have any cousins? And what did Rebecca like to eat, did she like music, did she have a job, or did she play tennis—a hundred details. How did you meet her, did you have a big wedding?"

Jim groaned. "In short, write a biography."

"Yes. And memorize it, and never make a slip. Anybody in Laura's position would want descriptions. Laura's already sharp, and she'll grow sharper."

Jim groaned again. "I don't know how to start inventing this life."

"I'll help you. When I go to Atlanta next month, I'll get a photograph from some framing shop. I'll find a young woman with dark hair like Laura's."

"And where did we live? And are there any pictures of a house, or of Rebecca and me together? Or pictures of anything? There's no end to it. Don't you see how impossible it is?"

"All right. When you were practicing law, you must have tried some cases that seemed impossible. Lawyers have to twist plenty of stuff out of shape, I'm sure."

"They have holes to patch up, that's true, but they don't invent things out of whole cloth."

"In this situation, you'll just have to invent."

"I feel horrible. I can't describe it. How can I look Laura in the face while I'm spewing out these lies?"

"What choice is there? Listen, I just remembered something that really did happen. I knew some people who put everything they owned in a storage warehouse while they served in the Vietnam War. The warehouse had a fire, and all their things were destroyed. So that's your story."

Jim considered. "All right. It's far-fetched, but

it happened once, so I suppose it could happen twice."

"Let me handle it. I'm already constructing the whole thing in my head. The reason you know nothing about her parents is that Rebecca was an immigrant from Russia, or anyplace. Her family got caught up in the troubles. For all you know, they died before she did."

When Kate had an idea, she pursued it just as she was pursuing her work in the greenhouse. There was no stopping her.

"They were educated people, so that's how she came to study English. But she wanted to perfect the language, and that's why she came here. She hoped to go home eventually and teach English there, but then she met you."

In a pocket park, where she was eating an orange and I almost dropped my papers, he thought, and blurted, "I don't want to talk it over. I don't want to think about it."

"Laura is already asking questions," Kate said quietly. "She wanted to know, for instance, why we live in separate houses. Other daddies and moms live in the same house."

He knew very well what Kate wanted. But for her inherent pride, the subject would have come up again now. However, she had made her point once and was not about to repeat it. She wanted marriage, and he owed it to her. The pattern of their lives, afternoon meetings in his cottage or a rare night in her house when Rick and Laura had both been invited to the Scofield grandchildren's for the night, were highly unsatisfactory to them both. It was well over a year since she had been widowed, and marriage now would be seemly enough. But he was afraid for her.

When he glanced at the newspaper, still spread out before them, she followed his glance. There stood Mrs. Arthur Storm in full, smiling glory. And here next to him stood Kate Benson in her own true glory, worth ten thousand Lillians.

His thoughts came and went. The debts were already half paid off. The farm belonged safely to Kate and Rick, and he would keep it so, for it was their inheritance, not his. He himself could live well enough on his salary. Then if there ever should be any penalty to be paid in his future, it would be his penalty alone. It was feasible, and yet—

"If I could only be sure that you would never suffer because of me," he murmured, thinking aloud. Yet in being so protective of her, was he not also hurting her?

The crinkle at the corners of her eyes told him that she was smiling inside her head. "So? If you could, what would you do?"

"I'd have a little wedding next month on the lawn, right out there."

"Then let's do it, Jim. You can't go on living in fear like this. I'm not afraid, and you shouldn't be. We'll make a proper home for the four of us. You owe it to Laura, and to hell with Mrs. Arthur Storm."

⁂

Mr. and Mrs. James Fuller stood on the grass in the shade receiving the congratulations of their guests. In a lovely kind of fog, as if he had been drinking champagne—without having yet had a drop—everything blended before Jim's eyes: the day, clear green and gold, Kate in something creamy with her bright hair hanging loose to her waist, Rick important in his dark blue blazer, and Laura in a long pink dress that he had himself selected from a catalog. The guests, all obviously approving, were laughing and chattering. There was an astonishing number of them, too, mostly from the town, where as Kate said, he had made more good friends in his few years there than many people make in a lifetime.

He looked over at the freshly painted house. Indoors a reasonable prosperity had prepared it for the new united family. The cramped desks in what had been the living room had been moved to the spacious cottage, where Kate and he had separate offices. The ceiling of Laura's room had been papered like the sky, blue with summery

white clouds. He had not yet looked at the bedroom where he was to sleep with Kate tonight.

She had asked him whether he wanted to have
a look at it. "Soft colors," she said, "pine green
and peach. I hope you'll like it." And she had
had a worried little frown which, laughing, he
had kissed away.

"Oh, I'll like it," he had said. "I'll like it very
much."

Late in the evening after everyone had departed, the now-united family went up to sleep
for the first time in the big house. For a few minutes, Jim stepped out and stood on the porch.
The moonless night was silver, and utterly still.
Not a leaf moved. And a perfect peace de-
scended, a peace such as he had not felt since
leaving New York, which seemed a century ago.
Perhaps indeed he had never felt such a peace.

"What a day," Kate whispered, coming up behind him. "What are you feeling? What are you
thinking?"

"All day I've been feeling as though I had just
won a long battle. I'm thinking of a quotation."

"You and your quotations! Tell me."

"It's from Stonewall Jackson, something like
this. 'Let us cross the river and rest in the shade.'
Well, I've just crossed the river, and now we will
rest."

# Chapter 16

There were times when Laura liked to be alone in her room. She liked to look around at the things she owned, the pink bathrobe hanging so that it would show on the inside of the open door, the jewelry box that played music when you opened it, and, most important, the diary that Dad gave her last year for her ninth birthday.

Red leather, with a key, it lay right out on her desk. And if she locked it, nobody would be able to read her secret thoughts. She often liked to read what she had written, as if it were a story in a book.

*I love to read. There are all sorts of things in books that can make you forget your troubles, like the broken finger that hurt so awfully. And I re-*

member I read the story about Eskimos and igloos that almost made the hurt go away. I read every day when I come home, except sometimes when I feel sleepy, I don't read. I stretch out on the floor and look at the beautiful ceiling with white clouds on it. Then I can think about the summer when you float on the lake and look up at the sky. You wonder what is really there, in the sky. Doesn't there have to be something? I wonder whether Felicia the cat, who lies beside me on the rug, ever thinks about things like that. Dad says that of course animals think, but we don't know what they think.

People always ask why I named my cat Felicia, but it's a secret, and I don't tell them. Felicia is Rick's girlfriend's name, and one day I wanted to make him angry. Only he wasn't angry. It's funny how he's gotten to act like a grown-up since he's been in junior high school. When I say things, he sort of looks at me the way grown-ups do, as if they were thinking how cute you are, you little kid. But sometimes I get angry because I am not a little kid, I'm ten. But I don't really mind because Rick is really my friend, even more than some of my best friends like Megan and Julia in school.

One day I saw him naked. I didn't know he was in his room, and I opened the door. I don't know exactly why I went in. I think I was

*looking for the candy that he hides. He's not sup-
posed to eat it because it makes pimples when
you're in junior high school. I hope I never get
pimples. He jumped and grabbed a towel, but I
saw. It looked funny. I guess he told Mom because she said I should remember to knock on
doors before I go in. You know better, she said.
But she said I shouldn't feel bad about seeing
Rick. It wasn't bad, only impolite to look at people when they have no clothes on. So I don't
think much about it anymore, only sometimes,
because it did look funny.*

*Rick and I do good things together. Now that
I'm ten, I don't have to ride the pony anymore.
Dad promised me a horse, and we're going soon
to look at a small mare that will fit me, or I'll fit
her. But we're going to keep my pony. He has
lived here all his life, so now he should stay and
just enjoy himself in the pasture. Dad says an
animal isn't a piece of furniture that you can sell
or give away without hurting its feelings.*

*Dad says that the white rabbit who stays on
our front lawn eating grass most of the time was
probably an Easter present to somebody who
didn't want it anymore and just dropped it off
along the road. It doesn't play with all the brown
rabbits that are wild here. Maybe they don't like
him, but I do. I miss him when I don't see him*

*for a few days, and I hope he hasn't been run over or eaten by a dog.*

*When I get my horse, I'd like a pinto like Mom's. Then I'll go riding when everybody else takes the long trail up through the hills. I was there once when I rode with Dad on his horse. I was very small then, but I remember it. When you get to the top, you can see a big waterfall, far down. It makes you dizzy to look so far down. You can't get there to swim. It's too wild. But you can tie the horses and have a picnic on top of the hill.*

*I like the things we do. A lot of my friends don't do the things we do. Rick says so too, about some of his friends. Last Saturday we planted two magnolia trees. One is Rick's, and one is mine. They look like little sticks now, but one day they'll be enormous and have pink flowers. Rick and I are responsible for them. We have to water them and put mulch, that's a silly word, around them. They haven't grown much yet, but Dad says we just planted them last Saturday.*

*The only thing we don't do is, we never go anywhere far away. It's because Dad hates big cities. Julia's family are all going to go to Washington in spring vacation to see the monument and the cherry blossoms, and maybe the president. I wonder whether they'll talk to him or maybe just peek at him over the fence. Anyway, I want to go too, but Dad won't and I am really angry. Really angry. Mom says I shouldn't be. She says Dad is the kindest man in the world, and I guess that's true. Yes, it is true.*

*Mom is very nice, too. She is hardly ever angry about anything. Dad isn't either. I mean really angry, like some people's parents who make them cry. Sometimes Julia Scofield's father is mean. He yells at her. So then she goes to her grandpop and grandma's house, and they make her feel better. Her grandpop is a doctor and he likes me. He says he knew me when I was two years old. I don't remember. He says that was when Dad brought me from Philadelphia. Once I heard Dad say to Mom that Dr. Scofield talks too much. But I don't think so. He tells jokes, and I like him. I wish I had a grandpop.*

*I wish all my family wasn't dead like my mother. I have her picture on my desk right next to this diary. I look at her picture a lot. I think she looks like somebody on TV. She has dark hair like mine. It's funny to think that she's the one who grew me inside her, and I don't even know her. Sometimes I wish I had red hair like Mom because I love Mom and I can't love Mother because I don't know her. But some days anyway I think about her, and I do wish I knew her.*

# Chapter 17

When in a warm wind the browning leaves rustle to the ground, dusk comes early. Crickets are singing and birds are silent. In another month at this hour, the leaves will have rained from the trees, and it will be too dark to be reading on the front porch.

So Jim reflected as he sat with his tired legs stretched out and the book fallen open. This tiredness, though, was the healthy kind that comes after a long day well spent.

In the far fields, since early morning, the men had been planting seedling firs, while on the near side of the creek, they had been shipping young firs. With a nice combination of thankfulness and pride, Jim had watched the products of the farm being loaded onto trucks and driven away.

Now Rick was following them down the

road. Jim had to smile. Ever since the boy had gotten his driver's license last month, he never missed an opportunity to use it.

They were going to miss him. Seniors in high school, now almost in college, were really wishing time away. At least most of them were, and it was entirely true of Rick. At dinner last night he had been full of information about the Appalachians, how millions of years ago these round, green mountains had been as high, rugged, and icy as the Alps, a fact that Jim had not known. No doubt Rick was going to be some sort of naturalist, a lover of the land as his father had been. And wistfully, Jim recalled his afternoons as umpire at the baseball games, the football games he had watched on the high school playing field, and the chess he had played with Rick on winter evenings.

Yesterday they were children, today they are adolescents, and tomorrow they will be their independent selves. Speaking of younger adolescents, he thought, surely his Laura was a textbook example! Thirteen now, and feeling very grown up, she often made droll remarks that brought a chuckle to Jim. And sometimes, as was only to be expected, she tried his patience.

"What are you thinking?" asked Kate.

So light were her steps, he had not heard her coming behind him. "Thinking about the kids.

Sit down. I miss you when you're not next to me. What have you been doing?"

"Preparing seed for next spring and jotting down some ideas for a catalog. It's high time for us to advertise, Jim. We need publicity. We need to settle on a name. Foothills Farm—how does that sound? It just popped into my head a few minutes ago. I've been thinking that we should go someplace for real advice. Maybe to Atlanta, or who knows, even New York. What do you think?"

"About the name? Not bad. Foothills Farm. But as to going to get advice, it won't be me who does it, Kate. I'll talk to anybody on the telephone as long as needed, but I won't be seen."

"You're still so sure about that?"

"You know I am, and that's final. What's Laura doing?"

"The last I saw, she was on the telephone, as usual."

He laughed. "What on earth can she talk about with those girls, whom she sees in school five days a week?"

"Darling, you were never a thirteen-year-old girl, so you wouldn't understand."

"Oh, there you are," said Laura, banging the screen door. "I've been looking all over for you, Mom."

"I was at my desk in the cottage up till five minutes ago. What's on your mind?"

"Well, I'm really upset. Everybody's going someplace during Christmas vacation, and we're not."

"Everybody is?"

"Well, not everybody. But Susan is going to visit her cousins in Denver, and they'll go skiing. Beth is going to Florida, where they have palm trees, and you can swim in the ocean. Gerry and Jane Parks are going to New York, and we're not going anywhere. We never do."

"I have an idea," Jim said slowly, while Laura's blue eyes, those alert blue eyes so disconcertingly like Lillian's, were turned up toward him. "Why don't the three of you pick a place and take a few days off during winter vacation? I'd like to take time off myself, but there's so much to do here that I don't see how I can. I'd love to have you all do it, though. I really would."

"You always say that, Daddy. You have to go, too. You're always too busy. Everybody's father goes. Why can't you? You have to."

"I told you I really have too much to do here. This is a very big, busy place."

"Other fathers have busy places. Susan's father is a lawyer, and he's very busy."

"Well, that's not quite the same, Laura."

"Lawyers are very busy. You don't know anything about them. How would you know without being one yourself?"

You might almost, if you wanted to, find this amusing. She was so in earnest, and so logical in her arguments.

At this point, Kate intervened. "I'll tell you what, Laura. We'll take a short trip for starters. You and I will go to Atlanta. I have some errands there, and you need a winter jacket. We'll have a good time."

"It's not the same as all of us going someplace. Why can't Daddy go to Atlanta with us?"

"Because," Kate said, firmly now, "because he can't. He knows what he can and can't do. You mustn't bother him like this."

Funny how she listens to Kate every single time, Jim thought, and only most of the time to me; she knows she can wrap me around her little finger, but she also knows when she can't.

"Can I go to the drugstore for a cone? Jennie called and asked whether I'd like to. She's driving some kids to the village. Can—I mean, may I go?"

"Of course. Have a double. Go ahead," Jim said.

As soon as Laura was out of hearing, Kate asked the question he expected her to ask. "Can you really not go to Atlanta with us, Jim? Whom will you meet in a crowd so far from where you used to live? You hear how much it would mean to Laura."

"Maybe I'm being unreasonable, I don't know. Anyway, it's getting too dark to read. I'm going inside."

"I haven't told you," Kate began when they settled in their usual chairs, "but Laura looked up Philadelphia on the map. She wants to see the house where you lived when she was born. I'm only telling you this now because she's going to ask you about it."

"Oh my God, I wish she would drop the whole subject once and for all."

"An odd thing happened, too. Rick heard her, and you know he's so grown up and hardly ever quarrels with her anymore, but he got really angry. He yelled at her: 'Will you shut up and stop bothering your father about that? Stop complaining, I'm sick of listening to it.' I suppose you are, too, Jim, but she's only a child, a very dear one, too."

"Yes," he murmured.

"I wish you could be less fearful. I wish for your own sake. It's not that we have to take trips, of course not. I don't give a hoot what other people do, and anyway, Laura's only pointing out a very few. Most people in town can't afford to go places every time there's a school vacation. No, it's your fear that makes me sad. It's eleven years now since you came here, and you see that nothing's happened, even when they had those photos on the milk cartons again last June. You haven't committed a murder. There's a limit to the money they'll spend on your kind of case."

"Don't be impatient with me, Kate."

"Darling, I'm not."

"It's because of her and you that I'm so terribly afraid every time there's talk of leaving this place even for a day. I never thought of myself as being especially cowardly, so it's strange that I can't get rid of the fear."

"Cowardly? That's the last thing anyone could accuse you of. So let's drop the subject. Read your book."

Such is the miracle of books that on a quiet evening in a familiar room, you are not there at all; you are in Tibet, or perhaps at the South Pole, struggling on an icebound ship. Then the clock chimes, a door slams, and you are back in the room.

"Who's that?" Jim asked.

"Just Rick."

"Where's Laura?"

"She came in half an hour ago."

"Then let's lock up. It's been a long day."

When he passed Laura's room, he almost always remembered not to look in. That dreadful photograph on her desk was in the line of vision.

Obviously, she could see it all the while she was doing her homework. He wondered what her thoughts might be. As for him, that young woman with the luxurious dark hair and perfect teeth always seemed to be grinning. He wished that something would happen to the picture, that the dogs would chew it up, or that somebody would steal it.

Oh, thank all that's holy for the gift of Kate, for her strength, her honesty, her laughter, her soft skin, her lips, and her open arms. So he went in to where she waited and firmly closed their door.

# Chapter 18

The desk stood between the two windows, which overlooked in the middle distance the stable and the barns, while behind them rose the hills. Upon the desk lay a solid geometry textbook, a photograph in a narrow mahogany frame, and a thick red leather diary.

Laura flipped through the pages. Now, at fifteen, she was amused at her ten-year-old self, and even slightly embarrassed by her present self. She was thinking that there was something so *adolescent* about pouring out all this *emotion* onto paper. Probably she ought to give up the diary altogether.

On the other hand, was it not also an *adult* thing to be doing? Think of all the famous people who had kept diaries, people one read about in the history books. Perhaps they, too, felt more comfortable writing down things they wouldn't want to talk about.

There are times, she thought, when on a perfectly ordinary day like this one, a good day, when I look down as usual and can watch Mom giving the dogs a bath in the tin tub, or I see Rick—he likes to be called Richard now that he's in college—coming back from the fields with Dad, times when I feel a quick, sharp sadness. It doesn't happen to me very often, but it happens. I suppose they've told me all they can and they must be sick of my questions: Who was the other half of me?

I've been seeing this picture for so long that I can see it in the dark. I think I look somewhat like her, but not really. Her teeth show more than mine do when I smile. I certainly don't look like Dad. What do I know about her? Not much, mostly that she liked to paint, although she wasn't an artist. She would have liked to be an artist. She was very smart, Dad says. He says he's sorry he doesn't have a whole lot to tell me because it must be hard for me to get so few answers. The fact is that they weren't together very long. He met her, married her right away, then I was born the same year, and two years later, she died. That makes only three years, or a little more. What a terribly sad story.

But still I think, if you lived with a person

even for only a month, you would know more than Dad knows. Not everything, but something not so vague. He only tells things about how she was a good dancer and played tennis and could speak fairly good French. What I want to know is: What was she *like*?

Mom says that when people you care about die, it hurts you to talk about them. You don't want to be reminded. But I don't think that's true. Rick—Richard—talks about Uncle Clarence pretty often. He and Mom even tell funny stories about things that happened, and they both laugh. Yet I know they loved him. And I remember when Coco, our springer spaniel, got sick and died, how for a long time nobody wanted to think of her. But lately when I speak of her, I remember how sweet she was, how happy she was in our house, and then I'm not so sad anymore. So is it possible that Dad didn't love my mother, and that's why he doesn't tell me things? My friend Emily's father and mother got divorced, and I'm very sure that if either of them should die, the other one wouldn't be sad at all, and wouldn't want to answer questions.

Or maybe it's the other way around. It's possible that Dad loved Rebecca more than he loves Mom. It's easy to see that he loves Mom, but you can't measure love in pounds and ounces, so maybe if he did love Rebecca more, he doesn't want to hurt Mom's feelings by mentioning her. But then, he really could tell me in private if he wanted to.

Once when I was about eleven and didn't know any better, I asked Mom an awful question: Did Dad love Rebecca more than he loves you? But I don't think I hurt her feelings very much because I remember she only told me very quietly that you can love two people in the same way. So maybe that's true. I'll never know because he surely won't ever tell me that.

He won't tell me anything about my ancestors, either. People around here are always talking about their ancestors. Julia Scofield has a great-great—I don't know how many greats—grandfather who fought at Gettysburg. Richard says the Bensons have lived on this property for two hundred years, since the time of George Washington.

Dad says he really has told me a lot. He's told me about his mother and the farm, and how he learned about his father's death on D Day in 1944. But I want to hear about the other half of myself. He keeps saying that he would tell me more if he could, that they lived in Europe and there's no way he can find out anything. It's almost as if I've been adopted. That I could understand, but this is different. Sometimes, although I know it doesn't make any sense, I feel a little angry. Not angry at Dad because I guess he can't help it, but just because it seems sort of unfair.

Even though I hardly ever mention all this to Richard, I think he understands it better than anybody else does. I think he knows that I have these moods. I don't know what makes me so sure, but I am. In some ways, he reminds me of Dad, sort of calm and serious, but he's much handsomer than Dad. Of course, he's a lot younger, nearer my age, so he can understand me better. I really miss him so much now that he's away at the university. Sometimes I think this is the beginning of love. Maybe I already am in love with him.

Once I put my arms around him and made him kiss me on the lips, the first time I ever kissed anybody that way, and I haven't done it with anybody else since. I remember he put my arms down and looked sort of scared.

"We mustn't," he said. "You're only fifteen."

Maybe he meant that when I'm older, we can do it. I hope so. We're not brother and sister, so we could get married if we wanted to, and the more I think of it, the more I want to. He will be a wonderful husband, very loving.

He wants to take care of the environment, polluted rivers, deforestation, and stuff like that.

He just joined the Sierra Club. I'm sure he'll live on this farm all his life. It's his inheritance. Dad teases him, calling him Daniel Boone. You can see that Dad loves him.

Richard says that Dad was a big help to him when Uncle Clarence died. Dad is very, very helpful to a lot of people in town. A lot of people come to him for advice because he is very smart. At first I did not realize that he helped me get my volunteer job at the hospital. Probably I would have gotten it anyway, but I got it faster because he is on the Board, whatever that means. I really like the job. It's quite important. I wear a pink uniform, which is professional-looking when I take the book cart around to the patients' rooms, or when I read to little kids on the children's floor.

Sometimes I think I might like to be a doctor. I get As in science, so maybe I would be one of those people who find out about cancer, that killed poor Uncle Clarence and my mother. Dad says it's possible. He told me that I have a very keen mind, and that's why he bought the microscope for me, so I can see things deep inside. It's interesting how an ant or a leaf looks so different under the microscope. Yes, I really think I might be a doctor if I work very hard. Dad says it's amazing what you can do if you try.

# Chapter 19

This is my last week at home. Next week, I'll be in the Midwest on the other side of the Mississippi, and I'll be gone for four years. I don't quite know how I feel. I'm excited, curious, and a little sad. Some of everything, I guess, filled as I am with random thoughts.

Dad really didn't want me to go anywhere in the Midwest. Actually, he would be happiest if I had chosen someplace in the South, near home, or if not that, at least some beautiful place like California. For some reason he didn't like the Midwest. But two of the girls from my class are going where I'm going, and that will be great.

The days are noticeably shorter now, but even so, you can tell it's summer's end by the locusts, drilling and rattling in the trees. I'll remember *that. I'll remember frogs croaking in the spring. You wouldn't imagine, in the life I've led in a quiet place like this farm and this town where I've gone to school, that there would be so much to remember.*

*Yet when I think about it, the days here have been very full. People are all remarking how the town has grown. Dad says he can hardly believe the changes since he arrived here fewer than twenty years ago. They've built a new spur to the main highway, and the mall is only six miles beyond that. You can hardly park on Main Street, especially on weekends. There's a new movie theater, really nice, with three screens and comfortable seats. There are at least fifteen new shops, a fancy hairdresser who gave me a great cut, and a gourmet food shop. The hospital has almost doubled in size, and somebody has built a beautiful new inn to accommodate people who are visiting patients.*

*Richard says Dad was the mover and shaker when they built the children's wing that brought so many new doctors to the hospital. I'm proud. I heard so much mention of him when I worked in the lab last summer doing slides.*

*"No backwoods town anymore," Richard said yesterday when we went in for the summer fair. It was our last day together until Thanksgiving, and we made the most of it. We had lunch in one*

*of the new restaurants, and it was fabulous. They made us chocolate soufflés, the first time I ever had one. It was an awfully expensive place, but Richard said this was a celebration for me and my going away.*

*When we got home, we saddled the horses and took a long ride up to the lookout, where we tethered them and sat down in our special spot above that stupendous waterfall. There's something mysterious about that spot. You can be having an interesting or even a hilarious conversation, and then suddenly a wistful thought interrupts it. Richard said thank goodness we live far enough away from the town so that this place will never be spoiled. The town isn't likely to spread in our direction because of the hills and all the big places like ours that people will probably never want to sell. I know Dad and Mom would never think of selling. I call Richard a hillbilly, too. He said he's glad to be one, and I agree because I love him just the way he is.*

*Yes, I truly, truly love him, and not as a brother. We were standing on the cliff ready to mount and ride home, when we kissed. We haven't done it more than three or four times that I can remember. There is always a feeling like a shock when we do, and I don't want to stop. I can tell he doesn't want to, either. And today, as on those other times, he let go of me.*

*"You're too young," he said, which is hardly true. "They trust us, Laura."*

*I know that, and I know he is right. He talks very wisely.*

*"Besides, you're going away, and you'll meet someone else."*

*But there he is wrong. I am not going to meet anyone else. If any two people can ever be perfect together, we are those two.*

# PART
# THREE

*Tornado*
1996

# Chapter 20

❦

Diary number four, bound like the earlier ones in red leather, lay on the desk, again between two windows, these overlooking the rolling grounds of the university. Above it hung a vertical row of photographs: Dad and Mom stood together on the front porch, Richard was on horseback, and Rebecca wore the only expression she had ever shown to Laura, her charming smile.

One other picture in the room was a large framed snapshot of Laura and Gilbert Maples taken on the day a few months ago when they had, albeit quite informally, acknowledged to each other their engagement. They both looked as if they had been laughing. While his light hair was windblown, hers hung long and smooth in a ponytail. His brown eyes smiled. She always thought of them as twinkling, as if he had a big secret that nobody could ever guess.

Next year they would be graduating, he from the law school, and she from the college, with medical school yet to come. It was all like a dream, she thought as she studied the photograph. This was one of those days when everything from the bright weather to the A on the biochemistry exam was perfect. And having a sudden urge to write in the diary, she began.

*When I read back what I wrote three years ago, I can see a tremendous change in myself. Is it merely the natural difference between the teens and twenty plus, or is it the fact that I am so far from home, forced to grow up because I have no dad and no mom to shelter me? But to be fair, they did much more than shelter me; they pushed me gently ahead on the way they knew I wanted to take. When I think back over those days, I clearly see how I was helped.*

*Dad got me the summer job in Dr. Barrett's office. I didn't do much there, but I looked and listened. So many people have helped me. The surgeon who pulled out my wisdom teeth gave me some articles about oral surgery because I was curious. Dr. Scofield wrote that wonderful recommendation for college. Mrs. Bondi, the chemistry teacher, and so many more, did the same. People are still helping me. When I volunteered to work in the university hospital talking to cancer patients, Dr. O'Rourke let me watch an operation; I thought I would be horrified, but I wasn't. I was fascinated. Then there was Professor Reich, who praised my paper on bioethics. He's promised to have it quoted in his article—quoted with my name on it!*

*I am so lucky. When I'm feeling superstitious, which I don't feel very often, I wonder whether all these things are too good to last. Gil says that's absolute nonsense. He has so much practical common sense. You have a legal mind, I tell him. I feel his strength. I felt it the first day we met. I didn't realize then how unheard-of it is for a student in law school even to notice an undergraduate. But as they say, something happened between us. And it's still happening wherever we are, in the cafeteria, on a hike, at the movies, or in bed—especially in bed.*

*I remember when I was in love with Richard. Now and then I feel a touch of guilt about him. It's not that any definite words were ever spoken, but hadn't our feelings been strong enough, it seems, to warrant some sort of mention now? On the other hand, maybe not. I still love him, but not in any way compared with the way I feel about Gil, or in any way I can easily describe. Maybe an English major could do it, but language is definitely not my field.*

*One thing I can say, though: Different as those two men are from each other, each of them reminds me of Dad. Of course it's true that women generally, without even realizing it, choose men who remind them of their fathers. Not one of these three, Dad, Gil, or Richard, is really like the others, but each is sensitive, determined, wise, and kind.*

When Laura closed the red book, she locked it and put it away. Someday, no doubt, she would read what she had written and see herself through the glass of distance much as she now could see her ten-year-old self. Oh, if you could witness the future . . .

She smiled, yawned, and having moved to the armchair, laid her head back. The day had been long, and the air was heavy with the scent of oncoming spring, not to mention the scent of Mom's gardenia plant. Mom had provided this chair and had dressed the bed with a flowered chintz comforter and pillows; lovingly, she had adorned the stark little room for her daughter.

"Dr. Fuller, I presume?" The door was ajar,

but Gil always knocked before opening. "Loafing again, while I've been in the library since two o'clock?"

"And I've been in the biology lab."

"Hey, what smells so good in here?"

"The gardenia. It arrived today. Mom raises them. That's her department, fancy shrubs and stuff."

"I liked her that time she came here. She's an interesting lady. And her son sounds interesting, too. I've never known anybody who has a degree in forestry."

"You'll like Richard. I guarantee."

"Was there ever anything between you?"

"Not really. What makes you ask?"

"Oh, a guy that good-looking, at least in the picture, and not related, growing up with a stunning girl. It's very possible, isn't it?"

"Anything's possible, darling. But I happen to be your girl, not anyone else's."

"Move over, the chair's big enough for two. My God, you've got the bluest eyes I've ever seen."

"They're my mother's, I'm told."

Gil turned toward the wall where Rebecca smiled, and then, looking back at Laura, shook his head, declaring that Laura did not resemble her at all.

"You must be your father's daughter."

"Well, you'll meet him when you come down to visit during spring break. Then you can decide for yourself."

"Has he never visited since you came here?"

"No, he doesn't like to travel. Doesn't like leaving the farm."

"A typical farmer. A man of few words? I always picture them like that."

"What on earth can a New Yorker like you know about farmers? No, he's quite the opposite. He's a historian, a scholar, even an orator. I've heard him at town meetings, and I hear him at home."

"How did he happen to end up on a farm?"

"I guess he just liked it. He grew up on a farm, in Maine."

"Well, I'm looking forward to the visit. He needs to know that I'm a responsible man. In the meantime, tomorrow's Sunday, so what about a five-mile hike, a few laps in the pool, and then a fancy dinner at Romeo's?"

"Romeo's? Hey, listen. It's not *my* father who's on Wall Street. I've got to watch my money."

"What? The daughter of Foothills Farm?"

"Dad's not the owner. Mom is, and he gets a salary."

"I was going to treat you, anyway. I'm old-

fashioned, behind the times. Haven't you noticed that I don't let women pay?"

"I've noticed that you're the sweetest man in
the world."

"I am? Fine. Show me how sweet I am. Get
up from this chair and lock the door."

# Chapter 21

"That oak you see over there by the fence," Jim said, "is a hundred years old at least, Gilbert. We're mostly oak and pine in this part of the country. Next time you visit, we ought to take you up for a day's outing through the Great Smokies. You'll see pristine forests, over half a million acres of them. You'll see boulders big as a small house, left over from the Ice Age, things you don't see where you come from."

"I hear you don't get up to where I come from very often, Mr. Fuller."

"I'm afraid not. I never cared much for traveling, and there's too much work to do here, anyway."

"But you have been in New York, haven't you? You must have visited when you lived in Philadelphia. It's only a stone's throw away."

"Well, I have, but mostly just passing through."

They were all sitting on the porch after supper, Laura feeling at ease with the quiet conversation and happy to be proud of her home. It was almost amusing to contrast this weekend visit to her visit with Gilbert's family in their apartment fourteen floors above an avenue crammed with cars. His were likable people, very bright, and most cordial, but so *quick* in their ways, and hence so different from the unhurried manner of her life at home.

"It's too bad Richard isn't here. He could tell you some interesting things about this part of the country. He's taking a short seminar in forestry and couldn't come home this week."

"I'd like to meet him."

"Why don't you take a walk to the overlook while it's still light?" Kate suggested. "That's really a spectacle, especially just before sunset. It's a bit more than two miles round trip, but worth it."

Gilbert, always eager to see something new, got up from the rocking chair. "Good idea. Let's do it."

"They're great people, your family," he said as they climbed the hill. "I admire their enthusiasm. I like them, and I hope they like me."

"Of course they do. Why shouldn't they?"

"I don't know. Your dad has mentioned

Richard so often that I was wondering whether there was anything . . . well, whether he had any reason to think that you and he . . . that he was in love with you, or you with him."

"I was when I was fifteen, but there's nothing left of that now. In fact, I was hoping you and he would meet this week," Laura said, although that was not quite the truth. She would have been uncomfortable sitting at table with these two men at the same time. Richard had known her most intimate thoughts. . . .

She laughed. "Richard is a wonderful person, but sometimes it seems that all he thinks about are the environment, conservation, trees, and animal rights."

"Then I'm glad. I don't want him to be thinking of you or you to be thinking about anybody but me. Those are my orders."

Gil makes light, she thought, when his heart's full. It seemed as if with every passing day she learned something new about him. And reaching upward, she stroked his cheek.

"Your eyes, Laura. Your grave eyes that I love."

Hand in hand they walked, scarcely speaking. The air was fragrant with pine. A fox streaked across the path and scurried into the crackling underbrush. At the final resting point they stopped and gazed, she to whom the sight was one of her first memories, and he who had never seen it before, equally in awe. Five hundred dangerous feet below them in the chasm, the waterfall plunged into the stream. In the distance between the horizon and the mountains lay a far blue haze.

"So those are the Great Smokies," Gil whispered. "Aptly named. Beautiful. Beautiful."

"We're miles away from them, though you wouldn't think so. This is only hill country where we live."

"And you love your hill country."

"It gets in your blood, as Dad says."

"I can see how it might."

"Let's start back. It'll be dark in ten minutes. We should have brought a flashlight. Dad put one in my hand, and I forgot to take it."

"He's a remarkable man. Sometimes he talks like a farmer, and then when we were discussing that spy case in Washington, he sounded like a lawyer, like one of my professors."

"People often say that about him. People on all the boards he's on, at the hospital, and the Board of Ed, and goodness knows how many others."

"They go well together, he and your mom."

"Oh, they do. But how can you tell after only two days?"

"I can't explain how. It's something I sense in

people. I don't mean I'm some sort of nut who reads tea leaves, but I have been right a lot of times. Wrong, too, I suppose." Gil frowned. "I think your dad is a worrier. Am I right?"

"Oh, definitely. But with a huge responsibility here—we've just added nine hundred acres to the place—I guess it's only natural."

"He's probably worried about you, too, my lady."

"Me? Whyever should he worry about me?"

"Because you're a treasure, and people watch over their treasures."

Laura could not have explained why, when packing for these two days at home, she had put the diary into her suitcase, but there it was on the table in her room. Nor could she have explained why, after getting ready for bed and about to turn off the light, she suddenly crossed the room, unlocked the red box, and began to write.

*So many times I start the page with the words, It is all a dream. Those are the times when everything in my life is going so well, that I feel as if I don't deserve it. I see so much suffering when I volunteer at the hospital. People are not only sick, but so often they have no love, no fam-*

*ily, no one to care about them, which is, I think, worse than having to worry about next month's rent. But then, what can I know when I have so much love and no worries about rent or anything else?*

*It is so good to see how Gil and Dad get along. They seem to have so much to say to each other, as if their minds run in the same groove. Although, it did bother me a little when Dad, very tactfully it's true, made that remark in private to me about love at first sight. When I told him how that happened to Gil and me at the very same moment, he said, "I don't believe in it. Maybe sometimes it happens, but I still don't believe in it."*

*Was he talking about himself? And if so, whom does he mean, Rebecca or Kate? But he is obviously so contented with Kate that he must have meant Rebecca, mustn't he?*

*It has always puzzled me to sense that sadness when her name is spoken. Or perhaps it is not sadness, but something else, something mysterious and vague.*

*Sometimes, now that medical school is only a year away, I think about my ultimate choice of a specialty and wonder about psychiatry. Often, I believe, I can tell when people are hiding their true feelings behind their ordinary, pleasant behavior, their earnestness, or their hilarity. In the library, I came across a fascinating book, The Anatomy of Melancholy, written by a man of the seventeenth century who says a lot of things that Freud wrote about in the twentieth century. Imagine that! Yet the whole thing comes down in a nutshell to the question: Why do we do the things we do?*

*I did not want to bring up the subject this week, and haven't done so in a long time, but eventually I shall tell him about the visit to Philadelphia. Actually, it was Gil's idea, on that weekend we flew to New York to visit his parents. It's only a short train ride, so we went, took a taxi to Spruce Street—or was it Pine? I thought I had the right street number, but not being sure, we tried both streets, and couldn't even find the number, so we gave up. I probably had it wrong. Someday, I'll try again. Although it isn't really that important, I want to see that house.*

*Richard says it's morbid to bother my father like this. He was annoyed with me when I asked Dad where Rebecca was buried. She was cremated, he said, and I shouldn't ask Dad about it. Maybe he is right. It is morbid.*

*The frogs are croaking in the pond behind the stables. It is a nostalgic sound for me, the sound of spring, of being three years old, which takes me as far back as I can remember. I probably don't even remember it then, or if I did hear the sound, I didn't know that frogs were making it. One wonders about the consciousness of a frog; obviously, it has some, but what is it?*

*All a mystery. Love is a mystery. At the table where we have our meals this week, there are so many kinds of love. There is Dad's love for Kate, hers for him, hers for me, mine for her, mine for my father, mine for Gil, and his for me. In time, I do believe and hope that Gil will love, and be loved by, Dad and Mom. And then there is Richard also, dear Richard, now and always.*

*Yes, it is a mystery and a dream. I don't know why I'm spilling this out on paper tonight. If I could go into Gil's room across the hall, I would spill it all out to him, and he would understand. But even though they certainly know that he and I sleep together, Dad and Mom wouldn't want us to do it in their house, so of course I won't go into his room.*

*I am so full of emotion tonight, that I could laugh, or cry, or both. When I look around the room, I remember Felicia my cat, long dead, and how I gave her the name of Richard's junior high school girlfriend. Really, I ought to get a cat tomorrow and name it Felicia to tease him. Every household should have a cat. Yes, that's what I'll do.*

*Now close the book and lock it. Good night.*

# Chapter 22

While Laura was writing in her diary, down the hall, Jim was taking a folded newspaper from a drawer and showing it to Kate.

"Here, look. I clipped this yesterday. I wasn't going to bother you with it, and here I am doing it anyway."

"Don't tell me. Another big event with a name you recognize?"

"Yes, in Venice this time. Well, Venice is a marvel in itself. I've been there twice. But when you add all these names, the money, the fashions of the transatlantic shoppers, and the jewelry, it's a dazzle. It's close to blinding. Look. Read."

For a few minutes, Kate scanned the page, a thick text with half a dozen photographs of partygoers in gondolas and people standing on flowery terraces.

"So what do you think this means?" she asked.

"It's obvious, they're separated. Storm's left her. He's finally had enough, I guess. '. . . *has taken up residence again at his home on Long Island. Lillian Storm and* her companion, *the well-known Swiss sportsman Luigi Di Something, have bought a seventeenth-century country house in Tuscany.'* Well, well. What else is new?"

"He looks pretty old, doesn't he? Well, old for her. She looks about twenty-five."

"Not bad for a woman of forty-eight. But she knows how to get herself in front of the cameras, and how to take the right pose."

"Look at those bracelets. And the lace bodice. She knows how to dress."

Hearing the scorn in his own voice, he said, "All it takes is taste and a few million dollars. She's had her lip plumped up, I notice."

Kate gave him a look of mingled concern and curiosity. "Dear Jim, still bitter?"

"I never was bitter, just furious until I got over it. Now I'm only afraid, still afraid."

"But think about it. Actually, you have less to fear than ever with Storm and his money and his detectives out of the picture. Not that they ever accomplished anything." And Kate, coming close to him, laid her head against his chest. "Your heart. I can hear it pounding. Oh, damn her for coming into your life. How do you explain a woman like her? How does she explain herself?"

"She doesn't, really. She doesn't even try except to say that she gets bored, restless. Nothing and nobody is ever enough for very long."

"I suppose one ought to feel sorry for her. In theory I do, if only because she must be suffering terribly, wanting her child."

"I think of that. You know I do. But I also think about what kind of life Laura would be having right this minute if I hadn't done what I had done."

"Darling, we must stop this. I ask you now to get those New York newspapers and those social columns out of your life."

"I suppose—oh, I don't know. I suppose I'll spend the rest of my time in fear. She always gets what she wants, Kate."

"Well, she hasn't gotten Laura after nearly twenty years of trying, and she's not about to get her. This fear doesn't make sense. There she is, floating around all over Europe, and here you are waiting for her to materialize all of a sudden like a ghost."

A great sigh eased Jim. "I know. I'm sorry. I must admit I don't get this way very often."

"No, only when you read this stuff. Stop thinking about it. You have so much to be thankful for, Jim. Do I need to tell you?"

Indeed, he knew that and she didn't need to tell him. Often, when riding over the flourishing land, or sitting at meals across from Laura, or fully asleep in the warm bed with Kate, he had such a sense of thankful rejoicing that he could have cried out with it.

"Laura has such a fine mind, and such charm. I hear that whenever I meet people in town. She may look like Lillian, but she's your girl. How many times have I said that to you?"

"Many, but I don't mind hearing it again."

"She has her feet on the ground, as they say. You don't need to worry about her. She'll take care of herself."

"I wish she wasn't applying to a medical school in New York."

"That's only because of your bad memories of the city."

"Ah, but they weren't all bad, not by any count." And for a moment, he saw himself walking to the office, feeling as bright as the morning, saw himself at the long conference table with some of the best legal minds in the city, heard himself push back his chair and rise to speak. . . .

"She'll be just fine, Jim. You can't object if that's where she wants to go."

He smiled at Kate. "Okay. You don't have to give me a pep talk."

"All right, I won't. Just one more thing, though: It's good that she'll have a young man like Gilbert in the city. At least we've met him and know who he is."

"Oh, she may have another boyfriend by then. Maybe two more. Who knows?"

Neither he nor Kate had ever put into words their mutual, small hope that Richard and Laura might eventually—but that was so ideal that it was unlikely to happen.

This fellow Gilbert was no Richard, although he certainly seemed to be very decent—his mind was quick and sharp; the opinion that he, as a student, had given about the insurance fraud that was in the news just now was impressive.

"Well, unless she has another boyfriend by next year, we'll have a busy commencement, Laura's from the college and Gilbert's from law school."

"I'm not looking forward to going there in that crowd, Kate."

"What are you talking about?" Kate cried with disbelief in her widened eyes.

"Nothing new. I don't want to go. It's too close to North Dakota. You and Richard should go."

"For heaven's sake, it's four hundred miles from North Dakota! This is really silly, Jim."

"It probably is. But—I don't know—I can't explain—I don't want to go. Let me have a sudden emergency here as my excuse, and when you come back, I'll have gotten a caterer in from town and all Laura's friends and our friends at a marvelous celebration. What's wrong with that?"

"Nothing, except that it's perfectly crazy. Not to go to your daughter's graduation? It's neurotic."

"Well, maybe I am neurotic."

"You are the least neurotic human being I've ever known, James Fuller. Except for this, and you are darn well going up there with Richard and me."

"It's a whole year off. Why talk about it now?"

# Chapter 23

A fresh snow had dusted the ground that morning, sparkling like spilled sugar. Now in the evening it lay here and there in patches with grass poking through it.

Jim had wanted this walk with his daughter. It was the last night of spring break, and they would not be seeing each other until commencement at the end of May. Laura had packing to do; she would be leaving shortly after dawn, so the walk, by mutual unspoken agreement, was very short. Unspoken, too, were their thoughts about another long separation. Who could say how long? It depended upon where life would take her, and who could answer that question? They were both keeping themselves from dwelling on that, thinking rather of the joy, the triumph, and the pride. Each knew from long association what the other was thinking. Or at least could make a pretty good guess: Laura that she had the strength of a solid family behind her and Jim that she had, thank God, known nothing but honor and goodness in this house.

At the front door the dogs went ahead to their beds in the hall. At the top of the stairs Jim gave Laura a kiss and a reminder: *six-thirty on the dot.*

"I forgot to bring my alarm clock."

"Mom or I will knock on your door."

"Dad? You're sure to come to the commencement? I want you to."

"I'll be there. Sleep well."

In his own room he said to Kate, "I'm ashamed of myself. All this emotion! You didn't seem to feel this way when Rick went away to graduate school."

"This is different," she answered gently.

Time, time, he thought, and saw himself as he still so often did, driving a long, dark road with his baby and her stuffed bear on the backseat.

# Chapter 24

"Honors," Jim repeated. "Graduated with highest honors. Summa cum laude."

From the hotel's window in the light of late afternoon, one looked out across a wide avenue to islands of fine old brick on an ocean of spring green that belonged to the university. He was, however, not seeing these; he was seeing, and no doubt would forever see, his Laura wearing cap and gown, coming down the walk in the academic procession that morning.

Kate was smiling at him. "Our Laura," she said.

There was certainly nothing unusual in her use of the word "our," any more than there was in his use of it when speaking of Richard, yet on this particular day, he was moved by the word.

But then, on this particular day, a feather's touch could have moved him.

Kate had begun to struggle with a row of buttons on the back of her dress, so he went over to help her. This was a small enough gesture, taken for granted, yet it, too, seemed to have greater significance at this moment; it was an intimate, a proprietary act, as when she straightened his tie, and from it his thoughts went, as if by inheritance, to the next generation.

In all the crowd and excitement of the day, Richard and Gilbert had not yet seen each other. Have I been having a foolish fantasy about Richard, he asked himself, that in the end there might be a chance for him? Gilbert is still hanging on, not that I have any objection, and not that it would do any good if I did have any. Well, that situation would work itself out by itself, as things do.

"There, you're buttoned. That's a nice dress. We'd better go down. Dinner's at seven, you said? I do wish she hadn't chosen a medical school in New York." And when Kate did not answer, "I know, I've harped on that before, haven't I?"

"You certainly have. Come on, and stop worrying."

He said hastily, "I'm not. I'm not worrying.

I'm glad Gilbert and his parents have their own party, so there'll just be the four of us at the table. It'll be like old times, just the four of us. Let's go."

In the dining room when they looked at each other, each knew very well that they were both thinking the same thing. They made a handsome pair, these two young ones of theirs. Richard, tall and tanned, was fairly unfamiliar in the jacket and tie, an outfit seldom worn at Foothills Farm. Laura's dress was light blue; did it come naturally for a woman to match her dress to her eyes? Jim wondered.

She was unusually vivacious. "Gil's found an apartment for me. It's about halfway between my school and his place. It has two big rooms and a tiny, clean kitchen, all new. Plenty of space for my stuff, computer and everything. And not too expensive, Dad, trust me."

"I always do," Jim said.

He could manage the cost. It would be a fairly tight squeeze, but he spent very little on himself, and he would manage. Through his head now there flashed a reflection of the funds he had regularly put aside for her during her first two years; the sum had not been a small one to begin with, and through all these years, it must have swollen to a figure that he had not even tried to estimate.

What was the use? It was lost and gone. Untouchable.

"Gil's in there. They took a private room," Laura explained, pointing toward the hallway. "They have three tables, an enormous family, all sorts of cousins. They're very close, so they've come from everywhere to see him get his law degree. It's so exciting."

Yes, yes, it had been, walking in to the music of "Pomp and Circumstance" and receiving his law degree . . . so many years ago now. His photograph had turned out well, eyes open, pleasant smile, no toothy grin, the camera just right. Forever lost, that moment, and that photograph, too, ground up in the trash on the last morning.

"I didn't tell you that Gil's had three different offers, from the best firms in New York. The one he's going to does a lot of international law, I think. Paris, London, Rome, you name it. All that traveling! No job for you, Dad."

Oh, he knew. Westminster Abbey, the Arc de Triomphe, the Forum, and much, much more: Cairo, Delhi, another life, another person . . .

Richard was staring at him, or perhaps not staring, for what was there to stare at? Unless there had been some odd expression on his face? Or probably he was only imagining the stare because Richard was saying something to him.

"How does the lobster bisque sound for starters, Jim?"

Ever since Richard had returned to work as assistant supervisor on the farm, he had, at Jim's insistence, stopped calling him "Uncle Jim." Richard was twenty-six, no boy anymore. A "practical idealist," Jim had named him. The woman who got him would be lucky.

"Sounds good to me," he answered, coming to himself. Fits of nostalgia were out of place today. Indeed, he very seldom had any, and most likely was having one now solely *because* Gil had gotten his law degree this morning.

"Yes, let's get to the menu," Kate said promptly. "I don't know about the rest of you, but I'm starved."

She had read his mind. He was sure of it, as he was sure there was mental telepathy between them. And he winked at her: *Sorry. Don't mind me. I'll be happy,* said the wink. *I am happy.*

So they ate, they talked, they had varied opinions about the chief speakers, and took their time and were deep in discussion when Gilbert appeared.

"I haven't seen you people since the procession this morning. I just had to break away from my table to say hello. They're all deep in reminiscences at our party. I haven't seen you all in a while, anyway, especially you, Richard."

"Hello, Gil. Let me steal a chair for you."

How young they were, the three of them, Laura between the two men. And again Jim thought, this could be an interesting situation. One never knew. Once in New York, where no doubt those two would be as good as living together, she might get tired of that, or he might. It happened all the time. Not that he knew much about such things anymore; he had long been away from those situations. Still, human nature didn't change, and being what it was, she might start remembering Richard—

"What did you think about the dean's speech, Mr. Fuller?" Gilbert was deeply earnest. "Frankly, I think he went a little too far when he made that comparison with the situation in Korea."

Jim, who with only half an ear had heard enough to reply intelligently, agreed. "Yes, but also when he went on to analyze the changes in Russia, it seemed to me that he knew exactly what he was talking about. I read his book this winter, and—does anybody see our waiter? We need more wine. Nobody's driving anywhere, so we can—"

"Rolls, too," Kate said. "I love those dark ones. I never see them at home, only in that restaurant when we go to Atlanta."

"Oh, I remember. It was such a lovely day, the

day we bought this dress, Mom. And on the way home we stopped at the kennel you read about and brought Clancy home—"

"When those two women go shopping, you never know what they'll bring back. Whoever thought we needed another puppy?"

A hard hand snapped Jim's shoulder. A hearty voice bellowed into his ear. "Don! Don Wolfe! Where the hell have you been all these years?"

There was a pause, a fraction of an instant in which time stopped.

*Steady now. Very, very steady. This is it. At last. This is it.*

"I'm afraid you've made a mistake," Jim said pleasantly. "That's not my name."

"What? I'd know you anywhere, Don."

"I'm sorry. My name's not Don."

"What the hell! Quit kidding, Don."

"You've made a mistake," Jim repeated, still pleasantly, and raised a forkful of mashed potatoes to his mouth.

"A mistake? Don Wolfe from Carter High, played catcher, Sycamore Street, number eighteen, was it? No, sixteen."

"Please," Jim said firmly now with blood racing cold, or was it hot, and was his face in flames? "You have the wrong man, mister."

The intruder persisted. "Cut it out. This isn't

funny. What the hell do you think you're doing?"

Half laughing, Kate exclaimed, "But it really is funny. Oh, these things happen. I once met a woman who swore that we had grown up together at the same school in Nebraska. In my entire life, I've never set one foot in Nebraska!"

Calmly, Jim cut a slice of meat, while the man stood hulking above him. For God's sake, how long would he stand there?

"I don't know what kind of act this is." In a large, angry face, the man's eyes narrowed, swiveled across the group, and returned to Jim. "If you're not Donald Wolfe, I'm a buffalo. If you're not Donald Wolfe, I'll eat my—"

"Then go sit down and eat it," Laura shouted.

Richard and Gilbert half rose in their seats. No doubt it was this movement of two brawny young men that put an end to the encounter, for, grumbling and with a hostile backward look, the visitor moved away.

"Of all the disgusting—" Laura said furiously.

Kate's cheeks were darkly red. "Ridiculous!" she cried. "Absolutely ridiculous. And so nasty about it, the fool."

"He's had a few too many," observed Gilbert.

Richard dismissed the subject. "It takes all kinds. What were we talking about? Oh yes, the dean's speech. Jim, Mom, do you remember the president's speech at my college commencement? It must have lasted an hour. Talk about being long-winded! He had a great theme, though. Do you remember . . ."

In his own deft way, Richard was trying to settle the atmosphere. Like his mother, he seems to read me, Jim was thinking as, without appearing to do so, he gauged the temperature of the table. It seemed to be normal. So then, no damage had been done? Apparently none, he decided, while his heart still drummed in his ears.

But the aggressive, loudmouthed boor—which he had always been—was only a few tables away; he had changed his seat so that now, with a turn of the head, he was able to see Jim, and Jim was able to see him, only three tables removed.

"Dad! The way he stares!" Laura was defiant. "Well, I'll just stare back at him."

"No, don't do that. Don't rile him. Don't, Laura."

Gil laughed. "Especially since there's no law against staring."

"Listen to you," Laura said. "How many hours since you received the degree, Gil? And already talking like a lawyer."

Jim was struggling not to get up and walk away. He had to get out of this place right now.

Now. If only they wouldn't all linger over dessert, first to select it, then to eat it, and linger afterward over coffee.

"Here come my parents. They've been wanting to meet you," Gilbert said.

There followed the usual scraping of chairs as the couple approached, as the men stood to greet the mother, as hands were shaken, as more chairs were brought, mutual congratulations exchanged, and cordial conversation begun.

Ordinarily, Jim would have wanted to observe Gil's family with care, but all he saw of them now was an impediment, a pair of simply but handsomely dressed people, urbane and gracious, using up precious time.

Could he be imagining that the enemy was still watching him from that corner and was perhaps about to return? Or could his terror be paranoid?

"Yes," said Mrs. Maples—her name was Harriet, and some fifteen minutes ago he had been instructed to call her that—"we have been getting your catalog for ages, and what a surprise it was when Laura told us that you were her parents. My brother-in-law has a lovely place in Westchester. The house is screened from the road with your trees, your beautiful Scotch pines. Foothills Farm. It must be delightful."

Kate's hand was fingering a spoon, the fingers

trembling, but her voice was even. "Well, any-time you travel in our direction," she said, "we'd love to show it to you."

"Clive and I are great travelers, so maybe we will. Who knows?" Meaning, of course, who knows whether our son and your daughter will still be together.

Jim looked toward Laura: a "find" if there ever was one. If he had a son, he would want him to find a young woman like her, with her charm and her intelligence.

Yet there was a sword hanging over her head. Long had he been aware of it hanging over his own, but now, abruptly, he saw that she was standing under it next to him. What would these people think of her if they knew the truth?

"Mom has all kinds of unusual things in the greenhouse," Laura was saying. "Bellflowers, lilies that bloom in the fall, and of course, her gardenias."

Kate objected. "Gardenias aren't unusual."

"I know, but yours are especially sumptuous. Dad, I would absolutely, positively love to have a soufflé for dessert."

"You should have ordered it before dinner. It takes too long to make," Richard said.

Had he read Jim's mind, or as so often, guessed his mood?

"I know, but I didn't notice it on the menu.

I've hardly ever had one—no, I've only had one once, come to think of it."

"At the midsummer fair," Richard reminded her. "Four years ago."

"So isn't it time she had one again? It's her big day," Gilbert said. "She'd like chocolate, I'm sure. She always does."

"Do you see the waiter, Richard? We're ready to order dessert," Kate prompted. And then, assuming what Jim when teasing called her "wifely tone," Kate turned toward him. "You've been such a good sport all day, dear. Why don't you go on up to the room?

"Jim's had a stomach upset since early this morning," she explained, "and now he's eaten a full dinner, when he should have had just tea and toast. Now go, Jim," she scolded. "Go on, take care of yourself. We're only family and friends. Nobody'll mind."

"Shall I go with you?" Richard asked Jim.

"No, no, no. Kate's too cautious, as usual. I'm fine. It's nothing. I'm sorry. Take your time, everybody. Have two desserts, one for me. Glad to have met you, Harriet, Clive. Thanks, everybody."

He heard himself, staccato, absurd, smiling and stumbling toward the doorway. Crossing the lobby to the elevator, his fear that the enemy had risen to follow him was so palpable that it chilled his back. When the elevator door slid shut, he took a deep breath; it was as if he had not breathed properly for a long, long time— although that, too, was absurd.

Once in the room, he locked the door and lay down on the bed. After a moment he got up and went to the window, where a golden evening lay spread above the university's trees. A highway curved into the distance. If you followed it in no matter what direction, you would reach an ocean. When you crossed the ocean, there would be more land, mountains, plains, great inland seas, then more oceans, a vast world. Yet not vast enough.

Drawing the curtains, he cast the room into shadow and lay down again. *Donald Wolfe.* The voice roared into his ears. But Donald Wolfe died a long time ago, don't you know? I'm Jim Fuller. Kate will come back and tell me this was a chance in a—in a what?—in a million, she'll say, as people say about airplane crashes, or cancer of the brain, or giving birth to sextuplets, or winning the lottery, or any other crazy thing that people talk about, gabbing, just gabbing without knowing the first thing about tomorrow or next year or the next hour, for that matter—oh my God, we know nothing.

Softly the door was opened, and softly Kate entered. When she sat down on the edge of the bed, she laid her hand over his, not speaking. Her wedding ring grazed his, metal sliding on metal. She's blaming herself, he thought, for making me come here and assuring me that there was no reason to fear.

"I had to come," he told her. "What would Laura have thought if I had not been here. It's not your fault."

"Thank you," she said.

"Did I look odd? Shocked or anything?"

"No, except for a flush. But that could be from having been startled, or from the wine."

"It's thirty-five years since we were in high school, since he saw me. I thought I had changed. Glasses, some graying hair, ten pounds heavier, or close to it. What's he going to do next, do you think?"

"I really believe he'll do nothing. He'll realize that he made a mistake."

"But I recognized *him,* Kate! I made no mistake!"

"Well, even so. He won't know how to begin looking for you if he does want to."

"What if he happens to read one of those notices that years and years later come on a milk carton or in the mail: *'Have you seen them?'* "

"So he goes to the authorities with information that he's seen you in a hotel restaurant. That's all he knows. What good is that?"

"He'll probably be leaving here in the morning. We can't let him see me a second time. This place is filled with people come for the commencement."

This was a state university town, only a few hundred miles from where he had grown up, so there might well be somebody else here who would recognize him. Thoughts came rushing now, pictures fleeting in front of his eyes: the lobby, the elevator stopping at every floor, the airport . . .

"The airport," he said. "There'll be people from all over the country going home after the commencement."

"It's so unlikely, almost impossible with all these crowds—rushing—"

"But you can't say it's impossible, can you?"

"I know." And Kate fell silent.

More grim thoughts came to Jim: a familiar recollection of the tax evader who, after being sought for nine years, was finally run to ground in Indonesia; the serial killer tracked down after leaving a bloody trail a thousand miles long. He was neither of them, and yet—

"We have to rent a car," he said, "and get home."

"We're supposed to have breakfast with Richard and Laura, then fly back with them."

"All right, you've all been harping on the fact

that I never take a vacation. So now I want one. I want to see where my great-grandmother came from in Louisiana, in the Cajun country. Does that make sense?"

"It's eccentric, and absolutely not your style. Better blame it on me if you want to use that for an excuse."

"I haven't been this terrified in years, Kate. I'm ashamed of myself."

"That's the macho business. You have a right to be afraid."

When the phone rang, Kate picked it up and spoke briskly. "Oh, he's a little better, Laura. It's a bad sick stomach, that's all, with a little fever to go with it. Goodness knows the lobster bisque probably didn't help it. We certainly won't be flying back with you and Richard tomorrow, though."

Jim went into the bathroom, and shutting the door, closed out the sound of Kate's excuses. He looked at himself in the mirror. This last hour had added ten years of age to his face.

"Jim? Open the door. Are you all right?"

"I'm sorry. I didn't mean to frighten you. Did you tell her about Louisiana?"

"No, that's no good. It sounded foolish. I simply said we'd stay here for another day or two before flying home. I said we'd call a doctor in the morning if you weren't feeling any better.

That we'd get him here early to leave time for them because I know if you were really sick they wouldn't leave without you, although I am sure you aren't really that sick. I said that right now you were asleep." Kate stopped, hesitated, and then resumed. "Gil's mother suggested that we should all get together when Laura starts the medical school in August. Then Laura said that you never travel, and that we should all make you do it because it would be good for you. And Richard really surprised me because he argued that we should leave you alone—oh, argued in a very nice way, of course—because you're happy the way you are. Haven't you noticed how he always takes your part? Men stick together, don't they?"

That last remark, whether exaggerated or true, was meant to warm the atmosphere for him. She was hiding her own fright, too.

There was no time to waste, and he spoke fast. "Listen to me. After they've left tomorrow morning, you go rent a car and drive it back here. I am not going to fool around with any airports. Meanwhile, I'll have packed our stuff. You phone up to this room and tell me where you've parked the car down the street. Then I'll walk downstairs with the suitcases. It's only five flights, and I'll take no chance on meeting that fellow in the elevator. And we'll drive toward home on a straight line. In two days we'll be there. And believe me, Kate, once I go down Main Street and out onto our road, I'm never going to leave it again. Call it neurotic, call it whatever you want, but I never will. Never."

# Chapter 25

⚮

They stood above the waterfall, that unspoken destination of their evening walks. Below them rushed the living water, making a distant music, while behind them lay the quiet land, alive with spring. Without a turn of his head, Jim saw those acres as if their map were imprinted on his brain. He saw the twenty years of proud growth swaying in the wind, and the seedlings, row upon prim row. Even as he took pride and pleasure in all these, he was able also to recall the droughts, the fungi, and the winter's floods. Here was life. Here were trials and achievement, and over all, abiding peace.

Kate said suddenly, "Laura writes such marvelous letters."

"I think you miss her more than I do, if that's possible."

"I doubt that. Can you believe she's almost finished with her first year of medical school, Jim? She's changed. It's as if she had grown ten years in one, I thought when I visited last month. Well, you can tell by her letters, can't you? Sometimes they sound almost like poetry. Do you know what I mean?"

He knew what she meant.

*"They thought I might faint or be sick. I know they thought I shouldn't be invited to watch, but I was fascinated. It was perfect, the way the instruments were used. It was like a mathematical problem, so calm and purposeful, and you know that the result is going to be exactly what it turns out to be. I thought it was a little bit like bringing a jet plane down from five miles in the sky, the way the wheels touch, bump a little, and stop in the right place. Maybe you could think it was like a symphony, eighty or ninety instruments under the conductor's baton, each coming down at exactly the correct second. In time. In place. Perfection. Last week it was a man's red heart that I was seeing, his red heart exposed. And this week when I saw him, he was sitting up reading the newspaper and having a good breakfast. When I looked at him, my own heart was speeding."*

"I hope she's having some fun, too," Jim said.

"Oh, that she is! She has Gil, and he likes his good times, you remember. He took us to dinner at the top of some tower on Fifth Avenue. I couldn't believe the prices. But the view was marvelous. On Saturday and Sunday afternoon we went to the museum. I couldn't believe the art, the paintings, Jim, things from all over the world that I've only known in books. There was the Chinese section, absolutely beautiful, all those delicate branches and blossoms. Laura can't understand why you won't take a little time off and see New York again, Jim. She wants you to come. She must have mentioned it every day while I was there."

"I can't believe you're saying these things to me," he said, feeling the rise of anger.

"All right. I'm sorry. I don't mean to hurt."

For a while they were silent. Into their silence the waterfall resounded like a distant thunder. This talk of Kate's, these memories of a past life went swirling through Jim's head: He did not need or want these reminders to intrude upon the present peace.

"Can you guess what Laura did with your birthday check? Spent almost all of it on an illustrated history of medicine, beginning with the Egyptians. They did cataract surgery, I think."

She was making up for her remarks about visiting New York. And she continued, "Isn't it typical of her, when she's usually so careful with money, to spend extravagantly for a book?"

"Yes, typical." And he thought of his leather-bound *Jefferson,* bought on Fifth Avenue so long ago. How like himself she was! Jim's child, but luckily for her, with Lillian's face, those incredibly blue eyes, and that alluring, yet faintly wistful smile.

"Has Richard told you he's going to New York next week? Actually, there's a meeting in Boston of that wilderness preservation group, but he's going to stay over in New York one night to visit Laura."

"Yes, he said he might."

Kate's glance met his. *Wouldn't it be a marvel if those two were to become a couple and settle nearby,* it said. Laura could practice medicine right here in town, maybe there in the hospital's new wing, for which Jim Fuller was partially responsible. Oh, it was much to ask for, in these days when young people, exercising their rights, went roving across the country and families were split among half a dozen states.

"It'll be dark soon," Kate said. "We'd better go down."

At the bottom of the hill, Richard, crossing the yard, hailed Jim. "I've just been in the north field past the creek. I think we've beaten that fungus, Jim. I examined ten trees and didn't find a sign of anything."

"Good work! Great. That's a worry off our minds. Come on in and let's have a drink on it."

"Bring it outside," Kate said. "Jim likes to hear the tree frogs."

She knew. She always knew what he liked. Well, almost always she did.

So the tree frogs drilled and sang, and the evening air was sweet.

# Chapter 26

Laura's room, in the light of a single desk lamp, was filled with forest shadows, while the streetlight one floor below was a full white moon that really belonged above. Only the sounds of passing cars, very few now so late in the night, were proof that she was not home at Foothills Farm.

Part of me will always be there, she thought. But the larger part of me knows that here where I am is where I belong. And drawing toward her the diary, still bound in red leather, number six since the first one was begun thirteen years ago, she began to write.

*I'm still wide awake and my mind is crowded. Probably it's because the day was so full: all morning at lectures taking notes like mad, with finals coming along in six weeks. After that Dr. Lambert invited me to visit a few patients with her. She reminds me of the doctors who, when I was still in college, sometimes let me watch a procedure and were surprised when I didn't get sick at the sight of raw flesh and blood. People have been so nice to me, so encouraging, even in high school, and I am very grateful when I think about it.*

*Dr. Lambert says medical school is different now from what it used to be in her early years. We go directly from books to the reality much sooner now. I think that's a very good thing. You might say it gets from your head to your heart right away.*

*I spent this afternoon in the emergency room for the first time, and there I saw somebody die. It is the first time I've seen death actually when it is happening, and it is surely not like the descriptions in a novel, even a very well-written novel. The man had been hurt in a car crash. Something in me felt disaster when I looked at him, although I don't know what made me feel it because he didn't look as bad as one might expect. I wonder whether he felt disaster the way I did. He was wide awake. . . .*

*And now I wonder: If a person is very ill because of something that cannot be cured, but doesn't know it, does a doctor tell him the truth?*

*And if so, how does the doctor find the right words? Perhaps I should be an obstetrician. That's probably ninety-nine percent cheerful work.*

*On the other hand, perhaps I should not cringe from the sorrowful. My life has been so easy and protected that I almost think I owe a debt to a good fairy. I have never had a real problem, except sometimes when I was younger, a long time ago, and used to wonder too much about my mother; I suppose, though, that that was only natural.*

*Yes, definitely, I should aim for the harder things and pay my debt to that good fairy. Yes, I should.*

*I had another new experience after dinner. On the way back to my apartment, we happened to pass one of those famous auction houses, where you can get a nice little painting for as low as half a million or as high as thirty million. Or heaven only knows how many millions. So being curious, the three of us, Gil and Richard and I, went in. Some of the things were marvelous. I can imagine how it might feel to come home, open the front door, and be greeted by something as beautiful as one of those Provençal landscapes. Some of the most expensive ones, though, I wouldn't take as a gift. Granted, art is not my forte.*

*We watched for a while, and then when we*

*left, another man, an acquaintance of Gil's, joined our walk home. He was a big talker, another lawyer with an endless story about somebody's divorce case and an art auction. I would hate to be married to anybody like him. He looked shrewd and tough.*

*Gil tells me I am sometimes too serious. Not heavy or dull, he says, to the extent that anybody would mind, but too thoughtful for my own good. Maybe, but I don't really think so. I'm never unhappy, just thoughtful. And if your life is going to be about treating the sick, you have to be a thoughtful person, don't you?*

*Our minds, his and mine, work differently. His is much quicker. I guess it has to be because law seems to be about not letting anyone outwit you. He calls it a kind of intellectual game, and he loves it. A great part of his charm, I think, are his own sharp wits and his humor.*

*I had a good time tonight, although I'm sure Gil wasn't pleased to meet Richard here in New York, and I'm fairly sure Richard would have preferred a quiet dinner without him, too. As for me, I wore my flowered silk and enjoyed being out in a fancy restaurant with two men. A new experience!*

*So Gil felt cheated out of a night with me. I've been so busy studying for exams that he hasn't had one in a week. But probably he wouldn't have wanted to make it all so public in front of Richard, anyway. I don't know why, but somehow I don't like to emphasize Gil in front of Richard. I have no reason to think he would mind—I'm sure he must know about us—and yet perhaps he would mind. We have a very unusual relationship, loving but yet not quite loving, if that makes any sense.*

*Enough for tonight. It's almost another day.*

The three dogs, who were racing down the path ahead of the two hikers, were the first to see the strange car near the house.

"That car! Were you expecting anybody this evening, Jim?"

"Not a soul. Look, the kitchen door's open."

"Who could have gotten in?"

"Don't worry. Prince wouldn't be wagging his tail unless he knew everything was all right. But who—"

"It's Rick! What's he doing here?"

He was waving, so there couldn't be anything too wrong. He even had what looked like a sandwich in his hand.

"What's up?" Jim cried. "You're supposed to be in Boston, aren't you?" And as always, an alarm bell rang in his head. "Laura? Is Laura—"

"She's just fine, couldn't be better. We, she and

Gil and I, had a great dinner last night. She had two helpings of dessert, her own and half of mine. Come in. I opened a can of soup and in another minute, it'll boil over."

"Are you feeling okay?" Questions shot across the kitchen table. "What happened in Boston? What changed your mind?"

"Oh, a mix-up, a last-minute thing. The head man, the speaker, couldn't come. And since he was the person I wanted to hear, it didn't seem worthwhile to make the trip. This is pretty good soup to come out of a can."

Vaguely irritated by such a careless attitude toward what had been a mission with a purpose, Jim contradicted Richard.

"I'm sorry, but you're not making any sense. The entire three-day conference on land preservation doesn't depend upon one man, no matter who he is."

"Well, maybe I made a mistake in judgment. If I did, I'm sorry. Down, Prince. Go eat your own food that your doctor ordered for you. That's the good boy."

Kate, speaking even more softly than usual, had a question. "There's something else. What really brought you home, Rick? Come out with it."

"Well, there are a couple of things, but let me finish my soup and sandwich first."

"It's got to be something about Laura, and you can't bring yourself to tell us," Jim said.

"No. No, Jim, I swear it isn't. Laura is absolutely fine. Healthy and happy as ever."

Yet the alarm bell in Jim's head was still ringing. A few minutes passed during which the only sounds in the kitchen were small familiar ones: dogs crunched their hard kibble; the teakettle whistled until Kate got up to turn it off; Rick's spoon struck the side of the soup bowl.

But the hand that held the soup spoon was shaking, dribbling the soup over the table. Finally, at the sight of this unmistakable agitation, Jim could wait no longer.

"Out with it," he commanded. "Don't spare us. Don't tease us. What's wrong?"

Rick pushed his chair back and raised eyes so troubled that they seemed to be making a plea for understanding and mercy.

"Perhaps we should go where the chairs are more comfortable," he said. "I have a long story. Then again, maybe I'll make it short."

In the room called the "den" and sometimes the "library," where Kate's books and his own had long been commingled, Jim glanced up to where, in the third row from the top, stood his leather-bound *Jefferson*. He would remember later how he had had a totally irrational premonition that this simple object would in some way have a connection with what Rick was about to say.

"After dinner the three of us went for a walk and stopped in at one of those art auctions, museum arts, tycoon stuff you know, worth millions. Of course, neither Laura nor I had ever seen anything like it, but Gil had, and he told us a great deal about it.

"Walking home, we met another man, a lawyer who works in the same building as Gil does, but not in the same firm. It was late, so we dropped Laura off at her place first. This man then told Gil and me that one of the paintings had just been withdrawn from the sale by court order, and he had simply stopped by to check whether the order had been carried out this afternoon. The piece is in litigation between a divorced couple, both of whom claim it."

Rick stopped and sighed, as if speech was exhausting him. He shifted his chair, and there was a long pause.

"Go on," Jim said.

"The woman, a client of this man's firm, has an interesting history. There was no real reason for him to mention it, so it turned out, except that he found it interesting. One of her ex-husbands had kidnapped their two-year-old daughter some twenty years ago or more, and there has been no trace of her, or of him, ever since. No trace, none at all, he said. It was long before his time, of course, but he also had heard plenty of talk about it at the office. The man's name began with a 'D,' Douglas or Donald something, he wasn't sure. And the last name began with a 'V' or maybe a 'W,' he thought."

Once more, Jim stopped to draw his breath, and again said, "Go on."

Kate's hand, reaching over the arm of the chair, was laid upon Jim's. And Richard's eyes, now meeting Jim's, were suddenly as compassionate as was that hand.

"The odd thing is that the man is—was—well-known, a top-drawer lawyer, a big shot. You could write a book about something like that, couldn't you?" he said.

What is silence other than the absence of sound? It is an awful hush. It stuns. It is like death.

After a minute or two, Jim broke the silence. "What else?"

"That's all," Richard answered.

"How long have you known about me before last night?"

"A long time, Jim."

"And how long is that?"

"Since I was seventeen. Does it matter?"

"Yes. I want to know."

So Richard, staring down at the floor, out the

window, and at the cat asleep on the rag rug, in any direction except toward Jim or his mother, began.

"It was the day after Thanksgiving. There was an extra pumpkin pie, supposed to be saved for the freezer. And I had such an appetite for it . . . you remember. So I went down the back stairs on bare feet and sneaked into the kitchen. And you two were talking. Hushed, but still loud enough for me to hear through the kitchen door that was ajar. I could tell by your voices that you were very frightened about something, and I couldn't help listening, simply because you were so frightened, and it scared me, too. You were talking about something in the newspaper, about people looking for Jim because he had stolen Laura. Before I went downstairs, I remember, I had been thinking that our lives were going to end in some awful way.

"But they didn't, so I went to school and tried all day not to think any more about it. After a few days, I stopped being terrified. I only knew that I must never let you know I had overheard you, because then you would be afraid that I might tell somebody, even let it slip out by accident, and it would be terrible for you to live with that fear for the rest of your life. I knew I could trust myself not to speak. But how could you know that I would never speak? So I buried it. I had to pretend I had never heard it. I had to."

Kate began to cry, and Jim said, "Come here. The chair is big enough for us both."

Through their two thin sweaters, he felt her heartbeat. What had he done to her? For his disaster would now be hers, as he had always known it would be, as he had warned her once that it would be.

*Steady. Steady. This is it. This time it really is.*

He looked toward Richard. Poor boy. Seventeen, he had been, no longer a child, but not an adult, either. Poor boy.

When he could speak, he spoke to Richard. "What can you have thought about me?"

"That it couldn't have been your fault." Richard's eyes were filled with tears. "That you must have had a good reason. I remembered how you had treated my dad, how kind you are to Mom, to all of us, and to everybody. But I was—I am—so afraid for you."

Afraid for me? Ah no, for Laura, who has never known and should never need to know. Laura, his little girl. What of her? And the silence flowed back. It was as though everything had been said.

The springtime sun, now low in the sky, cast its last gleam where the bare floor met the rug. In the middle distance beyond the windowpane where Jim was sitting, the old, old pony, Laura's first mount, grazed in his fenced yard. The sweetness, the simple, unchanging innocence of it all . . .

"I'm thinking that maybe you and Mom should go away, leave the country before anything happens."

"No. Running away is never an answer."

"I'm not saying that something is bound to happen, but it could."

"You haven't given me the whole story, have you? Tell me every word that was spoken, if you can recall. Every word is important. I need the whole story."

"Gilbert said he had a feeling he had heard something someplace. Names and incidents leave impressions in his head that often bother him, he said, because while he knows they are there, he can't place them. The funny thing is that days, even months later they can come back to him while he's brushing his teeth, maybe, or listening to the news. Then suddenly everything is there again. The other fellow laughed and warned him not to call up at one A.M. if that should ever happen because he didn't need the information, anyway. He called Gil a typical nit-picker."

"Gil will remember it. Mark my words."

"What makes you so sure, Jim?"

"Because Gil has a very, very sharp mind. He's orderly, he's ambitious, and he *is* a nitpicker."

Now Kate, recovering her courage, gave a caution. "Jim, darling, you're a super-worrier, you know you are. You worry when one of us has a cold. You're afraid it's pneumonia. You worry when the dog's paw is infected. The only thing you don't worry about is yourself. Am I right, Rick?" She was trying to soothe him, and soothe herself, too. "Isn't he a super-worrier, Rick?" she persisted.

"I can't say, Mom. That name may pop into Gil's head, or it may not. If it doesn't pop, then nothing will happen. How will we find out?"

"We'll find out," Jim said.

"Tell me," Kate begged, clasping his hand. "You think you're sparing me. Tell me what you really think."

"I think we'll know if and when anything happens. And in the meantime, we'll live just as we've been doing all these years."

So the seasons passed at their accustomed, normal pace. Laura came home for a brief summer stay. The countryside sizzled through a heat wave, and the town held its usual Fourth of July parade, after which the Fullers invited their friends to a grand barbecue; the Scofields, of course, and others like them, were there, all the busy people on the council, in the schools and the hospital, the energetic, good people whom Jim had collected through the years. "Movers and shakers," Kate called them. The Fullers, the Fuller family, fell back into its old routine of lake swims and six-mile hikes into the coolness of the hills. Richard put down a first payment on a twenty-five-acre piece of land, thus "rounding out the property into a perfect square," as he liked to say. Orders for early fall planting came in so fast that Kate hired a part-time secretary to keep up with the paperwork. And Jim worked so hard as overseer of Foothills Farm that he had little time to think about anything else.

Surprisingly rare was any mention of the event that Richard had reported. Only once, when Laura came for Thanksgiving with her lively talk of work and play in New York, as well as her store of comical reminiscences, was a real jolt felt.

"Ah, pumpkin pie," she said with a mock sigh. "I used to think you'd kill yourself with it, Rick. The portions you stole! Two at the dinner table, and a third one you'd sneak afterward while we were cleaning up the kitchen or asleep."

Three pairs of eyes flickered for an instant, met, and parted. Perhaps, Jim thought, we have all, without admitting it, been succumbing to some kind of superstitious feeling that if you don't think or talk much about a bad thing, it will go away. Or perhaps we are simply behaving like fairly intelligent people who refuse to waste precious today in fear of tomorrow.

Still, at random moments in disjointed fashion, a thought would stab him. Really, there had been no need for Kate to hear what Richard had heard in New York. Since there was nothing that she or anyone could do about this, why should she have to carry this dark thought with her? And then he would marvel at Richard, at his courage and his decency, hiding for so many years what must be his fears for his mother, for Laura, and for them all.

A rain-soaked winter passed, followed by another fragrant spring, and it would soon be a year since the shock. So Gilbert apparently had not associated the name of Donald Wolfe with James Fuller.

Then one day in midspring, Kate brought home a fashion magazine that she had read at the hairdresser's.

"I thought maybe you'd want to see this," she told him, "or maybe you don't want to?"

"This" was a page full of fashionable people at a fashionable event held in some tropical place.

And there was Lillian again, wearing some designer's dress with that vivid smile on her face, standing beside a new man.

"He is a new man, isn't he? The last one looked half her age, if I remember. This one looks twice her age."

Kate spoke with scorn, while Jim was merely reading rapidly and calculating. The caption described Lillian's new man as her "devoted companion, who rarely visits the United States, but has been staying here for the past two months because she has urgent business to take care of."

That painting, perhaps? *If I ever am rich, I will collect great art.*

But then again, it might be something else that was "urgent business," might it not? On the other hand, it's been two years since that man appeared at Laura's commencement, and nothing had come of it.

"Now I've spoiled your evening," Kate lamented. "Your expression tells me what you're thinking. I shouldn't have shown you this."

"I'm fine," he said lightly, "just amused at the sight of her holding those tiny dogs on a leash. She never liked dogs. She couldn't stand them around, as a matter of fact."

"These are the current fashion, though."

"Ah, so that's it. Now I understand," he replied, as though the whole thing were a joke.

When the magazine went into the wastebasket, the subject was dropped—or only dropped between Jim and Kate. For on the next day, it came to light again between Jim and Richard.

"Mom's worried. She told me about that stuff in the magazine, about—about *her* being in New York on business. What do you think?"

"I have no idea."

"But if Gil remembered the name, you surely would have heard from him, wouldn't you?" Richard hesitated. "I'm sure he wouldn't delay if he knew. Or maybe that other guy's law firm would have reported something to the police."

"It doesn't work like that. It can take a couple of weeks, or even a couple of months to get a case properly put together. The New York district attorney has to get in touch with the local D.A. here, and show evidence. It probably seems quick and simple to you, and I can understand why. But there are procedures to be gotten through before you can make an arrest. And Laura is not a little child who could be in danger, so there's no risk, no hurry, in this case."

"Well, I'm no lawyer, that's sure, but still it seems to me that Gil can't have recalled the name. I've been thinking that he wouldn't believe it possible, even if he could recall it. He'd tell himself he was making a mistake."

Jim gazed out over the placid landscape. The

corn was poking through the earth in the vegetable garden, and the dogs were stretched out asleep in the shade.

"I'm not so sure of that," he murmured, thinking that no lawyer worth his salt wouldn't believe it possible.

"No, Rick, it will come like a thunderclap on a sunny day if it comes."

# Chapter 27

❧

On a happy morning in Laura's pretty room, where the April sun bathed the windowsill, where her smart patent-leather loafers were brand new, her assignments for the week were already finished, and she was ready for her Saturday workout at the gym, there came the startling, shrill sound of the doorbell. Now who on earth could be so impatient at a quarter to eight?

She opened the door. Before her stood two men, one with some sort of elaborate camera that he thrust toward her face.

"Bettina Wolfe?" one shouted.

"No! What do you think you're doing?" For the one with the camera had put his foot past the door.

"What do you want? Get away, or I'll call the police."

"There's nothing to be afraid of, miss. You're in the news, that's all. It's about your mother."

"My mother? For God's sake, what's happened? Where is she?"

"Right now? Somewhere in Europe. Nothing's happened to her. She'll be coming back now that she's heard. Listen, we only—"

The elevator door had barely opened when Gil came rushing down the hall. "What are you guys doing here?" he shouted. "You're bothering this woman. Get away, and hurry up!"

"No harm, mister. We're not bothering her. This is news, that's all. We're from the paper."

"No, no! Get away! Let her alone."

Gil shoved his way into the apartment, closed and locked the door, and put both hands on Laura's shoulders.

"You're scared to death, and I don't blame you. The fools! Fools!"

"But what's this all about? What are you doing here?"

"I have an appointment near your gym, so I thought we might walk over there together."

"Tell me the truth," she said, "because I don't believe you. Did you know those men were coming? And who's on the plane flying back from Europe? What's he talking about?"

"I'm not sure . . . I heard . . ."

"Will you please stop stammering?"

"I don't know. There's some mix-up." Gil made a small, helpless gesture. "I think you should speak to your father."

"Why? Is anything wrong with Dad?"

"No, no. It's just that he can answer your questions better than I can. Really, darling. It's something to do with him, his affairs. But he's not sick. Don't worry. Just call him."

"Oh, this is crazy! Haven't people got anything better to do than send able-bodied men around to annoy ordinary citizens with nonsense? What can my father know about it? You don't answer me. . . . What's the matter?"

"I'm still thinking that you ought to talk to your father. He'll explain. I don't know about it."

"All right, I will. This is ridiculous."

The telephone rang and rang at every extension, Kate's office, Dad's office, upstairs, and the kitchen. Where could they all be? Yes, something had happened, maybe to Rick. He drove too fast. They were always lecturing him about it. Please let it not be Rick, or anybody. Please not—

"Hello?" said Jennie.

"Jennie? What are you doing over there? Is everybody all right? What's happened?"

"They're—they're all in town. They had

business there. Some errands. So I came over to answer phone calls for them."

The voice was strange, with a sudden, unnatural brightness, as when one speaks to a person who's very ill, or when one is dodging a subject.

"What are you hiding, Jennie?"

"I? Hiding? Why, nothing, dear. But I'm sorry I have to hang up. There's a pot boiling on the stove. I'll tell them you called."

When Laura replaced the receiver, she looked at Gil. He was fidgeting with a pencil that had been lying on a table, pushing the lead in and out.

"This game of secrecy is not fair to me," Laura said angrily. "First you, and now Jennie."

"Jennie?"

"You've met her. The nursery school down the road. Oh, do put that pencil away and talk to me, will you?"

When he came close to draw her to him, she retreated. "You had better talk to me," she said fiercely.

Gil did not answer. He was looking at his fingernails.

After a moment, he said slowly, "I really think you should go home. If you had people at your door, your dad may have had them, too."

All through her blood and bones there surged an awful nameless fright.

"Yes. Yes, of course I have to go."

"I'll go with you."

When she laid her head back with her cheek on a pillow, she heard the throb of her heartbeat in her ears. The sky flew past the window. She was in a hurry to reach home, and at the same time afraid to reach it because of what must be waiting for her there. Perhaps there would only be some oddity, nothing to fear? Gil held her hand, and with his other hand, held a book that he had not read since he had taken it out of the carry-on. Neither had he spoken.

Late in the afternoon, they landed and rented a car. "You'll have to guide me over these roads," he said.

"Gil, I'm terribly afraid of what I'll find."

"It won't be the end of the world, whatever it is. Try to remember that."

Houses, villages, highways, and scattered farms were unchanged. At a crossroads they came to a small sign with an arrow pointing the way to Foothills Farm. Someone had spilled a load of gravel; the car crunched over it and stopped in front of the house, which looked unchanged. So perhaps there was nothing wrong after all.

One of the old workmen, Bob, came to the door. He had tended the cows for Richard's grandfather and although he wasn't quite "all there," still did small jobs around the place.

"Hey, how're you, Laura? Didn't know you were coming. Nobody told me. Nobody told me nothin'. All topsy-turvy here. Bad day. Bad days. Never thought I'd live to see anything like it. I said to myself, I—"

"Like what?"

But Laura's intended interruption was itself interrupted. "Took poor Mister Jim away this morning. Never thought I'd live to see such a thing, him dressed up in his good suit—"

"Took him where, Bob? Where?"

"Why, jail, Laura. Captain Ferris come from the police in town, and I know it hurt him plenty to haul off Mister Jim, but—"

Before she could make a sound, Gil led her to the sofa. "Sit down, sit down. Your dad'll be okay. It's just some kind of what you might call a formality. He'll be back here and he'll tell you about it himself. Please. Believe me. He's okay."

"Here," Bob said, "look here. It's all in the paper, county news, come this morning. Read what happened."

**Jim Fuller is Donald Wolfe, long sought as kidnapper.**

**Reached by telephone at her home in France, Lillian Storm, a tearful mother,**

described her agonized yearning for her baby, Bettina Wolfe, stolen from her more than twenty years ago by the baby's father, a prominent New York lawyer turned farmer.

The words blurred, the room revolved, and Laura read on.

Mr. Wolfe, known to this community as Jim Fuller, proprietor of Foothills Farm, has been active in local affairs in this community as a generous benefactor, an advisor to the Board of Education, St. Clare's Hospital administration, and . . .

She screamed. The paper fell to the floor. The room was filled with her eerie screams. Even as she heard them, she was able to understand that this was hysteria. It could push you over the edge and down, down, with your own appalling voice in your ears.

"Give her a drink," Bob said. "Mister Jim keeps brandy in the cupboard over there. I seen where he keeps it, time I run a saw over my finger."

Laura was clinging to the arm of the sofa. Oh God, oh God, she was going to be sick. She was

sick. She wanted to die. It wasn't true. Dad
wouldn't do that. It couldn't be true.

"Is it true, Gil? No, it's not true. You knew,
Gil. You knew, and you didn't tell me."

"Ah, Laura, don't blame me. What can I do
for you? It wasn't my story to tell. I didn't know
it all, anyway. Oh, don't cry. No, do cry. Cry it
out, it's better—"

"She needs a drink. Make her take it. Here,
let me—"

"No, no, Bob, it's too strong for her. She's not
used to it. She won't keep it down. Ah, darling,
you always wondered so much about your
mother. Now you can have her. You'll be all
right. You'll be fine again, you'll see."

"All my life, the lies, the lies! Even my name
isn't my own! Read the rest of it to me. Is it true?
Yes, it has to be. They wouldn't print a long
story like that if it wasn't."

Lillian Storm, recently divorced from
Arthur Storm, the financier, divides her
time between New York and her home
abroad. Well known in social circles, she
is renowned for her charities, as well as
for her art collection. Bettina, who is her
only child, grew up on Foothills Farm
and is now a medical student in New
York. Her many friends in this area have

long known her as Laura Fuller, a top
student, swimmer, and basketball star—

"How could he have done this to me and my
mother? I want to see her! My mother! Oh my
God, how can a man do such a thing?"

"They're home," Gil said, "and Rick just
drove in. Somebody's with him."

"Oh, poor Kate! He lied to her, too. Poor
Mom!" Laura cried, and stretched out her arms
as Rick and Kate came into the room.

"No, darling, not 'poor Kate.' It's 'poor Jim.'
Oh, how brave. My heart's breaking for my Jim.
So you heard so soon? And you flew here to be
with him? God bless you."

A few seconds passed before these words
arranged themselves into some comprehensi-
ble shape: "came to be with him" . . . "how
brave" . . . "poor Jim" . . . And Laura sprang up,
almost throwing Kate off balance. A volcano
erupted and scorched her chest.

"What are you saying? I came to be with him?
A fraud. A liar. Destroyer of—of a whole world,
my world and yours, and you tell me how brave
he is? I am going insane. Yes, I'm losing my mind,
I'm dreaming this, why don't I wake up? And if
it's only a nightmare, why am I having it? Yes, I'm
sick. I'm sick. Who am I? What's my name? Bettina Wolfe, it said. Yes, I'm losing my mind."

There they stood, all of them looking at her, shocked and helpless with their foolish, staring faces, the old man scared, Kate's cheeks wet with tears, Gil numb, and Richard, standing with Dr. Scofield in the rear, like two statues.

Dr. Scofield moved his hand across his forehead. "You are not going to lose your mind," he said steadily. "You are understandably in shock."

"Yes, shock." She turned to Kate. "Is it for him you feel sorry? What's wrong with you? He lied to you, turned your whole life into a lie, and you—"

"No," Kate said very low, as if it was a tremendous effort to speak. "No, no, your father told me the truth."

"Are you saying that you've known this about my mother and me?"

Kate's despairing eyes looked straight into Laura's. "Yes."

"You! Whom can one ever believe? And you, Rick? Have you known, too?"

"Yes."

"Gil?"

"Not really. Just something vague—unreliable. A couple of days ago I didn't know what to believe."

"Dr. Scofield?"

"No."

Scanning the silent room, Laura felt only hatred. A prisoner must feel such hatred for his captors; all the triumph and strength belonged to them; could Richard and Kate ever be made to take back the wrong they had done her? Could they undo this humiliation, these blank years?

And suddenly before anybody could stop her, Laura ran into the hall where old Bob had sought refuge, and raced, stumbling, up the stairs into the room where the pretty woman smiled from her pretty frame. She seized it, ran back downstairs, and thrust it before Kate.

"This! Is this my mother? Or is this another lie? Tell me the truth, if you can."

"It is as close as I could find to your father's description of her. He had no photo, and you needed one."

Frantic in her rage, Laura raised the picture overhead and flung it into the fireplace.

"Then everything you people ever told me or did for me was a fake and false. How can I ever trust anybody in the world again, if you could do this to a child?" She sobbed. "How can a man, a father, do this to his child? And to the child's mother, too—how she must have suffered! Things come back to me, that man at my graduation, I never suspected he could be right. Why should I suspect? Why would anyone? But now . . . No wonder we never went anywhere, just stayed here, hiding—oh, now I see, I see it all. I know."

"All this didn't just happen of itself," Richard said quietly. "You need to listen to the other side, talk to your father, it's only right, and then—"

"Fine. I will. Take me to him now. Gil, you drive me. Let's go. Yes, I want to hear what he can possibly have to say."

Richard put his hand out as if to stop her. "Not now, Laura. It's not allowed."

Ah, yes. In jail. Her father. And she said aloud, not asking a question, but making a statement: "In jail."

"He will be arraigned on Monday before a magistrate," Richard explained. "It was too late today. Tomorrow's Sunday, so we can't do anything before Monday. But we do already have a lawyer. In fact, one offered himself, Harold McLaughlin. He knows Jim and wants to represent him."

Dr. Scofield asked, "What will happen on Monday?"

"He'll plead guilty and be released on bail. Mom and I will provide it with the farm. Naturally, the trial will be held in New York."

"Does it have to be?" Kate pleaded.

"Mom, it all happened in New York."

Dr. Scofield sighed. "They're saying he was a big-shot lawyer there."

"Jim never called himself big-shot anything,"

Kate said. "He was always simple in his ways." And she sat down with her hands over her face.

"Yes, simple," Richard said, "and wise. Anytime I had a problem, or there were decisions—"

Laura's cry interrupted him. "You're forgetting the real victim. The mother. *My mother!* Gil, take me to her. If there's no plane, we can drive. I feel so sick. . . . I can't stand up. I'll lie down on the backseat. Start now. You'll do this for me. Please, Gil?"

"Listen here." Dr. Scofield spoke up with severity. "I'm going to prescribe something that will give you a night's sleep, Laura. One of you young men take it to the pharmacy now, before it closes."

"No," Laura said. "I'm not staying in this house. And I don't take drugs. I'll face reality, not escape it."

"This is medicine, Laura. I'm not a drug dealer."

"I won't stay here in this house!"

"There's noplace else for you to stay. You'll stay here. And anyway, you're not fit to travel. Kate and I will take you upstairs and get you into your bed."

⸎

When she awoke, the room was gray, and rain was spattering the window glass with the force of anger. Even before she left the bed, she knew that a gale had come down from the north.

Something, Dr. Scofield's pill or perhaps some curious quirk of her nerves, hormones, genes—no matter which—had turned yesterday's helplessness into determination. Whatever it was, it pulled her upright and set her feet onto the floor.

Tomorrow she would be united with her mother. *Mother.* The woman who had borne her. And she looked at the desk where the fake had stood, the smiling fake that she had loved enough to have it duplicated for her other desk in New York.

Someone tapped on the door. "May I come in? I heard you moving around. They asked me to be here so you wouldn't wake up in a vacant house," Jennie said.

She seemed shy. She seemed small, this teacher who had once been tall in her authority. No doubt she knew the whole story, while I knew nothing, thought Laura. *She* knows everything about *my* life!

"Your friend Gilbert left early to catch a plane home. He wants to find out what's happening, to see how he can help your father. He'll phone you later today, he said. I should be sure to give you that message. I should be sure to tell you he loves you. He wants you to be calm."

"Thank you. I am calm."

"Your father called, too. Said not to wake you. He'll be home and try to explain everything. It's an unbelievable shock, he knows that, but in the end he's sure you will understand and forgive."

"So he's sure, is he? How nice for him!"

"Will you come down and have a late breakfast or an early brunch? It's half-past ten. Kate took corn muffins out of the freezer. Corn with raisins. She said you love raisins."

Muffins! Are they supposed to make up for twenty years of deception? Nevertheless, Laura went downstairs and sat with Jennie at the familiar kitchen table, across from the dog's water bowl and Rick's raincoat on a wall hook in the corner.

There was nothing to say. Or rather, there was too much to be said. Jennie got up and brought to the table Kate's treasured copper-trimmed coffee pot. The clock in the hall chimed eleven. Clancy came in, lapped water noisily, and rested his wet whiskers on Laura's knee.

Strange that it should be a dog who brought forth the tears she had just vowed not to shed! Be calm, Gil said. Be strong. Cope with disaster as a person must, and people do every day, everywhere.

Jennie spoke softly. "Is there anything you want to ask me, Laura?"

"There's so much that I don't even know how to begin."

"When you telephoned yesterday, I wasn't able to talk to you. I think I said something about a pot boiling on the stove. They had just come for Jim—for your dad. They were expected, so Kate had asked me to be here. Old, old friends, you know. Not that she seemed to need me or any support. She held her head up. Jim—your dad—had put on a business suit. He answered the officer with his correct name, Donald Wolfe. The officer was a nervous wreck, I could see. Of course, he must have known Jim for years. Everybody knew Jim, and loved him," Jennie faltered.

A fascinating topic, this would be, from the courthouse to the beauty parlors and the coffee shops, all through the town. The crowds that collect around a four-car accident on the highway are full of pity at sight of the blood and guts, but there is more than a touch, a thrill, of drama along with the pity.

"A fellow was here this morning," Jennie hesitated. "A reporter. I forget what paper he was from. I told him you weren't here. You were in New York."

"That was kind. Thank you."

There was a silence. Jennie got up, rinsed the

few plates, and tidied the kitchen counters while Laura stared out at the windy sky.

"You won't mind if I go home, Laura? It's Sunday, and it's our turn for the family's get-together at our house."

All of a sudden, the most innocent words, "the family," were sharp as a knife. Whose family? Where? Who?

"No, I don't mind. And thanks again for everything."

"Sure you're all right? What are you going to do while I'm gone?"

"I guess I'll just read the paper or something."

"I took it in from the front step. Maybe I shouldn't have. I didn't think. Don't bother with it, Laura. It's just a scandal sheet."

Dear, forgetful Jennie. Yes, probably she shouldn't have brought it into the house.

**Friends are rallying on behalf of Lillian Storm. Early rumors yesterday from authorities in Georgia reveal that Donald Wolfe, her former husband, will defend his kidnapping of their child by charging her with being an "unfit mother," have shocked people here and abroad. Not one person out of the several who have already been interviewed during the last**

two days has failed to be outraged by the charge. The consensus of opinion is that she has spent the last twenty years in a brokenhearted, fruitless search for the girl, Bettina, whom Donald Wolfe took away from her nurse in Central Park and has hidden in Georgia, where they now live on a tree farm owned by Wolfe and his second wife.

The girl, now known as Laura Fuller, is a medical student in this city.

So the mother, *Rebecca,* is *Lillian.* The daughter, *Laura,* is *Bettina.* And they would not even recognize each other if they were to pass on the street.

"I cannot bear this," said Laura.

Beyond the window swept the gale, ripping early blossoms from the trees, twisting and crippling their branches. Any living creature would be grateful for any kind of shelter on such a terrible day, yet if she could have walked through it to reach Lillian Storm, she would have done so. For a long time, she stood there staring out into the rain.

She was still looking out when a bedraggled little group—Mom, Richard, Dr. Scofield, and another man—came into the room.

"Laura," Richard began, but she stopped him.

"You're forgetting. The name is 'Bettina.' "

"Ah, don't," Kate pleaded. "This is Mr. McLaughlin. He's kindly come here to talk to us."

Mr. McLaughlin might indeed have come kindly, but he had clearly not missed the little exchange about names; his quick glance encompassed everything from Kate's reddened eyes to Laura's retort.

"I have had my understanding with Jim," he said. "It was effortless on my part. He had all the answers almost before I asked the questions. But I haven't yet laid things out on the table for the rest of you. It's a tragedy." He shook his gray head and continued. "Shakespeare could have written it. Yes, it's a blow to you, young lady. I understand that. But believe me, it's even worse for your father."

"Young lady." The old-fashioned term would have amused her if she had been in a mood for amusement.

"It seems you are only thinking of him," she replied coldly. "Of course. You're his lawyer. But I am thinking of my mother. Have you by any chance read this?" And she handed the newspaper to him. " 'Punishment to the fullest extent of the law,' she wants. Well, I have to tell you, that's what he will probably get, and he should. I have a different point of view from yours, you see."

Richard, who had been standing beside his mother with shoulders bowed, seemed suddenly to come to life.

"Laura doesn't know the other side," he said. "I know Jim wouldn't want me to tell it straight out to her; in fact, he forbade me to do so, but I'm going to do it anyway. That kind of life was—it was indecent. And so, to remove his child from it, he sacrificed everything he had achieved for himself."

McLaughlin had settled into a chair as if he were exhausted. His voice was low and agitated.

"Kidnapping is a federal crime. The best we can hope for is a reduction in prison time. Let me put this to you bluntly right from the start, though it hurts me like hell to do it."

Richard put his arm around his mother, who, having released one cry, was still.

"I've already heard from Mrs. Storm's lawyers. They lost no time, not an hour's worth. But I cannot defend Jim in New York, that you know. I'll have him out on bail tomorrow morning, but that's as far as I can go. You'll be needing counsel in New York, and I suggest you hire the best you can find."

"I thought," Laura said, "there would be an enormous fine. I didn't realize that they put a man in prison for taking his own child."

"For kidnapping? You didn't know?"

McLaughlin's thin smile was astonished. "You'd better stick to medicine then, not law. Your father was telling me—he's very proud of you. Yes. They put you in prison for kidnapping."

In a low, strained voice, Richard managed a question. "For how long?"

"It depends. It can be as long as twenty or thirty years, and usually is."

Kate began to weep, making fearful, choking sounds while she rested her head on Rick's shoulder.

A woman whose child had been run over on the street where Laura lived had made just such awful sounds. . . . "Thirty years," Laura whispered, watching Kate, who never cried. Then she turned to McLaughlin.

"Thirty years," she repeated. "Is that the fullest extent of the law?"

"I would expect so. It could be more if Jim had mistreated or neglected you, but since that's not the case—at any rate, that's what they'll aim for."

"And they will get it?"

"It's safe to say he'll serve some years. I wish I didn't have to say it."

"But all the people who know him, people in town, surely they'll vouch for him, a citizen like him. Won't that count for anything?" asked Richard.

"Frankly, I doubt it will help much. Shouldn't you get a doctor for your mother?" McLaughlin asked with pity, and glanced toward Kate, whose body seemed about to collapse.

"I have those pills I took last night," Laura offered.

"Yes, give her one. I'm sorry that I've had to talk as I've done, but you wanted the truth. I'm always sorry when I have to give people news that they don't want to hear. But you need the truth in order to do your best for Jim. A tragedy," McLaughlin repeated. "A splendid man. An eminent lawyer, well on his way to the very top, they tell me. I myself have known him for a long time, but of course I never knew who he really was. I never guessed. How could I have? Well, I'll see you in the courtroom tomorrow. You know you have to bring the deed to the farm," he added as he went to the door.

"We know," Rick said.

❧

The house was still. Only the creak of the top step as Richard mounted the stairs disturbed the stillness. Then came the small thud of his door as he went to his room. From Kate's room there came no sounds; she must have taken one of Dr. Scofield's pills.

Now finally, long after midnight, the rain had

ceased and with it the last gurgle in the spout near Laura's window, through which there poured the poignant scent of wet grass. On the rim of the hills there rested a gibbous moon, faintly green. Living as long as she had in the city, she had long forgotten to look outside except to question whether to carry an umbrella.

Dad and Richard always searched the sky. Should they irrigate today? Was that a rain cloud, or was the sun about to break through the mist? After breakfast, Dad always put on a jacket and drove to town, or else wore jeans and worked in the office, or else wore jeans and surveyed the farm. So it had always been.

Yesterday morning, thirty-six hours ago, everything had made sense. Laura Fuller had made her tidy plans for Saturday; she had had plans for Sunday and would be back in class on Monday. Now, like the victim of earthquake or war, she had no plans. She was not even Laura Fuller anymore.

Needing to steady herself, she grasped the back of a chair and stared about the room, at the bed, the chest, and the desk, where until yesterday had stood that fake photograph, and where, next to it, still stood the smiling family, herself in the midst of them, wearing cap and gown. There they were, for all time together, and now split apart.

*Is that really you, Donald Wolfe? What have you done with your life? Oh, I am so angry, I am enraged, I am crushed. I have come home and found my house bombed and everyone in it dead.*

An unfit mother, he says. And she has spent the last twenty years with a broken heart! How they must have despised each other. Oh my mother, I need to talk to you!

The morning dawned, this morning that should be taking her back to New York, where she would wait for that *Rebecca*, now to be known as *Lillian*. Yet she could not leave here without knowing what the day would bring. Dressed and ready within ten minutes, she went downstairs to find that Kate was already in the car, and Richard was about to join her.

"I can't talk, we have to hurry," he said.

"I'll be quick. I accused you last night. I was pretty frantic."

"Understandably. It's okay. We'll talk about it later."

"Is Mom all right?"

"No, but she'll manage. She has to."

"Shall I go with you now?"

"No. He doesn't want you to see him where he is."

Laura nodded at Richard, and the door closed.

The county newspaper had been delivered and put on the table. On the front page in a column next to the state election ran the black heading:

## *FULLER BAIL, VERY HEAVY, EXPECTED TO BE SET TODAY*

It seemed as if every nerve in her body was quivering. She needed air. And going outside, she walked up the slope and farther up the hill to the cottage where once she had lived. A sense of panic overcame her, a claustrophobic feeling such as one can have in a locked space where nobody hears one's call for help, or conversely, a panic that one can feel at the junction of roads where the signs are in a language one cannot read.

What happened? What happened? Why did he take me away from my mother? Why did he ruin our lives? I look down at the window of my room; I think of all the books he bought for me, the blue ceiling with the stars on it, and the dog bed he got for Clancy because he likes to sleep in my room. I look at all these things and I am so angry at my father, at everything, at life.

Kate left them alone. She had set before Jim a cup of coffee and a sandwich, neither of which he had touched. All of a sudden he looks older than Dr. Scofield, Laura thought.

She had been prepared to rage at him when they brought him home, to fling at him all the pain and despair that were choking her throat, but instead there seemed to be only this icy scorn that one feels toward some white-collar embezzler who has robbed the poor and now stands alone without defense, beneath contempt.

"I wanted to talk to you first," he said, "but they came for me unexpectedly. You were in New York, and this was nothing I could tell you over the telephone. Even now the right words don't seem to be coming to me. It's a long, sad, complicated story, Laura. I've told you what I could. I don't seem to have the energy for any more right now."

"You keep forgetting that the name is Bettina. And yes, it's a sad story, but it doesn't have to be such a long one. Actually it seems rather simple to me. You robbed me of my mother. You're not the first man who's done that, nor will you be the last."

Jim shook his head. "It's never that simple."

"How did they find out?" she demanded.

"It isn't a pretty story."

"I didn't think it would be. But I want to hear it."

"Well . . . well, it was Gil. He recalled that

man at your commencement, as I thought he would. I said so to Rick. Of course, it seems like an awful thing that he would report his girl's father, and I can't feel very loving toward him. And yet I can't blame him too much, either. A lawyer has to obey the law or lose the right to practice it. And I am guilty of the charge. It's as simple as that."

"A minute ago I heard you say things are never that simple."

"I wasn't talking about the same thing, was I?"

"Lillian's on her way back, Gil told me. I'm going to New York to see her, you know."

"Of course. You should."

Now Kate came into the room looking as though she had not slept; her eyes were weary, and her hair was untidy. Gently, she scolded Jim.

"Can't you even manage a small sandwich? You have to eat something! Tell me what else I can get you. And you have to go upstairs to take a nap right afterward. Please. Please, Jim. And Gil phoned for the third time, Laura. I told him you were talking to your father and I wasn't going to disturb you. You'd better call him back. He says he has something important to tell you." And taking the tray with the plate and cup, Kate added sharply, "I can't for the life of me imagine what else he could possibly add to the damage he's already done."

Upstairs in her room, Laura gripped the telephone. "So you really knew more about all this than you admitted to me," she said.

"That's true. I haven't told you everything." His voice wavered. "I've put off telling, because I hadn't the courage."

"My father said you remembered that awful man at the commencement. So obviously it's you who notified the proper people?"

"Laura, I was just about knocked for a loop. I wasn't able to keep it all to myself, so I told my parents, and my father hit the ceiling. 'When the friend of yours who works for that woman's lawyers reveals that you knew—and you can be sure he will reveal it, since it's too good a story to keep to oneself,' he said, 'you'll be in a pickle. Don't you know you'll be questioned? My God, you've been going around with Laura for how many years now?' I couldn't answer, didn't have the wits or the strength. And then he pointed out the publicity that I'd have unless I were one of the first people to go to the authorities with the facts. And I told him that it would break my heart to do that. And he said, 'Okay, do as you please. What do you think the senior partners in your firm will say about it?' So I knew I had to do it, and I did it. I went to the district attorney."

They knew it by then, anyway, Laura thought, so I suppose it really doesn't matter. And yet it breaks my heart, too.

"Please don't hate me, Laura. I'm trying so hard not to hate myself."

From the tabloid newspapers spread out on the kitchen table, a picture of Lillian, standing before a grand Fifth Avenue hotel, smiled up at Jim.

"I'm surprised she's given up the impressive name of 'Storm,'" he said. "Well, she's had a lot of names: born Morris, married and divorced Wolfe, then Buzley, then Storm, and now back to Morris."

Kate spoke bitterly. "It must be quite a nuisance to keep replacing monograms on all your things. Didn't you say that everything had to be monogrammed? Oh, Jim, we really should stop reading this stuff."

"It will die out soon. And it won't be born again until the case comes to court."

But he was not sure about the dying out. He had never known—how could he have known?—the extent of human meanness. A woman had actually written a letter to the editor of the local paper saying Jim Fuller was not only a kidnapper, but a sponger who had married to get hold of a tremendous business and an easy life. In another letter someone predicted that a little more investigation would reveal that he had a criminal record in New York. Worst of all now, most devastating of all, were the words of Lillian herself: *People as cruel as he is don't deserve to live.*

Right here in this house, we are all detached from one another, he thought. We hardly speak anymore. Each one of us is sunk in his own wretchedness: Richard keeping busy at unnecessary labor outdoors, Kate keeping up her spells of false optimism, and Laura sunk into depression. Like delicate shrubbery, we are wrapped in burlap against the winter storms, waiting for spring. The difference is that for us, there is no spring in sight.

As well as Jim could without revealing things that would be best for Laura not to hear, he had tried to explain to her what had gone wrong between her parents. But always he had been stopped on the threshold of the unspeakable; as vividly as if it had been yesterday, he found himself back on that rainy Sunday morning at the hotel in Italy. Long ago that had been, and long the trail afterward from there to here, with—had McLaughlin not told him?—as many as twenty years ahead.

What have I done? he asked himself, and chided: You could have done nothing else.

∽∾

"I thought you should read this," Richard told Laura. "I found it on the kitchen table. It's one of those tabloids they have in the supermarket. Hot off the press overnight."

There she stood, this time above the heading:

## JUST ARRIVED, LILLIAN MORRIS, OVERJOYED AND FURIOUS, IS IMPATIENT TO MEET WITH HER LONG-LOST DAUGHTER

The long-suffering mother, accompanied by friends from France and Italy, has arrived in America with some words about that daughter's father, Donald Wolfe.

"I have turned heaven and earth to find my child. They talk about twenty or thirty years in prison for him, but they could put him to death as far as I'm concerned. There is no punishment severe enough to compensate me for my lost years with my child. The man hasn't a decent bone in his body. He is a criminal and should suffer for the rest of his life."

Before Laura's dizzy vision there appeared a striking face, curiously not unlike the fake photograph with which she had grown up. She had a strange awareness of herself looking at this face, and feeling that this was perhaps the most dramatic moment of her life so far. And then suddenly, unbidden, there appeared another picture: iron bars, bars on doors, on windows, and on gates, while between them peered great pleading eyes in pleading faces.

*He is a criminal and should suffer for the rest of his life.*

Anger, yes. Oh, yes, she thought. But so much hatred?

*People as cruel as he is don't deserve to live.*

✌

"I don't understand you," Gil said over the telephone for what was possibly the fifth time in the last two days. "Ever since I've known you, whenever you mentioned her, I could feel your longing. And now when you could actually meet her, you're not doing it."

He was waiting for an explanation that she was unable to give him. There were no words to describe, possibly no words existed, that could describe the tumult within her.

"Gil, my mind is barely functioning."

"They say she wrote you a letter. Is that true?"

"Yes. I returned it unopened."

"I can hardly believe what you're saying. Are you afraid of something?"

"I don't know how to describe how I'm feeling. But something has changed."

"Well, one thing hasn't," he said gently. "You've already missed a week of classes. It's time you came back here. You need to go on with your life, Laura."

"I'm not going back."

"What? You're quitting? Giving up medical school?"

"I don't know. I don't know anything anymore. Can't you feel what's happening to me? I'm tired of trying to think. And now, I'm sorry, but I have to hang up. Let's talk again tomorrow."

Still her thoughts whirled. If only she didn't want to put Dad in prison! I keep having that vision of iron gratings, and the faces. Neglect, they say. Neglect of a child. I wish I knew the whole story because that can't be all of it. But nobody wants to talk about it. Rick says I should not bother Dad with so many questions. Now I see why he always seemed to take Dad's part when he refused to go with us on a trip. I remember, too, the time we were all trail riding and I was asking Dad a lot of questions about my mother; Rick told me to "shut up and leave your father alone." I was furious with him, which was in itself very strange, because in a certain way I loved him.

Perhaps if he had not known the secret, he would have loved me, too, and would have been less reserved and solemn. But since he never said anything, I could hardly say anything, either. And then came Gil, with all that fun and laughter.

There is such confusion in my head. Everything is haphazard. Yesterday when I approached our front door, I had a horrible, weird sensation of fright. I seemed to see myself running through the rain, needing to get inside. I don't know why. There is a cat sitting on the step, and it wants to get in, too.

There is so much that we do not know about ourselves or, I suppose, about anybody else, either.

On sudden impulse, Laura got up and went outdoors. The day was fair and warm; it seemed impossible that everything, sky, grass, and a pair of doves at the feeder, could be as they had always been. It seemed impossible that terror could exist in such a world.

Yet how terrified Dad must be today, and every day! All these years, he has walked around with an awful fear inside.

*Twenty or thirty years. He doesn't even deserve to live.*

Uncertain, quite alone, her glance fell on a pair of magnolias just coming into blossom. Rick and she had planted them years ago. *If you take care of them, water and feed them, they'll be three times your height ten years from now,* Dad had told them that day. And so they were. Two chipmunks emerged from their homes in a stone wall and chased each other up to the top of these trees. Once a car had run over a chipmunk and killed it on their driveway. Dad had shown her its tiny feet with their five toes like her own. He had hoped that it hadn't suffered before it died. She remembered that she had wanted to bury it in a flowered candy box, and that he had helped her give it a funeral.

So did the past close over Laura as if to drown her.

∽○∽

In her room again, she sat down, huddled in the corner by her desk. And then, for no other reason than that a partly open drawer revealed a battered old diary, she drew it out and read.

*Dad says I can have tennis lessons. I asked him whether my mother played tennis, and he said she did. That's funny because I know I asked him once before, and he had said she didn't. Sometimes he forgets things like that, and I wish he wouldn't.*

*When I volunteer in the children's part of the*

*hospital, I see Dr. Scofield. He tells me I was a "fresh kid" when I was two. He teases me, but I like him. He likes Dad a lot. He says people all like Dad, and I am very lucky. I know I am because my dad never yells at me the way some fathers do.*

*Sometimes when I am feeling sorry because my mother is dead, Dad tells me I am lucky to have another mother like Mom. She is a little more strict than he is. She makes Rick and me watch our table manners. But we love her anyway.*

*Yesterday we all rode up into the hills and had a picnic. Dad roasted marshmallows. When we went home, he helped me with fractions because I am not that good at math.*

She began to cry. When, many minutes later, the tears stopped flowing, she wiped her eyes and wrote a few words on a large piece of paper: I LOVE YOU, DAD. She would put it on the table in the kitchen where he would see it. She went upstairs again and waited. After a long while, she heard voices below. Then came the well-known tread on the stairs. And afraid to look at his weary face, she did not turn.

*Twenty or thirty years.*

Then she heard her name and felt the gentle touch of his hand on her bowed head.

# Chapter 28

"Jim," Kate said, "Mr. McLaughlin just called. He has a lawyer for you, a very competent person."

"I know, I know. He thinks I should consult somebody who once knew me well. He probably got in touch with somebody at Orton and Pratt."

Shame, in a wave of heat, flowed through him. To ask Ed Wills or to stand before Pratt, exposed, condemned, and forlorn—oh, it was hard, too hard! Nevertheless, it might have to be endured.

He got up and went to the mirror that hung between the windows. Eighteenth century, the woman had said when Kate and he had bought it at the secondhand shop in town. The glass was wavy, turning his tense cheeks to a geographical map with hollows, plains, and rivers.

"You're wrong, Jim. McLaughlin's been inquiring everywhere for you. Yesterday he heard from three different sources that there's a woman in New York who's been steadily making a name for herself. She sounded interesting, so he checked some more. He even telephoned Gil at his law firm. And Gil made inquiries—"

Jim interrupted. "At this point, it might be a very good idea for Gil Maples to stay out of my affairs."

"Who can blame you? I feel the same way. But McLaughlin did say that Gil was very frank about his part in what happened to you; he's sick with guilt, and—"

"He needn't be. He did what was legally correct and saved himself. I just don't want to hear any more about him, that's all."

"Well, all right. But McLaughlin thinks you should see this woman. Her name is Ethel Rice," Kate said.

Jim sighed. "I'll think about it."

"Jim, you're saying that because you want to get rid of me. It's been ten days already, almost two weeks. She—the other side—has probably been working on the case all last winter."

"Maybe it's because I'm dreading to be told what I already know."

"You don't *know* anything. It's not like you to be defeated before you've even begun."

She meant well. She was doing her best. You entered a sickroom with a cheerful face. You grasped at straws, so goes the old saying, to save a drowning man, even though the dying or the drowning man knows that you know how weak are your straws and your cheer. When they talked about his "situation," it hurt; and if they didn't talk about it, that hurt, too.

Kate folded the newspaper and put it into the bag to be recycled. When her posture was rigid like this, he did not need to see her face to know that she was holding back tears. He wondered how long she would be able to keep up the effort. He wondered how long it would be before, one night as they lay together in their bed, he would blurt the question: What will become of you when I am locked away?

He walked out of the kitchen and sat on a chair, bent, dangling his arms between his knees. Clancy came over and laid his head on one of his knees. Was it possible that the dog, even the dog, felt the oppression in the beloved house?

He was still sitting there when Laura came into the kitchen. "I know this is unbearably hard for you, Dad," she began. "You, a lawyer, now under the thumbs of lawyers! All the questions and all the probing—"

She read his mind. And suddenly he realized that she always had done so. Even as a tiny child she had seemed to know when he could be coaxed and when he meant what he said. This recollection brought a very faint smile to his lips as he replied.

"Who is she, this interesting, promising person?"

"She is a feminist. Very clever. She likes to represent women whom men have mistreated," Laura said.

"Then why on earth would she want to represent me?"

"For the novelty, for the challenge. Are you upset because Gil approved of her, too? If you are, I'll understand because I feel the same. But we both know why he did it. And of course we'll never forget it. But he does want to help you now. And anyway, it was Mr. McLaughlin who asked him. Will you see her, Dad? Will you?"

"I'll go. I don't believe she or anyone can do much. It's a clear-cut case." A long sigh struggled out of Jim's chest. "But I'll go," he repeated.

# Chapter 29

"You really didn't expect to hear anything very different, did you, Mr. Wolfe?" When he raised his eyes Jim saw, past Ethel Rice's shoulders, a room where a younger woman sat at a word processor. A long time ago, back in the 1890s, that room had been a family kitchen and this spacious office had been divided into a dining room and a parlor. The people who had occupied this house had known another world from the present one. The people who would occupy this ground when the house was torn down to make way for an office tower would know yet another world. So his mind roved.

"You really didn't, did you, Mr. Wolfe?"

*Mr. Wolfe.* It rang so strangely in his ears.

"I guess—I guess I only hoped," he said.

"After all I've told you—yes, I hoped. Then there were other times when I knew better."

"Of course you did, you of all people. Twenty years ago I was only starting out, so I didn't mingle with people like you. But I've heard a great deal about you since, and naturally . . ."

The voice, softer now, faded away. The eyes that had been alert and searching turned toward some chirping sparrows on the windowsill. He understood that she did not want to embarrass him by witnessing his pain.

"I thought that after all I've told you just now you might be able to find some mitigating circumstances. I never practiced family law or divorce law."

"Think. You have no corroboration for anything you've told me, no proof of her morals or lack of them. There are no witnesses to conversations held in bedrooms."

"The neglect? Being out of the city when the child was so sick?"

"The pediatrician was five minutes away. The child was left with a competent, highly paid nurse. In Lillian Morris's circles, there is nothing so unusual about that."

Her "circles," he thought, recalling the drab flat in which she had lived with Cindy.

"Prominent people, active with her in every charity you could think of, have spoken to everybody from journalists, TV reporters, and last but hardly least, to the prosecutor on her behalf."

He was about to answer when she read his mind. "Your friends in Georgia have known you only since you arrived there with your baby. They know nothing about what happened before you committed the crime."

"It must seem absurd to you that the word 'crime' can still startle me," he confessed. "When I look at my daughter and see what she has become under the care of my wonderful wife and myself, there seems to be no sense in all this. Three divorces, God knows how many lovers during and in between, each marriage a climb up the financial ladder—"

"Not enough. There are no laws forbidding that sort of thing. You have only to look at Hollywood."

Outside, a fire engine or an ambulance or police car shrieked, rending his eardrums. The cacophony of the city had never disturbed him; he had indeed seldom noticed it. My nerves are failing, he thought, and steeled himself to ask a concluding question.

"So, what is it? Thirty years, or twenty?"

"I shall fight for less. I suppose I don't need to tell you that the best thing we can do is to avoid a trial. We'll plead guilty and go for a plea bargain. Do you agree?"

"You say less. What's less?"

"I'll fight for ten. I'm rather good at fighting, too."

Ten years. He would be well over sixty. Worn down, never the same afterward.

"I'm in your hands," he said. And then, rising, he thanked her courteously and went out.

Heat lay upon the city's concrete walls and sidewalks; from its source in the sky, it seemed to be returning to the sky where, like a muffling gray blanket, it spread itself.

"She didn't take very long," Richard said as they met at the door.

"No. Short, and not so sweet."

"You didn't like her?"

"I liked her very well. She respected me enough not to sugarcoat the facts, with which I am as well acquainted as she is."

One of Richard's many good qualities was his awareness of mood. Right now it was time to be silent, and so they continued down the long street in silence. Not two blocks distant, quite within view, was the building that housed the offices of Orton and Pratt, where Jim—no, Donald—had occupied a room that looked southward down the avenue. Yesterday, that had been, or else in another century, depending upon the way one happened to feel at any particular moment.

My God! Could I ever, could the people there in that office, could anybody who ever had known me, have believed I would commit a *crime?* I, whose father died for his country? I, a felon, subject to imprisonment for no one could yet predict how long?

No, it could certainly not go to a trial, to a jury filled perhaps with parents of young children. In his mind he had predicted that Ethel Rice would advocate a plea bargain. In that case, all would depend upon the prosecutor's state of mind. Twenty years, or ten . . . Shut away from the world, from life, from Laura and Kate. And from the young man walking beside him, this young man who had become a son to him.

"Let's turn the corner here," he said.

Yes, turn before we pass the building where Augustus Pratt, or anyone else, might be going in or coming out. Hiding for twenty years out of fear, and now, here where it all began, hiding out of shame!

"We ought to have some lunch, don't you think so, Jim?"

Turn again, and walk past the pocket park where once a man had paused for a few minutes in the shade and there, without knowing it, had met his future. Now, out of rage and hatred, he looked away. "Only if you're hungry. I'm not. And we have to catch the plane home."

"I checked while you were with Ms. Rice. We've more time than we need, and Gil wants to meet us."

"I don't want to be seen in the kind of fancy place he'll choose."

"No, he thought of that. He said I should tell you it's a quiet little place uptown. We'll need a taxi."

"I'm sorry. I should have known Gil would consider my feelings. He's trying hard to be helpful. I'm cranky, Rick."

"You're not cranky, you're overwhelmed."

"I won't deny that."

In the "quiet little place," Jim let the young men do the talking. He ordered a sandwich and coffee, but hardly touched either one.

On the wall there hung an amateurish painting of some blue and white Mediterranean village, perhaps Amalfi, as he recalled it. No place could be more unlike the mountains above Foothills Farm, yet its effect upon him was the same. The beauty! The beauty in the world!

People came and went. Two old men, probably retired and partly deaf, held loud, enthusiastic dialogue. A young woman coaxed her little girl to eat her vegetables. Before his eyes, a drama was unfolding, his last drama, with the curtain about to descend.

After a while, he became aware that Richard and Gil were talking about the World Series. Out of consideration for him, they had neither questioned him nor discussed the day's events. Gil, no doubt, would be in touch with Ethel Rice before the afternoon was over. Then it occurred to Jim that he had not even thanked Gil. But it was hard to talk; it would be easier to express his thanks with pen on paper, so he would do that tonight.

When Richard excused himself to telephone home with the time of their flight, Gil made a brief mention of what was on all their minds.

"I wanted you to know one thing: I shall always be there for Laura. You have my word."

"I know," Jim said, and looked toward Amalfi to hide the tears in his eyes.

❦

The airport, too, was a drama. "International Arrivals and International Departures," he read. There they went, the honeymooners with new luggage and new clothes for the journey. There they rushed, the gray-haired and the young in their dark suits with their attaché cases in hand, bound for London, Moscow, and any other place you might think of. Well, he had done it all too, had loved it and given it away for something more important.

The plane made a wide curve, crossing the Hudson, rising over the flat clusters of suburbia through which he had once hurried with Laura and her stuffed bear, and over the clouds. Beside him Richard was reading the newspaper. In an odd way, as if he were a child being led by a strong adult, he thought, I'm glad he offered to come with me today. I am not at my best.

Suddenly Richard spoke. "Jim, I've been wanting to tell you something. No matter what Laura does, whether she goes back to medical school or not, whatever she does or wherever you may be, I want you to know I will watch over her."

"I know that, Rick. I never had any doubt."

Sometimes Jim had a feeling of haste, an awareness of speeding days with so much yet to be done before "things" should happen.

Because Foothills Farm had been pledged to provide his bail, money was short for the first time in many years. Rick, who had spent his time in the field, had had very little business experience at a desk. Kate's realm was the greenhouse. Who, then, is to take my place, he asked himself, when finally "things" do happen? There was a great deal of teaching to be done before they would all be prepared to take over his responsibilities.

Sometimes, on the other hand, he had a feeling that time was crawling. It seemed as though months had passed since the meeting with Ethel Rice, yet when he looked at a stand of pin oaks turning russet, as they do in the fall, he reasoned that the worst had already happened and was behind him.

Then, then always, there was Laura. He worried; he lay awake with his worry. She must, she clearly must return to medical school. But her blue eyes were darkly ringed, and her silences were too long. He argued, tried logical reasoning, did everything short of commanding, and failed. Dr. Scofield alone had been able to pierce the fog of her depression. Pleading the need for some help in his office, he had asked her to take a job there, if only temporarily.

"Because at least you can spell," he had said, trying to be jovial. No doubt she had seen through his kindly ruse, but had nevertheless accepted the offer as a way to get out of the dreary house.

God bless Scofield, and all the other people who had been so thoughtful with their visits, their small friendly gifts of flowers or pies, and most of all, their tact. Yet his own moods ebbed and flowed. Could it be possible, he asked himself, that if the delay were long enough, he might somehow be overlooked, lost in the mass of papers that collect in a city of eight, or is it nine, million? And a moment later he knew how terrified he must be to have had an absurd, crazy thought like that one.

But then again, there were other thoughts. These came at night when his book was put down—the book in which he tried to flee from reality—and the light was turned off in the room where he slept with Kate. What of their last night? For surely it would come, that last night when they would lie down together and part in the morning. Kate and he, before the long, dark, separated years would begin.

And still, they were all trying to live normally now. She invited him to "come look at the Dutch bulbs that have just arrived." The greenhouse reminded her of an Edwardian conservatory, where ferns hung out of baskets fastened on the ceiling, and the chair in the tiny office was made of white wicker. Look here, she would say, there aren't too many nurseries in this country where you'll find forget-me-nots, or Turk's-cap lilies. And these blue echinops—if you didn't know, would you ever guess they were simple thistles?

Then he would tell her that she need not put forth such an effort in his presence, because he knew she was just as frightened as he was.

"Oh, it's not fair!" she would cry. "You don't deserve it, as good as you are to everybody. It's not fair. It's rotten. There's no sense in it."

"Kate, oh Kate, I broke the law and I have to pay for it. It's as simple as that."

Once, filled with anger, she fought him. "Stop talking like a saint."

"I'm hardly a saint. I only know that you can't have a country, a civilization, any other way. This is just what it's all about."

And in spite of all, he meant it; at least until despair returned and struck him down again, he meant it.

❧

Laura's notes were short, only a fraction of a page. On most days, she wrote nothing.

*Why record and repeat? I already know that she was—is—a frivolous woman, which really means very little. I have no proof of that except for what Rick tells me, and that has to be second- or thirdhand information. And why, if it is true, why should I care? I don't. But that she is vengeful, that I do care. What benefit to her will it be when my father is locked away?*

*We are all too busy. There is a feverish energy here at mealtimes, with everybody talking at once about crops, planting, hiring, buying, and selling. No one wants to ask outright how this huge place is going to be run when Jim Fuller is no longer here, yet everyone is thinking about it.*

*Last week Rick told me that very possibly the farm would be sold; the family would disperse and this little family would move who knows where? Then I think he was sorry he had told me that. They don't want to alarm me because they want me to go back to medical school.*

*Yes, I loved every minute of it there, but not anymore. Can a person concentrate on personal pleasures when there is death in the house?*

*Ethel Rice telephoned Dad this morning, the day before Thanksgiving. He is to appear before the district attorney in New York next week. Richard says that she told Dad not to get his hopes too high, especially because this man is a new D.A., inclined toward the tough side, and eager as they all are to make a name for himself.*

*"Not that it isn't the job of a prosecutor to be tough, anyway," Rick said.*

*Dad will not allow any one of us to fly to New York with him. I think that is his way of saying that he must learn to live without us.*

# Chapter 30

Gilligan was his name. A large man with ruddy cheeks, a brusque voice and eyes like X rays, he's about the age, Jim estimated, that I was when I became a partner at Orton and Pratt. Ambitious and competent, he's preparing to rise in the hierarchy, and he will. So there wasn't much hope here, not that there had ever been much to start with.

It was a dark afternoon with electric lights blazing at three o'clock, an hour when people are tired and impatient to finish their day. Jim was chilled, though his palms were sweating.

"So you are positive you want to enter a guilty plea?" asked Gilligan.

"Yes, sir, I am."

"Given your past in the profession, I assume there's no need to describe the procedure: that you will appear in court and plead guilty, which will eliminate any trial. You cannot withdraw the plea once the judge accepts it. You will then await the court's decision as to your punishment."

"Sir, I fully understand."

*I fully understand, too, how much of the court's decision depends upon your prosecution of the case. . . .*

Suddenly Gilligan, leaning forward, shot the question as if it were a bullet: "Why did you do it, Mr. Wolfe?"

The small gray eyes were curious. Well, naturally they would be; this was, after all, a most unusual case, even for a prosecutor who must have seen and heard just about everything.

"Sir—she, the mother, had a different way of life. She lived in a different world, and I did not want my child to grow up in it."

"A different world? Ms. Morris is known for her labors on behalf of charity both here and abroad. She's prominently named in connection with refugee and war relief, among other good causes. She is a woman highly respected. There are no marks against her. So I have tried, but do not quite understand what you mean."

"Much can be hidden, Mr. Gilligan."

Ethel Rice, who was judiciously allowing Jim to make his own defense, now objected. "My client is also widely respected, as is evidenced by the reports you have of his activities over the last twenty years in Georgia, not to mention the years before here in New York."

"But you are omitting the reason that he is here in this room, Ms. Rice. What do you say to that, Mr. Wolfe?"

The repetitious drilling had begun to exhaust Jim. Now all he could do was to make a helpless gesture.

"To all appearances, yours is a classic case, in which an angry divorced husband takes revenge on his former wife by stealing their child. Ms. Morris claims that the wife here is the one who suggested the divorce because you were not getting along with each other. In short, as I see it, she rejected you and your pride was wounded."

What sense does that make? Jim wondered. If I were so proud a man, would I have damaged myself as I did when I fled with the baby and threw my whole life away?

"Excuse me, sir. It is true that she is the one who suggested that we end the marriage, but excessive pride is not among my faults."

*Benumbed and sodden in her disheveled clothes, with her wet hair tumbled and her mouth half open, she lay on the sofa.*

"She asked for nothing from you, no alimony,

nothing but her freedom. She even returned to you the valuable ring you had given her. Is that or is that not correct?"

"It is correct."

"A mark of unusual character, I would say. She still asks for no damages, other than a rather large contribution to one of her charities. But she asks for nothing to compensate for her pain and suffering, which must have been indescribable, Mr. Wolfe."

"I very much regretted her pain and suffering. I never wanted to hurt her."

"Yet you did."

In his authority, he sits here *judging* me, or I should say *prosecuting*. Of course. He's the prosecutor.

"I know you're trying not to delve too deeply into the very personal, Jim, but you're hurting yourself," said Ethel Rice.

*My lawyer is annoyed with me. Still, she has the consideration to address me as* Jim, *rather than* Donald, *a name I have begun to despise.*

Gilligan's quick glance passed from Ethel Rice to Jim. "What do you mean by 'delving deeply,' Ms. Rice?"

Jim answered for her. "She means that I am thinking solely of my daughter."

"The daughter you took to Georgia?"

"The only one I have. I want to protect her.

There are things about her mother—that she need never know."

His heart raced, and his head pounded so, he had to come to a stop. If he could have made an escape from this room, this room of a kind once so familiar, with the diplomas on the wall and the flag in the corner, this room that was turning into a torture chamber, he would have done so.

Gilligan coughed, and moving his chair closer, formed a circle of three. Filling a glass from a water pitcher, he handed it to Jim, and with surprising gentleness, spoke to him.

"You surely know very well that anything said here goes no farther, Mr. Wolfe."

"Yes, sir, but still . . . Sometimes accidentally . . . I don't want to hurt her any more than I have to. She's been studying medicine, she's had enough of a shock and will have more if I—when I—receive my punishment."

"Please go on, Mr. Wolfe. Tell me why, in the first place, you allowed her mother to have sole custody."

"I didn't think, didn't care. The baby wasn't even born when we divorced. I said I would provide for it, and I have done so. There's a considerable sum in the bank in Laura—in Bettina's name. At that point, though, I didn't really want a baby, although I wouldn't let her abort it, as she wanted to do."

"When did you decide that you really wanted the baby enough to take her away?"

"I didn't decide to take her away until much, much later. I've told about that."

It was so hard to speak; it was like pulling his heart out of his chest so people might watch it beat. "I loved her when she was four months old. She knew me. She smiled at me." And Jim paused as if reflecting. "It's funny, whenever I had any vague thought about having a child, I always pictured a boy."

"Can you tell me what is the main, immediate reason you put her in the car and drove off with her that Sunday? Why that day?"

"Of course it was the accident and all the carelessness. But it was other things from long before that I had been trying to forget. Then suddenly I couldn't forget anymore."

*"Whom did you sleep with last night, Lillian?"*

*"I wouldn't even recognize him if I should ever see him again."*

Abruptly, a torrent of passionate words came rushing out of Jim's mouth. It startled the decorum of the room, and astonished the listeners.

"She wanted what she called 'fun.' She called me a puritan, a bore. Oh yes! There was a party once with beds on the lawn under the trees. You picked your partner. I knew she would have gone with someone if I had let her, or hadn't

caught her on the way. I began to think that perhaps we had made a mistake in our marriage.
But I didn't want to think it because I had loved
her so.

"When I purposely made her pregnant, we
went to Italy. I wanted to make a new commit-
ment. She loved art, she knew so much about it,
and I thought it would be wonderful together.
Then she met some friends there, and I learned
things that she had never told me. She had had
lovers there, married men; she had become
pregnant and had had an abortion. That was
when I saw that I had never known her. We did
not know each other. She had lied, lied to me
from the start."

*The rain was wild and angry that morning along
the river, on the old covered bridge, and on the other
side where I walked. . . .*

"The baby she didn't want?" asked Gilligan.
"That's Laura?"

"Yes. That's Laura."

Behind Ethel Rice was a desk with the usual
photograph on it, this one of twins, a boy and a
girl about two years old. Perhaps it was unconsciously that Gilligan had turned half around in
his chair to face it. There was a long silence before he looked back at Jim.

"And so it all came to an end?"

"Yes. Especially when I asked her with whom

she had slept the night before, after I had refused to join a party."

"And she answered?"

"That she wouldn't even recognize the man if she should meet him again."

"You see," said Ethel Rice, "why Jim doesn't want Laura to know all that. And you also can see how hard it is to prove any of it."

Hard to prove? Impossible, Jim thought. Lillian had everything on her side. It was he who had committed the crime. Her slate was clean.

*Ah, let it all go. Submit. Accept. You've lost your will to fight.*

There was a long silence before Gilligan spoke again. "Pull up your chairs to the desk," he said. "I will lay out some papers for you to read, some unusual mail that came to me this week. I wanted to compare them with what your client had to say, Ms. Rice, before showing them to you. Here, look."

There was a longer silence while Ethel Rice read what seemed to be two or three letters. God only knew what Lillian had come up with.

"Astonishing," said Ethel Rice, pushing them in front of Jim.

"Are you acquainted with Arthur Storm, Mr. Wolfe?"

"The man from whom Lillian was recently divorced? No, I am not."

"Have you ever seen him? Met him? Spoken to him?"

"My answer is no to all three."

"Then you will be surprised to read this."

On thick, monogrammed paper, there was a page of strong, black script. Storm lost no time before getting to his point. Because he and Donald Wolfe had each been married to Lillian Morris, he had been especially interested in following this unusual case. Knowing what he did about what he would call her "propensities," he well understood why any man who cared about his child would want to move her into a different environment. He also understood that, since he himself had left his first wife, he was hardly an example to be admired; yet never had he expected to witness the things he had seen as the husband of Lillian Morris. Moved by the threat of imprisonment hanging over Donald Wolfe's head, he now took it upon himself, purely out of sympathy, to speak on the poor man's behalf.

There was a postscript. His first wife was taking him back.

"Extraordinary," murmured Ethel Rice, while the lump in Jim's throat kept him silent.

The second letter, scrawled on office stationery and covering three pages, came from Howard Buzley. It was filled with indignant outrage. For nine years, he had been loyal to his bedridden first wife, loyal, that is, in that he had come home to her every night, acting on the theory that what she didn't know wouldn't hurt her. She had died in comfort and peace. When he married Lillian, he had given her the same loyalty, but she didn't know the meaning of the word. She was a cheat, a beautiful cheat who took everything as a good-natured joke. How he had loved that baby of hers! He loved kids anyway; why, he already had two grandchildren! But she—she only liked to show the kid off. Ask anybody; they would tell you how good he was to Tina, and she wasn't even his kid! A good thing the father took her away, poor man. Of course it's a crime, but from what he sees of Tina on TV, he knows the girl is far better off. He, Howard Buzley, knows what it is to bring up good children, and he wants to put in his two cents on behalf of Donald Wolfe, a man he doesn't even know. Donald Wolfe. He's hardly spoken two words to him, except perhaps a couple of times on the telephone.

Again, no one spoke until Gilligan turned to Jim and asked him to take off his jacket. "It's hot for November. We don't have to be so formal here, anyway. Go on, take it off. And read this."

On lined paper such as one uses for laundry or marketing lists, Jim read the signature first. It was Maria's, and could only be that of the one Maria he had ever known.

"The baby's nurse," he said. "She's learned to write English! We used to speak Spanish together."

" 'Dear Mr. D.A.,' " he read aloud. " 'My boss where I take care of baby give me your address, so I write you about Mr. Wolfe. I work for Cookie Wolfe long time. I read, I see on TV my baby Cookie Wolfe. I see father take her away. Mrs. Buzley wants put him in jail. Is terrible thing. He love that child. I can tell Cookie is big now on TV. She love father. I know right away that Sunday. I can guess and glad because mother no good for her. No good. Everybody know, cook know, doorman know, she have too many boyfriends. Only Mr. Buzley, he don't know so soon, but when he find out, he leave. Same minute. He kiss baby, very sad. Don't think I tell things about Mrs. Buzley because she bad to me and I angry at her. Not so. She always very nice to me, talk nice and give me presents. So I not angry at her. She not *bad* person that way. Only like too many boyfriends and that bad for child. Wrong. Wicked. And Mr. Wolfe, he must not go to jail. Thank you. Your friend, Maria Gonzalez.' "

It was too much. Unashamed of his tears yet

not wanting to display them, Jim got up and walked to the window, where he stood looking out at the coming dusk.

Gilligan coughed again. When he is moved, Jim thought, he covers up with a cough. Ethel Rice rustled papers and made conversation.

"Imagine! All the way from California. And after twenty years. Or more than that, isn't it? Extraordinary."

The little room, which had for a few minutes become almost a gathering of friends in somebody's house, became again the office of the prosecutor, with flag, framed documents, and voices passing in the outer corridor. Then a chair leg scraped the floor. Jim turned, and knew that the interview was over.

"I don't know what all this can mean, if anything," Jim said, "but I thank you for your kindness, Mr. Gilligan."

On the sidewalk he stood for a minute with Ethel Rice before they walked off in opposite directions.

"Naturally, D.A.s get letters," she said. "I've had letters, too, in support of defendants, but I personally have never seen anything quite like these."

"I guess not. Any mail you've been getting would be in defense of a woman."

"Well, perhaps this has been a lesson for me in keeping an open mind."

"As you look ahead, what do you see for me, Ethel?"

"This can't have hurt today, especially that letter from Maria Gonzalez. How much it helped, how can I say? Anyway, you should know very well that's a question I don't dare guess at."

"I do know it. But there's no harm trying."

"Go on. Don't miss your plane. You'll be seeing me next time in court, but of course we'll be in touch half a dozen times before then. Try to enjoy the holidays, Jim."

# Chapter 31

Melted snow lay in the gutters. Valentine candy was on sale, and spring clothes were in shop windows when Laura went back to the hotel and took out her diary.

*This is the year that was. Maybe it would be better for me to wipe it out, forget that it ever happened. But maybe it would be better to set down what I know, rather than let time and selective memory take over, leaving for Dad's great-grandchildren little more than a legend.*

*I felt sometimes that I was watching a play. There on the bench sat the judge in his black robe, and below him stood my father.*

*"You have signed an agreement pleading guilty, Mr. Wolfe. Do you now again admit you are guilty of this charge?"*

*"I do,"* Dad said.

*"Are you saying this willingly? Do you understand what you're saying?"*

*"I do."*

*"Has anyone in any way brought pressure on you to plead guilty?"*

*"No one,"* Dad said.

*"Explain to me why you committed this crime, please."*

*You could feel the movement, like a wave or wind, as everyone craned to hear. And the center of it all, my father, replied. His voice was firm.*

*"I took the child away because she was being neglected. I wanted to give her a solid, normal home."*

*On the other side of the courtroom sat Rebecca/ Lillian. It was the first time we had seen each other except for all those miserable interviews on television and in the newspapers. I was thinking that she looks just like her picture, and that I look a little like her, without any of the glamour. She was quietly dressed, a "portrait of a lady." I was wondering what she thinks of me.*

*As for my feelings toward her, this woman who would, if she could, put my father into prison for thirty years, there was only fear and rage.*

*I must write down these bits and pieces of argument before they fly out of my mind.*

*"This father was generously given the freedom of his ex-wife's home. He was free to visit the child whenever and wherever he wanted to, but all he ever did was to pass her by in Central Park on a Sunday," said the lawyer.*

*"This father was the one who took the sick child to the doctor when the mother, away on a ski trip, could not even be reached by telephone," came the response.*

*"This child was seized from her home where she would have had every educational advantage and was hidden away on a farm in Georgia."*

*"This child has grown up to study at one of the leading medical schools in the country."*

*Bickering. Endless bickering. What do I really know, except that it's over at last?*

*FINISHED, Laura wrote in large, black letters. Five years in prison, but sentence suspended unless the defendant should commit a crime. Hardly likely! That, and an enormous payment to Rebecca/Lillian for her charities.*

*A difficult case, the judge said.*

*Difficult? There are no words for it.*

*Gil says there must be a great deal more to the story than we'll ever find out, or the prosecutor would not have made such a weak case. And Richard says that it looks to him as if the prosecutor actually wanted Dad to go free.*

*Here are Rebecca/Lillian's remarks on the late-afternoon news. I took them down word for word.*

*"I did not pursue my aims as I could have done. I am much calmer now that I have seen my daughter. There is nothing anyone can give me to make up for my long agony, but at least I have seen that she has been well cared for. Putting her father in prison would undoubtedly be a terrible punishment for her, too, so that is another reason why I shall not appeal the judgment and fight on."*

*For months, ever since I learned what she wanted to do to Dad, I hated her. But now that she is behaving this way, I really don't anymore. Clearly, Dad doesn't want me to hate her, either. I am also sure that there are things he doesn't tell me about her. Probably it's because when you've had a miserable marriage, there's no pleasure or point in talking about it. I am truly sorry that things turned out this way for them both, but at least it's all over now and we are at peace.*

*"Perhaps sometime in the future, Bettina will want to know me. I hope so," she said.*

*I do not think I ever will.*

*We stayed on this extra day and a half after Mom and Rick went home because Dad wanted to give me a little history lesson. This is where we used to meet in the park on Sunday afternoons, he told me; this is the building where I lived when I first came to the city. And he told me that we're having our name changed legally, so I'll still be Laura Fuller. I had had the idea of going to that cemetery where Dad found the name, but everyone said that was absolutely crazy, and I see that they're right.*

*They all tell me I must now "move on." Well, I am moving. I have a choice among three medical schools, north, south, and west, that will let me resume my interrupted studies. "Not east?" Gil asked, although by then he surely must have known better.*

*I am surprising myself by being able to write these words without tears. It's partly because I've shed so many recent ones all during the last awful year, but mostly it's because, without my being aware of its happening, the red-hot love between Gil and me has been cooling off. I know he felt bad about having talked too much, especially since my father completely forgave him. I know he's been embarrassed about his parents' dropping me with such a resounding, unmistakable thump. I guess they didn't want any part of the publicity.*

*We didn't have to do much explaining. We had, after all, been apart all winter when I was home. When we met over dinner back here in New York, we had not spent a night together in almost half a year, and neither one of us said a word about when we were going to do it again.*

*So we part tactfully, with no resentment, a little sadness, and on my part, much thanks for the way he saw everything through to Dad's deliverance at the end.*

*The trouble that drew me away from Gil has drawn me even closer to Richard. (When I am having serious thoughts, I call him Richard. Otherwise, he is Rick.) It's hard to believe that he has known about Dad and me for the last ten years. He must have known, and worried, that the truth was somehow bound someday to come out. And now that it has, he is almost a different person with me. He's more lighthearted, more at ease.*

*When I told this to Dad, he agreed. But then he gave me this advice.*

*"Don't rush into another love affair just yet. Go live your free life first. Go back to school with a free mind. You need that now, after all you've been through. It's what you really want, anyway."*

*And that is the truth.*

# Chapter 32

"I'll be back by noon," Jim told Laura on the last morning in the hotel. "We'll have a quick lunch and catch the plane home. It'll feel good to get there."

All he had truly missed over the years were the collections of old books, where you could browse for a couple of hours and come out with as many treasures as you could afford or carry. That would be his first stop. The only other one would be the shop in whose window Kate had looked so longingly the day before yesterday at an emerald green leather handbag. But it was, she said, "ridiculously expensive," not to mention that one had so little use for the color. He had to chuckle when he imagined her opening the package and exclaiming over it. Her cheeks would turn almost as bright as her hair. And then she would carry that bag wherever they traveled because now, Kate Fuller, he said to himself, we are going to travel wherever you want to go.

"A woman is coming along who will change your life," Augustus Pratt had once told him long ago, and so it had happened.

It had not surprised Jim to see a few tears skimming under Pratt's eyelids when he had brought Kate and Laura to visit. It was a visit that never would have been paid save for certain horrendous recent events; otherwise, he would have lived out an uneventful life in Georgia. The whole of Pratt's firm had followed Jim's trial and ordeal, and this last visit had been full of more emotion than Jim could have expected. Indeed, the whole week had been full of more emotion than he would ever want to experience again.

He supposed he could be forgiven for the pride he had surely showed when he had stood before them all with his two lovely women beside him. It was as if Kate and Laura had been reborn since the court's decision, each of them restored to her best self.

"I'm going back to the day I met this man," Pratt had said. "I wish we had a few days—we'd need that long—for me to tell you both about him. He was extraordinary."

Kate nodded. "He still is, Mr. Pratt."

"But we can come back, Mom! Now that Dad can travel again, we must!"

"Yes," Pratt agreed, "you must."

Well, we will, Jim reflected now, as he walked past that same office on his way to the bookstore. But he had no wish to return to that first life with all its challenges and its achievements. Too many things had changed, and he along with them.

You would think, he reflected as he walked with his packages under his arm, I was purposely reliving my past today. For here is the pocket park where we met, and two blocks farther on is the place where we had the pizzas and a couple of poodles tried to sniff at them. Farther east is the apartment where I lived, and a few steps farther north is the apartment where we lived together. . . . Oh Jim, forget it! Look the other way.

"Don't miss your plane," Rick had warned. "They're preparing a welcome party for you. Dr. Scofield seems to have invited close to a hundred people, and they're all bringing food. Mom's supervising things to make sure you have all your special favorites. That's why she left New York a day ahead of you. You know how she is."

Yes, he knew very well how she was. And he walked on, hastening.

Suddenly, as he crossed a street, he had the feeling that a man on the opposite sidewalk had recognized him.

"Long time no see," said Cindy's boyfriend.

There was no mistaking the man, still after twenty years the same: the rippling, rumpled hair fell to the shabby shoulders; the sardonic, intelligent face was sullen.

"Yes, a long time," Jim agreed, wondering whether the fellow knew about him and what he would say next.

"You've had your small troubles. Tough luck."

Small? And why the ironic grin?

"Yes, tough. And how's everything with you?"

"Doing okay."

"Working?" He had no idea why he asked, and he would have liked to move on. But the other man stood still, blocking the crowded sidewalk.

"From time to time. As the spirit moves me."

The vocabulary and the accent were so incongruous with the speaker's appearance that, for some reason or other, Jim was moved to pity.

"Do you need money?" he asked.

"Not particularly. Of course, one can always use more. Right?"

When Jim took out a wallet thick with

currency to pay the hotel bill, the man showed his own wallet, which was even thicker, and laughed.

"Thanks, but I don't really need it. She takes good care."

"Takes care? Who does?"

"Why, Lillian. Takes care of everybody. Ask, and she'll give it. Always did."

"I don't understand."

"What's there to understand?"

"Why she takes care of you, or of 'everybody.' "

The man laughed again. It was disturbing to Jim that he was unable to remember his name. Then it occurred to him that probably he had never known it.

"Yeah, everybody. Rich men empty their pockets for her, she takes care of guys like me, and it trickles down and everybody's happy. I'm happy. You should know. You knew her long enough."

Obviously he had not known her long enough to know all this. And he stood there, puzzled and troubled by some disconnected shreds of memory.

"Wasn't it you who told me when I met you long afterward that Cindy was Lillian's sister?"

"That's right."

"What else have you not told me?"

"How can I answer that? I told you everything I wanted to tell you."

"And you—aren't you—didn't you say you grew up across the street from them? You were some kind of distant cousin, I think?"

"If I said so. If we go back far enough are we not all cousins? Descendants of Adam and Eve?"

Again the mocking grin crossed the face that was suddenly and incredibly familiar, although he had never before spent so many moments paying any attention to it.

But now above the scruffy beard, he saw a pair of shining, clever eyes, light blue and wide with amusement.

And as if pierced by a knife blade, Jim was pierced with a shocking certainty. "My God!" he cried. "You're Lillian's brother! She's hidden you the way you both hid Cindy!"

"Well, if you say so, I am. I guess I must be."

"But why? Why? I feel as if I'm standing inside a puzzle that's inside a riddle that's inside a—"

"An enigma. Keep your shirt on, man. It's human nature, that's what."

"This secrecy! It doesn't make any sense."

"Maybe not to you."

The face! There was no mistaking it. It was her face above his beard! It was her expression, and her enjoyment of his bewilderment.

The two men stood there, the one thunder-struck and the other, quite without any mean intent, just simply amused.

"You're all worked up, so I won't keep you guessing, man. Yes, I'm her brother. You've got to remember that it takes all kinds. So good luck to you, better luck than last time. Well, I'll run along. Keep the faith."

Jim watched him till he had gone around the corner and out of sight. *Her brother.* But why? It would have been so simple to find out before this. Why had he never done so? He could have insisted. But, he had tried from time to time to find out what she was hiding and she had strongly resisted. And after all, when everything started to go downhill, he had no reason to pursue the problem. Besides, it would have done no good anyway. When a person builds a life around a lie and you manage to penetrate that lie against his will, there is nothing left except a terrible, bleeding wound.

Walking back to the hotel, Jim was filled with a troubling sadness. What horrors might possibly have lurked in the home of her childhood? What sordid evil, or what tragedy?

Heaven alone knew how much strength and courage it had cost her to rise above it, to learn her charming ways, how to eat that orange with such dainty fingers, how to speak with such grace, to dress with such elegance, to have studied and so loved art!

Who was it, or what was it, that had done such damage to her? Or was it only some careless conglomeration of the genes? You'll never know, he said to himself.

Yet she had realized everything she could have wanted, including a proud name. Even the scandal over possession of that painting had been settled amicably, as she and Storm had made it a gift to a museum. All of it, all of it, was a mystery.

And it seemed to Jim that perhaps the wisest way to look at life might be to expect the unlikely. For no one seeing Lillian would ever imagine what was hidden within her. Nor would anyone expect that Maria would write that astonishing letter; he must send her a note of warmest thanks and a fine photograph of Laura. And no man would expect to sit in a train next to an uninteresting woman who turned out to be the love of his life.

Judge not, he said to himself, and went into the lobby, where his daughter—and Lillian's daughter—was waiting for him.

Later that day, Rick met them at the airport and drove them home. The driveway was filled with so many cars that they had to park far down the road and walk the rest of the way. Behind their split-rail fence, two Guernseys and three horses were cropping new grass. The air was full of twitterings from the trees. And just past the curve appeared their house, low and white in a sea of green.

"What are you thinking of, Dad?" Laura asked.

"That I already smell barbecue and I'm starved."

She was standing there with such gladness in her face!

"And you?" he asked.

"It's a funny thing. Looking down at the house from here, I can imagine it's alive. The windows are eyes, the front door smiles, and the wings are like open arms that are asking me to come in."

# About the Author

BELVA PLAIN lives in northern New Jersey. She is the author of the bestselling novels *Evergreen, Random Winds, Eden Burning, Crescent City, The Golden Cup, Tapestry, Blessings, Harvest, Treasures, Whispers, Daybreak, The Carousel, Promises, Secrecy, Homecoming, Legacy of Silence, Fortune's Hand, After the Fire,* and *Looking Back.*